A world of mysteries and wild meetings—
You never know who you'll run into on Riverworld!

CROSSING THE DARK RIVER
by Phillip José Farmer
Trapped in a feud between Vikings and Monguls, a failed idealist and a crazed surrealist must become bizarre partners on a desperate spiritual quest...

EVERY MAN A GOD
by Mike Resnick and Barry Maltzberg
Huey Long's back on the road to populist power—his only problem's his new ally, Emperor Caligula...

THE MERRY MEN OF RIVERWORLD
by John Gregory Betancourt
Robin Hood and Abe Lincoln must save Jules Verne's utopia from the conquering armies of Al Capone...

UNFINISHED BUSINESS
by Robert Weinberg
Davy Crockett, Jim Bowie, and Socrates aim to refight the Alamo—but Riverworld throws some unexpected twists and characters in their plans...

GRACELAND
by Allen Steele
You can't kill rock 'n roll! John Lennon, Sid Vicious, Keith Moon, and Brian Jones are the supergroup on the pleasure isle of Graceland, where Elvis really *is* the King—and his blood enemy is none other than... the Lizard King...

✳

The greats of science fiction join forces
to create an all-star romp in
TALES OF RIVERWORLD

TALES OF RIVERWORLD

EDITED BY

PHILIP JOSÉ FARMER

WARNER BOOKS

A Time Warner Company

WARNER BOOKS EDITION

Questar is a registered trademark of Warner Books, Inc.

Cover illustration by Don Ivan Punchatz

Warner Books, Inc.
1271 Avenue of the Americas
New York, NY 10020

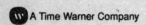 A Time Warner Company

Printed in the United States of America

First Printing: August, 1992

10 9 8 7 6 5 4 3 2 1

ACKNOWLEDGEMENTS

CONTENTS

Foreword by Philip José Farmer   *ix*

CROSSING THE DARK RIVER
by Philip José Farmer   *1*

A HOLE IN HELL by Dane Helstrom   *65*

GRACELAND by Allen Steele   *73*

EVERY MAN A GOD
by Mike Resnick and Barry N. Malzberg   *101*

BLANDINGS ON RIVERWORLD
by Phillip C. Jennings   *141*

TWO THIEVES by Harry Turtledove   *173*

FOOL'S PARADISE by Ed Gorman   *207*

THE MERRY MEN OF RIVERWORLD
by John Gregory Betancourt   *237*

UNFINISHED BUSINESS by Robert Weinberg   *283*

CONTENTS

Foreword by Philip José Farmer

CROSSING THE DARK RIVER
by Philip José Farmer

A HOLE IN HELL by Dane Helstrom

GRACE NOTE by Allen Steele

EVERY MAN A GOD
by Mike Resnick and Barry N. Malzberg

A SAUCER ON THE RIVERWORLD
by Philip C. Jennings

TWO THIEVES by Harry Turtledove

RIVER OF DREAMS by Ed Gorman

THE MERRY MEN OF RIVERWORLD
by Tom Clareson

THIRTY-ONE RIVERMEN by Robert Weinberg

FOREWORD

by Philip José Farmer

What we have here is a gathering of stories by different writers about one planet. This is the Riverworld, the first novel about which was written by me and was published in 1971. This novel was called *To Your Scattered Bodies Go*. The second, *The Fabulous Riverboat*, appeared the same year. Then came *The Dark Design*, *The Magic Labyrinth*, and *Gods of Riverworld*. My novelet, *Riverworld*, is part of the series but is not concerned with the main plot or main characters.

The book at hand is a shared-world anthology. That is, each of its stories takes place on the Riverworld but is by a different writer. These writers were given carte blanche with their situations and characters but had to follow the structure and strictures of the Riverworld as laid down by me. However, when the action takes place on a planet where there is a river almost eighteen million miles long, and which is populated by over thirty-six billion and six hundred million human beings who lived and died on Earth from circa 100,000 B.C. to A.D. 1983, the writers are not very confined.

My "Crossing the Dark River" is the lead story. "A Hole in Hell," a very short but powerful story, is by Dane Helstrom, a name appearing in print for the first time. Jennings's "Blandings on Riverworld" is the first humorous Riverworld story to be written. Betancourt's "The Merry Men of Riverworld" is about a character who is well known in the Western world. Well, it is in a way. "Fool's Paradise" is by Ed Gorman, a well-known mystery writer, and is his first science-fiction story. His protagonist, as might be expected, is a detective-turned-writer well known in the twentieth century. Weinberg's "Unfinished Business," Resnick's and Malzberg's "Every Man a God," and Turtledove's "Two Thieves" exhibit the inventive virtues and high imagination we have come to expect from these writers.

In fact, as one of the editors choosing these stories for inclusion in the anthology, I was very pleased with their handling of another writer's basic concept and of the historical characters they chose to write about.

I hope you enjoy these stories as much as I did.

Crossing the Dark River

Philip José Farmer

"What? You prescribed lemon juice to cure cholera?"

"What? You had a sure cure for infants who held their breaths until their faces turned blue? And for young females in a hysterical seizure? You stuck your little finger up their anuses? Presto! Changeo! They're rid forever of infantile behavior and the tantrums of the body?"

"What? You're searching for the woman who's supposed to have given birth to a baby somewhere along the River? A baby? In this world where all are sterile and no woman has ever gotten pregnant? You believe that's true? How about buying the Brooklyn Bridge?

"No? Then how about a splinter from the True Cross? Ho! Ho! Ho! And you believe that this baby reproduced by parthenogenesis is Jesus Christ born again to save us Valleydwellers? And you've been traveling up-River to find the infant? Who do you think you are? One of the Three Wise Men? Ho! Ho! Ho!"

And so Doctor Andrew Paxton Davis had not stayed long any place until he had been detained by Ivar the Boneless. He had wandered up the Valley, seldom pausing, just as, on Earth, he had been the peripatetic's peripatetic. During the late 1800s and early 1900s, he had traveled to many cities in the United States. There he had lectured on and practiced his new art of healing and sometimes established colleges of osteopathy. Denver, Colorado; Quincy, Missouri; Pittsburgh, Pennsylvania; Cincinnati, Ohio; LaFayette and Indianapolis, Indiana; Dallas and Corsicana, Texas; Baker City, Oregon; Los Angeles, California, and many other places.

Then he had originated Neuropathy, an eclectic discipline of healing. It combined all the best features of osteopathy, chiropracty, magnetism, homeopathy, and other systems of drugless medicine. He had preached that God-inspired gospel throughout the country. And he had written four thick books that were used by osteopaths and ophthalmologists and read by many laymen throughout the United States.

"From going to and fro in the earth and from walking up and down in it."

That was Satan's answer to God when He said, "Whence comest thou?" That could be said also of Andrew P. Davis. But Davis loathed Satan, and his model was Job, who "was perfect and upright and one that feared God and eschewed evil."

Since Davis had awakened on the Riverworld, he had suffered the torments of Job. Yet he had not faltered in his faith any more than had Job. God must have made this world, but the Great Tempter was here too. To realize that, you just had to look around at the inhabitants.

Riverworlders dreamed most often about lost Earth. The one exception to this was the nightmare about their mass resurrection, the Day of the Great Shout when all the dead had screamed at one time. What a cry that must have been!

Doctor Andrew Paxton Davis had often awakened moaning, sometimes screaming, from that nightmare. But he had another dream that distressed him even more.

For instance, on this early and still-dark morning of the fifth anniversary of The Day, he had painfully oozed into wakefulness from a Riverworld-inspired nightmare. Not terror but shame and humiliation had written the script for that sleep-drama.

He had gotten his M.D. from Rush Medical College in Chicago in 1867. But, after many years as a physician in the rural areas of Illinois and Indiana, he had become unhappy with the practice. Always a seeker after truth, he had become convinced that the new science and art of healing devised by Dr. Andrew Taylor Still was a breakthrough. Davis had been in the first class (1893) to complete the courses of the newly established American School of Osteopathy in Kirksville, Missouri.

But, ever questioning, ever seeking, he had decided that osteopathy alone was not enough. Hence, his own discipline and his founding of the College of Neuropathy in Los Angeles. When he died at the age of eighty-four of stomach cancer—he also had nightmares about that long agony—he was still the head of a flourishing practice.

However, medical science had improved considerably from his birth in 1835 to his death in 1919. And, from then on, it had accelerated at an incredible velocity. His late-twentieth-century informants made it sound like one of those scientific romances by H.G. Wells.

In the first two years on the Riverworld, he had proudly, at first, anyway, told the doctors he met of his knowledge and accomplishments. He had also confided his belief that the Savior had been born again. So many had laughed at him that he became very reserved about telling any M.D. that he had practiced the healing art. He was almost as reticent about revealing his Quest to laymen. But how could he find the Holy Mother and the Holy Infant unless he told people that he was searching for them?

He had awakened this morning and lain in a sweat not caused by the temperature. After a while, he vaguely remembered a dream preceding the one about the mockery and jeers.

He was outside the tower on top of the hill and just starting to walk down the hill when he heard the king calling him. He turned and looked up through the twilight that enveloped most of his dreams. Ivar the Boneless was staring down at him from the top of the tower. As usual, the king was half smiling. Beside him, Ann Pullen, the queen not only of Ivar's land but of all the bitches in the world, was leaning through a space in the top wall. Her bare breasts were hanging over the top of the stone. Then she lifted one and flipped it at him.

Suddenly, Sharkko the Shyster appeared beside the two. Sharkko, the man who would have been utterly miserable if he could understand how detestable he was. But Sharkko was unable to imagine that anyone could not like him. He had been given solid proof, kicks, slaps, curses, and savage beatings, that he was not loved by all. Yet his mind slid these off and kept his self-image undented and unbreakable.

These three were the most important beings in Davis's life in Ivar's land. He would have liked to have put them in a rocket and fired them off toward the stars. That way, he would keep them from being resurrected somewhere along the River and thus avoid meeting them again. Except in his nightmares, of course.

Later, a few hours after dawn, Davis was walking up the hill to the tower after fishing in the River. He had caught nothing and so was not in a good mood. That was when he met the lunatic gotten up like a clown.

"Doctor Faustroll, we presume?"

The man, who spoke in a strangely even tone, held out an invisible calling card.

Davis glanced down at the tips of the man's thumb and first finger as if they really were holding a card.

"Printed in the letters of fire," the man said. "But you must have a heart on fire to see them. However, imaginary oblongs are best seen in an imaginary unlighted triangle. The darker the place, the brighter the print. As you may have noticed, it's late morning, and the sunlight is quite bright, At least, they seem to be so."

The fellow, like all other insane on Earth, must have been resurrected with all traces erased of any mental illness he had suffered there. But he was crazy again.

His forehead was painted with some kind of mathematical formula. The area around his eyes was painted yellow, and his nose was painted black. A green mustache was painted on his upper lip. His mouth was lipsticked bright-red. On his chest, a large question mark was tattooed in blue. A dried fish was suspended on a cord reaching to his belly. His long, thick, and very black hair was shaped into a sort of bird's nest and held in place by dry gray mud.

And, when the man bent his neck forward, he exposed the upper part of an egg in the nest. Davis could easily see it because the man was shorter than he. It did not roll with the movement of the head. Thus, it must be fixed with fish glue to the top of his head. The wooden and painted pseudo-egg, Davis assumed, was supposed to represent that laid by a cuckoo. Appropriate enough. The stranger was certainly cuckoo.

A large green towel, the clown's only garment, was draped around his hips. The gray cylinder of his grail was near his bare feet. Most people carried a fish-skin bag that held their worldly possessions. This fellow lacked that, and he was not even armed. But he did carry a bamboo fishing pole.

The man said, "While on Earth, we were King Ubu. Here, we are Doctor Faustroll. It's a promotion that we richly deserve. Who knows? We may yet work our way to the top and become God or at least occupy His empty throne. At the moment, we are a pataphysician, D.Pa., at your service. That is not a conventional degree in one sense, but in all senses it is a high degree, including Fahrenheit and Kelvin."

He started to put his imaginary card in an imaginary pocket of an imaginary coat.

Davis said, "I'll take it," and he held out his hand. Humoring the pataphysician, whatever that was, might prevent him from becoming violent.

He moved his hand close to his bare chest to suggest that he was pulling out a card from an inner pocket of his coat. He held it out.

"Andrew Paxton Davis, M.D., Oph.D., N.D., D.O., D.C."

"Where's the rest of the alphabet?" the man said, still keeping his voice even-toned. But he pretended to take the card, read it, and then put it inside his coat.

"I made soup of it," Davis said. His blue eyes seemed to twinkle.

Doctor Faustroll's dark-brown eyes seemed to reflect the twinkle, and he smiled. He said, "Now, if you'll be kind enough to conduct us to the ruler of this place, whatever his or her or its names, we will present ourself or perhaps more than one of our selves and will apply for a position or positions."

Davis was startled. He said, "What? You don't know where you are? The guards did not stop you? How did you get by them?"

Doctor Faustroll indicated an invisible object by his right foot. "We carried ourself through the border in our suitcase. The guards did not see the case. It was midnight and cloudy. Also, they were drowsy."

"It must be a very large case to hold you. All of you?"

"It's very small, but there's enough room for us and our conscience," Doctor Faustroll said. "We take the conscience out of the case only when we intend to use it, which isn't often, Or when it needs airing."

He picked up his grail with one hand and his fishing pole in the other.

Davis hitched up the towel Velcroed to his waist and then grasped the handle of his own grail. His good humor had vanished. He was getting impatient with the fellow, and he did not want to be late for his appointment with the king.

Looking serious, he said, "If I were you, I'd get out of this place as quickly and quietly as possible. If you don't, you'll be working with those wretched people down there."

He pointed at the riverbank. Faustroll turned around to stare at the swarm of sweating, straining, and shouting men and women. Tiny figures at this distance, they were

striving to pull or to push a roughly cube-shaped and
bungalow-sized block of granite on log rollers into the
River. Its forward edge was on two wooden runners,
heavily lubricated with fish fat, that dipped into the
water.

"They're building a pyramid beneath the surface of
the River?" Faustroll said.

"Must you keep up this nonsense?" Davis said. "And
why don't you ask me why I'm giving you this advice to
scoot out of here as fast as your feet can carry you? If,
that is, you're able to do so, which I doubt very much."

"There is no such thing as nonsense," Faustroll said.
"In fact, what you call nonsense makes greater sense
than what you call sense. Or, perhaps, there is no
concrete abstraction that we term sense. But, if there is
no sense, then there is also no nonsense. We have
spoken. Selah."

2

Davis sighed, and he said, "If you don't mind risking
slavery and perhaps torture, come along with me. Don't
say I didn't try to warn you."

They had been standing at the edge of the grass-
carpeted plain. Now they trudged up the slope of the
foothills. Davis, a red-haired man of medium height and
build but with abnormally large hands, led the way. The
madman was slower because he was observing the whole
milieu. Though the mountains towering straight up to
20,000 feet, the mile-wide foothills, and the mile-wide
plains on either side of the mile-wide River were typical

of most of the Rivervalley, the human activity was not. Many men and women were cutting away large blocks of stone in the vertical face of the mountains and were sliding the blocks down the foothills. The grass in the path of the very heavy weights was crushed, and the earth had sunk in. But the grass was so tough that it had not died out.

Near the lower edge of the foothill were extra oak log rollers for moving the blocks across the plain. Halfway along the plain, several crews were pulling on ropes tied around the blocks while gangs shoved against the rear of the blocks. When these got to the River's edge, they were placed on runners and slid into the water.

As in most areas, the River was shallow for several yards beyond the banks, which were only a few inches above the River. Then the level bottom abruptly became a cliff. That plunged straight down at least a mile before reaching the cold and lightless bottom in which was a multitude of strange forms of fish.

Not only was the bank swarming with people, the River itself was jammed with boats small and large. And two gigantic wooden cranes on the bank were close to being completed.

The other side of the River showed a similar scene. Even as Faustroll watched, a huge stone block on that side slid on runners into the water and disappeared. A huge bubble formed above the roiling water and burst.

Suddenly, Faustroll caught up with Davis.

"We don't leap to quick conclusions," he said, "or even walk to them. But it seems to us that those workers are trying to fill the River. They're not having much success at it."

"Building a dam," Davis said. He quickened his pace.

"Ivar and that other fool across the River, King Arpad, plan to dam the stream with all those blocks of stone if it takes them a hundred years. Then they'll be able to keep any boats from slipping through past the guards at night. They'll also tax the merchant boats going up and down the River past this point. Also, Ivar thinks that he'll be able to cut through the mountains to the other side of the Valley. He'll invade the state on the other side and rule it. And the tunnel will be a conduit for trade from the other side. Ivar also has this dream that the tunneling will reveal large deposits of iron.

"Pride goeth before a fall. He'll suffer the fate of the arrogant Nimrod, who built the Tower of Babel thinking that he could conquer the hosts of Heaven."

"How can they cut granite with flint tools?" Faustroll said.

"They can't. But this area was blessed—or cursed— with underground deposits of copper and tin. The only such for thousands of miles either way from here. Ivar and his army of Vikings and Franks grabbed this land three years ago, and that's why he has bronze tools and weapons."

Going up the hill, they heard a loud explosion as rock was blasted with black gunpowder. When they stopped at the top, they heard a loud clanging. Beyond the shallow valley below them was a higher hill on top of which was a large round tower of granite blocks. Circling it at its base was a moat.

Below the two in the valley were the smithies, the molds, and great chunks of tin- and copper-bearing ore and the round bamboo huts with cone-shaped and leaf-thatched roofs in which the workers lived. The din, heat, and stench rolled over the two men in a nauseating wave.

"Men have brought Hell from Earth to this fair place," Faustroll said. "They should be seeking spiritual progress, not material gain and conquest. That, we believe, is why we were placed in this purgatory. Of course, without the science of pataphysics, they won't get far in their quest.

"On the other hand, left or right, we don't know, it may all be accidental. But accidental doesn't necessarily mean meaningless."

Davis snorted his contempt for this remark.

"And just what is pataphysics?" he said.

"Our friend and fellow doctor, let us charge through the breach created by our conversation and assault the definition of pataphysics. It is an almost impossible task since it can't be explained in nonpataphysical terms.

"Pataphysics is the science of the realm beyond metaphysics. It lies as far beyond the metaphysics as metaphysics lies beyond physics—in one direction or another, or perhaps still another.

"Pataphysics is the science of the particular, of laws governing exceptions. You follow us so far?"

Davis only rolled his eyes.

"Pataphysics, pay attention, this may be the heart of the matter, pataphysics is the science of imaginary solutions. But only imaginary solutions are real."

Davis grunted as if struck a soft blow in the stomach.

"For pataphysics, all things are equal," Faustroll continued. "Pataphysics is, in aspect, imperturbable.

"And this, too, is the heart of the matter, one of them anyway. That is, all things are pataphysical. Yet few people practice pataphysics."

"You expect me to understand that?" Davis said.

"Not at once. Perhaps never. Now, the last castle to be

conquered. Beyond pataphysics lies nothing. It is the ultimate defense.''

''Which means?''

Faustroll ignored that question. He said, ''It allows each man or woman to live his own life as an exception, proving no law but his own.''

''Anarchy? You're an anarchist?''

''Look about you. This world was made for anarchy. We don't need any government except self-government. Yet men won't permit us to be anarchists—so far.''

''Tell this to Ivar,'' Davis said. He laughed, then said, ''I'd like to see his face when you tell him that.''

''Ah, but what about the brain behind that face? If he has a brain?''

''Oh, he has brains! But his motives, man, his motives!''

They descended the hill and then climbed to the top of the next hill, much steeper and higher than the previous ones. The tower drawbridge was down, but many soldiers were by its outer end. Most of them were playing board games or casting dice carved from fish bones. Some were watching wrestling matches and mock duels. Their conical bronze helmets were fitted with nose- and cheek-pieces. A few wore chain-mail armor made of bronze or interlocking wooden rings. All were armed with daggers and swords and many had spears. Their leather bronze-ringed shields were stacked close by them. The wooden racks by these held yew bows and quivers full of bronze-tipped arrows. Some spoke in Esperanto; others, in barbaric tongues.

The sentinels at each end of the drawbridge made no effort to stop the two. Davis said, ''I'm the royal osteopath to King Ivar. Since you're with me, they assume you're not to be challenged.''

"I like to be challenged," Faustroll said. "By the way, what is an osteopath?"

"You've never heard of osteopathy?" Davis said, raising his reddish eyebrows. "When did you die?"

"All Saints' Day, though I'm no saint in the Catholic sense, in 1907. In Paris, which you may know is in France, who knows how many light-years away?"

Davis said only, "Ah!" That explained the man's madness and decadence. He was French and probably had been a bohemian artist, one of those godless immoral wretches roistering in the dives of Montmartre or the Left Bank or wherever that kind of low life flourished. One of those Dadaists or Cubists or Surrealists, whatever they were called, whose crazed paintings, sculptures, and writings revealed that their makers were rotten with sin and syphilis.

There wasn't any syphilis on this world, but there was plenty of sin.

"My question?" Faustroll said.

"Oh, yes! One, osteopathy is any form of bone disease. Two, it's a system of treatment of ailments and is based on the valid belief that most ailments result from the pressure of displaced bones on nerves and so forth. Osteopaths relieve the traumatic pressure by applying corrective pressure. Of course, there's much more to it than that. Actually, I seldom have to treat the king for anything serious, he's in superb physical health. It could be said that he retains me—enslaves me would be a better term—as the royal masseur."

Faustroll lifted his eyebrows and said, "Bitterness? Discontent? Your soul, it vomits bile?"

Davis did not reply. They had gone through the large foyer and up the stone steps of a narrow winding staircase to the second floor. After passing through a small room, they had stepped into a very large room, two stories high and very cool. Numerous wall slits gave enough light, but pine torches and fish-oil lamps made the room brighter. In the center, on a raised platform, was a long oaken table. Placed along it were high-backed oaken chairs carved with Norse symbols, gods, goddesses, serpents, trolls, monsters, and humans. Other smaller tables were set around the large one, and a huge fireplace was at the western wall. The walls were decorated with shields and weapons and many skulls.

A score or so of men and women were in a line leading to a large man seated in a chair. The oaken shaft of a huge bronze-headed ax leaned against the side of the chair.

"Petitioners and plaintiffs," Davis said in a low voice to Faustroll. "And criminals."

"Ah!" Faustroll murmured. "The Man With the Ax!" He added, "The title of one of our poems."

He pointed at a beautiful bare-breasted blonde sitting in a high-backed chair a few feet from the king's throne.

"She?"

"Queen Ann, the number-one mare in Ivar's stable," Davis said softly. "Don't cross her. She has a hellish temper, the slut."

Ivar the Boneless, son of the semilegendary Ragnar Hairybreeches, who was the premier superhero of the Viking Age, stood up from the chair then. He was at least six feet six inches tall. Since his only garment was a sea-blue towel, his massive arms, chest, legs, and flat corded belly were evident. Despite his bulk, his quick and graceful movements made him seem more pantherish than lionlike.

His only adornment was a wide bronze band around

the upper right arm. It bore in alto-relief a valknut, three hunting horns meeting at the mouthpieces to form a triskelion, a three-legged figure. The valknut, the knot of the slain, was the sacred symbol of the greatest of the Norse gods, Odin.

His long, wavy, and red-bronze hair fell to his very broad shoulders. His face would have been called, in Davis's time on Earth, "ruggedly handsome." There was, however, something vulpine about it. Though Davis could not put a verbal finger on the lineaments that made him think of Brer Fox, he always envisioned that character when he saw the king.

Ivar was not the only general in the ninth century A.D. Danish invasion of England. Many native kings ruled there, but the king of Wessex would be the only one whose name would be familiar to twentieth-century English speakers. That was Alfred, whom later generations would call The Great, though his son and grandson were as deserving of that title. Though Alfred had saved Wessex from conquest, he had not kept the Danes from conquering much of the rest of England. Ivar had been the master strategist of the early Dane armies. Later, he had been co-king of Dublin with the great Norwegian conqueror, Olaf the White. But Ivar's dynasty had ruled Dublin for many generations.

As Davis and Faustroll approached the king, Davis said softly, "Don't call him Boneless. Nobody does that to his face without regretting it. You can call him Ivar, though, from what he's told me, it was Yngwaer in the Norse of his time. Languages change; Yngwaer became Ivar. His nickname in Old Norse was The Merciless, but it was close in sound to a word meaning "boneless."

Later generations mistranslated the nickname. But don't call him Merciless either.

"If you do, you'll find out why he was called that."

3

Doctor Davis was surprised.

He had been sure that the king would hustle the grotesquely painted and nonsense-talking Frenchman to the slave stockade at once. Instead, Ivar had told Davis to get quarters in the tower for Faustroll, good quarters, not some tiny and miserable room.

"He's been touched by the gods and thus is sacred. And I find him interesting. See that good care is taken of him, and bring him to the feast tonight."

Though this duty was properly the province of the king's steward, Davis did not argue. Nor did he ask Ivar what he meant by referring to the gods. On Earth, Ivar had been a high priest of the Norse god Odin until a few years before he died. Then he had been baptized into the Christian faith. Probably, Davis thought, because the foxlike Dane figured that it couldn't hurt to do that. Ivar was one to make use of all loopholes. But, after being resurrected along the River, the Viking had rejected both religions. However, he was still influenced by both, though far more by his lifelong faith.

Ivar gave his command in his native language, instead of Esperanto. Ivar referred to it as "that monotonously regular, grating, and unsubtle tongue." Davis had learned Old Norse well enough to get by. Two-thirds of its speakers in the kingdom came from Dublin, where Ivar had been king of the Viking stronghold when he had died in 873. But most of these were half-Irish, equally fluent in the Germanic Norse and Keltic Gaelic. Davis could speak the latter, though not as well as he could Norse.

Since the Franks made up one-fourth of the population of Ivar's kingdom, having been resurrected in the same area as the Dane, Davis had some knowledge of that tongue. The Franks came from the time of Chlodowech (died A.D. 511 in Paris), known to later generations as Clovis I. He had been king of the western, or Salian, Franks and conqueror of the northern part of the Roman province of Gaul.

Andrew Davis and Ivar's queen, Ann Pullen, were the only English speakers, except for some slaves, in the kingdom. Davis only talked to her when he could not avoid it. That was not often, because she liked him to give her frequent treatments, during which she did her best to upset him with detailed stories of her many sexual encounters and perversions. And she brazenly insisted that he massage her breasts. Davis had refused to do this and had been backed by Ivar, who seemed amused by the situation.

Ann Pullen had never told Davis that she was aware that he disliked her intensely. Both, however, knew well how each felt about the other. The only barrier keeping her from making him a quarry slave was Ivar. He was fond, though slightly contemptuous, of Davis. On the other hand, he respected the American for his knowledge, especially his medical lore, and he loved to hear Davis's stories of the wonders of his time, the steam iron horses and sailless ships, the telegraph and radio, the automobile, the airplane, the vast fortunes made by American robber barons, and the fantastic plumbing.

What Davis did not tell Ivar was what the late-twentieth century doctors he had met had told him—to his chagrin. That was that much of his treatment of his patients on Earth had been based on false medical information. However, Davis was still convinced that his neuropathic treatments, which involved no drugs, had enormously benefited his patients. Certainly, their recovery rate had been higher than the rate of those who went to conventional M.D.'s. On the other hand, the physicians had admitted that, in the field of psychiatry, the recovery rate of the mentally disturbed patients of African witch doctors was the same as that of psychiatrists' patients. That admission, he thought, either down-valued twentieth-century medicine or up-valued witch doctors.

A few of his informants had admitted that a large number of physically sick people recovered without the help of medical doctors or would have done so without such help.

He explained this to the painted madman on the way to the room, though he was irked because he felt compelled to justify himself. Faustroll did not seem very interested. He only muttered, "Quacks. All quacks. We pataphysicians are the only true healers."

"I still don't know what a pataphysician is," Davis said.

"No verbal explanation is needed. Just observe us, translate our physical motion and verbal expressions into the light of truth, vectors of four-dimensional rotations into photons of veracity."

"Man, you must have a reasonable basis for your theory, and you should be able to express it in clear and logical terms!"

"Red is your face, yet cool is the room."

Davis lifted his hands high above his head. "I give up! I don't know why I pay any attention to what you say! I should know better ! Yet..."

"Yet you apprehend, however dimly, that truth flows from us. You do not want to acknowledge that, but you can't help it. That's good. Most of the hairless bipedal apes don't have an inkling, don't respond at all. They're like cockroaches who have lost their antennae and, therefore, can't feel anything until they ram their chitinous heads into the wall. But the shock of the impact numbs even more the feeble organ with which they assumedly think."

Faustroll waved his bamboo fishing pole at Davis, forcing him to step back to keep from being hit on the nose by the bone hook.

"I go now to probe the major liquid body for those who breathe through gills."

Faustroll left the room. Davis muttered, "I hope it's a long time before I see you again."

But Faustroll was like a bad thought that can't be kept out of the mind. Two seconds later, he popped back into the room.

"We don't know what the royal osteopath's history on Earth was," Faustroll said, "or what your quest, your shining grail, was. Our permanent grail is The Truth. But the temporary one, and it may turn out to be that the permanent (if, truly, anything is permanent) grail or desideratum or golden apple is the answer to the question: Who resurrected us, placed us here, and why? Pardon. Not a question but questions. Of course, the answer may be that it doesn't matter at all. Even so, we would like to know."

"And just how will you be able to get answers to those questions here when you couldn't get them on Earth?"

"Perhaps the beings who are responsible for the Riverworld also know the answers we so desperately sought on Earth. We are convinced that these beings are of flesh and blood, though the flesh may not be protein and the blood may lack hemoglobin. Unlike God, who, if It does exist, is a spirit and thus lacks organs to make sound waves, though It seems to be quite capable of making thunder and lightning and catastrophes and thus should be able to form its own temporary oral parts for talking, these beings must have mouths and tongues and teeth and hands of a sort. Therefore, they can tell us what we wish to know. If we can find them. If they wish to reveal themselves.

"It's our theory, and we've never theorized invalidly, that the River in its twistings and windings forms a colossal hieroglyph. Or ideogram. Thus, if we can follow the entirely of the River and map it, we will have before us that hieroglyph or ideogram. Unlike the ancient Mayan or Egyptian hieroglyphs, it will be instantly understandable. Revelation will come with the light of comprehension, not with the falling of the stars and the moon turning blood-red and the planet cracking in half and the coming of the Beast whose number is 666 and all those delicious images evoked by St. John the Divine."

Davis spoke more hotly than he had intended. "Nonsense! In our first life, faith and faith alone had the answers, faith in the divine work as recorded in the Bible. As on Earth, so here."

"But there is no Holy Scripture here."

"In our minds!" Davis said loudly. "It's recorded here!" And he tapped a fingerpoint against his temple.

"As you know, no afterlife depicted in any religion faintly resembles this one. However, we do not argue. We state the truth and move on, leaving the truth behind us yet also taking it with us. But truth is arrived at when one ceases thinking. That's hard to do, we admit. Yet, if we can think about abandoning thought, we will be able to quit thinking. Thus, with that barrier to mental osmosis removed, the molecules of truth penetrate the diaphragm."

"Lunacy! Sheer lunacy! And blasphemy!"

Faustroll went through the doorway. Over his shoulder, he said, "We go, yet that is an illusion. The memory of this event remains in your mind. Thus, we are still here; we have not left."

Andrew Davis sighed. He sure had a lot to put up with. Why didn't he just take French leave and continue his quest up-River? Why didn't he? He had compelling reasons not to. One, if he were caught sneaking out of Ivar's domain, he'd be a slave and probably flogged. Two, if he did get out of the kingdom's boundaries, he still would not be safe from recapture for several days. The kingdoms for a fifty-mile stretch up the River had an agreement to return slaves to the states from which they had run away. Three, he could take the guaranteed foolproof way of escape. But, to do that, he'd have to kill himself. Then he'd be resurrected far away, but the thought of killing himself was hard to contemplate.

But, though his mind knew that he'd live again, his body didn't. His cells fiercely resisted the idea of suicide; they insisted on survival. Furthermore, he loathed the idea of suicide, though it was not rationally based. As a Christian, he would sin if he killed himself. Was it still a sin on the Riverworld? He doubted that very much. But his lifelong conditioning against it made him act as if it were.

Also, if he did do away with himself, he had a fifty-fifty chance of being translated downstream instead of upstream. If that happened, he'd have to travel past territory he'd already covered. And he could be captured and enslaved again by any of hundreds of states before he even got to Ivar's country.

If he awoke far up the River, he might have the goal of his quest behind him. Not until he had come to the end of the River would he know that he had skipped it. Then he would have to retrace his route.

What if the story of the woman who gave birth in the Valley was false? No, he would not consider that. He had not only faith but logic behind his belief. This world was a final test for those who believed in Jesus as their savior. Pass this test, and the next stage would be the true Paradise. Or the true Hell.

The Church of the Second Chance had some false doctrines, and it was another trap set by Satan. But the Devil was subtle enough to have planted some true doctrines among the false ones. The Second Chancers did not err in claiming that this world did offer all souls another opportunity to wash off their spiritual filth. What that church overlooked or deliberately ignored was that it also gave Satan a second chance to grab those who had eluded his clutches on Earth.

He looked through the wide, arched, and glassless window. From his height, he could see the hills and the plain and the River and the plain, hills, and mountains on the opposite bank. Arpad (died A.D. 907) ruled that twelve-mile-long area. He was the chief of the seven Mongolian tribes, called Magyar, who had left the Don

River circa A.D. 889 in what would be Russia and migrated westward to the Pannonian Plains. This was the area that would become Hungary. Arpad had been resurrected among a population that was partly ancient Akkadian, partly Old Stone Age southeast Asiatics, and ten percent of miscellaneous peoples. Though he was a Magyar, a tiny minority in this area, he had become king. That testified to his force of personality and to his ruthless methods.

Arpad was Ivar's ally and also a partner in the dam project. His slaves worked harder and longer and were treated much more harshly than Ivar's. The Norsemen was less severe and more generous with his slaves. He did not want to push them to the point of revolt or of suicide. Arpad's slaves had rebelled twice, and the number of suicides among them was far higher than among Ivar's.

Nor did Ivar trust Arpad. That was to be expected. Ivar trusted no one and had good reason not to rely on the Magyar. His spies had told him that Arpad had boasted, when drunk, which was often, that he would kill Ivar when the dam was finished.

If the Dane planned to jump the gun and slay Arpad first, he had not said so. Though he drank deeply at times, he reined in his tongue. At least, he did so concerning matters of state.

Davis was convinced that one of the two kings was not going to wait for the dam to be completed. Sometime, probably during the next two years, one was going to attack the other. Davis, on the principle that the lesser of two evils was to be preferred, hoped that Ivar would win. Ideally, each would knock the other off. Whichever happened, Davis was going to try to flee the area during the confusion of the battle.

4

He must have been looking through the window longer than he had thought. Faustroll had left the tower and was walking downhill, the fishing pole on his shoulder. And, some paces behind him, was the inevitable spy, a woman named Groa. She, too, carried a fishing pole, and, as Davis watched, she called to the Frenchman. He stopped, and they began talking. A moment later, they were side by side and headed for the River.

Groa was a redheaded beauty, daughter of a ninth-century Norwegian Viking, Thorsteinn the Red, son of Olaf the White and that extraordinary woman, Aud the Deep-Minded. Thorsteinn had been killed in a battle after conquering the northern part of Scotland. It was this event that caused Aud to migrate to Iceland and become ancestress of most Icelanders of the twentieth century.

No doubt, Thorsteinn was somewhere on the River and battling some foe while trying to get power over the foe or else battling to keep a foe from getting power over him. Power had been the main fuel of humankind on Earth. As on Earth, so here. So far. Until the Savior— Savioress?—grew up and worked God's will on His creations.

Groa must have been ordered by Ivar to attach herself to Faustroll. She was to find out if his story was true. Though the king had seemed to accept Faustroll at face value, he would wonder if the fellow had been sent by

Arpad to assassinate him. Groa would test him, probe him, and go so far as to lie with him if it was necessary. Perhaps, even if it was not necessary. She was a lusty woman. Then she'd report to Ivar later.

Davis sighed. What a life the afterlife was! Why couldn't everybody live in peace and trust? If they could not all love each other, they could at least be tolerant.

They could not do this for the same reason they had not done so on Earth. It was the nature of *Homo sapiens*. Of most of men and women, anyway. But . . . their situation was so different here. It was set up so that none need work hard for food and housing and other necessities. If people could all be pacifists and honest and compassionate, they would need no government by others. The Frenchman was right, though Davis hated admitting it even to himself. Given a new type of people, anarchy could be workable here.

Obviously, Whoever had placed humanity here had designed the Rivervalley so that humans, not having to spend so much time working, had time to advance themselves spiritually. But only those who understood this would advance themselves, change themselves for the better, and go on to whatever stage the Whoevers had built for them.

The Whoevers, however, had to be God. For Davis, there was no doubt or mystery about the identity of the creator of this place. The big mystery was why He had prepared a halfway house for the once-dead instead of the heavenly mansion the Bible had described.

He admitted to himself that the Bible had been very vague about the specifics of the abode of the saved, the saints. It had been much more concrete about the abode of the damned.

He could only accept that God, in His infinite wisdom, knew what he was doing.

Why, as so many complained, had not God given them some reassurance? A sign? A beacon toward which they could go as a moth could fly to the flame? Though that was not the best of comparisons, now he considered it. Anyway, where was the sign, the beacon, the writing in the sky?

Davis knew. It was the birth of a baby to a virgin. In a world where men and women were sterile, one woman had been the exception. She had been impregnated with the Holy Spirit, and she had conceived. God had performed a miracle. The infant, so the story went, was female. At first, hearing this, Davis had been shocked. But, thinking about it calmly and logically, trying to overcome his preconceptions, he had concluded that he should not be upset, not kick against the pricks. On Earth, the Savior had been a male. Here, the Savior was a female. Why not?

God was fair-minded, and who was he to question the Divine Being?

"Davis!" a harsh voice said behind him. He jumped and whirled, his heart beating hard. Standing in the doorway was Sharkko the Shyster, the ever-egregious slave of whom he had dreamed last night.

"Hustle your ass, Davis! The Great Whore of Babylon wants you for a treatment! Right now!"

"I'll tell the queen what you said about her," Davis said. He did not intend to do so, but he wanted to see the loathsome fellow turn pale. Which he did.

"Ah, she won't believe you," the slave said. "She hates your guts. She'd take my word against yours any time. Anyway, I doubt she'd be insulted. She'd think it was a compliment.''

''If it wasn't against my nature, I'd boot you in the rear,'' Davis said.

The slave, his color now restored, snorted. He turned and limped down the hall. Davis left the room. He watched the man as he walked behind him. Though the man had been resurrected in his twenty-five-year-old body, his vision restored to 20/20, he was now a human wreck. His right leg had been broken in several places and reset wrong. His nose had not been reset after the bridge had been shattered. He could not breathe properly because of his nose and some ribs that had also lacked proper resetting. One eye had been knocked out and was not yet fully regrown. His face twisted and leered with a tic.

All of this had resulted from a beating by slaves whose overseer he had been. Unable any longer to endure his bullyings, kicks, and other unjust treatment, they had worked on him late one night and thus worked out their hatred of him. His hut had been too dark for him to identify his attackers, though he, and everybody else, knew his men were the malefactors. If you could fairly call them malefactors. Most people though the deed was justified self-defense.

Ivar thought so, too, after hearing testimony. He decided that Sharkko had broken the rules laid down by the king. These were mainly for the sake of efficiency, not of humanitarianism. But they had been disregarded, and Sharkko's back was bloody from forty lashes with a fish-hide whip. Each of the overseer's slaves had administered a stroke. Ivar, witnessing this, had been highly amused.

Sharkko had then been degraded to a quarry slave. But his injuries had kept him from doing well at the hard work, and he had been made a tower slave after six months. Ivar used him for, among other things, a human bench when he wished to sit down where a chair was unavailable.

The Shyster had been so named by a Terrestrial client who was now a citizen of Ivar's kingdom. From what the client said, he had been cheated by Sharkko and had been unable to find justice in the court. The ex-client was among those who had beaten Sharkko.

The Shyster had been indiscreet enough to tell some cronies that he meant to revenge himself on all who had wronged him. Though Davis did not think that he had earned Sharkko's hatred, he was among those named for some terrible retribution. The Shyster had not been so full of braggadocio that he had said anything about revenging himself on Ivar. He knew what would happen to him if the king heard about such a threat.

Sharkko, hunched over, dragging one foot and mumbling to himself, continued on down the hall. Sharkko was a veritable Caliban, Davis thought, as he followed the monster down the hall to a steep and spiraling staircase.

He felt unusually uneasy. It seemed to him that events were coming to a head, a big, green, and pus-filled boil on the face of this kingdom. The coming conflict between Arpad and Ivar, the arrival of the grotesque and disquieting Faustroll, the increasing tension between himself and the queen, and Sharkko's hatred added up to a situation that could pop open—like a boil—at any time. He could feel it. Though he could not logically predict that the eruption would occur soon, he sensed it.

Or, perhaps, this was caused by his internal conflicts. He himself was ready to break open and out, much as he wanted to wait until the right moment for flight.

The virgin mother and the baby were waiting for him up the River. They did not know it, of course. But he was to play a strong part in the events that would bring on the revelation of the second Savior to this world. Though it might be egotistic to think so, he was sure of it.

He entered the large room where Queen Ann waited for him. She was on the osteopathic table that he had built. But, spread out naked there, she looked as if she were waiting for a lover. Her two attendants giggled when they saw him. They were blacks who had been slaves of an early-twentieth-century Arabian family on Earth. They had been free for only one year after their resurrection. Now they were slaves again.

They should be sympathizing with his plight. Instead, they were amused.

5

"Massage my inner thigh muscles," Ann said. "They're very tight."

She kept talking softly while laughing loudly between sentences. Her remarkably bright and leaf-green eyes never left his face. Though he kept it expressionless, he longed to snarl at her, spit in her face, and then vomit on her. The Jezebel! The Scarlet Women! The Great Whore of Babylon!

"When you're on your back, rotating your pelvis,

your legs up in the air for a long time, you put a strain on those muscles," she said. "It's almost an equal strain when I'm on top. Sometimes I have to rest between up-and-downs and hip gyrations. But then I squeeze down on him with my sphincter muscle and so don't really get a rest. It is the sphincter, isn't it, Doctor?"

He knew the human body so well he did not have to see what he was doing. His head turned away from her, his eyes half closed, he kneaded her flesh. How soft her skin was! What a muscle tone! Sometimes, when he was in that drowsy twilight state between dreaming and awakening, he knew his fingers were working on flesh. Not hers, of course. The reflex was caused by a digital memory, as it were, of the thousands of bodies he had treated while on Earth.

"Don't get too close to the king's personal property," she said. "You touch it, and he might cut your hands off."

If he did that, Davis thought, scores of the males in the kingdom would be without hands.

"You're not much of a man," she said. "A real man's tallywhacker would be lifting that towel right off his waist, rip the Velcro apart."

The slave girls giggled though they did not understand English. But they had heard similar phrases in Esperanto for a long time. They knew that she was saying something taunting and demeaning.

Davis envisioned closing his hands around the queen's throat. It wouldn't take long.

Then he prayed, Oh, Lord! Save me from such sinful thoughts!

"Perhaps," he said, "I should massage your knees, too? They seem to be rather stiff."

She frowned and stared hard at him. The she smiled and laughed.

"Oh! You're suggesting . . . ? Yes, do. I have spent a certain amount of time on my knees. But they're on pillows, so it's not so bad. However . . ."

Instead of flying into a rage, as he had expected, she was amused. She also looked somewhat triumphant, as if goading him into saying something insulting to her, even an innuendo, was a victory. However, she probably did not regard his comments as an insult. The bitch was more likely to think he had complimented her.

What did he care what she thought? To be honest with himself, he cared a lot. Unless she was stopped by Ivar, she could make his life unbearable, torture him, do anything with or to him. Davis had not heard any stories about her being cruel, except for her sexual teasing, which could not be ranked with torture or killing. But he had no guarantee that she might not become so. Especially in her dealings with him.

Ann Pullen was a fellow American, though a nauseating example as far as he was concerned. She had been born about 1632 in Maryland. Her family had been Quakers, but when it converted to Episcopalianism, she had gone to hell. Those were her own words. She had been married four times to tobacco plantation owners in Virginia and Maryland. She had survived them all.

No wonder, Davis thought. She'd wear any man out, if not from her incessant sexual demands and infidelity, then from her TNT temper and willfulness.

Mostly, she had lived in Westmoreland County, Virginia, which was between the Potomac and Rappahannock rivers. In her day, the area had many thick forests and large swamps but no roads. Travel was mainly by river or creek. Nor did the plantations resemble those of a later era. There were no beautiful many-pillared mansions and broad well-kept lawns. The owners' houses were modest, the stables were likely to be made of logs, and chickens and hogs roamed the yards. Pig stealing was common even among the plantation owners. Cash was scarce; the chief currency was tobacco. The people were unusually hot-tempered and litigious, though no one knew why.

By her own testimony, Ann had once been sentenced to ten lashes on her bare shoulders because of her libelous and scandalous speeches against a Mister Presley. She also had once attacked her sister-in-law with bare hands.

It had been recorded in the Order Book of the county in A.D. 1677 that Ann Pullen had encouraged her daughter Jane to become "the most remarkable and notorious whore in the province of Virginie." But Davis had to admit that, in the strict sense of the word, she was not a whore. She fornicated because she liked to do so and never took money.

The Order Book also said that Jane's mother, Ann Pullen, had debauched her own daughter by encouragement to commit adultery and break the whole estate of matrimony.

The daughter's husband, Morgan Jones, had enjoined more than once (as the court had recorded) any man from entertaining or having any manner of dealing with Jane or transporting her out of the county or giving her passage over any river or creek.

It was also recorded that Ann Pullen had declared that Jane had no husband at that time, Jones having died, and she (Ann) did not know why her daughter should not take the pleasure of this world as well as any other woman.

Also, Ann did not care who the father of her daughter's child was, provided one William Elmes would take her to England, as he had promised.

Ann was a feminist ahead of her time, a lone pioneer in the movement in the days when it was dangerous to be such. She had also been a libertine, though Davis thought that automatically went with the desire for female equality.

However, such Terrestrial attitudes should not apply on the Riverworld. Even he admitted that, though insisting that there were limits to that viewpoint. Ann had certainly overstepped them. With seven-league boots.

Ivar's kingdom was basically Old Norse. Since women (though not female slaves) in the pre-Christian era had had many more rights than those in the Christian countries, they had even more rights on the Riverworld. In this state, anyway. Theoretically, Ann could divorce Ivar with a simple statement that she wished it, and she could take her property with her. Not half of the kingdom's, that is, the king's. Her grail, her towels, her artifacts, and her slaves were hers.

But divorce didn't seem likely. Ivar was greatly amused by her, even when she became angry at him, and he reveled in her uninhibited and many-talented lovemaking. He knew that she had lovers, but he didn't seem to care. He doubted that she would plot with a lover to assassinate him. She knew well on which side her vagina was buttered.

So Andrew Davis had to suffer the indignities she piled on him. Meanwhile, he dreamed of the divinely begotten infant far up the River. He also tried to think of foolproof ways to escape this land. And how to prevent capture by the other slave-holding states between him and his goal.

Doing his Christian duty, he had tried to pray for Ann. But he sounded so insincere to himself that he knew God would ignore his requests that she be forgiven and be made to see the Light.

When her treatment was over, he left the chamber as he always did. He was angry, frustrated, and sweating, his stomach was boiling, and his hands were shaking.

Oh, Lord, how long must I endure this? Do not, I pray You, continue to subject me to evil and the temptation to curse You as you did Job!

At high noon, the grailstone in the tower courtyard erupted in lightning and thunder. He left the room in which he had been waiting until this happened. To stand in the yard near the stone was to be deafened. Though his grail was full of excellent food and drink, he had no appetite. What he did not eat, he shared with his cronies at the table in the big hall. The cup of brandy and the pack of mingled tobacco and marijuana cigarettes he put aside. He could have kept half of the booze and the coffin nails for himself, but he would give them all to Eysteinn the Chatterer, Ivar's chief tax and tribute collector.

Thus, he paid his taxes at a double rate. That enabled him halfway through the month to pour the daily quota of the liquor down a drain and to shred the cigarettes. He did this secretly because many would have been outraged at this waste. They would report to the king, who would confiscate the extra "goodies" and would punish him.

He had never, during his two lives, tasted any alcohol or smoked. In fact, on Earth, he had not even drunk ice water because of its unhealthy effects. He loathed having to contribute to the king and his vices. But, if he didn't, he would suffer the cat-o'-nine-tails or become a quarry slave. Or both.

That evening, shortly after sunset, he went to the great hall built near the bank. This was where Ivar preferred to eat supper, to drink, and to roister among his cronies and his toadies. (Davis admitted that he was one of the latter. But he had no choice.) The hall was built in the old Viking style, a single huge room with Ivar's table on a platform and at the head of the floor-level tables. The platform had not been used on Earth among the semi-democratic Vikings. It was an innovation adopted by Ivar. The support poles were carved with the heads of humans, gods, beasts, and symbols from the old religion. Among these and often repeated were gold-mining dwarfs, dragons, the Earth-encircling Midgard serpent, stags, bears, valknuts, frost giants, Thor and his hammer, one-eyed Odin with, sometimes, his ravens Hugin and Munin on his shoulders, right-handed swastikas, runic phrases, and Skidbladnir, the magical ship that could be folded and carried in a bag after use.

Tonight, as usual, the men and women drank too much, the talk was fast and furious, boasting and bombast thundered in the hall, people quarreled and sometimes fought. Ivar had forbidden duels to the death because he had lost too many good warriors to them. But the belligerents could go at each other with fists and feet, and the king did not frown on gouging of eyes, crushing of testicles, ripping off of ears, and biting off of noses. Though it took three months, the eyes, noses, and ears would grow again, and the testicles would repair themselves.

Davis had grown used to these nightly gatherings, but he did not like them. Violence still upset him, and the air stank of tobacco and marijuana smoke and beer and liquor fumes. Also, the sickening odor of farts, followed by loud laughter and thigh-slapping, drifted to him now and then. Queen Ann, who was sitting on Ivar's left, was one of the loudest in her laughter when this form of primitive humor erupted. Tonight she wore a towel around her neck, the ends of which covered her breasts. But she was rather careless about keeping them in place.

Mingled with the other smells was that of the fish caught in the River and fried in one end of the hall.

Davis sat at the king's table because he was the royal osteopath. He would have preferred a table as far away as it could be from this one. That would give him a chance to sneak away after all were too drunk to notice him. Tonight, however, he was interested in watching and occasionally overhearing the conversation of Doctor Faustroll and Ivar the Boneless. The Frenchman sat immediately to the king's right, the most favored chair at the table. He had brought an amazing amount of fish to the feast, far more than any other anglers. Once, during a lessening of the uproar, Davis heard Ivar ask Faustroll about his luck.

"It's not luck," Faustroll had said. "It's experience and skill. Plus an inborn knack. We survived mainly on fish we caught in the Seine when we lived in Paris."

6

"Paris," Ivar said. "I was with my father, Ragnar, son of Sigurd Hring, when we Danes sailed up the Seine in March, the Franks not expecting Vikings that early in the year. A.D. 845, I've been told. The Frankish ruler, Charles the Bald, split his army into two. I advised my father to attack the smaller force, which we did. We slaughtered them except for one hundred and eleven prisoners. These my father hanged all at once as a sacrifice to Odin on an island in the Seine while the other Frankish army watched us. They must have filled their drawers from horror.

"We went on up to Paris, a much smaller city then than the vast city others have told me about. On Easter Sunday, the Christian's most holy day, we stormed and plundered Paris and killed many worshipers of the Savior. Odin was good to us."

Ivar smiled to match the sarcastic tone of his voice. He did not believe in the gods, pagan or Christian. But Davis, watching him closely, saw the expression on his face and the set of his eyes. They could be showing nostalgia or, perhaps, some unfathomable longing. Davis had seen this expression a score of times before now. Could the ruthless and crafty hungerer for power be longing for something other than he now had? Did he, too, desire to escape this place and its responsibilities and ever-present danger of assassination? Did he, like Davis and Faustroll, have goals that many might think idealistic or romantic? Did he want to shed the restrictions of his situation and be free? After all, a powerful ruler was as much a prisoner as a slave.

"The One-Eyed One blessed us," Ivar said, "though it may just have been coincidence that Charles the Bald was having serious trouble with other Frankish states and with his ambitious brothers. Instead of trying to bar us from going back down the Seine, he paid us seven thousand pounds of silver to leave his kingdom. Which we did, though we did not promise not to come back again later."

Faustroll had so far not interrupted the king, though

disgust sometimes flitted across his face. He drank swiftly and deeply, and his cup was never empty. The slave behind him saw to that. He also gave the Frenchman cigarettes after he had smoked up his own supply. The slave was Sharkko, apparently delegated by the king to serve Faustroll tonight. Sharkko was scowling, and, now and then, his lips moved. His words were drowned out by the din, and a good thing, too, Davis thought. Davis could lip-read both English and Esperanto. If Ivar knew what Sharkko was saying, he would have him flogged and then put into the latrine-cleaning gang.

Finally, he banged his wooden cup down, causing those around him, including Ivar, to look startled.

"Your Majesty will pardon us," he said loudly. "But you are still as you were on Earth. You have not progressed one inch spiritually; you are the same bloody barbarous pirate, plenty of offense meant, as the old hypocrite who died in Dublin. But we do not give up hope for you. We know that philosophy in its practical form of pataphysics is the gate to the Truth for you. And, though you at first seem to be a simple savage, we know that you are much more. Our brief conversation in the hall convinced us of that."

Many at the table, including Davis, froze, though they rolled their eyeballs at each other and then gazed at Ivar. Davis expected him to seize the war ax always by his side and lop off Faustroll's head. But the Viking's skin did not redden, and he merely said. "We will talk with you later about this philosophy, which we hope will contain more wisdom and less nonsense than that of the Irish priests, the men in women's skirts."

His "we," Davis knew, was a mimicking and mocking of Faustroll.

Ivar rose then, and silence followed three strokes on a huge bronze gong.

Ivar spoke loudly, his bass voice carrying to all corners of the huge hall.

"The feast is over! We're all going to bed early tonight, though I suppose many of you will not go to sleep until you can no longer get it up!"

The crowd had murmured with surprise and disappointment, but that was followed by laughter at the king's joke. Davis grimaced with disgust. Ann, seeing his expression, smiled broadly.

"We haven't run out of food or drink," Ivar said. "That's not why I'm cutting this short. But it occurred to me a little while ago that tomorrow is the third anniversary of the founding of my kingdom. That was the day when I, a slave of the foul Scots tyrant, Eochaid the Poisonous, rose in revolt with Arpad, also a slave, and with two hundred slaves, most of whom now sit in honored places in this hall. We silently strangled the guards around Eochaid's hall. He and his bodyguards were all sleeping off their drunkenness, safe, they supposed, in their thick-walled hall on a high mound of earth. We burned the log building down and slaughtered those who managed to get out of the fire. All except Eochaid, whom we captured.

"The next day, I gave him the death of the blood eagle as I did on Earth to King Aella of York and King Edmund of East Anglia and some of my other foes whom I sacrificed to Odin."

Davis shuddered. Though he had never seen this singular method of execution, he had heard about it many times. The victim was placed facedown, his spine was cut, and his lungs were pulled out and laid on his back,

forming the rough shape of an eagle with outspread
wings.

"I have decided that we will go to bed early and get up
early tomorrow. The slaves will be given the day off and
given plenty of food and drink. Everybody will celebrate.
We will all work to collect much fish, and that evening
we will start the festivities. There will be games and
archery and spear-casting contests and wrestling, and
those who have grudges may fight to the death with their
enemies if they so wish."

At this, the crowd shouted and screamed.

Ivar lifted his hands for silence, then said, "Go to bed!
Tomorrow we enjoy ourselves while we thank whatever
gods made this world that we are free of Eochaid's harsh
rule and are free men!"

The crowd cheered again and then streamed out of the
hall. Davis, the handle of his grail in one hand, was
heading for the tower and halfway up the first hill when
the even-toned voice of Faustroll rose behind him. "Wait
for me! We'll walk the rest of the way with you!"

Davis stopped. Presently, the Frenchman, in no hurry,
caught up with him. Heavy fumes of whiskey mixed with
fish enveloped him, and his words were somewhat slurred.
Mon ami! Mia amico! That which treads on day's heels is
beautiful, is it not? The beings that burn in the nocturnal
bowl above in their un-Earth patterns, how inspiring!
Wise above the wisdom of men, they will have nothing to
do with us. But they are generous with their splendor."

"Uhmm," Davis said.

"A most observant remark. Tell me, my friend, what
do you think is the real reason behind Ivar's ending the
feast?"

"What?"

"I do not trust the goat who leads the woolly ones. Statesmen and politicians, generals and admirals, they seldom reveal their real intentions. The Boneless is up to something his enemies won't like. Nor will his people."

"You're very cynical," Davis said. He looked across the River. The plains and the hills in Arpad's kingdom were dark except for the scattered fires of sentinels. There were also torches on the tops of the bamboo signal towers a half-mile apart and forming a ten-mile-long line.

"Cynical? A synonym for experience. And for one whose eyes have long been open and whose nose is as keen in detecting corruption as the nose of the hairy one some claim is man's best friend. Remember, our leader comes from the land where something is rotten, to paraphrase the Bard of Avon."

They had resumed walking. Davis said, "What did Ivar say to make you suspicious?"

"Nothing and everything. We do not accept anything at face value. The meaning of words and of facial expressions, the hardness of objects, the permanence of the universe, that fire will always burn skin, that a certain cause always leads to a certain result, that what goes up must come down. It isn't always necessarily so."

He swung the cylinder of his grail around to indicate everything.

Davis did not feel like talking about metaphysics or, in fact, anything. Especially not with this fellow, who made no sense. But he accepted Faustroll's invitation to sit down in the tower courtyard and converse for a while. Perhaps he might find out just why Faustroll suspected that Ivar was up to something. Not that it made any difference. What could he do about anything here?

There was a table near a row of torches in wall

brackets. They sat down. The Frenchman opened his grail and drew out a metal cup half filled with whiskey. Davis looked at the formula painted on the man's forehead. He had attended lectures on calculus at Rush Medical College, and he was familiar with the markings. But, unless you knew the referents of the symbols, you could never know what they meant or how to use them. He read: $- O - a - + a + O =$

Faustroll said, "The significance of the formula? God is the tangential point between zero and infinity."

"Which means?"

Faustroll spoke as if he had memorized this lecture. "God is, by definition, without dimension, but we must be permitted . . ."

"Is this going to be long?" Davis said.

"Too long for tonight and perhaps for eternity. Besides, we are rather drunk. We can visualize all clearly, but our body is weary and our mind not running on all eight cylinders."

Davis rose, saying, "Tomorrow, then. I'm tired, too."

"Yes, You can understand better our thesis if we have a pen and a piece of paper on which to lay it out."

Davis said good night, leaving the Frenchman sitting at the table and staring into the dark whiskey as if it were a crystal ball displaying his future. He made his way up to his tiny room. It was not until he was at its door that he remembered how astray his conversation with the Frenchman had gone. Faustroll had not told him what he had concluded from his suspicions about Ivar.

He shrugged. Tomorrow he would find out. If, that is, the crazy fellow's tongue did not wander off again. To him, a straight line was not the shortest path between two points. Indeed, he might deny the entire validity of Euclidean geometry.

Davis also had an uneasy feeling that Faustroll's near-psychopathic behavior hid a very keen mind and a knowledge of science, mathematics, and literature far exceeding his own. He could not be dismissed as just another loony.

Davis pushed in the wooden-hinged and lockless door. He looked out through the glassless opening into the darkness lit only by the star-crowded sky. But that light was equal to or surpassed that of Earth's full moon. At first, it seemed peaceful. Everybody except the sentinels had gone to bed. Then he saw the shadows moving in the valley below the tower. As his eyes became more adjusted to the pale light, he saw that a large body of men was in it.

His heart suddenly beat hard. Invaders? No. Now he could see Ivar the Boneless, clad in a conical bronze helmet and a long shirt of mail and carrying a war ax, walking down the hill toward the mass of men. Behind him came his bodyguard and counselors. They, too, were armored and armed. Each wore two scabbards encasing bronze swords, and they carried spears or battle-axes. Some also bore bundles of pine torches or sacks. The containers would, he knew at once, hold gunpowder bombs.

Faustroll had been right. There would be no celebration tomorrow unless it was a victory feast. The king had lied to cover up a military operation. Those not involved—as yet—in the military operation had been lied to. But selected warriors has been told to gather secretly at a certain time.

Suddenly, the starlight was thinly veiled by light clouds. These became darker quickly. Davis could no longer see

Ivar or, in fact, any human beings. And now the sound of
distant thunder and the first zigzag of lightning appeared
to the north.

Soon, the raging rain and the electrical violence that
often appeared around midnight would be upon the kingdoms of Ivar and Arpad. Like the wolf on the fold, Davis
thought. And Ivar and his army would be like the ancient
Assyrians sweeping down from the hills on the Hebrews
as that poet—what was his name?—wrote.

But who was Ivar going to assault?

7

The wind spat raindrops through the window into
Davis's face. Another layer of darkness slid in and cut off
his view of the men. Thunder rolled closer like a threatening
bully. A lightning streak, brief probing of God's lantern
beam (looking for an honest man?), noisily lit up the
scene. He glimpsed Ivar's group running over the top of
the nearest hill to the River. He also saw other dark
masses, like giant amoebae, flowing onto the plains from
the hills. These were warriors hastening to join Ivar. The
larger body of plains dwellers waiting for the king was,
as it were, the mother amoeba.

Another blazing and crashing streak, closer this time,
revealed a great number of boats in slips that had been
empty for a long time. These had to have come in
recently from upstream. Just off the bank many vessels:
rowboats, dugouts, catamarans, dragonships, and the
wide-beamed merchant boats called dromonds. Their
sails were furled, and all bristled with spears.

Under cover of the night, Ivar's warriors from every part of the kingdom had slipped down here. Of course, there would be other parties who would attack the opposite bank, Arpad's domain, up-River. The attack had to be against the Magyar's kingdom. Davis did not know why he had wondered what the king was up to. However, Ivar was unpredictable, and it was chancy to bet on any of his next moves.

The secrecy with which the operation had been carried out impressed Davis. He had had no inkling of it, yet he was often in the king's company. This operation, though it involved thousands of men who had somehow not revealed the plans to their female hutmates, had been exceedingly efficient.

But the lightning was going to display the invaders to Arpad's sentinels. Unless, that is, some of Ivar's men had crossed the River earlier and killed the guards.

After a while, the heart of the storm raged over the area within his sight. Now the warriors were grouped on the bank and embarking. So frequent and vivid were the bolts, he could see the invaders moving. They were many-legged clumps the individuals of which were not visible from this distance in the rainy veil.

He gasped. A fleet was putting out from the opposite bank.

A few seconds later, more groups began to gather behind Ivar's forces on the bank. He groaned, and he muttered, "Arpad has pulled a sneak play!" His force had come ashore farther up the River and sneaked along the banks to come up on the Ivarians' flank. And now the Arpadians were charging it. The surpriser had been surprised; the fox had been outfoxed. The Magyar was going to grind his former ally between two forces. But that was easier planned than done. Ivar's men on shore, though taken by surprise, had not fled. They were fighting fiercely, and their shore force outnumbered the enemy's. Soon, Ivar's warriors in the boats would join those on the bank. As quickly as the oars could drive the boats, they were driving toward the slips and the open bank. Though the boatmen could not get back to the bank to disembark swiftly, they should be able to get all ashore before the enemy's second force arrived from the opposite bank. And they would overwhelm the ambushers—if Ivar had anything to do with it. He was a very cool and quick thinker. His men, veterans of many battles, did not panic easily.

Meanwhile, Arpad's fleet was about a quarter of a mile from their destination. Its commander, whom Davis assumed was Arpad, not one to hang back behind his army, would be considering two choices. He could order the boats back to his shore and there await the inevitable assault from Ivar's forces. Or Arpad could keep on going straight ahead, hoping that the ambushers would keep Ivar's men entangled long enough for him to land his army.

The rain thickened. Davis saw the conflict now as if through distorted spectacles. And then, five or six minutes later, the downfall began to thin. The worst of the storm had passed over, but thunder and lightning still harried the land. Intermittently, starlight between masses of clouds revealed that a third force had entered the fray. It was a large fleet that must recently have come around the River's bend a half-mile to the north. Davis could not identify who its sailors were. But the only ones liable to come from the north were the men of Thorfinn the Skull-Splitter.

Thorfinn had been on Earth the earl of the Orkney

Islands and part of northern Scotland. Though a mighty warrior, as his nickname testified, he had died in A.D. 963 in bed. The "straw death," as the Norse called it, was not the fate he wanted. Only men who were killed in battle went to Valhalla, the Hall of the Slain, where the heroes fought each other during the day and those killed were resurrected to fight the next day, where the mead and the food was better than anything on Earth, and where, at night, Odin's Valkyries screwed the drunken heroes' brains out.

But Thorfinn had awakened in the Rivervalley along with everyone else: the brave and the cowardly, the monarchs and the slaves, the honored and the despised, the honest and the crooked, the devout and the hypocrite, the learned and the ignorant, the rich and the poor, and the lucky and the unlucky.

However, the Riverworld was, in many respects, like Valhalla. The dead rose the next day, though seldom in the place where they had died; the drink and the food were marvelous; nonfatal wounds healed quickly; a chopped-off foot or a gouged-out eye grew back again; women with the sexual drive of a Valkyrie abounded. Of course, Valkyries never complained or nagged, but they were mythical, not real.

And what was he, Andrew Paxton Davis, a pacifist, a Christian, and a virtual slave, doing standing here and watching the battle among the heathens? Now, now, now was the time to escape.

He quickly stuffed his few possessions in a fish-skin bag and grabbed the handle of his grail. Like the Arab in the night, I steal away, he thought. Except that I don't have to take the time to fold my tent. He walked out of his room swiftly and sped down the narrow winding steps. He met no one until he got to the courtyard. Then he saw a dark figure ahead of him. He stopped, his heart beating harder than his running accounted for. But a lightning bolt revealed the face of the person who had struck such fear into him.

"Doctor Faustroll!"

The Frenchman tried to bow but had to grip the side of the table to keep from falling on his face.

"Doctor Davis, I presume?" he mumbled.

The American was going to hurry past him but was restrained by a charitable impulse. He said, "There's uproar in Acheron, my good fellow. Now is the time to gain our freedom. Ivar was going to make a sneak attack on Arpad, but Arpad had the same idea about him. There's the devil to pay, and Thorfinn, Ivar's ally, has just shown up. Chaos will reign. We have an excellent chance of getting away during all the commotion."

Faustroll put a hand on his forehead and groaned. Then he said, "Up the River? Our quests for the probably nonexistent?"

"Think, man! Do you want to remain a slave? Now's the time, the only chance we may ever have!"

Faustroll bent to pick up his grail and fishing pole. He groaned again and said, "*La merde primitive!* The devil is using our head as an anvil."

"I'm going," Davis said. "You may come with me or not, as you please."

"Your concern for us is touching," the Frenchman said. "But we really don't have to run. Though we've been in lifelong bondage, we have never been a slave. Unlike the billions of the conventional and the swine-minded, we have been free."

A distant flash faintly illuminated Faustroll. His eyes

were rolling as if he were trying to see something elusive.

"Stay here, then, and be free in your miserable bonds!" Davis shouted. "I felt it was my duty to tell you what is going on!"

"If it had been love compelling you, it would be different."

"You're the most exasperating man I've ever met!"

"The gadfly has its uses, especially if it is equipped not only with a fore sting but an aft sting."

Davis snorted and walked away. But, by the time he had started down the hill from the tower, he heard Faustroll call out to him.

"Wait for us, my friend, if, indeed, you are that!"

Davis halted. He could not say that he liked the grotesque fellow. But...something in the absurd Frenchman appealed to him. Perhaps, Davis thought, it's the physician in me. The man's mad, and I should take care of him. I might be able to cure him someday.

More likely, it's just that I don't want to be alone. Crazed company is better than none. Sometimes.

The thunder and lightning had rolled on down the Valley. In a few minutes, the bright zigzags and the vast bowling-pin noises would be out of sight and out of ear. Then, as almost always, the downpour would stop as if a valve had been shut. The clouds would disappear within thirty minutes or so after that. And the star-filled sky would shed its pale fire on the pale weapons of the warriors and their dark blood. It would also make it easier for Faustroll and him to be seen.

Now he could faintly hear the frightening sounds of the clash. Shrill screams, deep cries, swords clanging, drums beating, and, now and then, the bellowing of a black

gunpowder bomb as it destroyed itself in a burst of light.
He also became aware that the tower, in which he had
thought was no living soul, was as busy as a disturbed
anthill. He turned to look back. Faustroll, panting, was
just about to catch up with him. He was silhouetted by
the many torches of the many people streaming from the
tower.

Among them was Ann Pullen. She had put a heavy
towel over her shoulders and a long one around her
waist. But her white face and streaming blond hair were
vivid under the flaming brand she held high.

And there was Sharkko walking as fast as his dragging
leg would permit him. He carried a grail in one hand, a
sword in the other, and a large bag was strapped to his
back.

The others passed Davis on their way down the hill.
Apparently, they were going either to join Ivar in the
battle or to find a place where they could more closely
observe it. The latter, more likely. If they thought that
things were going against Ivar, they would be running,
too.

Davis grabbed a torch from a slave woman as she
passed him. She protested but did not fight him. He held
it up and pointed up-River.

"Let's go!"

Easier said than done. Just as they reached the edge of
the plain, they were forced to stop. A large body of men,
many of them holding torches, jogged by. Davis looked
at the round, wooden, leather-covered helmets, the broad
dark faces, and the eyes with prominent epicanthic folds.
He groaned. Then he said, "More of Arpad's men! They
must be a second flanking force!

These were not Magyars but soldiers from Arpad's

ancient Siberian citizens, forming ten percent of the kingdom's population. They looked much more like the American Indians than Eskimos or Chuk-chuks. A group of six or seven men broke off from the mass and trotted toward them. Davis yelled, "Run!" and he fled back up the hill. Behind came the sound of bare feet on the wet grass and wet mud under it. But it was Faustroll.

When he was halfway up the hill, Davis looked behind him. The invaders were no longer in pursuit. Finding that they could not kill the two men easily, they had rejoined the army.

After a while, he and Faustroll quit climbing along the sides of the hill and went down to the edge of the plain. Within ten minutes the starblaze was undimmed by clouds.

"Time to look for a boat," Davis said.

They went slowly and stealthily among the huts. Now and then, they had to go around corpses. Most of these were women, but some had managed to kill invaders before they had been cut down. "The never-ending story," Davis said. "When will they learn to stop killing and raping and looting? Can't they see that it does nothing to advance them? Can't . . ."

"They didn't see on Earth, why should they here?" Faustroll said. "But perhaps it's a weeding-out process here. We get not just a second chance but many chances. Then, one day, poof! The evils ones and the petty, the malicious, and the hypocritical are gone! Let's hope that that does not mean that nobody is left here. Or, perhaps, that's the way it's going to work out."

He stopped, pointed, and said, "Eureka!"

There were many boats along here, beached or riding at anchor a few feet from the short. They chose a dugout canoe with a small mast. But, just as they were pushing it off the grass into the water, they were startled by a yell behind them.

"Wait! For God's sake, wait! I want to go with you!"

They turned and saw Sharkko hobbling toward them. He was dragging another bag, a large one, behind him. No doubt, Davis thought, it was filled with loot Sharkko had picked up on the way. Despite his fear, his predatory nature had kept the upper hand.

Davis said, "There's not enough room for three."

Panting, Sharkko stopped a few feet from them. "We can take a larger boat."

Then he turned quickly to look down-River. The distant clamor had suddenly become closer. The starlight fell over a dark and indistinct mass advancing from the south. Shouts and clanging of bronze on bronze swelled from it. It stopped moving toward Davis for several minutes. Then the sounds ceased, and the group moved again, more swiftly now.

Whoever the men chasing after those who fled were, they had been killed. But another hue and cry rose from behind the survivors. The men coming toward Davis began to run.

"Get in one of the boats!" Sharkko squalled. "They'll grab them, and we won't have any!"

Davis thought that that was good advice, but he did not intend to take the fellow with him. He resumed helping the Frenchman push the canoe. It slid into the water. But Sharkko had splashed to it, thrown his grail and bags into it, and started to climb in. Davis grabbed the bags and threw them into the water. Sharkko screamed with fury. His fist struck Davis's chin. Stunned, Davis staggered back and fell into the water. When he rose, sputtering, he saw that Sharkko was going after the bags. He got to the boat and threw Sharkko's grail after him. That made the man scream more loudly. Without the grail, Sharkko would either starve to death or have to live from the food he could beg or the fish he could catch.

Faustroll, still standing in the water, was doubled over with laughter.

Davis's anger ebbed and was replaced by a disgust he felt for himself. He hated Sharkko, yet despised himself for hating him and for losing his temper. It was hard to act like a Christian when dealing with such a "sleazebag" (a word he had learned from a late-twentieth-centurian).

But he now had no time to dwell on his own failings. The running men had stopped near him. They seemed out of breath, though that was not the only reason they had halted. They were Ivar and about fifty of his Norse and Frankish warriors and a dozen women. Ann Pullen was one of them. Ivar was bloody though not badly wounded, and the bronze war-ax he waved about dripped red. He seemed to be in favor of making a stand of it against the pursuers. Some of his men were arguing against it. Davis did not know what had happened at first. By listening to them while he was getting into the canoe, he pieced out their situation.

Apparently, the rear attack had caught Ivar by surprise. But he had rallied his men, and Arpad's had been routed. No sooner was this done than Arpad, leading his fleet, had stormed the shore. In the melee, Ivar had killed Arpad.

"I hewed off his sword arm!" Ivar shouted. "And his forces lost heart and fled. We slaughtered them!"

8

But Thorfinn the Skull-Splitter had his own plans. He had sent a part of his army to overrun the west bank. While they were doing that, he had attacked the rear of Arpad's fleet. That was partly responsible for the panic among Arpad's men on the east bank.

Thorfinn had decided then, or perhaps he had long ago decided, to betray Ivar. Thus, he would become master not only of his own kingdom but of Arpad's and Ivar's.

Ivar and his soldiers had not expected betrayal, but they had rallied quickly and had fought furiously. But they had been forced to run, and Thorfinn's hounds were baying close to their heels.

Ivar yelled in Norse, "The traitor! The traitor! No faith, no faith! Thorfinn swore by Odin on the oath-ring that we would be as brothers!"

Davis, even in the midst of his anxiety, could not help smiling. From what he knew about Norse kings and their brothers, he was sure that there was nothing unusual about their trying to kill each other. That, in fact, had been typical of most medieval royal kin, whatever their nationality.

Oh, he was among barbarians, and he had been just about to be free of them when the Norns decreed that they should catch up with him. No, he thought, it's not the Norns, the three female Fates of the ancient Scandinavian religion. It's God who's destined this. I've been among the Vikings so long, I'm beginning to think like them.

By now, Ivar had quit raving. In one of the sudden

switches of mood that distinguished him, he was laughing at himself.

"After all, Thorfinn only did what I might have done, given the circumstances. Seize the chance turn of events! Get the power! The power!"

Faustroll, now sitting in the canoe, called out, "Your Majesty, true descendant of the great King Ubu! We believe that Power is what motivates almost all of humanity, and Power is responsible for more rationalizations and false justifyings than Religion is, though the two are by no means unconnected! You are a true son of Adam, not to mention of Eve, and perhaps of a fallen angel who saw that the daughters of men were fair and went unto them and lay with them! Go, go, go, our son! Consider Power, worship it, obey its ten thousand commandments! But we are a voice crying in the Wilderness! Crying in the jungle fertilized by the never-ending flow of desire for Power in its ten thousand manifestations, the true shit of the true universe!

"Yet somewhere there is the Holy Grail! Seek it, find it, seize it! Be redeemed thereby and by It! In the Grail you have the greatest fountain of Power! But it renders all other Powers powerless!"

Ivar's counselors had been babbling while Faustroll spoke, but they fell silent when their leader lifted his hand. From a distance, not far enough away to damp the writhing of Davis's nerves, came the yells of Thorfinn's men as they ran toward the fugitives.

"For God's sake!" Davis murmured. "Let's get into the boats and get away!"

Ivar shouted, "You are a strange man, Doctor Faustroll! One touched by whatever gods may be! You may have been sent by them! Or by Chance, of which I have heard so much from men of the latter days since I came to this world. Either way, you may have been sent to me. So, instead of slaying you, which would do little good except to get rid of your presence, and I might run into you again, I will go with you! Perhaps . . ."

He was silent for a moment while the others about him looked more than uneasy. Then he roared, "Into the boats!"

No one protested, though a few of the more aggressive warriors sighed. They scrambled, though not in a panicky manner, into the vessels. Ivar roared orders, assigning each to a particular craft. Davis was commanded, along with Faustroll and Ann Pullen, to get into the largest craft, a single-masted merchant boat with oarlocks for fourteen rowers. Ivar took the helm while the rowers began pulling and the big sail was unfurled.

He laughed uproariously and said, "The Norns have smiled on me again! These must be the boats Arpad's men used to bring them to this bank for the flanking attack!"

Davis, Pullen, and Faustroll were sitting on a bench just below the helm deck. The Frenchman called up, "Perhaps it's a sign from them that you should leave this area forever!"

"What! And allow the troll-hearted Thorfinn to crow that he defeated Ivar Ragnarsson?"

He shouted in Norse at the warriors who had not yet gotten into a boat. "You there! Helgi, Ketil, Bjorn, Thrand! Push the empty boats into the stream! We will jeer at our enemies while they dance frustrated and furious on the bank and utter threats that will harm us no more than farts against the wind!"

Helgi the Sharp yelled back,

"Boatless will they be.
Boneless makes them bootyless.

Boneheaded Thorfinn,
Bare is your bottom!''

Those within hearing broke into laughter. And Ivar laughed until he choked, which relieved Davis, who had become even more anxious on hearing the stanza. The Dane became very angry when someone slipped up and used the surname he did not care to hear.

"I love the words," Ivar called out. "But, Helgi, your meter is blunted. Wretched. However, considering our haste and that your meter always scans as if it were a newborn foal trying to walk . . .''

He laughed again for several seconds. Then, recovering, he bellowed, "Row as if Loki's daughter, the hag Hel, clutches your ankles with corpse-cold hands to drag you down into Niflheim! Bend your backs as if you are the bow of Ull and your arms are the god's hundred-league arrows! Row, row, row!''

There might have been rowers as mighty as the Norse, though none was better. However, these men had been in face-to-face battle, and nothing funneled the energy out more swiftly. Nevertheless, they dug in as if they had had a long night's sleep. Their enemies on shore were left far behind. But the starlight glimmered on a large mass along the eastern bank moving up-River. It was about a half-mile behind them. Thorfinn's fleet, part of it, anyway, was hot on their trail. Not so hot, perhaps, since his men would also be battle-weary.

"We make for the kingdom of my brother, Sigurd Snake-in-the-Eye!'' Ivar said loudly. "It's a long long way off, but our pursuers will tire before we do. We'll be safe then, and we can loll around, drink all the thickly sugared lichen beer and the grail-given liquor we want. We will also have our fill of the beautiful women there. Or vice versa.''

The rowers had no breath to laugh, though some tried.

Sigurd was one of the few men Ivar trusted and was probably his only trusted brother. He had been a mighty Viking when young. But, in his middle age, he had hung up his sword and become a peaceful and just ruler of Sjæland, Denmark's largest island. The kingdom he had established since coming to the Riverworld was four hundred miles from Ivar's. He had visited his brother once, and Ivar had visited him twice. Davis had seen Sigurd every time. The slender, wriggly, and red birthmark on the white of his right eye had given him his Terrestrial surname. Though it was gone when he was resurrected, the nickname stuck.

Davis's thoughts were broken by cries behind him. He stood up and looked around the raised helmsman's deck. The boat holding Helgi and three men was passing by a man in the water. Though Davis could not see the swimmer's face, he knew that he had to be Sharkko. Apparently, he was asking to be taken into the boat. But they were laughing as they rowed, and presently, Sharkko, still screaming, was left behind them.

A thrill of sympathy, though fleeting, ran through Davis. Sharkko was a liar, a cheat, a blusterer, a coward, and a bully. Yet the man could not believe that there were people, and they were many, who did not like him. It was pathetic, which was why Davis pitied him at that moment.

He sat down and looked sidewise at Ann, who was sitting near him. A small thin blue towel was draped over her head like a scarf that women wore in church on Earth. She had a strange expression, a mixture of sweetness and longing. Or so it seemed to him, though who knew what the bitch was thinking. Yet she looked like a madonna, mother of the infant Jesus, in a painting Davis had seen in a cathedral.

He wondered if that was what she had looked like when an infant. What had erased that sweetness, that goodness?

Then she turned her head and said, "What in hell are you staring at, you lascivious lout?"

Davis sighed, relishing the moment when he had pitied her because of her lost innocence. And he said, "Not much."

"You may think you can talk to me like that because of the situation," she said. "But I won't forget this."

"Your Majesty is like King Louis XIV of France, of whom someone said that he never forgot anything," he said. He added, under his breath, "And who also said that he never learned anything."

"What?"

Most un-Christian of me, Davis thought. Why can't I learn to turn the other cheek? I should have said nothing to her. The silence of the martyrs.

Later, Ivar transferred the four men from the rear boat to his. By late morning, the lead boat in Thorfinn's fleet was far ahead of the rest of the pack. An hour before high noon, it was within arrow range of Ivar's craft. Ivar turned his vessel around, picked off seven men with his arrows, rammed the enemy, and then boarded him. Davis and Faustroll sat in the boat while the battle raged. Ann Pullen used her woman's bow to wound several men. Whatever she may be, Davis thought, she has courage. But I hope she doesn't turn around and shoot me, too.

Ivar lost six men but killed all of the enemy except those who jumped into the River. Thorfinn's other boats were still out of sight. Ivar took over the enemy's vessel

and abandoned his own. He and his crew sailed on while
they sang merrily.

By the time they got near to Sigurd's realm, they had
passed through at least forty waking nightmares. Or so it
seemed to Davis, though the Norse obviously enjoyed it.
There was one fight after another and one flight after
another. The states for hundreds of miles up-River from
Ivar's ex-kingdom and probably down-River, too, were
in a state of bloody flux. The invasions of Ivar's land
seemed to have had a violent wave effect on others, none
of which was very stable. Slaves were revolting, and
kings and queens were trying to take advantage of the
deteriorating situations to attack each other. Davis believed
that only this semi-anarchy enabled Ivar's fleet to get this
far. Even so, all but four vessels of the original fleet had
been sunk or abandoned. The survivors had lived chiefly
on the fish they trolled for while sailing up-River. Now
and then, they had been allowed to go ashore and fill their
grails. But even when the people seemed peaceful and
cooperative, the Vikings were nervous. Behind the smiles
of their hosts might be plans to seize the guests as slaves.

"Oh, Lord," Davis prayed, "I beseech you, stop this
killing, torturing, robbing, and raping, the heartbreak and
the pain, the hatred and viciousness. How long must this
go on?"

As long as men permit themselves to do all the
horrible deeds, he thought, God wasn't going to inter-
fere. But, if He didn't, then He had a good purpose in
His mind.

A few hours past dawn, the fleet arrived at Sigurd's
kingdom. Or what had been his. It was obvious that it,
too, had been torn apart by the strife that seemed to have
been carried by the wind. Men and women capered

drunkenly while waving weapons and severed heads. Most of the bamboo huts and wooden buildings were blazing, and bodies lay everywhere. As the fleet drew near the bank, a horde climbed into boats and began paddling or rowing toward Ivar's boats.

"Who are they?" Ivar said. Then, "It doesn't matter. Sail on!"

"What about your brother?" Davis said.

"He may have escaped. I hope so. Whatever happened to him, I can't save him. We are too few."

After that, he was silent for many hours, pacing back and forth on the small afterdeck. He frowned much, and, several times, he smote his breast with an open hand. Once, he startled all on his boats when he threw his head back and howled long and mournfully.

Bjorn the Rough-footed, standing near Davis, shivered and made the sign of Thor's hammer. "The cry of the great wolf Fenris himself comes from his throat," he said. "Ivar acts as if he's about to go berserk! Get ready to defend yourself! Better yet, jump into the River!"

But Ivar quit howling, and he stared around as if he had suddenly been transported here from a million miles away. Then he strode to the forward end of the deck, and he called down.

"Osteopath! Clown! Come up here!"

Reluctantly, knowing that the Dane's actions could never be predicted and were often to be dreaded, Davis went up the short ladder with Faustroll. Both halted several feet away from Ivar. Davis did not know what Faustroll was thinking, but he himself was prepared to follow Bjorn's advice.

Ivar looked down at them, his face working with some unreadable expression.

"You two are of lowly rank, but I've observed that even a slave may have more brains than his master. I've heard you speak of your quests, the spirit of which I admit I don't quite understand. But you've intrigued me. Especially when you spoke about the futility and emptiness of always striving to gain more land, more property, and more power. You may be right. I really don't know. But, a few minutes ago, I was seized by some spirit. Perhaps I was touched by whatever god made us, the unknown and nameless god. Whatever strange thing happened, I suddenly felt emptied, my mind and blood pouring out of me. That terrible feeling was quickly gone, and I saw the sense in your wisdom, I also was overwhelmed, for a moment, with the uselessness of all I had done. I saw the weariness of forever fighting to get power and then fighting to keep it or to get even more power. Glory seems golden. But it's really leaden."

He smiled at them, then looked past them toward the north. When he resumed talking, he kept on staring past them. It was as if, Davis thought, Ivar was envisioning something really glorious.

Faustroll murmured softly. "He sees, however dimly, the junction point of zero and infinity."

Davis did not speak, because Ivar was glaring at him and the Frenchman. When Ivar spoke, he wanted your complete attention, no interruptions. But Davis thought, No, it's not that, whatever that means. It's . . . can't remember the Greek theological term . . . it means a sudden and totally unexpected reversal—a flipflop—of spirit. Like the reversal of attitude and of goal that Paul of Tarsus experienced on the road to Damascus . . . he had been fanatically persecuting the Christians . . . the great light came even as he was plotting death for all

Christians . . . he fell paralyzed for a while . . . when he arose, he had become a zealous disciple of Christ. Sudden, unexpected, unpredictable by anyone. Your spirit, hastening you toward the South Pole, turns you around without your will and shoots you toward the North Pole. There were records of similar mystical or psychological reversals of spirit.

He felt awed. It was several seconds before the cold prickling of his skin faded away.

However, he reminded himself, this sudden turnabout was not always for the good. Though it was rare, a flipflop from good to evil occurred. As if Satan, imitating God, also touched a man with his spirit.

"The god did not speak with words," Ivar said. "But he did not have to do so. He said that I should go up the River until I came to its source, no matter how far away that is. There I will find a Power beyond power."

"Always power," Faustroll murmured. He spoke so softly that Davis could barely hear him, and Davis was sure than Ivar could not.

"You, kneader of sore flesh, and you, the mocker of all that men hold to be good sense," Ivar said, "also have your quests. One wants to find the baby born of a virgin. The other hopes to find the truth that has eluded all men from the birth of mankind."

He paused, then said, "Though you are no warriors and have some strange attitudes, you may be the kind of companions I need for the long journey. What do you say?"

His tone implied that he was condescending to give the invitation. Yet he intended it as a compliment.

Faustroll said, "King Ubu and his two fools looking

for the Holy Grail? Ah, well, I will be pleased to go with you.''

Davis did not hesitate. He said, ''Why not? Perhaps we are all seeking the same thing. Or, if we're not, we'll find the same thing.''

Author's Note:

It's obvious that the adventures of these three will continue and be concluded in volume 2 of the Riverworld shared-world anthology.

I have a strong sense of historical continuity that was strengthened while I was researching into my genealogy. As of this moment, I have 275 confirmed American ancestors and several thousand European ancestors. So, I thought, why not use some on the Riverworld, where everyone who has lived and died now lives? And I did so.

Thus, every named character in this story, except for Faustroll (Alfred Jarry) and Sharkko, is a direct ancestor of mine. Doctor Andrew P. Davis is my great-great-grandfather (1835–1919). He was an extraordinary man, an eccentric, a quester after the truth, and an innovator. Ann Pullen is my nine-times-great-grandmother. She was, according to the court records, a real hellraiser, spitfire, and liberated woman in an age when it was dangerous for a woman to be so. As for my remote forebears, Ivar the Boneless and the other Viking men and women herein, their living descendants as of 1991 would number many millions. It's reasonable to assume that at least three-quarters or more of my readers will be descended from them.

A Hole in Hell

Dane Helstrom

His pen had hurled many into Hell. Now he, who should be in Heaven with his adored Beatrice, was in a pit such as he had depicted in *The Inferno*.

For years, he had searched along the River for the only woman he had ever deeply loved, the light of his life and his poetry. Now he was imprisoned by a man whom he deeply hated.

The eight-feet-square and twelve-feet-deep pit was on top of a foothill. Its sides were oak logs that slanted inward. (This whole world, he thought, slants inward and imprisons me.) The pit was in shadow except when the sun was directly overhead. Oh, blessed sun! Oh, swiftly moving sun! Stay in your course!

Ankle-deep in sewage, Dante Alighieri stood, his face turned upward. Dawn was an hour old. Soon, Dante's accursed enemy, Benedict Caetani, Pope Boniface VIII from 1294 to 1303, would come. Dante would know when Boniface was nearing because he would hear the barking and the howling of dogs. Yet there were no dogs in this place, which might be Purgatory or might be Hell.

A few minutes later, he stiffened. The yapping, barking,

and howling sounded faintly. It was as if he had just detected the sounds erupting from the three heads of Cerberus, Satan's unnatural hound that guarded the entrance to Inferno. Presently, the noise became a clamor, and he saw the man who owned the dogs.

"Another God-given morning," Boniface said. "Time for my first piss. I baptize thee, Signor Alighieri, in the name of those whom you so hatefully consigned to Hell!"

His eyes shut, Dante endured the rain that did not come from the heavens. A minute later, he opened them. The pope had shed his robes and his wooden beehive-shaped tiara. The dogs—naked men and women on hands and knees or on hands and toes—prowled around the edges of the pits. Their fish-skin collars were attached to leashes held by men and women of Boniface's court. The male dogs, by the edge of the pit and parallel with it, lifted legs to piss into it.

Boniface stuck his buttocks over the pit while two men held his hands to keep him from falling backward.

"In the name of those whom you wrongfully put in Hell in your vicious poem, I give you the bread and wine of the unblessed! Eat thereof, and glory in the transubstantiation of your fallen god, Lucifer!"

At the same time, a dozen dogs loosed their bowel contents. Only by standing in the center of the pit could he avoid being struck.

After a year of this, Dante thought, he should have been suffocated by the filth daily expelled into the hole. But the many excrement-eating earthworms kept the level of filth down to his ankles. Boniface had been pulled erect but again bent over as a series of slaves spat water between the pope's buttocks. Meanwhile, the dogs barked, howled, whined, and yipped.

Dante shouted, "May God force you for eternity to wear an iron tiara as white hot as His wrath!"

"Dante Alighieri never learns!" the pope screamed. "Does he get down on his knees, that stiff-necked Florentine, and beg forgiveness of those whom he has cruelly wronged? Not he! His mind is as the shit in which he lives!

"You committed blasphemy when you wrote of me in your Inferno as being in Hell while I was still living! Even God does not put sinners in Hell before they die!"

"You were and are evil!" Dante cried. "Would a godly man make dogs out of men, no matter what their offense?"

Boniface screamed, "Down on your knees, Guelf pig, and confess that you have wronged me and be truly contrite! Then you may continue your journey to find your beloved Beatrice! Though you should be seeking the Truth and God, not a slut such as she!"

"A fig upon you!" Dante screamed. And he bit his thumb and stabbed it at Boniface.

"Dante empits himself; he confesses his guilt and sin. Continue to suffer your rightful punishment!"

Then the pope, slaves, henchmen, and dog pack left. Four guards stayed behind to make sure that he did not find some means of killing himself.

Tonight, as every night, it would rain so hard that he could lie down in the water and drown himself. To do that would be to commit an unforgivable sin, one that automatically damned a soul. Would that be a sin in this world? Here, when a man died, he rose to life twenty-four hours later, though far away from where he had

died. Was it then a sin to kill himself? Logic said that it
was not. Yet he could not be sure. What God forbade on
Earth should also be forbidden in this world. Or had the
commandments been changed somewhat here to fit the
situation?

Unheeding the soft squishy stuff under his feet, he
paced back and forth. His mind went from the unanswer-
able question of suicide here to the conflicts raging
during his lifetime. When he was calm and logical,
which was not often, he told himself that the bloody
quarrels between Ghibellines and Guelfs and between
Black Guelfs and White Guelfs over politico-religious
issues no longer mattered.

The huge majority of resurrectees had never heard of
these conflicts and would yawn if they did. Only in this
area, where Italians of his era lived, did the hatred burn
fiercely. Yet it should be forgotten. Far more important
things stalked the Rivervalley and should be dealt with.
If they were not, salvation would be beyond their reach.

But he could neither forget nor forgive.

At high noon, the grailstones thundered. The echoes
from the mountains had just ceased when he heard the
dogs coming toward him. Presently, the barking and the
howling, mixed with the crack of the dog-tenders' whips,
were above and around him. Dante looked upward,
shielding his eyes against the sun. He cried out and sank
to his knees. He said then, "Beatrice!"

Boniface, standing naked by the edge of the pit, a
leash in his hand, said, "Your long quest is over, sinner!
Your beloved whore was brought in this morning by slave
dealers! Here she is, a lovely bitch who must surely be in
heat!"

Dante had averted his eyes, but he forced himself to look again. Once more, he cried out with horror.

She was naked and down on her hands and knees. She was weeping, her face so twisted that he should not have been able to recognize her. Something, some divine element, a sort of lightning flash between heaven and earth, had flashed from her to him. He had known instantly that she was Beatrice.

Boniface, grinning like a fox about to eat a chicken, pulled on her leash and kicked her, though not hard, in the ribs. She obeyed his orders to place herself parallel with the edge of the pit and very close to it. Then he gave the leash to a guard and got down on his hands and knees behind her.

"A bitch must be mounted from behind!" he shouted.

She cried out, "Dante!"

A whip wielded by another guard cut her across her shoulders. She cried out again.

"Do not speak!" Boniface said. "You are a soulless dog, and dogs do not speak!"

He eased himself forward over her. She screamed when he penetrated her.

Dante was leaping upward again and again and yelping like a dog. But he could not jump high enough to grab the edge.

"Look, look, sinner!" Boniface cried. "I am no dog, yet I am humping doglike the bitch you love so much!"

Dante wanted to close his eyes but could not.

And then Beatrice heaved upward and lifted Boniface with her. Though the guard jerked savagely on her leash, he could not stop her. She was at this moment as strong as if an avenging angel had poured his holy fierceness into her. She turned around and grabbed Boniface. Both screaming, they fell into the pit, the leash jerking loose from the guard's hand. She landed on top of the pope and knocked the wind out of him. Immediately, she began tearing at his nose with her teeth. She ceased biting when a spear cast by a guard from above plunged deep into her back.

She gasped, "Mother of . . . wish . . . die forever," and died.

The guards shouted at Dante to stay away from the pope. He had pushed the woman's corpse aside and was scrambling to his feet. Dante, crying out with grief and rage, jerked the spear from the beloved flesh and drove its point into the pope's belly. Then he yanked it out and started to turn.

A guard who had just dropped into the pit ran toward Dante, his spear held level. But his feet slipped in the filth, and he fell hard on his face.

Dante raised the spear to stab the guard. He hesitated. If he spared the guard, he, too, might be spared. But the pope's men would only do that to torture him and then, probably, cast him again into the pit.

As the guard, slipping in the filth, tried to get up, Dante cried out, "Beatrice! Wait for me!"

He rammed the spear butt against the log wall and pushed the blade into the pit of his stomach. Despite the agony, he kept on pushing until the blade was buried in him.

He was committing the sin of suicide. But it was the only way of escape. Someday, he would find out if it was unforgivable. If he eventually went to Hell because of his evil deed—if it was evil—he was willing to pay the full price.

Beatrice had been little more than an arm's length from him. Then, within two minutes, she was gone.

But she could be found again.

Though he might have to search for a hundred years, he would find her.

Surely, God understood his great love for her. He would not be jealous because his creature, Dante Alighieri, loved Beatrice more than he loved his Creator.

Dante's last thought dwindled into darkness. Forgive . . . didn't mean tha . . .

Graceland

Allen Steele

1

"...strange days, it seems..."

"I miss me gold tooth," Keith said.

He was sitting on the edge of the oak stage, his bare legs dangling over the bamboo-slat front. The Mersey Zombies were taking a break during the sound check. A couple of Titanthrop stagehands were making themselves busy, checking the electrical cables for burn-throughs in the fish-skin insulation and rearranging the massive stacks of speakers. In the sound booth, located in the middle of the open-air amphitheater's seating area, the King was haranguing some luckless techie about the recurrent feedback problems from the mikes; they couldn't hear what was being said, but the King's ring-encrusted forefinger was jabbing back and forth and the techie's head was alternately nodding, shaking, nodding, shaking, as if keeping time: yes sir Elvis, no sir Elvis, yes sir Elvis, no sir Elvis ...

"You miss your tooth." Sitting next to Keith, his bare back resting against a monitor speaker, John lit a limp

73

joint with a firestarter and sucked the smoke into his lungs. "So what? I miss my glasses. . . ."

" 'Coo, you always looked like a fairy with them on. . . ."

"I most certainly did not," John croaked. He held in the toke for a second, then slowly exhaled. Behind them, Sid was sullenly practicing the opening riffs of "Anarchy in the U.K." on his bass. Brian was nowhere in sight, as usual. "And just for the record, I never believed that story about how you busted your mouth after your drove a Caddy into a Holiday Inn swimming pool. . . ."

"It wasn't a Caddy," Keith insisted, "it was a bloody Lincoln Continental, and I did so break out me front tooth, when I climbed out of the water and slipped on the pool deck while running from the coppers. . . ."

"Yeah, yeah. We've heard the whole sodding story many times." John passed the joint to Keith. "And I didn't look like a fag with my glasses on. I loathed those contact lenses Epstein used to make me wear. . . ."

"Heard from him again lately?"

"Not since he joined the Dowists . . . besides, Yoko liked the glasses. . . ."

"Oh, for God's sake, man, when are you going to stop talking about your old lady?" Keith picked up one of his drumsticks and idly scratched his sunburned back with it. "I mean, you're getting more pussy than Frank Sinatry. . . ."

"Lord!" John looked at him sharply. "Is Sinatra here?"

Keith shrugged. "Not that I've heard. It's just a line I picked up from one of the Yanks." He took a quick hit off the joint and passed it back to John. "Pigpen told me that one," he gasped. "Or maybe it was Lowell. . . ."

"Okay, so I get laid regular." John gazed dismally at the rows of empty bamboo benches in front of the stage.

He absentmindedly reached beneath his kilt and scratched. "But I miss the missus, all the same," he said softly. "She was a good woman. Good singer, too."

Keith made a face, but wisely kept his mouth shut. They were both quiet for a moment, listening to Sid as he struggled through the bridge of "God Save the Queen," the punked-out version that the three other members of the Mersey Zombies refused to play during their shows. Keith cocked his head toward the kid. "I mean, you think young Mr. Ritchie there misses Nancy?" he asked softly. "The bloody wench was nothing but poison. Even when she showed up here two months ago, he told her to shove off or he'd stick her again. . . ."

Sid's head jerked up. "I did *not*!" he shouted.

John looked over his shoulder at him. "Easy, lad," he murmured. "The Moon here was only joking."

Sid wasn't satisfied. He unplugged his guitar, hauled the strap over his shoulder, and threw the instrument down on the stage, startling one of the Titanthrops. "You geriatric old farts make me want to vomit," he muttered as he stalked toward the curtained door leading to the backstage area.

"Then go vomit," Keith called after him. "Just make sure you don't do it in your lunch pail again. *Ah-ahaha-hahaha!*"

Keith's maniacal laugh was one of the few traits that endeared him to John. He shook off the lingering memory of his wife's face as he reached over to pluck the joint from Keith's fingers. "He doesn't miss Nancy," he said, "but I think he does miss riding the old white horse."

"Just as well. The shit killed him in the end." Keith frowned, pensively tapped his drumsticks between his legs. "Come to think of it, so did all the booze I was putting away. . . ."

"You both bought it within weeks of each other, as I recall. . . ."

"Yeah. So it did." The wicked smile reappeared on his homely face. "But at least I managed to get old before I croaked. The kid, now, he was barely old enough to shave. . . ."

" 'Hope I die before I get old. . . .' " John sang.

"Roger was full of shit and so was Pete. Ox didn't say enough to be full of shit. . . ."

"S'truth. Way I felt about George."

"*Ah-hahahahahahaha!* Lord love a duck . . . or a bass player!" Keith reached up to touch his youthful, undamaged front teeth. "But I still miss my front tooth, you know. It was quite classy. The birds thought it had sex appeal. You reckon I may find another one from . . . ?"

"Hey! What're y'all think you're doing up there?"

John and Keith looked up at the sound of the baritone, southern-accented voice. The King was stalking down the right aisle from the sound booth, clapping his hands for attention. "Shit," John murmured, discreetly stubbing out the roach behind him and palming it.

"I thought I told you," the King bellowed, " no drugs while we're working!"

Keith looked at him blandly. "But we're not working, mate," he said in a maddeningly mild tone of voice. "We're having tea." He pointed up at the midafternoon sun. "See? It's teatime."

The King's face became livid. "I don't see any tea up there, son! All I see is that goddamn mari-hoochie I told you not to smoke during rehearsals! Now you get Sid and Brian back up there and you make sure you can play your asses off tonight, 'cause we got a riverboat coming in this afternoon, now you hear me?''

"Who's the headliner?" John asked.

"The other band!" the King yelled. "And they're gonna headline all week because you English assholes can't get your shit together and an American band can and I don't like your attitude and I think y'all play like a bunch of English queers and I don't give two shits if you were one of the Beatles . . . !"

"Frankly," John calmly interrupted, "neither do I."

That shut him up, but John couldn't resist twisting the knife a little more. He cleared his throat as he rested his chin in the palm of his right hand. "Tell me," he inquired, "are you *still* blaming me for your movies?"

The King scowled at him but said nothing; he was never good for a wicked comeback. Keith hid his bemused smile behind his hand. "Goddamn fucking English eel-suckers," he finally muttered as he turned around and began stalking back toward the soundboard. "Think you invented rock 'n' roll. . . ."

Sunlight off the letters embroidered in semiprecious stones across the back of his redfish vest: *TCOB*. Taking Care Of Business. John watched the King walk away, feeling somewhat sad for him. A couple of years ago, when Elvis had started managing them, he still had his just-resurrected slimness and handsomeness, a sexuality reminiscent of his Sun Studios vintage years. Now he was becoming an obese wad again, much to everyone's disgust, only worse than before: he had let his hair grow unchecked and his mammoth ass stuck out from beneath his kilt. Worst of all, he had developed into a mirror image of his old manager, albeit without the Colonel's redeeming qualities. And he couldn't sing worth a damn.

But he was the King of Graceland; if you didn't want to be a dragonfisher, a farmer, or a slave, you played by his rules.

"He was a lot more fun before he died," Keith whispered.

John popped the roach into his mouth and chewed on it thoughtfully, savoring its burnt-herb flavor on his tongue. He stood up, giving the drummer a rough slap on the shoulder. "We were all more fun," he replied. "C'mon now, mate. Back to the grindstone."

"Rock 'n' roll," Keith murmured.

2

"...long live rock..."

The island was known as Graceland.

Thirty years after Resurrection Day, it was the only place in the new world where live rock 'n' roll could be heard, and its existence was largely due to Elvis's considerable influence and charisma. Through the course of many high-level trade agreements, the enlistment of a handful of loyal Titanthrops, a couple of years of seeking out resurrected musicians, and (so it was rumored) at least half a dozen translations, Elvis had managed to establish a small colony on a small island a hundred miles up-River from Parolando, an undiscovered rare bit of dirt and rock where two unclaimed grailstones lay. Not unexpectedly, he had decided to call the island Graceland. This was the way it was listed on the riverboat charts, the name by which it was known to hundreds of thousands of Valleydwellers who had heard of it.

Graceland had only one industry: rock 'n' roll, played live and loud. Elvis had been canny enough not to put his bands on riverboats to tour up and down the great river; there were too many uncivilized places where his groups could not only lose their grails and hard-won equipment, but also their lives. Instead, he settled an island and sent out word that two supergroups performed there six nights a week, eight months a year, and let everyone come to him. Tickets were bought at the dock through barter: whatever Graceland's fifty permanent inhabitants needed—fishmeat, cloth, refined metals, tools, open grails, new firestarters, precious and semiprecious stones, riverdragon products, extra liquor and cigarettes, groupies (especially groupies)—were gained in trade for a week's admission into the stockaded Graceland amphitheater.

Each week, another riverboat landed at the dock, unloading another hundred-odd passengers who had bartered their way up-River or down-River to Graceland. They surrendered their goods at the dock, then went to the lean-to cabins on the island's leeshore, where the visitor's grailstone lay. Admission to Graceland was for exactly a week, with admission to the amphitheater coming extra. However, since all weapons were confiscated at the dock by the Titanthrops and the accommodations were relatively pleasant, few minded the cost. It was the closest many of the resurrected could get to having a real vacation in the new world.

Of course, Graceland had its own dues to pay. Not only did neighboring river-nations have to be consistently bribed to keep them from contemplating invasion, but all of the amphitheater's belongings—from the electric guitars to the relatively sophisticated sound equipment to the upstream hydroelectric generators that powered everything—

had been custom-built by the inhabitants of Parolando and New Bohemia, who in turn received the lion's share of Graceland's gate receipts. There were few creature comforts available to Graceland's permanent inhabitants as a result of the system. However, as the King was known to frequently observe, it beat hell out of working. If picking one's fingers to the bone each night on crude copper strings couldn't be considered working, that is. . . .

There were two regular house bands on Graceland, alternating sets each night during the concert season. One was the American band, the Wonder Creek Revival: Lowell George on local vocals and rhythm guitar, Duane Allman on lead guitar, Berry Oakley on bass guitar, Rod "Pigpen" McKuen on harmonica and keyboards, Dennis Wilson on drums and —when she was sober and able to take the stage—Janis Joplin as guest vocalist. The Creeks had a laid-back, Marin County sound that appealed to most of the Valleydwellers, considering the agrarian circumstances they had faced since Resurrection Day; it was easy to relate to a rendition of "Proud Mary" or "Watching the River Flow."

The Mersey Zombies, on the other hand, were at an inherent disadvantage. Given the mixed heritage of the Beatles, the Rolling Stones, the Who, and the Sex Pistols, the quartet could manage a few numbers that were palatable to the average Valleydweller, but their sound was more geared toward British Invasion (both of them), guitar-driven hard rock, which seemed to be unsettling to most audiences. Songs like "Cold Turkey" and "I'm So Bored With the U.S.A." didn't have much to say to an audience far removed from either heroin withdrawal or Uncle Sam. And then there were the contradictory reputations of the two bands. If Janis was incoherent and mumbling off into a bluesy, lichen wine-ramble, there was always her old boyfriend, Pigpen, to shore her up. On the other hand, the Mersey Zombies had a nasty rep for breaking into on-stage bickering, backstage fistfights, short huffy sets . . . and Sid couldn't be restrained from sometimes spitting into the front rows when they began to jeer.

More than a few times, Elvis had been asked by Graceland's patrons why other resurrected rockers couldn't be found and hired. Elvis usually mumbled off with one of his usual excuses—"good idea, buddy, I'll work on it" or "we're straightening out the contract, y'know"—but the fact of the matter was that the musicians who had been found during his long talent search were the only ones who still considered themselves to be music people. Jimi Hendrix was alive, but he now lived in Soul City, where he played an occasional blues duet with Robert Johnson; no one who didn't live in the African-heritage nation-state had ever heard them perform. Hank Williams and Patsy Cline were married and owned a farm far downstream, as did their nearby neighbor, the Big Bopper. Ronnie Van Zandt and Steve Gaines were dragonfishermen; Buddy Holly and Richie Valens co-owned a small airship company flying out of New Bohemia. Bob Marley was reputed to be a revolutionary, secretly traveling along the Rivervalley to infiltrate and foster rebellions within slave-nations wherever he and his gang of Rastafarians could find them. Bon Scott was a hopeless dreamgum addict without a grail, squatting wherever he could and begging for the basic necessities in whatever village would next accept him.

And no one knew what had happened to Jim Morrison

. . . if, indeed, he had truly died in Paris when everyone thought he did.

3

". . . please to introduce myself . . ."

Shortly before sundown, the grailstones had delivered dinner with all its usual sound and fury. Once the audience had removed their grails, the Titanthrops had opened the wooden gates of the amphitheater's stockade and allowed the newcomers inside. Now, beneath the torchlight surrounding the seating area, a hundred of the resurrected were standing or sitting on the bamboo benches, waiting for the first band to come on stage. The summer-evening breeze carried mixed odors—fried fish, lichen wine, tobacco and marijuana smoke—along with the low buzz of voices, impatient whistles, and hand-clapping. The sounds and smells of rock 'n' roll. . . .

"Ten minutes to curtain, John."

John let the redfish curtain fall back into place; he had parted it a half-inch to peer out at the audience from the entrance of the backstage area. He turned to look at the skinny young woman who had come up quietly from behind him.

"Already beat you to it, love," he said stoically. She blinked rapidly in apparent confusion; he pinched a fold of the curtain. "See?"

Mary West Wind blushed and looked down at the floor, embarrassed at having not caught the awful pun. John flashed her a smile to show that he didn't mind and she visibly relaxed. Mary West Wind had been a San Francisco flower child until six tabs of particularly nasty LSD had dispatched her to strawberry fields forever. Here on Graceland, she served as stagehand and permanent groupie-in-residence to both house bands. She was so sweet and innocent, however, that none of the rockers—not even Sid, even in his most repugnant moments—had the heart to seduce her, although John was completely aware that she had a crush on him in particular.

"The King asked me to ask you to find Brian," Mary said meekly. "I mean, I know where he is, but I can't . . . I mean, I shouldn't . . . ."

John sighed and rubbed his eyelids between thumb and forefinger. His vision was now perfect, but he still missed his glasses. Like Keith and his rotten gold tooth. "I know, I know," he murmured. "Bloody damn . . . all right, I shall go track down our errant stone."

He began walking away from the curtain; Mary deferentially stepped aside to let him pass to the short flight of stairs leading to the dressing rooms. On sudden impulse, John paused, leaned over, and gave her a quick brotherly peck on the cheek.

"Always stay the way you are, dear," he whispered in her ear. Mary giggled and blushed again as John hopped down the stairs.

Backstage was a long wooden shed, partitioned into individual, closet-size dressing rooms and a larger "green room" located just behind the stage entrance. The member of the Wonder Creek Revival were gathered in the green room, waiting for their nightly gig; Duane was practicing licks on his unplugged guitar, Berry, Lowell, and Pigpen were playing poker, Dennis was catching a nap on the couch in the corner, and Janis, as usual, was getting drunk. Like John himself, all were wearing simple kilts, sandals, and redfish shirts or vests.

The days of elaborate stage outfits were long gone, along with stretch limousines and overworked roadies, Dom Perignon in chilled buckets and five-course catered meals, crystal punch bowls filled with cocaine, and contract riders that stipulated that five pounds of M & Ms had to be available, with all the red ones removed first. On the other hand, also missing were the usual backstage hangers-on: overdressed radio jocks with their flunky photographers, ready to accost you while a camera flashed in your face so that a self-serving picture could be published in the next issue of *Billboard*; studio reps hovering in the corridor, hand-grabbing and shoulder-hugging, trying to hustle another sleazy deal; fawning winners of local record-store contests with copies of your most hated album, babbling inanities while you tried to find your way to the lavatory; and, of course, the groupies with their mall hair and blowjob lips, eager to fuck a rock star so they could write it all down ten years later in their memoirs, or at least to make their regular boyfriends insanely jealous.

All things considered, John was only too happy to see all that posturing and pretense removed from the scene. What was left was the music, pure and simple, like a neglected rose garden that had been cleaned of broadleaf vine and chokeweeds. Some things, though, had remained much the same. . . .

He passed through the green room and walked down the short, narrow corridor to the dressing rooms. Sid was in his room, apparently passed out on a cot, his bass guitar propped against a wall. John stuck his head through the door, stuck his fingers between his lips, and whistled sharply.

"Wakey wakey, you killer junkie!" he shouted. "It's showtime!"

Sid's eyelids fluttered. "Fuck off, you fuckin' ol' hippie," he muttered from the depths of his dreamgum hallucination, but John had already strode down the hall, passing a short side-corridor leading to the exit door. He heard voices down the hallway, but he didn't pause to look. Probably the King, raising hell with someone else for some real or imagined transgression. . . .

The door of Brian's room was shut. John stopped and pressed his ear against the hollow-core panel; from within, he could hear faint gasps of pleasure amid the ruthless pounding of flesh against flesh. He grinned; Brian was getting his customary preshow lay. Different girl each night; all he had to do was scout the nearby audience camp until he found a bird who didn't mind being fucked by the man who had taught Mick Jagger how to sing. If it weren't for the fact that all Valleydwellers had been made sterile on Resurrection Day, Brian could have probably populated an entire village with his illegitimate offspring by now. . . .

Enough was enough, though. Time to go to work. John took a deep breath, then reconsidered the urge to shout. Instead, he gently rapped his knuckles against the door, pinching his nostrils with the thumb and forefinger of his other hand. "Telegram for Mr. Jones!" he called in a nasal voice.

An exasperated sigh and a feminine giggle from the other side of the door. "Coming!" Brian called gaily.

"I'm certain you are," John replied. "Five minutes."

"See you in four and a half." More muffled laughter.

"Very good, sir." John didn't have to worry about Brian making it to the stage; it was always Sid who gave everyone trouble. Next, to find Keith; from farther down the hall, he could hear the hyperactive *ratta-tap-tap* of drumsticks against a piece of furniture. Keith was wired and ready to perform, as usual. Now, if only he hadn't destroyed his dressing room again...

As he turned to walk down the corridor, John was startled by a hard tap on his shoulder. He jumped a half-inch off the floor, then spun around to find a massive, hairy shape filling the hallway.

John sagged against the wall, laying a hand against his thudding chest. "Oh... Billy, it's you," he gasped. "You scared the life out of me, mate."

Billy was one of the Titanthrops who worked on the island. Although the bands rarely had any problems with audience members seeking their way to the dressing rooms uninvited, Elvis had insisted upon having one of the titans enlisted as backstage security. Billy guarded the exit door that John had just passed. No guest list was necessary; if Billy was told a name—as Brian did every night—then Billy would remember that name for weeks, even months, to come. And if someone tried to con or muscle their way into the dressing rooms, they were usually treated to a flying lesson over the stockade wall.

"Thorry to interrupth you," Billy said in his usual deep-throated lisp, "but there'th thomeone at the door who inthith upon theeing you."

Billy looked annoyed, if only because he had to bend almost double to keep from banging his huge skull against the ceiling. John sighed; rock stardom was dead in the afterlife, but it still didn't prevent zealous fans from seeking out his autograph at exactly the wrong

time. "Tell them I'm about to go onstage and I'll see
them after..." he began.

"He'th rather thee you now," Billy persisted. Before
John could respond, he added, "He'th from the Church
of the Thecond Chanth, and he thaid he knowth you from
back then."

He paused, then added in a low voice, "He thaid it
wath important... he thaid hith name wath Jim."

John looked askance at the Titan. "Jim? I don't know
anyone named..."

He stopped. For a long moment, John stared at Billy,
deciphering what he had said. When it struck home, his
first impulse was to yell for Keith and Brian... hell, not
just them, but for Duane and Pig and Janis and Mary
West Wind and anyone else who remembered the magic,
anyone within earshot who remembered the Lizard King....

John sucked in his breath. "Pardon me," he said, then
he ducked beneath Billy's right armpit and slowly walked
back toward the intersecting hallway. Behind him, he
heard the nervous rattle of drumsticks, a woman's faint
cry of orgasm. All around him, there was sound: the
twang of Duane's muted guitar strings, someone laughing
at an old joke, the faraway clapping of hands by an
audience waiting to see rejuvenated legends of their past.
John broke into a trot....

He stopped at the crossway, staring at the open door.
Torchlight from outside illuminated a robed figure, standing half-seen just outside the doorway.

No call to him, though. No gesture of recognition, no
familiar all-fucked-up amble down the corridor to meet
him. Only a monkish figure in severe brown robes, a
hornfish helix draped around his neck, waiting just outside the dressing room. And, within the dark pit of the

hood, the barest hint of a familiar face, first seen long ago in Toronto when they were sharing the bill. . . .

"Jim?" he whispered. "Jim, is that you?"

"After the show, John." The voice was very low, but it was the same unmistakable voice. "Back here when you're through."

The figure then melted into the shadows, allowing the door to slowly swing shut again.

John stared at it until Keith goosed him with one of his drumsticks and reminded him that the crowd was waiting. For the first time since anyone in the band could remember, John was late coming on stage.

4

". . . no future for you. . . ."

The Mersey Zombies set lasted for an hour; to nobody's great surprise, least of all John's, it was a lame night.

John had long since learned that the intrinsic problem with the band was that, because of the all-star lineup, everyone expected to hear their favorite Beatles or Rolling Stones or Who or Sex Pistols songs. However, there were many differences between each band member's sensibilities that could not be easily paved over by the excuse that they were all British rockers; it was like expecting Nat King Cole and Jimi Hendrix to successfully collaborate because they were both black American musicians.

While it was perfectly possible, for instance, for Keith to hammer out the nuclear-attack percussion of "I Can

See For Miles,'' John had trouble singing the lyrics. Although John and Brian were more than happy to perform ''Ruby Tuesday''—the only song which their two former groups had ever had in common—Keith would almost fall asleep at the drums and Sid would make I'm-bored faces at the audience. John would all but give up on keeping up with Sid on ''Anarchy in the U.K.''; Brian made weird faces at the bassist's maniacal pogoing and guitar-thrashing, and Sid barely tolerated Brian's woodwinds during ''You Can't Always Get What You Want.'' The only song on which all four musicians meshed together was ''Helter Skelter,'' even though it was clear from the audience reaction that that particular number was still associated with Charles Manson; even while the band kicked out the jams, too many faces out there looked as if four giant cockroaches had suddenly crawled onto the stage. Manson and his killers had ruined that song for all eternity, literally.

It was only when the other three band members left the stage to allow John to sing ''Imagine'' as the finale that the crowd seemed to awaken from their glassy-eyed stupor, even singing along with the final refrain. This was not unusual, though; that particular song struck a chord among the Valleydwellers, who had found themselves, after all, reborn in a world without borders, countries, or flags. At the song's conclusion, John stood up from the makeshift piano amid rousing applause; he bowed once, then gratefully strode off the stage.

A party was already in full swing in the green room: Keith was arm wrestling with Duane; Brian had joined a conversation with Janis, Berry, and Dennis; and Sid lurked silently in the corner, glaring at everyone with once-fashionable punk disdain. John walked past them, completely unnoticed; he stopped by his dressing room to lay his guitar on the bed, then stood for a few moments, gazing indecisively at a fish-skin packet of joints that rested on a table. "What the hell," he murmured to himself, then picked a joint out of the packet before he left the room and headed back down the corridor toward the rear door.

Billy was minding his post, sitting on an enormous oak stool next to the open door. The titan stood up as John approached. "He'th thtill waiting for you," he rumbled. "I athked if he wanted to come back to your room, but he didn't want to."

"It'th . . . oops, sorry . . . it's okay, Billy." The Titanthropic lisp was rather infectious. "I'll talk to him outside." Billy nodded sagely and stood aside; John patted his hairy forearm as he stepped outside.

The wooded area behind the backstage shed was dark, illuminated only by a couple of flickering, half-spent torches that marked the way to the outhouses. He could hear the rhythmic hand-clapping of the audience as they urged the second band to come on stage. John's eyes, unaccustomed to the gloom after the bright lights of the stage, sought the shadows.

"Jim?" he called softly. "Hullo? Jim?"

The robed figure he had seen earlier detached itself from the shadows beneath an oak tree. "Here," a quiet voice said from within the raised hood.

John took a step forward, then stopped, uncertain. "If it's truly you," he replied, "then let me see your face."

There was a moment of hesitation, then the figure's hands moved from within the dark folds of the robe and

lowered the cowl. After another moment, he stepped
farther into the light, revealing himself to John.

It was Jim, all right, but not the Jim he remembered.
His dark hair no longer reached down to his shoulders;
instead, it was cut very short, almost monkishly. The face
was still starkly handsome, but the familiar mannish-boy
glower had completely vanished, leaving behind only a
neutral, almost beatific expression. Jim, by all accounts,
had died overweight and bloated, his innate sensuality
stolen by liquor and drugs. Now he was rejuvenated, but
as a cloaked figure standing in the half-light, as if
materialized from one of the William Blake poems that
had so influenced him as a UCLA art student.

"You've changed a bit," John said.

Morrison's heavy-lidded eyes blinked. "We were never
close, John, so how would you know how I've changed?"
He raised his arms, the sleeves falling back from his
arms. "Perhaps this was how I've always been."

John chuckled. "I never saw you wearing *that* on the
cover of *Rolling Stone*." Jim only stared at him, unamused.
John held up the joint he had grabbed before leaving the
dressing room. "Care to join me for a little smoke?"

Jim said nothing. "Don't do drugs anymore, hmm?
How 'bout we go out and find some girls to ball, then?"
Again, no reply. "Well, why don't you just go out there
and flash 'em your dick, just for old times' sake, eh?"

Jim's eyes shut for a second, seemingly to control
himself. "I'm beyond these things now," he intoned.
"But, yes, you're right. I have changed."

"So I noticed." John stuck the joint between his
lips, lit it with a firestarter, and sucked in the
ragged-tasting smoke. In one life a man's wearing
ass-tight black leather and French silk shirts, the

next he's decked out in sackcloth and ashes. Figures.
"Did you hear the show?" he asked, exhaling through
his nose.

"I heard."

"Not exactly a rave review. . . ." John cocked his head
toward the door. "Hey, why don't you come on in and
I'll reintroduce you to the other band? Most of 'em think
you didn't make it over, but I'm sure they'd be willing to
let you sit in on their set. Christ, at least you could do
better justice to 'Light My Fire' than they do. . . ."

The slightest flicker of a smile. "Perhaps . . . but I no
longer sing."

"Really?" John started to take another toke, but suddenly felt foolish. He bent down to stub the joint out in
the grass, then tossed it away. "What a waste." He
paused, looking in the direction of the discarded joint.
'Y'know, I don't think I ever told you this, but you were
really very, very good. I was even a little envious of your
voice. And some of the things you wrote, particularly
your poetry . . ."

"That's not why I've come here, John."

"Then why the hell have you come here, Jim?" In
exasperation, John folded his arms across his chest
and stared back at the disciple. "Come to stand by
haughtily and laugh up your sleeve at the fool who's still
singing 'Day Tripper' five nights a week?"

'I'm not laughing at you. . . ."

"Jesus!" he shouted, suddenly fed up with the conversation thus far. "You sound like a bloody priest!"

John impulsively whirled around and began to stalk
back toward the door. He was almost inside the shed—
Billy, half rising from his stool, was about to get out of
his way—when he impulsively turned again. "Of all the

people in the world," he snapped, thrusting his finger at the robed figure, "I would have expected at least *you* to be honest!"

Jim's face remained impassive, but for an instant there was a brief flicker of irritation in his eyes. "I have said very little to you," he said quietly. "So far, you've done most of the talking."

They stared at each other for a few moments. Through the door, John heard a shouting match in the corridor— "you fuckin' fucked-up fuck-off, why can't you handle a simple fuckin' song like..." and "Bugger off, you bloody sod..."—Keith and Sid, from the sound of it, having one of their usual post-gig tantrums. In a few minutes, they would be attempting again to flatten each other's noses.

"Billy, go break it up, please," he murmured without looking over his shoulder. He heard the stool scoot back as Billy maneuvered his Buick-size body down the corridor. Unless Sid unwisely attempted to kick Billy in the nuts again, the squabble was as good as settled. John hesitated, then walked back out to the edge of the glade where Jim was patiently waiting for him.

"So talk, then," he said.

5

"...this is the end..."

Long after midnight, John lay in his tent, gazing up at the long wooden rod of the ceiling pole.

Mary West Wind was fast asleep next to him, most of the bedsheets curled around her nude body. Out of sheer impulse, he had brought her back to his tent after the show; they had made love in a frantic, almost adolescent sort of way, yet despite her fervor she had fallen asleep almost as soon as she had climaxed. John felt almost relieved, however; he didn't feel like talking, just as, indeed, he had felt a strange detachment from her even in middle of their sexual throes. They had used each other for their own purposes; she had finally fucked the sexy-looking guy on the back sleeve of the *Meet The Beatles* album, and he had found temporary surcease from the dark thoughts in his mind.

Now he lay naked atop the blankets, listening to the cool night-breeze, remembering another late night in a different lifetime.

Getting out of the car with his wife, the boxed tape of that day's studio session under his arm. The usual crowd of autograph-mongers and fans hanging around the front door of the Dakota. Walking down the sidewalk, Yoko passing in front of him, heading into the open archway of the building. Feeling pleased with the day's work, looking forward to playing with his young son before going to bed . . .

A young man's voice calling from somewhere behind him: "Mr. Lennon?"

Turning, seeing a shadowed figure in combat stance barely five feet away, aiming a pistol directly at him . . .

Barely a moment of confusion, wanting to say something . . . then loud gunfire, muzzle flashes, the horrible force of five bullets slamming into him . . .

Turning around, body screaming in anguish, mind numbed by what had just happened, disbelieving that he had just been shot . . . staggering toward Yoko . . . Christ, he's been shot . . . he collapses, saying something he can't remember to his dear wife as the doorman dashes toward him . . .

Ambulance sirens, voices shouting, policemen all around, cold sidewalk concrete . . . a glimpse of a young man standing on the curb reading a paperback book . . . being loaded on a stretcher . . . nausea, weakness, the sense of passing from time and space . . .

"Do you know who you are?" the disembodied voice of a cop asks softly just before the end. . . .

Well, constable, at least I think I do. I mean, it was right there on the tip of my tongue just a moment ago, right before some deranged asshole shot me. I once shook hands with the Queen, and I'm pretty positive that I once played Shea Stadium, if that's what you're asking. But if you'll only give me a few minutes, I'm sure I can give you a correct answer. Umm . . . you wouldn't mind making it multiple choice, would you?

"Not very bloody funny," he whispered to himself.

We can't allow you to continue, Jim had said. *You're much too dangerous.* . . .

Without really thinking about it, John slowly slid his legs over the side of the bed; the soles of his feet came to rest on the coarse wooden boards of the tent-platform, and for a few moments he peered into the darkness, listening to Mary's rhythmic breathing.

We've been given a chance, don't you see? Jim's voice had almost been pleading. *We've been brought here by the ancients, every one of us from time immemorial, to achieve personal salvation through our personal actions. We can yet achieve union with the Godhead, John, but only if we give ourselves the chance.* . . .

He could hear the wash of the River through the darkness. Downstream, somewhere close by, dugout canoes were stealthily making their way toward Graceland, paddled by Second Chancers who had been waiting for this hour when everyone on the island would be sound asleep.

But you and the others have revived the old ways. You brought technology to this island where only life-sustaining grailstones had once existed, and you use it to preach evil. You've brought back idol worship, debauchery, lust of every kind . . . all those very things that I myself once practiced before the resurrection. . . .

John bent and picked up from the floor the kilt that Mary had torn off him; he stood up and slid it around his waist. His eyes searched various objects resting on tables and chairs around his tent—spare clothing, his grail, a carved wooden tobacco box and other handmade ornaments given to him by visiting fans, his guitar—until his gaze found a long, flat thing in the corner.

I had hoped you might join us, but I see now that's impossible. All I ask now is that you receive my testimony, and understand why we've done what we shall do, why I've led them here. . . .

John reached out and picked up the dragonfish knife, sliding it out of its scabbard. As he did so, a dim, reddish glow was reflected off its sharp, polished-white surface.

Rock must die, John. . . .

He looked around; through the open tent-flaps, he saw a sudden blaze of firelight from the amphitheater.

You must accept this. . . .

Then he had vanished into the deeper shadows of the night.

"Bloody hell I will," John whispered to the fire. Clutching the knife in his fist, he strode out of the tent.

Already there was shouting from the campsites: cries of surprise, anger, shock, desperation. He could see people emerging from their tents, staring in disbelief at the bonfire that was erupting from the stage area. Now there were new, smaller blazes being set; the backstage shed, the speaker stacks, the sound board, all in turn were being set ablaze by distant cloaked figures who had scaled the stockade walls and were now committing arson on the amphitheater. Everything was made of wood; once set afire, it would all go up in minutes.

There was a wash of heat against his skin. He could hear Elvis bellowing in rage. Through the trees, he glimpsed audience members moving toward the besieged stage. From somewhere not far off, there was a harsh scream of mortal pain, suddenly cut short as another knife found the passive throat of a Second Chancer. "John?" Mary called from somewhere behind him. "John, what's going on?"

John ignored her. Somewhere in the heart of the furnace, Jim was waiting for him, capering with a torch in hand, igniting precious sound-equipment and acoustic baffles and his own crude yet irreplaceable piano. The technology of music, deemed the root of all evil by a group of religious fanatics, was being systematically destroyed.

John took a few more steps into the night. It wouldn't be very difficult to find Jim. He must have known that he would die again before he left Graceland; he had all but told John what he intended to do, and John had attempted to escape the blunt reality of the threat by taking home a sweet little hippie-chick. If you smoke enough pot and fuck long enough, you can avoid coming to grips with anything. Hell, when it came down to it, he was a world-class champion when it came to avoiding responsibility.

No more. Not when something he loved was being torched.

Mary was still calling his name as he took a few more steps into the darkness, the palm of his hand sweating against the handle of the knife. Find the fucker. Grab him by the neck. Slash his goddamn throat . . .

Do you know who you are? the nameless policeman in the ambulance asked again.

He stopped in his tracks. He felt his knees buckle as he sagged to the ground.

He remembered the Cavern Club. He remembered the Royal Albert Hall. He remembered the first American tour and the groupies who sobbed over a patch of ground he had walked across. He remembered going to India while Epstein was dying. He remembered the final rooftop performance in London with the lads before they called it quits. He remembered falling in love with Yoko. He remembered their bed-in demonstration, and all the other countless protests and demonstrations against war and violence. He remembered Julian's birth, then Sean's. He remembered the one and only time he met Morrison, backstage in Toronto when the Plastic Ono Band and the Doors had been the headliners. He remembered writing a song about how it was permissible to give peace a chance. . . .

"Good Lord," he whispered, "what am I doing?"

He didn't remember dropping the knife. In fact, he didn't remember much else until Keith sat down next to him on the dew-soaked ground, lit up a joint, and offered it to him.

6

"... with a little help from our friends ..."

"Haven't seen anything like this since we played the pubs, eh, mate?" Keith said dryly.

John looked at the joint and shook his head. "Not exactly the proper sound," Keith went on, "but it's got a good beat and you can dance to it. *A-hahaha*..."

For once, his laughter was forced. John continued to silently stare at the burning amphitheater. Firelight reflected off the treetops, silhouetting figures rushing back and forth past the stage; the air smelled of burning wood. The Titanthrops had managed to muster a bucket brigade from various musicians and standbys, but it didn't look as if it was doing much good. Graceland's amphitheater was well on its way to becoming history; it would take much more than the King's considerable charisma to rebuild the venue. Keith picked up the knife and toyed with it, almost as if he were considering a quick round of mumblety-peg. "You could have stopped him, y'know," he said quietly.

John looked sharply at him. "I mean," Keith continued, "I saw you two out there having a chat, so I suppose you must have known what was going to happen...."

"Not worth killing him, though."

"Hmm, got a point there. But why didn't you at least let on to the rest of us?"

"Didn't really think he meant it. Not until it was too late." John thought about it for a moment, then shrugged. "Not sure if it would have made any difference. Elvis would have thrown 'im off the island, but that wouldn't have been the end of it. Even if we had stopped him this time, he would have just returned later."

His gaze returned to the flames. "This way, the arseholes got what they wanted. They won't be back again."

"Right." Keith stuck the knife into the ground between his legs, then sucked another hit off the joint and offered it again to John. John looked at it for a moment, then pinched it out of the drummer's fingers. "Well, I suppose it makes a daft sort of sense. . . ."

"You're not going to tell anyone, are you now?"

Keith exhaled and scowled at him. "What do I look like, a narco?" He shook his head. "But what makes you think there's going to be a next time?"

John *tsk*ed, letting the joint burn between his fingers. "Here, mate. You should know better than that. You can't kill rock 'n' roll that easy." He looked at the joint again, then stubbed it out on the ground. "I mean, you can ban it from school and burn all the Beatles records and get the holy rollers to carry on about how it's the devil's music and so forth, but it's a tough beast to knock off."

He waved a hand at the bonfire. "So they torch a stage. Big hairy deal. We can always build another. Rock 'n' roll will never die."

"If you say so." Keith picked up the joint again, straightened out the bend in the paper, and carefully relit it. From somewhere far off, they heard another harsh scream. John idly wondered if it was Jim. . . .

"Next time, though," Keith muttered, "you wonder if we can get Elvis to sing?"

John smiled slyly. "Only if he gives me back my glasses," he said, watching the smokes and flames rising into the first light of dawn over the endless River.

"Yeah," said Keith. "Right. And me gold tooth . . ."

"Now don't start with that gold tooth shit again. . . ."

Every Man
A God

Mike Resnick and Barry N. Malzberg

Selous crept silently down the heavily wooded trail, shooting an occasional glance behind him. He wasn't especially worried; the rustle of the dried leaves and branches would alert him if his pursuer was getting too close.

He came to a small stream, stopped to slake his thirst, then waded halfway across it, turned to his left, and began walking down the middle of it. He continued for a quarter of a mile, then finally climbed out.

The bush was denser on the other side, and he had more difficulty passing through it. He looked off into the distance with practiced eyes, found the crooked tree that he had spotted before entering the wooded depression, and using it as his landmark, made a large semicircle around the worst of the thornbush.

Eventually he reached the tree. Beyond this, he knew, was a grassy plain, not large enough to be a savannah, but one that he must nonetheless cross, alone and unarmed. He continuously examined the ground for animal sign, but found none.

He broke through the last of the bush and stood at the

edge of the plain. The silence was almost tangible: no birds, no monkeys, no grazing animals, not even the hum of insects. He estimated that he could trot across the plain to the safety of the forest beyond it in perhaps three minutes, but he hesitated to present any predators with the sight of a running man, so he began to walk slowly, carefully, his every sense alert.

To his surprise, he made it to the trees without seeing any sign, any indication of life, not even so much as a butterfly. For a moment he was plagued with self-doubt: could his bushcraft be deserting him on the strange new world? Then he saw the signs, barely visible: the broken twig, the crushed leaf, the human hair snagged on a low-hanging branch, and he knew he was still on the right trail. Burton *had* passed by here.

Of course, Burton couldn't know that Selous was following him; the latter had awakened on the Riverworld less than a day ago. The two men had met only once, for no more than twenty minutes, in Zanzibar. But when Selous had awakened on the Riverworld and started out to hunt for answers, the few people he had met had mentioned that another Englishman, an explorer, had come this way before him, and by putting together bits and pieces of information he had determined that it was Burton, and had immediately begun tracking him. Separately, the two of them had opened up half of Africa; together, they might find some way to solve the mysteries of the Riverworld.

And yet, during the past three hours, he had become aware that while he was tracking Burton, someone else was tracking *him*. It could be friend, it could be foe—but alone and unarmed as he was, he had no intention of remaining an easy or a stationary target if it *was* a foe.

He'd meet his pursuer, but he'd do it under conditions of his own making.

He walked another mile, constantly alert, still unwilling to believe that such a primitive, untouched forest was totally devoid of animal life. Finally he slowed his pace. The trees were thinning out, and if he was going to lay a trap, there was no guarantee that he would find any better place for it up ahead.

He took the rope he had woven, sought out a sturdy tree with a branch that overhung the trail he was blazing, and slung the rope over it. He manipulated it to the edge of the branch and used his weight to pull the branch down to where he could reach and position it. Next he secured one end of the rope to the bole of the tree, being careful to make it invisible to anyone approaching from the direction he had just come. Then he set the trap, covering the loop with leaves and small sticks.

Not satisfied, he found some large fallen branches and positioned them carefully and naturalistically along the approach, so that the trail narrowed gradually and his prey would *have* to set one or both feet inside the prescribed circle.

Finally he stood back to examine his handiwork. It would never fool a leopard, that most cautious of animals, but he could think of no other living thing, including a human, that would notice a single twig out of place. He was a hunter, not a trapper, and he missed the heft and feel of his rifle in his hands, but he'd spent too many years in the bush not to take careful notice of how those natives who didn't own rifles, and probably would use them like clubs if they *had* possessed them, trapped animals for the pot.

For a moment he wished his friend Theodore were

there with him. Bushcraft got you just so far, and then, even in the midst of the bush, you found that you needed statecraft even more. And nobody could charm a crowd, be they Republican, Democrat, British or Maasai, like Roosevelt.

Selous thought back to the last time he had seen him. It had been just eight years ago—or was it eight millennia? —that he had arranged the first professional safari in the history of the continent, and had inadvertently created an enormous new business, when he had hired hunters, trackers, skinners, porters, chefs, and camp boys—five hundred of them in all—for the ex-President's African hunting trip.

Then Roosevelt had gone back to run for the presidency again, and the Great War had started, and though he was in his sixties and had spent most of the past forty years in the bush, he was still British to the core, and had immediately volunteered to put a regiment together to drive the Hun out of Tanganyika.

Yes, it was all coming back to him now. Taking his men across the border, then rafting down the Rufiji River. The battles, the victories. And then, from nowhere, as he sat taking breakfast before his tent, the German bullet slamming home in his throat. He had tried to cry out, but had choked on his own blood.

He had always expected to die in Africa, perhaps beneath the claws of a lion or on the tusks of an elephant, perhaps of some tropical disease, possibly in the midst of battle against the Hun. But to die like this, sitting and sipping his tea . . .

Now he remembered what he was trying to scream: *"Pointless! Pointless!"*

For a man's life to mean something, his death also had

to have meaning, and it was as if the war and the German bullet had conspired to rob his life of its meaning. What mattered the books he had written, what mattered his slow conversion from hunter to ecologist to conservationist, what mattered his service to the Empire, if the ultimate act of his life was to clutch at his throat while spitting out a mouthful of tea and blood? His life read like a book that built to a climax, and then, on the last page, turned into a farce. Maybe this new land, this Riverworld, was created to give him a second chance, and as his hand gingerly sought the wound that no longer existed, he silently resolved not to botch it.

Suddenly he heard the sharp *crack!* of a small branch being broken, and he was once more the hunter. He melted silently into the bush, waiting as his pursuer walked closer and closer to what he now thought of as the killing ground, then crouched down and waited with the terrible patience of one of the predators he had hunted so often.

The footsteps came closer, and he resisted the urge to peek through the bushes to determine the nature of his pursuer. That would be made clear in less than a minute, unless he did something foolish to give his position away, and he hadn't lived into his seventh decade by being foolish.

Thirty more meters, Selous estimated. Now twenty, now ten, now—

"What's going on?" demanded an outraged voice. "Put me down this instant!"

Selous leaped out of his concealment, and found that his trap had netted a blond white man, who now hung upside down, one foot suspended by the makeshift lasso.

"Who are you, and why are you following me?" replied Selous.

"Who do I look like, fool?" snarled the man.

"You look like a man who is in no position to make demands," replied Selous.

"*Man?*" shrieked his prisoner. "Do you not recognize a god when you have captured one?"

Huey Long looked at Beethoven and thought, Oh, you sly bastard. You are more cunning than I would have ever thought—but you're closed in here too, aren't you? It's no different for you than for me.

Around them as they slogged their way from the city to the plains, the struggling forms of the rednecks—that was how *he* thought of them, anyway—seemed to rise and fall in the mud, clamoring at him to get moving, get back, get out of there. Or maybe Huey had made it all up in his head, maybe they were saying nothing at all. Maybe there were no rednecks, and he was hallucinating the whole bunch of them. Maybe this was all just some ghastly dream and he was lying on his back in the capitol building, the judge's slugs in his belly, his blood streaming away, the people weeping as they carried him off. Maybe he would wake up in a white room with tubes running in and out of his head, and all this would be behind him.

Beethoven seemed real enough, though. Stolid Germanic fellow, five feet six, solid build, pustules all up and down his cheeks.

Huey kept on moving, stretching, rocking, easing back and forth in the mud, making small progress in the pelting rain, the rednecks in the distance cheering him on (or so he would like to think).

It was a real bitch, a down-home Saturday-night fish-fry son of a bitch, slogging through all this mud, with this Beethoven stuck next to him, matching him stride for stride. It's a long way from the capital to here, and a longer way back, he thought.

But nothing could be done about it. It had been Beethoven's idea to quit the city. That made some sense to him: there was certainly no reason to hang around there, fighting for food, fighting even harder for attention, trying to clear some space among the mottled hordes, all of whom wanted him dead. (That was the conviction that had come over Huey in this place, an insight that he trusted, had relied upon from the immediacy of old experience: there people were so caught up with themselves that they could kill him.) If Beethoven wanted to get out, that was all right with Huey Long. Beethoven had his reasons, Long had others, but the idea was to put distance between themselves and the rest of them.

Oh, he wished he could get rid of this character too, but Beethoven had fixed him with those shining eyes, those deep, yearning, Boss-obsessed eyes that Huey Long could understand, having seen them at a thousand rallies.

"There is no emperor," Beethoven had said. "I thought he was there, but I was wrong."

Well, that was all right with Huey. There were no emperors in America either, not with every man a king. *Every man a king:* it had gotten him this far. It would get him farther still.

"The emperor is dead," Beethoven had said again. "Everyone is dead, everything is dead. That must be the only explanation. That is why we are here. In death there is nothing but betrayal. Of course, I saw that in the *Missa Solemnis*, that solemn mass. By the end, deaf and crazy, I could see through to the bottom of it all. I'm not deaf here, though; I am filled with sound and light, but for no purpose. There is no emperor."

"You're wrong," Huey had lied. "Sometimes there *is* an emperor."

Anything to pacify, to jolt Beethoven from those strange and sullen rages that would overtake the man. Meanwhile, you kept on going, regardless of the company you kept. The Boss still had his plans. Give him a break, give him an even chance at this fish-fry, and he would find a way to make it work for him. Getting out of the city was a decent enough first step. It wasn't so much a city as an encampment anyway. Beethoven had called it a city, but that was wrong, really, a different terminology from a different time and place.

All right, he said to himself: just keep moving.

"Pfui!" spat Beethoven.

It was strange how Huey could understand some German monosyllables and not others, how Beethoven's language wavered back and forth between foreigner talk and understandable Esperanto. It was yet another thing that was just too complicated for him, something that he didn't need to talk about, didn't want to consider.

"The emperor betrayed me," said Beethoven. "First he, and then the others. All of them. And they left us here to deal with that betrayal."

"You seem to be a little bit wound up, son," said Huey. "You should calm down a little."

"We need a new start," said Beethoven. "That was what they had promised, what I was looking for. But how can there be a new start when it is all *da capo* again and again and no *fine*?''

"I don't understand you," said Huey, not unkindly. "I can follow some of your talk, but not all of it." He paused, trying to find some common ground. "This is pretty shoddy goods for me too, you know. One moment I'm walking through the capitol building and the next I have a slug in my heart that hurts like an explosion, like a firecracker lifting your balls to heaven, and I'm looking up at that damned ceiling, and then I wake up here. That isn't too easy, you know. It wasn't easy for you, I know—I was *killed*, son. I was murdered—assassinated. They killed me because they knew I was going to be the next president." He paused for breath. "That's a hell of a transition to make, you know, from being maybe the next president to waking up in this stinking place. It is a strange, strange business.''

Oh, he could go on if he wanted. The old talent was still there, the line of language that he could unreel, turn out there to fend for itself in that nest of the world. Every man a king, and me their president, he reflected. Even Beethoven seemed awed, seemed to shut up at last, and backed away from him.

Huey smiled a secret smile. Going on and on in the Senate, opening up, filibustering from the Constitution of the United States, his favorite document, the greatest document in the history of the world, something that could make Huey cry with its coiled language and beauty of intention if he thought about it, going on and on like that with the can strapped to his thigh so that he could piss right in the middle of a speech without having to leave the floor, break the filibuster—*that* was finding a new dimension for the meaning of the word "talk." If he considered the truth of it, it was much more difficult and challenging than anything that had happened to him here. This little bit of carrying on he had done on the Riverworld was for nothing, was little more than a practice shot in a small hall. The real stuff had been what he had managed in the Senate and on the campaign trail. Yes, he had been a wonder in his age, that was for goddamned sure. Then he had gotten gut-shot on the floor of the capitol, and now here he was.

Except now there was no one to listen or give a damn. Everyone here, even the pretty women, the models and the fifty-dollar-a-night hookers whom he could tell right away, all of them had troubles, *big* troubles, and pretty much the same ones at that.

For one thing, they were all dead. They had closed their eyes and given up the ghost gently or in some violent manner, and the next thing they knew they had come to consciousness in this stinking place with a million other troops. That was a hell of a trauma, and it seemed to be pretty much the general condition of the place—and you had to understand that, grant everybody a little weight on that basis alone. Apparently the only way you made it here was to die, which was one hell of a thing.

"You know I'm right," said Beethoven. He was back to talking again. He produced one of his filthy handkerchiefs from some inner pocket, wiped his streaming forehead in the style of his period, and offered it to Huey in a friendly way.

Huey shook his head disgustedly. *Pfui* was the word, all right, it pretty well summed it up.

"Forget it," he said. "I don't want it. It's not necessary." Nothing like this, nothing, never in the history of the world, that was what he thought now. He remembered standing on the shoulders of the bayou, battling his fear of alligators while half expecting the beasts to crawl from the swamp and swallow his ankles, all the time trying to keep the crowds at bay. That was one thing—but *this*, this was infinitely another. It was amazing how you could feel that your experience had prepared you to deal with a whole range of activity, and then it turned out that the experience was of no use whatsoever. In actual point of fact, he was counting on Beethoven more than the composer was relying on him. None of this made it any easier to take when the German seized his elbow, dragged him to a halt, and fixed him with shining eyes.

"Listen!" said Beethoven. "Do you hear them?"

"All right," said Selous, cutting the pale blond man down. "Why have you been following me?"

"I owe you no answer, mortal," said the man, rubbing some life back into his leg.

"What makes you think you're a god?"

"*Think* I'm a god?" was the reply. "I *am* a god. I have proclaimed it."

"That's all it takes?" asked Selous with an amused smile.

"Enough of your insolence!" snapped the man. "I've slaughtered whole cities for less!"

"Have you indeed?"

"Yes. Now help me to my feet."

Selous placed a foot against the man's chest and shoved, hard.

"Either strike me dead for that, or get ready to do some explaining," he said.

"I will kill you!" screamed the man, starting to get up again. Once more Selous shoved him down.

"I'm running out of patience with you," he said. "Who are you, and why were you following me?"

"I am Gaius Caligula Caesar, and I explain myself to no one."

"Caligula?" repeated Selous, arching an eyebrow.

"You know of me?"

Selous nodded.

"Then bow down and pay homage to me, and perhaps I shall let you live."

"Answer my questions, and perhaps I'll let *you* live."

"I am immortal," said Caligula. "I cannot die."

Selous chuckled. "Where do you think you are, and how do you suppose you got here?"

Caligula concentrated for a moment. "I had a dream," he said. "I dreamed that my retainers stabbed me, cut me to ribbons. And then I seemed to awaken on the bank of a broad river. But it was only a dream, for here I am."

"It was not a dream."

"Then this must be heaven."

"It is not heaven," answered Selous. "I assure you of that."

"It *must* be heaven," Caligula said again. Suddenly he looked around. "But where is Jupiter? Where are Mars and the fleet-footed Mercury? More important, where is Venus? Where is Aphrodite? Where are the Helens of our mission? Where are the women?"

"That I cannot tell you," said Selous, "though I know of your reputation."

"And well-deserved it is," said Caligula. "Who but I would know all the hundred and one ways to pleasure

Venus and take her pleasure for his own?'' He paused and stared at Selous. ''And what god are you?''

''My name is Frederick Courtney Selous, and I'm no god. On the other hand, you do not strike me as a pleasurer of women or anything else.''

''Then you simply demonstrate your ignorance,'' said Caligula. ''You do not know the splendid technique to which I am privy. But, of course, you would not have an emperor's phallus, a god's constancy.''

''You *do* think well of yourself, don't you?'' said Selous.

''And why should I not?''

''At any rate, I assure you that no gods exist here.''

''No?'' said Caligula, touching himself in a familiar and, to Selous, disgusting way. ''Then I am the last and thus the greatest. I command you now to let me rise.''

''You seem to do that quite well on your own.''

''I will show you a rising in time of which you could not dream.'' Caligula glared at him. ''You must be one of the gods' servants. Let me up and take me to them, or it will go hard with you, Frederick Courtney Selous.''

''I've killed more elephants and lions and buffalo than you can count,'' said Selous. ''Don't make me add a god to the list.''

''I cannot die,'' answered Caligula confidently. ''They tried in Rome, and all that happened is that I ascended to heaven.''

''This isn't exactly heaven,'' said Selous.

''If I am here, then it must be.''

Selous stepped back and allowed Caligula to get to his feet, watching him every second. ''Why were you following me?''

''I seek the city of the gods,'' answered the Roman. ''I

saw you disappear into the forest, and I decided that you knew where it was and would lead me to it.''

"You were wrong."

"A god cannot be wrong," said Caligula. "Therefore, you must be lying."

"It is true that I seek a city," said Selous. "*Any* city. There must be some force governing this world, some set of rules and rulers, and since they have not manifested themselves along the riverbank, I decided to go in search of their civilization. I was following the trail of Sir Richard Burton, whose name will be as unknown to you as my own. It seems to have vanished, but I hope to pick it up again. I do not know where he is headed, but I assume he also has the intelligence to seek out the rulers of this place, and I hope to join forces with him before he reaches his goal. That is the whole of it.''

"Why should I believe you?"

"You are free to believe what you wish," said Selous. "You are also free to go your own way. I warn you now not to follow me: my next trap may not be so pleasant."

He turned and started walking off.

"Wait!" cried Caligula.

Selous stopped and turned to face the Roman. "What is it?"

"I am tired, and my leg pains me. I shall permit you to carry me until I regain my strength."

Selous chuckled. "That's very generous of you, but it's an honor I think I can do without."

He turned to leave, and the Roman hurled himself on his back, clawing at his eyes and biting his shoulder.

Selous dropped to the ground, rolled over once, then managed to grab one of Caligula's hands and twist it sharply. The Roman screamed and released his hold, and Selous scrambled to his feet.

"If you touch me again, I'll kill you!" he snapped.

"You *hurt* me!" said Caligula. Suddenly he began crying like a baby. "Why would anyone want to hurt me?"

Selous stared at him and said nothing.

"Don't you know that you are not permitted to touch the person of a god?" wept Caligula. Suddenly the tears vanished, to be replaced by a smile. "Still, I admire your courage, Frederick Courtney Selous. Perhaps I shall let you be my general. We shall cut a bloody path through my enemies."

"That's a generous offer," said Selous sardonically, "but right now I'm the only enemy you've got."

"Nonsense," said Caligula. "Is not the forest our enemy? Does it not hide the path we seek?" He ripped a small dead branch from a nearby tree. "I shall take this plunder to prove we have conquered it!"

"I think Gibbon understated the problem," murmured Selous, staring at the Roman as he went around gathering up more tokens of victory.

"Well?" demanded Caligula, his arms filled. "Don't just stand there! We've got a city to find and a world to conquer!"

"I think we'll find the city much faster if we split up," said Selous.

"An excellent suggestion," said Caligula. "But then who would draw my bath for me and bring me my meals?"

"I thought I was a general."

"You are whatever I want you to be," said Caligula.

"Otherwise, what's the purpose of being a god in the first place?"

"You have a very short memory," said Selous.

"My memory is perfect."

"But you have already forgotten what happened the last time you tried to give me an order."

"That was different," said Caligula. "That was before I made you my general and we brought the forest to its knees." He paused. "Tomorrow morning I shall create some women for us to enjoy, and perhaps some birds to sing of our coming, and we shall march off to find the city."

Selous shook his head. "I'm leaving now."

"Then I will follow you."

"I might not wait by my next trap. You could spend all eternity hanging upside down, or impaled on sharp sticks at the bottom of a pit."

"I *allowed* you to catch me," answered Caligula. "I was tired of chasing you, and it seemed the easiest way to meet you."

"Sure you did," said Selous.

"Be not clever with me, mortal, or you risk bringing down my godly wrath upon you."

"It's a chance I'll have to take," said Selous, unimpressed.

"At the very least, I will have the members of my guard run you through."

"First find them, and then I'll worry about it."

"Then I shall do it myself," said Caligula, picking out the longest, sharpest branch he could find and brandishing it like a sword.

"You take one step closer and I'll wrap that thing around your neck," said Selous.

"You are but a mortal," said Caligula with a maniacal laugh.

"I didn't give in to the whims of madmen the first time around," answered Selous. "I don't propose to change my ways in *this* life."

Caligula stared at him, puzzled. "Why didn't it all end when I died?"

"The Empire?"

"The world. How could it go on without me?"

"It managed quite well without you," answered Selous.

"Who succeeded me? Did Jupiter himself descend to sit on the throne?"

"You were succeeded by Claudius."

"That crippled old fool?" yelled Caligula. "Now I know you lie! He could barely speak his own name!"

"But *he* didn't go to war with a bunch of trees," noted Selous.

"I always knew he was a coward." Caligula paused, trying to remember the thread of the conversation. Finally he shrugged. "Well, don't just stand there. We've got a city to find!"

Selous stared at him for a long moment, and decided that he'd probably be better off knowing where this lunatic was every second than having him pop out of the bush at the most inopportune moment. Finally he shrugged.

"Follow me," he said.

"Do you hear them?" repeated Beethoven.

Huey Long swayed to a halt and looked over Beethoven's shoulder, far past the composer into the smoke and haze of the fading Riverworld.

"Hear *what*?" he said. "I don't hear anything. Just

the gulls, maybe—the bird calls. That's all. Nothing exceptional.''

"Horses," said Beethoven. "Napoleon's troops. They're coming after us.''

"I don't hear horses," said Huey.

"They are sending the troops on horseback with spears and muskets," said Beethoven with total conviction. "They know where we are. That was their plan all the time. We're going to be killed here like pigs.'' He turned to Huey. "I warned you," he continued, "we should have gotten out of there days ago. I said, let's go, let's leave, but you wanted to stay.''

"Wait a minute, now," said Huey. "You're wrong. There are no troops, no horses, no muskets. Just the usual sounds.'' *Agitato*, that was one of Beethoven's words. Excited, frenzied. That was what was happening before him. "Just stay calm, son," said Huey Long. "Ain't nothing happening that we can't control.''

But Beethoven was a trembling, palsied mess before him now, tears leaking from his astonished eyes, that huge forehead clotted with sweat. The musician gasped, grabbed a big towel that he used as a cloak, then fell gracelessly to the mud and rocked there, grasping his knees.

It's an epileptic fit of some sort, decided Huey. I should have stumbled off, kept to myself, tried to understand this place before things began to happen. But when I came to myself on the banks of this crazy place, he was the first I saw; he helped me and guided me to some kind of consciousness. How could I have left him?

Still, it was confusing. One moment surrounded by your bodyguards, striding through the lobby of the capitol into history, the future and your destiny ahead like a dream, the next minute crushed to the ground, astonished, surely dead and quaking with this German musician.

How much could a man take? How much could a man truly understand? It was all too much for him. You did the best you could, after all, and you tried to make sense of the senseless, but this was really too much.

Beethoven began to cough, shudder, and shake.

I should never have done this, thought Huey. I should have stayed at fish fries, stayed in the back woods, aimed for the legislature. All right, maybe that wasn't enough for me, maybe I had to be governor. But *that* was enough, surely. I could have taken steamboats up and down the river and played with honeyed tits and taken casual graft forever. . . . But instead what did I do? I went to Washington and drove FDR crazy and then came back to the capitol to meet the bullet they had prepared for me. Every man a king, but sometimes even kings get killed.

Too late now, he thought, too late. They got me, they just goddamned *got* me. Hell, maybe those *were* horses Beethoven heard in the distance, maybe Beethoven was right, maybe the whole goddamned Napoleonic guard is heading toward us.

"Come on, Ludwig," he said. "Get up! Let's get the hell away from the city. It was *your* idea, remember?"

Beethoven finally heaved himself to his feet, mumbling about betrayal and heroes and the brutal blows of fate, and Huey knew that he would be all right. As long as the man sounded like himself, he *was* himself. That was something you came to understand quickly on the Riverworld.

"Why have we stopped?" demanded Caligula.

Selous squatted down, staring at the ground. "Someone passed this way not too long ago."

"Doubtless it was your friend Burton."

"He's not exactly my friend," said Selous. "And it wasn't him. I lost his trail miles ago. This was someone who came by in a hurry, at kind of a half-run. Also, whoever it was has never worn shoes. The toes are all straight, not bunched together at the edge."

"What is that to us?"

"I don't know yet."

"Then why are we pausing?"

"There may be people ahead of us, and they may not be friendly."

"They will fall to their knees and worship me, and perhaps, in my magnanimity, I will let some of them live," said Caligula, striding confidently past Selous.

For a moment the Englishman was tempted to grab his arm and hold him back. Then he shrugged. What the hell, if someone was going to take the first shot or the first arrow, far better this madman than himself.

He fell into stride behind the blond god.

Beethoven had turned to Huey Long in the first flush of their acquaintance, a few days earlier, and said, "They lied to us. From the beginning, from the very start, we were lied to."

"Lying is what it's all about," the politician had said. "Without lies, son, there woudn't be any politicos at all. There would just be a bunch of people hitting each other with clubs to see who came out on top. It's the lies that bring structure to the whole mess, you understand what I mean?"

"No," Beethoven had replied, "I don't understand what you mean." Everything seemed so clear in his mind until he started talking, and then it drifted away, simply left him. It was an embarrassment, a disgrace of sorts to be out-talked and out-thought by this fool of an American. "How could I understand?" he continued bitterly. "But surely you see they are not telling the truth about this place. It is not like something we have seen before, but is something else."

"That's true, son," Huey agreed. "Everything is something else, which is why we must apply our higher reasoning powers to the situation."

"But the situation is not as you think," Beethoven said, and wanted to continue in a long speech to the politician about the nature of thought and the different kinds of liars with whom he had had to struggle all his life, but a shocking C Minor triad directly out of the first movement of the C Minor Symphony, the loudest he had heard since the deafness had been stripped from him in this place, came thundering through with the force of light and left him surprised and numb.

"C Minor, C Minor!" he said wildly. "That's all of life, don't you understand, tonic to dominant C and back again!" He remembered how it had been in the last years before the deafness struck, when the music had seemed so absolute in its purity and force that even the *Hammerklavier* had seemed to be only a preparation for what he might do. And then to lose hearing, lose patience, lost all of the fawning, miserable *dilettantes* who had made ease possible, all of the time understanding that he was sinking slowly beneath his own shame.

"Enough!" he shouted suddenly. *"Enough!"* He heard the triad shift to the major, now a clashing C major triad signaling the opening of the final movement after the crawl through the *bassi*.

"I can't understand how this happened," he said to

Huey Long. "Of this destiny there was not any indication at all. Not a hint of prayer or light. Even when I tore the curtain aside in the *Missa Solemnis*, it was nothing like this, it was acres and acres of the graveyard, the encased dead, the unwrapped dead, rising, singing, ascending slowly. . . ."

"Oh, son," said Long, not unkindly, "you're really gonna have to stop with this nonsense. You're just tearing yourself up with the anxiety, and you ain't getting nowhere at all."

All this was before Beethoven realized that they must leave the city, that the way to redemption lay in the empty spaces far beyond the enclosure, when he was still trying to piece some meaning out of these circumstances.

How foolish he had been then! He seemed years older now, though of course only a few days had elapsed. Conferring with the wretched Long, whom had he seen arriving in the same stunned and disastrous state that Beethoven remembered so well, he had felt not only sympathy but indeed a kind of necessity, a need to reach out and rescue this man from the horror embodied always in that first view of the Riverworld. As the peasant boy from Stockholm had done it for him before vanishing into the tablelands, so he had done it for Long, had soothed him, calmed him, eased the ferocity of the terror as his new situation first opened up before him, then conveyed him to a safer and more secluded space where Long could finally make some sense of what had happened to him.

Beethoven had not understood much of the Riverworld then, either, but what he knew he tried to impart in short, gentle phrases that would give Long the little material he needed to somehow recover himself and move past that first point of terror.

Now here they were, and Long had slowly become acclimated.

"Son," said Long, touching Beethoven gently on the top of the head, propelling him gently forward, "we'll just stop and rest a spell now if you don't mind."

"But we are being followed! They'll be here any moment."

"I know," said Huey, "but I feel a speech coming on. I just want to make a little address to the troops. I was a mighty fine speechmaker in my day, and now I think it is time to make my position known."

They had finally come to the end of the forest. The trees had been thinning for the past mile, the scrub was sparser, and now Selous stared out across a large clearing. He stood, hands on hips, trying to make up his mind which way to go next. Far in the distance to his left was a small lake.

Suddenly he heard a savage, almost inhuman scream behind him. He whirled around instantly, just as Caligula was swinging a huge log at his head. He raised a hand, slightly cushioning the blow, but fell backward before the Roman's onslaught.

"You're a brave man!" muttered Caligula, pummeling him with both hands. "I will take your bravery unto myself!"

Selous tried to roll free of the blond man's weight, but he was still dizzy from the blow to the head.

"Get off me!" he snapped. "You're crazy!"

"As I ate my unborn son, so shall I eat your heart!"

Selous felt consciousness slipping away from him, and

then Caligula lowered his head to the Englishman's chest and took a huge bite of it.

It was the horror of what would happen should he pass out more than anything else that seemed to provide Selous with a fresh burst of adrenaline, and he brought his knee up hard into Caligula's groin. The Roman emitted a falsetto shriek, rolled over on the ground, and began screaming incoherently.

Selous, blood flowing down his torso onto his belly, leaped to his feet and examined himself as best he could. It really could use some stitches, but wounds seemed to heal magically on this world. Besides, he'd received worse from lion and leopard; if Caligula's teeth weren't septic, and there was no reason to assume they were, it would be only a temporary annoyance.

Still, it hurt like the devil, and he walked over to the fallen god and kicked him again, this time on the side of the head. There was no further reaction from Caligula, who was still howling and hugging his groin, and all he got for his trouble was a sharp shooting pain in his foot.

He searched around for the rope that he had been carrying coiled over his shoulder, found it where he had fallen, and brought it over to Caligula. Before the Roman could resist, Selous had tied his hands behind his back and then wrapped the rope a few times around his neck, giving him about a ten-foot slack.

"All right," he grated. "On your feet!"

He jerked the rope, and Caligula, gasping and choking, rose awkwardly.

"You *hurt* me!" he said accusingly.

"*You* tried to *kill* me," answered Selous.

"But it is an honor to die for a god's pleasure," said Caligula, honestly puzzled by Selous's reaction.

"It's an honor I can do without."

"Then you are a fool."

Selous jerked the rope, and Caligula began gasping again.

"What about a god dying for *my* pleasure?" he asked.

"Blasphemy!" cried Caligula, charging at Selous with his head lowered.

Selous sidestepped him just as he would sidestep a rhino that had lowered its head to charge. Instead of putting a bullet in his ear, as he would then have done with the rhino, he simply waited until Caligula reached the end of the rope and gave it a quick, hard tug. The Roman did a complete flip in the air and landed heavily on his back.

"I think I broke my arms!" he wailed.

"I thought gods couldn't feel pain," said Selous sardonically.

"Help me!" whined Caligula. "I'm hurt!"

"I'll help you," said Selous, approaching him. "You've got three seconds to get up before I kick you in the groin again."

"No!" shrieked Caligula, jumping to his feet. "My person is sacrosanct! You can never touch it again!"

"Just so we understand each other," said Selous, approaching him and slapping his face.

He expected Caligula to curse, or cry, or perhaps even giggle. Instead the Roman looked at him as if nothing had happened, and said conversationally, "I think we're more likely to find a city by the River. Cities need commerce, and the lake doesn't afford much likelihood of that."

Once he got over his temporary surprise, Selous found

that he agreed with his prisoner. "All right," he said. "Let's start walking toward the River. You first."

"We could use some horses," commented Caligula as he headed off to his right.

"If we find any, I'll trade you for them."

"Gods are not property to be traded by merchants," said Caligula, suddenly haughty.

"What makes you a god, anyway?" asked Selous.

"I am a god by proclamation."

"Whose proclamation?"

"My own," answered Caligula.

"That's all there is to it?"

"No one has ever challenged it."

"No one?"

"Well, no one who was still alive an hour later."

"Nice work if you can get it," commented Selous dryly.

"I *am* a god," insisted Caligula. "Without me there would be no night or day, no rain or sunshine. When I die the heavens will open up and pour forth a stream of black lava that will kill all living things and cover the earth."

"That must comfort you in times of need," said Selous.

"You don't believe me?"

"If you're a god, create a pair of horses for us. If not, stop talking; you'll need all your strength for the march that lies ahead of us."

"I can create horses," said Caligula with conviction. "I can bring them to life right here this instant."

"Then why don't you?"

"Because you dared to lay your hand on a god. You don't deserve to ride."

"Do *you* deserve to walk, too?" asked Selous.

"I am a god. I feel no pain, no fatigue. The sun is my brother; it cannot burn my skin. The grass is my lover; it renews me with every step I take."

"How very fortunate for you."

"I require no nourishment, no water, no sleep," continued Caligula. "Later tonight, when you finally can remain awake no longer, I shall change into a snake and squeeze the life from you. Then," he continued conversationally, "I will eat your heart, and very possibly your eyeballs, for you have truly excellent vision, and I will go find my city."

"Since you are capable of all these things, I assume you won't mind if I tie you securely to a tree before I go to sleep?" said Selous.

"Not at all," said Caligula pleasantly. "I would expect no less of you . . . though of course it will do you no good."

They walked another mile in silence, and then Selous stopped, causing Caligula to choke when he reached the end of the rope.

"Are you tired already, mortal?" asked the Roman.

"Be quiet," said Selous, raising his free hand to shade his eyes from the sun.

"What do you see out there?" asked Caligula.

"I'm not sure. Something. It could be a group of men."

"Come to worship me, no doubt."

"Or to kill you."

"I cannot die."

"Try to stay sane long enough to remember that you are no longer an emperor and never were a god, and keep your mouth shut until I can find out if these people are friends or foes."

"I will turn myself into a hummingbird, so they cannot see me until I know why they are here," agreed Caligula promptly.

"A very quiet hummingbird," said Selous. "Start walking."

"Flying," corrected Caligula.

"Whatever."

"I can't fly," said Caligula suddenly. "You have bound my wings."

"Even birds have feet," noted Selous.

"True," said Caligula. "You are a very wise man. In a way, I will be almost sorry to rip you open and eat your innards."

And then, chirping very quietly to himself, the Roman began leading the Englishman across the savannah toward the distant cluster of men.

The command had seemed to come from inside him, as it always did when a real stemwinder was building.

"Here I stand my ground," said Huey Long. "Come around! I want to talk to you!"

In the dim light of the infernal sun, Huey thought he could see them beginning to stumble before him, but then again it might have been only an illusion. He had Beethoven's attention, though; the musician was crouched in place, squatting there, looking at Huey with those odd and flickering eyes, a crazy man's eyes.

"Let me tell you about my friend the great musician here," continued Huey. "He had plans. He wanted to enter the city and find the emperor, to settle old accounts with him, but he has changed his plans. Do you know why? Do you?"

There was no response to the question, just the sound of empty breathing and perhaps a rumble in the distance. You had to have confidence, however; then you could draw them in.

"He gave it up," said Huey, "because, like you, he thought that there was nothing in the city, that it was all random, that some would come and some would go, but that the reincarnation made no sense at all and there was no way that the emperor could be found because the emperor could be a thousand miles down the other way. And he grew discouraged, tired of the noise, the heat, the feeling that nothing at all could be changed, nothing could be done." Huey paused and looked around him, measuring their response. "But now I am here to tell you that my friend has seen differently, that he has understood the nature of his portion and he must recant his obstinacy, for the emperor *is* there, he is there for all of us and everything that we want can be found in that city of desires. The truth of Riverworld has been launched upon us."

Now he knew that he had their attention. "Do you know what the truth is?" he continued. "It is here for all of us. *That* is the truth. We have been granted all power, all possibility, all fundamental circumstance in this be-deviled place. Every man a king, every woman a queen! We can do anything we want, all of us kings and queens of our domain, waiting for that entitlement, for the cloak of possession to be put upon us. And that is why we are going to change our ways." He paused dramatically. "We are going to go back. We are going to reclaim the city."

"What are you talking about?" someone said. It was a British accent, clipped and almost indecipherable in the thick haze, but Huey could infer the message. "You're out of your mind," the voice said. "You Americans don't know shit!"

"Where is that man?" shouted Huey. "Let me see the man who said that! Bring yourself forward and confront me! If you have the courage to do that, then you have the courage to go back to the city."

"Not courage," the voice said, attached to a spindly figure who came through the haze and dropped to one knee before him, crouching in the mud beneath the tree stump upon which Huey stood. "Hey, mate, why don't you give it up and just face the truth? We are lost. We are as lost as we all have ever been. We are so lost that we don't even know the wood. Why don't you let us sleep? Why don't you let us buy out of this terrible place?"

"If you have the courage to say this," answered Huey, "then you have the courage to move on from here. We can take back the city. We can find our souls within that place. We can reclaim ourselves and we can begin anew."

He was sure of this, Huey thought. It was not only the sound of his own voice pounding that realization into him, but indeed some intimation of what they had become. He clambered down off his perch on the tree stump, staring at the Brit who had baited him, and behind that Brit the ragamuffin crowd that had assembled, the worst army he had ever seen—and yet it *was* an army, it could be taken in that direction.

"Beethoven," he said, "stand up and give us a march! Give us a march, do you hear me? We are going to take back the city!"

And without thinking about it further, without stopping to consider the amazing and preposterous dimensions of what he had somehow suggested, Huey Long pushed his way through them and began to advance upon the city.

Suddenly a voice rang out:

"It's a very big city, and you're a very small army. If you're going to take it, then you're going to need an advantage, something to even the odds."

"Yeah?" said Huey, turning to face the lean, bearded newcomer. "What have you got in mind?"

Selous smiled and displayed a youthful blond man who struggled against the rope that bound him. "A god," he said. "A genuine gold-plated god."

Caligula looked up at the man and said, "He's right. That's exactly what I am. You will unbind me immediately. You will release me from these ropes or I will strike a curse—"

"He talks like that," interjected Selous. "Up and down, like nothing you have ever heard. You might as well give him a try. After all, not only does he have plans, *big* plans for reckoning, but how can you be defeated with a god at your fore? In any event," Selous concluded with a sweeping gesture, "I turn the situation over to you. Deal with him as you will."

Caligula examined the others carefully: the wild-haired man with the poisoned features of a Claudius, the somewhat younger, smooth-faced man with funny hands and strange gestures. They were not the kind of troops he would have envisioned, but on the other hand, you had to use what you had. In court, out of court, in or out of the city, surrounded by fools or madmen, you lived as you must, transcendent, and you brought order from the sinister.

"Well," said Caligula with a haughty tilt of his head, fixing his attention on the smooth-faced man who seemed the most reasonable, perhaps the most reverent of them all, "are you going to release me? Are you going to serve my powers? Or will you defy me and bring down my terrible curse?"

"He talks that way," said Selous. "Almost all the time. I can't do anything with him; maybe *you* can."

"Yes," said the smooth-faced man, his eyes filled with reverence, or at least a decent sense of the occasion. "Yes, I think we can do that." He reached out, began to tug on the ropes. "Stand clear," he said, "and let me release this god from his altar." He smiled at Caligula. "My Latin ain't all it used to be, and truth to tell, it was never that good. What did you say your name was?"

"Quickly unbind me," said Caligula, "and you will know my name and my curse, all of my circumstances. . . ."

"He talks that way all the time," Selous said again. "I'm a solitary man, used to the silent places. *You* deal with him; I've had quite enough, thank you."

"We've all had enough," said the smooth-faced man. "It's amazing how much you can take, though." He stared at Caligula intently, knelt, tugged at a knot. "*Every* man a god, that's my philosophy," he said. "What else would have brought us here?"

"Godhood is restricted," said Caligula. "It becomes only one of us."

"Oh, calm down," said his rescuer. "Calm down and stop babbling, at least for a moment. Beethoven, come and step on this cord, will you? We're *never* going to get him loose at this rate."

They bent intently to minister to him. Caligula crouched proudly, his head inclined at an angle, seeking the sun, the thin blades penetrating the heavy rolling clouds. An image pressed upon his mind, an image that inserted itself, unbidden, and that he could not remove. Hunched as if in this position, clinging to the stones, his belly heaving and inverted, his knees feeling the cold damp of the stones as he clutched the handles.

The vomitorium.

Without instruments he could not carry a tune, and this place yielded not even percussion, but Beethoven gave them a march anyway as they labored up and down with the one called Caligula at their head. It was the Turkish March from *The Ruins of Athens*, not his favorite, but good enough for this rabble with its piercing woodwinds and rattling snare drums, effects that he could reproduce in his head if not his muttering, groaning voice.

Take the city, that was Selous's idea too, take back the city. Not that they had ever had it in the first place, not that the city was anyplace to take. What could you do with it? But the Roman emperor, the strange youth with the glaring eyes, seemed to know his business: he had the assurance of Napoleon and the madness of an archbishop, moving out at the end of them in a curious, shuffling stride that conveyed, if not regality, then a kind of determination that Beethoven could appreciate.

Selous and Huey Long seemed deep in conversation as they shuffled along. From time to time some form would leap from the crowd that streamed alongside them and slap at the Roman emperor, then fall back with a roar.

It was a procession unlike any Beethoven had ever known. He had written his share of marches and contradances in his time, junk and diversions for the rabble, but he had never seen a group such as this. He could tell that things had changed since they had come upon Selous and Caligula, had released Caligula from his bondage and started back toward the place from which he had come. Matters were not at all as they had been. The air was thicker, clotting his nostrils, and the crowds pressed with an insistence he had not known before. *Every man a god*, Huey Long had said, and indeed attention was being paid to this Caligula unlike anything Beethoven had ever seen. Maybe there really was something at the end of this trek; Beethoven did not know, and it was not worth thinking about. What you did was take the staff and make your way with the rest of it: Roman emperors, Gallic emperors, democrats, freedmen, archbishops or slaves, they were all the same. There was almost an insight there, but he would not think about it. Not with the music roaring in his head, the *cymballo* rattling, the pedal of the snare drum furious against the screen of his consciousness.

When they came to the rise and looked down upon the enclosure, the huts erected along the River, Selous felt a sense of triumph, of vindication.

"You see?" he said, turning to Huey Long. "I *told* you we could get here. I knew it was just a matter of turning around and coming back, that no one would stop us!" Indeed, no one *had* stopped them, and they had in fact gathered a considerable group that was not discouraged by the heat and the brutality of the conditions, nor by Caligula's ravings. "Now we go on to the next step."

"And what *is* the next step, son?" asked Huey Long. The walk had not winded him, nothing on the Riverworld seemed to have the effect that it might have had in what he had come to think of as civilian life. "Am I supposed to make a speech? Is there a place we're supposed to occupy? Are we empowered to take something?" His eyes twinkled with a mad light, and he suddenly seemed to Selous to be not only an odd but possibly a dangerous man. Then the intimation passed and he was just a fat American politician with no constituency.

"I'm quite sure that matters will resolve now," said Selous. "Once they see us, once they know we've returned here, they will make arrangements for us."

Huey Long stared at him with that odd, kindly expression that could so suddenly and awkwardly shift to brutality, and said, "I don't know what you're talking about, son. I truly do not."

Selous shrugged. "Do any of us? Do any of us really know what is going on in this damnable place?"

"*I* do," said Caligula. "I know exactly what is going on." He turned to them, his body at attention, his eyes ferocious and insistent. "Now," the emperor said, "now we will bring this to an end." He raised his hand, stared at Selous, then Long, then passed his gaze along the thin ranks that had staggered to surround them.

"Bring me a virgin," he said. "Bring me a virgin at once!"

But, of course, he had known that this was their mission, that this was what had been waiting for them all along. Caligula felt the godhood coursing within him, felt in these burning moments the fullness of his need, and as he cast his eyes slowly down the line of followers he sought out the women in the ranks. He could feel the familiar power of his sex stirring deep within him. They would not dare to refuse, for soon they would know his true power.

"Bring me a virgin," he repeated, "or soon all of you will be dead. I will pronounce a curse upon you that will bring you to the dung that you are." He reached out, snagged Selous in a surprising and huge grasp, then flung the man out of his way with a power born of the madness now inside him, and ran toward the dim line he saw before him.

"I'll have you!" he yelled. "I'll have you all!" Destiny filled his loins as gracefully as if it had been the blood and sex of the virgin he craved. "You will acknowledge my godhood!" he cried. "I will open the gates of this city in the game of the anointment and I will have you all, just as it was decreed!"

He reached out, snared a body, ran his hands cruelly up and down it, seeking breasts, seeking the familiar pudenda, an amazing sense of destiny overwhelming him. Why, this place was splendid! He had not judged its splendor until this very moment. For he was truly a god here. He could do as he wished to any of them. Why had he not understood this before? They were *all* gods.

He started to mount the body, his needs urgent. He had never dreamed there could be a place such as this, but here it was. This was surprising, enormous, absolutely astonishing to him. In his head there was a ribbon of screaming, and he seized on to it, held it, and let the screaming drag him home.

Beethoven stared in despair. He had never seen such things. Even when the mobs had stormed the gates of Paris in 1789 there had not been anything like this, he was sure. But here it was. Huey Long was staring, laughing. Selous was rubbing his hands and yelling at Caligula in Victorian outrage . . . but no one moved on the young emperor in the small space that he had opened as he continued his cruel and amazing act.

The cymbals in Beethoven's head had stopped, the piccolo too, and all that was left was the droning of the *bassi* in the trio of the C Minor Symphony, that grotesque dance toward Hell.

"What are we doing?" he said to Huey Long. "Is this what we have become? Is this the end for us?"

He had a sudden blazing insight: Long and Selous had talked them back to the gates of the city for precisely this reason, so that pillage and rape could be undertaken, and Caligula had been unbound to lead them because only Caligula could manage what was necessary without hesitation.

"Aren't you going to stop this?" continued Beethoven. Long bit his lip, shook his head, smirked a negative. Selous shrugged; he seemed fascinated with what was going on, engaged but disengaged.

"From here I can't even tell if it's a man or a woman," said Selous.

"Does it make any difference?" said Long.

"Then *I'll* stop it!" Beethoven, without quite realizing what he was doing, flung himself at the rounded, heaving flanks of the emperor, feeling a revulsion such as he had never known. That other emperor, Napoleon, had betrayed him, but that had been impersonal, it had not been like this. This was *revolting*. It was obscene, disgusting, it was the revocation of all that he had lived his fifty-seven years to negate. Freedom, yes, but freedom for *all*, not just the insane and the wicked.

"Stop!" he shrieked, lunging toward them. Then he

felt Huey Long's hands upon him, enormous, pulling him back.

"No!" said Huey Long. "Don't stop him! This is what we came here to see."

"Every man a god," said Huey Long. Selous stared at the American in shock and approval. "*That* is why we were taken to this place," continued Long; "so that we could do as we wished."

Beethoven struggled in his embrace, tried feebly to escape, but Long was much too powerful for him.

Selous looked upon the two of them in that embrace, looked further to see Caligula humping and scuttling away in the position of an insect, and thought: the man is right. The American is right, every man *is* a god, and we have come to this accursed place to make gods of ourselves, be they in the most despicable of fashion. *That* is the answer that lay in the heart of the city; that is what we have always understood. All of his life he had aspired, just as others must, to this position, and now that he had found it there was nothing to do but submit.

"Submit!" Selous screamed to Beethoven. "Let it be! Do as you will!" He scanned the land, the encampment in the distance, the near forms that in the intensity of Caligula's necessity had scattered to open ground. I'd do it myself if I could, thought Selous, and I will, I will. "Now I understand why we came back to the banks of the River," he said to Huey Long. "This was waiting for us all the time, wasn't it?"

Long smiled, shook his head, opened his hands to Selous. His expression was curious, abstracted. Beethoven, scrambling in Long's enormous hug, gave up suddenly, sunk to his knees, then leaned over the ground and rubbed his forehead in the mud.

"You won't stop him," muttered Beethoven. "None of us will stop him. Nothing will ever be stopped again. That's the answer, isn't it? That's what you wanted me to know, why you brought me back to humiliate me."

"I don't know anything about that, son," said Huey Long. He smiled easily and stared at Selous. "But we think we know the answer now, don't we?"

"Yes," said Selous. There was a dim and insistent haze in front of him; he could have whisked it away with a few motions of his hand, but he chose not to. "Yes, I understand. Every man a god." He looked at the entrapped, sullen Beethoven. "Even you," he said. "And me, and the rest of them. That is for us to discover."

Caligula's voice bleated through the haze, through the shocking stillness of the Riverworld. Selous heard the chanting of the emperor and then the dull scream of his release. I'll be damned, he thought, and then, Yes, I guess I am. I guess we all are. Which is exactly the same thing as being free.

"He sure put that chicken in the pot, didn't he?" said Huey Long. "Look at the man put that there car in the garage." He cackled and wondered what Selous would say to that. "Say, there," he said to Beethoven, who was now softly weeping beneath him, "what do you think the Englishman would say?"

"*Muss ess sein,*" Beethoven said. "*Ess muss sein.*"

Magnificent in his duties, triumphant in his discharge, the god Caligula rolled from the inert form that had served him so well—adequately, anyway, enough for the time being, though of course there would be better—and looked at his subjects encamped in the distance, fallen to their knees to revere and serve him.

"Oh, yes," he said quietly. "Oh, yes, reverence and service, they are the same thing."

He readjusted his garments, stood, pushed the husk of his revenant to one side, and strode to the small place that had been made for him by the servants of the Riverworld, his parapet from which he would speak. He would gather them to him and give them his orders, and then the true and final nature of his reign would begin. In the distance he heard the shrieks of homage, Claudius himself soon to come, to bear witness, to bow down in service. Every man a god, yes—

—But this god, granted the Riverworld, its indulgence, its folly and its treasure . . . *this god a man.*

Blandings on Riverworld

Phillip C. Jennings

"Has even death become unsure? Are we mockeries of ourselves? Are you the Mocker?"

The Big Cheese's voice echoed down from the throne. P.G. Wodehouse, Bart., was urged to his knees by the guards at his side, and the Grand Panjandrum—this "al-Hakim" chappie—took wind for another set-to in what Plum had to admit was exceptionally refulgent Arabic.

"To say that God speaks is to suggest he may ever be silent. This—this 'river world' is not reality, but a code, and therefore a message and not of God. But it implies a message very like the Druze da'wa, and therefore a thousand times deceitful. What do you know of the Deceiver?"

Hakim's mighty line of thought seemed almost logical. Some Oxford wallah might grasp how one sentence led to the next, each conclusion grimmer than the one before it. "Well now, dash it! I mean—codes and all!" Saddled with the habits of a myopic lifetime, Plum blinked about, trying to make something of a hall built of cyclopean slabs. His spirits certainly needed fortifying. A casual

141

viewer of these mustered ranks in black robes and white turbans—said viewer might easily hop to the conclusion that he was "in for it."

It was not a conclusion Plum Wodehouse liked to embrace. Death may have lost much of its sting by the third or fourth inning, but his last incarnation he hadn't even gotten a chance to eat, and his faith in the better nature of humanity was taking a beating. "If you think I'm the Devil, or that I've met him, I have to answer not to my knowledge. No. I mean, I don't think so."

"Truth knows what it means."

"I suppose it does," Plum conceded. In moments of desperate anxiety his smile widened to the straining point and became almost horrible. "But I can't vouch for anyone but myself, and I've met a lot of strange coves and covesses these last few lives. . . ." His eyes narrowed with sudden cunning. "Besides, didn't you say we might not be ourselves? Under the circ.s, I don't know how to prove my bona fides."

"We tolerate one people here, and one language. Assuredly I've never heard Arabic spoken as you do," al-Hakim thundered from his high and distant seat. *"Nevertheless, it is Arabic—of a sort."*

He pondered, and the flanking spear-carriers shifted in waiting, ready to extirpate this infidel at the crook of a finger. *"You've lived several lives? After the feast, attend us privately in our garden, and we will hear your testimony."*

Plum took this for good news, and breathed again. The four hours of this present existence might become eight, and then sixteen. . . . Socially inept, yes, but he'd always charmed—well, not everybody. In his last incarnation Hans Hörbiger had it in for him, with bells on. Still, al-Hakim bi'Amr Allah would feel better for a few rashers under his belt, and in a tête-à-tête encounter . . .

Plum felt a tap on his shoulder. His travail was over, but the business of court went on—the business of recessing for lunch in conformity with the inexorable schedule of the local grailstones.

One of the spearmen sat him in an alcove with a few heterogenous gents, and took his tiffin-tin. The usual magic was done offstage, and it came back not quite an hour later for Plum to open.

The fee for this service was all his cigarettes and alcohol. Plum hardly minded crossing the callused palm of the local IRS. At some date umbrage might set in, but for the nonce he took a larger view. Made affable by a mélange of chicken, paprika, onions, and sour cream, he tried his French on the swarthy gang around him. French, language of diplomacy, perfect for the exchange of secrets— but his halting attempts *ne marche pas*.

German? Latin? *Carpe diem* might as well be a Vietnamese fish recipe. After some diffidence and throat-clearing, the Apache-looking customer ventured his English. "Don't use Jesus dates. He'll ask you. Subtract six hundred thirty from everything."

Plum beamed mutely, his mouth full. The Apache went on. "It's not always the same number, because they got shorter years. But if you lived on Earth after 1200 *his* time, he'll be interested in you."

Plum did the math. The six hundred part was easy: Thirteen dah-de-dah. Thirteen forty-two. He might round it upward—fifty, sixty, seventy. "Do I want to be interesting?" he asked.

The Apache laughed. He might have said *touché*, but the Norman conquest had never reached Arizona.

After the pudding, Plum tried to ease himself among this crowd: "Ah, an afterlife of leisure." The irony, apparent in the English, did not survive translation. He reconsidered his cheerfulness, adopting the general silence until a pair of black-robes—lots of kiltcloth wasted here—strode in and grunted him to his feet.

The local gendarmerie marched him left through an atrium and out a roofless corridor. Under a semitropic sun the corridor doubled on itself, stones like polished incisors on both sides. *Giant chiclets,* Plum thought, always keen to improve a metaphor. His way ramped into a shallow pool and out again. The three left wet footprints for a distance, and the labyrinth opened to compass a field just too small for a cricket match.

The man Hakim waited under a tree. Close up, he boasted a heroically Semitic face: like an Assyrian fresh off the frieze, minus the beard and trimmings. A guard or two stood at wide distances, as unmenacing as they could get, but still Plum thought of those biblical stories—the ones involving wolves on the fold, and mountains of severed heads. He bowed, unsure of the protocol, and his escorts beetled away to join the others. "When did you die?" Hakim asked, getting straight to the point.

Plum took the plunge and exaggerated manfully. "The year 1380," he said. "—after Mohammed did whatever it was."

"You've worked it out. Good." *Good puppy,* he might have said. *Good infidel.* Hakim paced a circle. "You shall have a hut. See that row? A hut to each of my historical consultants. I labor under a disadvantage, and you will help me. Who have you run into?"

This al-Hakim bi'Amr Allah had one thing going for

him—he knew how to keep a chap off balance. "What? Where?"

"In your several lives," Hakim said. "Hitler? Lenin?"

Plum shook his head. "Queen Bilkis. That was my first resurrection. She and Madame Blavatsky set up an aunt-aucracy of women who lived long lives on Earth, and learned not to take backchat from me. La Blavatsky— she got this religion going when I was a schoolboy. Er—ah."

"Yes?"

"I do a splendid job of organizing things on paper; it's only in real life that I'm a broken reed. Do you want to know all the Hollywood types I met on Earth? Movie stars," he went on. "Clark Gable. Fred Astaire. Broadway chappies, too."

"Queen Bilkis is a mythical figure," Hakim said.

"There was a good muchness to her, for a myth," Plum answered. "She had the advantage on me of a stone or two, and made dashed sure I learned Arabic. Who else? Bilkis's neighbors across the river tugged their forelocks at Prince Fernando Montesinos, who claimed to be somebody. You couldn't prove it by me. I mean, I couldn't tell you if Rowena was Horsa's daughter, or Hengist's."

"Rowena?" Hakim had the gift of patience.

"Gossip drifted up-River that she'd married H. Rider Haggard, but Allah knows how many kingdoms away from me *that* was; somewhere the far side of Emperor Alexius. I got killed for Bilkis, don't you know. I walked into a spear because my new eyes were too good."

Since he had Hakim's attention, Plum took wind. "The *real* me used to be blind as a bat. I'd take my glasses off before going to sleep. I needed to get blurry, or it didn't go. All that time with Bilkis and her sanhedron of aunts, I had insomnia like nobody's business. I was groggy on my toes when Prince Fernando launched his armada. *'Invasion!'* the locals hued and cried. *'Invasion? What? Where?'* I yawned, fumbling for my bludgeon—''

Hakim's black eyes beaded steadily on despite this diversion. ''But perhaps you know about Lenin,'' he interrupted. ''And the Bolshevik movement? Had they achieved true communism by your time on Earth?''

Surely this wrench in topics meant something profound, Plum thought to himself. ''Lenin died—spare me the math—but fifty years before me. Russia kept going and picking up satellites. They bought my books, don't you know. Bought 'em like billy-o. I had the deuce of a time doing anything with their rubles, but my characters were all idiot English capitalists, and they liked that.''

''You wrote books.''

''Fiction. Music hall stuff. Funny.''

The man Hakim filed this away. ''Fifty years. And Lenin's cause was prospering?'' An eagle had the same way of plucking here, plucking there, and pausing between times to contemplate its dead fish. Hakim had an eagle's craggy face, and all the time in the world.

''The Reds? In a glum sort of way, rising on the stepping-stones of dead multitudes to higher things. Politics wasn't my game. When it's summer, one doesn't dwell on the torments of winter, and I'm a summer person.''

Hakim nodded at the metaphor. He spoke in ponderous sympathy. ''All these people in black robes: winter people. *Religion* does that. They migrate up-River and down, dozens a week, because they've heard that their *Hakim* is back from occultation. I have to conquer new grailstones to feed them all, and so my neighbors hate me. Perhaps they're right. Messiahs are evil, no?''

Plum shrugged. In his hours here, he'd gotten the impression that Mr. al-Hakim bi'Amr Allah was a god in the flesh to the Druze who dominated this bit of riverbank. He was a latter-day Mohammed. Tact required that he show some reluctance to damn the man to his face.

He cogitated—what *should* he say? As he ransacked his wits, Hakim went inscrutable. ''Your cabin. The last one in the corner. We'll walk there.''

They did. It had a bed, a small table, a door, and a window. During his internment in World War Two, Plum had endured worse than this. *Much* worse. Given the dearth of structure around Riverworld, this bamboo box was a suite at the Ritz.

The godlike and possibly evil Hakim made a gesture— *this is yours*—and left. Plum stepped inside, put his tiffin-grail on the table, and tested his frame-and-mattress. Ropes took the place of bedsprings, but it was comfortable. Privacy!

Plum's face fell. This was as good as it got, but Riverworld was still hell. No paper, no ink, no printing presses. How could he function? The one thing he did well was no longer an option. Except for that, he was a fool. His role as ''historical consultant'' was pure folly. No one forced to be there had paid less attention to the twentieth century.

Then there was Hakim. When Plum talked, the vagaries of his mind took play. Hakim was equally inconsistent, but here was the terrifying difference: He had depths behind him. In switching topics, he followed a cunning mental algorithm that left his victim plundered.

Literally speaking, Plum had always found it a bad

idea to get into the psychology of his villains. It ruined them. Now that he was *in* the story instead of writing it, his feelings were different. Plum regretted that he could guess nothing of his master's inner compulsions. He was Hakim's poor mule, goaded by carrot and stick, but why?

Why had Hakim hinted that he was not really the figment his followers worshiped? Something didn't wash. What was going on here? After a time Plum got up and went back outside, into the "garden"—this giant-chiclet-walled cricket meadow—to see if his fellow historical consultants had any idea.

They were fonts of information. The ex-haberdasher from Smyrna pointed off right, to the wall opposite this row of huts. "Beyond that's the women's side," he explained. "Hakim spends *much* more time with them. We're the second team. He uses us to check their facts. When Maria tells him that Kemal Ataturk did thus and so, he noses around to make sure of it."

"Maria?"

"We're not supposed to know their names," said Nabuch ad-Nasr, who was an expert on Middle East politics two thousand years *before* Hakim became Imam-Caliph. Plum thought it odd that a fellow of Old Testament times should bounce around in the vigor of youth, as giddy a lad as the Afghan resistance fighter—notwithstanding his love of makeup and elaborately pretty eyes, this last was an expert on nine guerrilla organizations fighting the Soviet invaders.

None of the aforementioned chaps came by Arabic honestly: they were Turkish, Amorite, and Pathan. But it was a condition of living here that they could make themselves understood, and so they had huts, while Jim the Apache was obliged to camp in odd corners until he grew fluent. Plum repeated the name in translation, as if "Maria" sounded different in English. Before he could laugh at himself for this stupidity, Jim answered in broken Arabic: "She's best. Queen of harem. She talk much Lenin."

"Hitler too," said the haberdasher.

"Hakim is jealous. He thinks *he* should rank in history with those two," said a junior prince of Iraq, assassinated in some coup in the 1950s. Plum was surprised at the princeling's open hostility, and at the general freedom of speech within these walls, but most of this cabal had gotten here the same way he had, by taking the "cheap trip." They were half ready and half willing to die again.

There were worse punishments than death. One heard of slaver kingdoms: blind, mutilated starvelings kept in confinement for the booty in their tiffin "grails." If Hakim wanted a reputation for villainy, he could have done the like. He hadn't. It gave one pause. It made one wonder if there was a goodish bloke inside Hakim, trying fitfully to make himself known.

Plum Wodehouse slept on the problem that night without coming to an answer. The daily rains came just before dawn. Breakfast was a bun and hot noodle soup, the guard absconding with the usual tax. There'd be no tobacco for Plum's nonexistent pipe, and afterward no typewriter to lay hands on, no audience for the latest adventure at Blandings Castle. What was left? How could life be worth living?

That afternoon, good bloke Hakim and his entourage visited the male side of his garden, filing from hut to hut for chats with the locals. Reaching Plum at last, the Occult Master of Druze-dom played the generous host.

"What is wrong?" he asked, after Plum made a botch

of gratitude for his lodgings. "Would you like to wander around this land of winter piety? I myself feel circumscribed, and so we organize hikes and tours and picnics. You mustn't think you're a prisoner."

Really? "No, it's not that. I just—I'm addicted to writing," Plum answered. "For sixty-plus years that's all I did. Writing, and a spot of walking, or wrestling now that I'm in my vigor again. Dogs. I liked dogs. But nothing quite does it for me like putting words on a blank page."

He averted his face, appalled at the surge of his emotions. He spoke on, brokenly. "I've never seen paper on Riverworld."

Hakim took Plum's hand, as a minister might pluck the limp hand of a mourning widow, and gave it a ministerial pat. "I can bring you paper! We make it out of bamboo. I knew there was something. People are sent to me for a purpose. Yesterday I didn't know what you were for, but now it becomes clear."

"Allah wouldn't send you P.G. Wodehouse to write funny stories," Plum answered. Even as his spirits launched upward on the giddy wings of hope, he recoiled against the grandeur of Hakim's concepts.

"You must have faith! The universe is broken," Hakim answered. "Logic demands that all the casual chains should cycle beginning to end, in a round of time, and each link of that round chain, when you come to it, is the *same* link as eighty billion years before. The same Hakim meeting the same P.G. Wodehouse, but thanks to Allah, the doom of that eternal cycle cycle of Big Bang and collapse is not for us. The universe of Physics has cracked, and His grace leaks in through His instruments. I know nothing except what I experience—I am a vessel of that grace. I trust in it. I use it. When I was younger, I used it very badly, although grace has a way of making bad things good.

"I was not sure yesterday. You seemed very bad: a mocker. A man of un-Druze-like character in a world that makes a joke of Druze beliefs. But now you can prove yourself. Come. We must whisper."

Bending away from his guards into Plum's hut, Hakim touched his finger to his lips. "This is a secret you will be unable to betray: my followers would kill you at the suggestion of the truth. Nine hundred years before your time, they say I left Cairo and fled my honors and titles. I wrote letters from hiding the next three decades. These letters instructed them in their religion. Lies, lies! But naturally I'd be interested in reading them myself! To know what I said! On Resurrection Day we all woke on Riverworld, naked and bookless, and I have no good way to quote myself."

Hakim went to the window to make sure no one was listening. After a moment he came back. "Hence my interest in paper and ink. All I need do—all I *can* do, is cause to have published as much of those texts as my elders here can remember. We are all enthusiastic about this project, for various reasons, mine being survival.

"Survival? But—"

"I know I'd resurrect if all they did was kill me. Consider that they could do worse. Consider also: I have not died once since the morning in Cairo when I 'went into occultation.' I'm not as used to the idea as you are. But I'm not merely a coward who plays a bully in self-defense: the fealty of these people gives me wonderful opportunities. What I told you is true. Unless I'm insane to say so, I am one of Allah's vessels of grace. I was born to it, and I have felt the power in me."

Plum cleared his throat. Why me? he thought to himself. If this cove unbosoms himself to every customer he meets within forty-eight hours . . . One possibility had to be that he really was insane.

Fortunately, Hakim kept up his end of the conversation without Wodehouse's active help. "In your life on Earth, al-Hakim bi'Amr Allah meant nothing to you. You never heard of me before yesterday."

"Er, ah . . . I guess—"

"Few people have, outside the Jebel Druze. Yet until my sister had me assassinated I was the Lenin of my age. I ruled from Cairo, and Cairo was as great a city as Byzantium had ever been. Greater than Damascus, much greater than Rome!

"Being a vessel of God, I hated religion. I was impartial—I hated them all. I destroyed the Church of the Holy Sepulcher in Jerusalem. I suppressed all pilgrimages, emphatically including the sacred Hadj to Mecca and Medina. But I ruled through my Shi'ite followers, and *they* were biased. Christians and Jews suffered much worse than Moslems.

"What use was it to drive people of the Bible into apostasy, if all they did was convert to Islam? My solution was to create a new religion without priests and real estate and vested interests, so fanaticism could work *for* me, and Allah sent me proselytes to do the work. If we'd had more than four years . . . if we'd had eight, or twenty . . ."

Hakim shrugged. "Before I came along, Moslems, Christians and Jews lived peacefully in my realms. I set the precedent of oppression, and did not survive to see it work properly—it was always *unjust* oppression, never *just*. For years afterward, rulers continued to harass Christians with biased zeal. A lifetime later, the Franks responded with the First Crusade."

Hakim paused at this dramatic juncture. Plum took up the slack. Apparently the man wanted blame—or credit. Yesterday he'd almost begged to be called evil. "So you caused all that."

"All that harm. Useless bloodshed in the name of religion, because I wanted to *break* those institutions, not *use* them. Should I not be famous over the centuries for my mistakes? Perhaps Lenin was greater than me. He succeeded where I failed."

Plum shook his head. "The verdict isn't in. Not as of my former life span. Anyhow, Lenin's religion of communism—I can't see it's better than the others. People die for it the same way."

Hakim smiled. "I like the way your mind works. But Maria and I have anticipated your reservations. Secrets within secrets! This is one I cannot give away. An extraordinary woman!"

He went to the window again and spoke in a more public voice: "For you, my women do not exist. You will never be useful in the same measure as my favorite among them. There is no scoundrel in you. No energy I can grasp and use. I must simply give you paper and ink, and trust in the results."

On this note he swept off, except this one-room shack lacked the dimensions. A good sweep needs three paces—two if there's a door one shuts dramatically. By Hakim's third pace he was well outdoors and talking about someone's prospective execution.

A tyrant's agenda was a busy one. Plum reconstructed

the last ten minutes, and decided the man had done it again. Overwhelmed him. What he was proudest of in his work wasn't his lyrical English, his mastery of the storyteller's rules. No, he prized those Rube Goldberg plots, full of hairsbreadth timing and improbable coincidences. It cost him half his efforts putting them together— the harder half. The easier half was slathering on the verbiage.

Hakim? Hakim was a plot on the hoof. You could hardly *help* having a story with a dervish like him whirling around. Wodehouse didn't like it. Reality was reality and fiction was fiction, and never the twain should meet. He'd always been fond of the characters in his stories, but did those characters like their author? The issue came up with a vengeance, because Hakim had an author's power over him.

Plum fulminated. What one had here in spades were: plush digs, servants, impostors. Familiar elements to any of his readers. What about the love angle? The dreaded aunt? Well, there'd be enough of that on the other side of the wall, in the women's garden.

Yes, he could work something out. It might be therapeutic. If Hakim made good on his promised paper, Plum might manage a story: Blandings-on-Riverworld. Something to restore his sense of balance. Something to put Hakim in his place.

Careful. 'Twere best to be subtle indeed, given all this bally fanaticism. The cast must play in disguise. It made a pretty problem, and Wodehouse devoted the rest of the afternoon and evening to working it out.

By morning he was adding details, and wishing he could remember them all. Hakim-and-crew came by again on their daily constitutional. ''People who die simultaneously—do they resurrect in the same place? Have you heard rumors? Lovers' compacts and the like?"

Plum blinked. "I—I don't know."

"We'll experiment. Nabuch and the Afghan can be lovers somewhere else, with my blessings." He shifted his voice, as newscasters did when they sat in front of a mike. "Unnatural vices are not tolerated here."

"Ah." Plum focused on the sight of two historical consultants being led to the big tree. Thrust up against the bark. Tied. If this happened often, no wonder there were empty huts for new arrivals like himself.

Hakim reached behind him and handed over a parcel. "Paper, pens, and ink. Don't watch if it distresses you."

Plum collected the treasured objects and ducked into his cabin. He heard spear thunks. They were not very simultaneous, after all.

For an hour afterward, Wodehouse found it impossible to write. The story was to have circled around an American rubber-toy magnate who funded a cult combining health and religiosity, a sort of Seventh-Day Adventism. The chap had a happy-go-lucky twin with a thirst for alcohol. . . .

Both twins were Hakim, the good Hakim and the bad one. But Plum's juices froze at any thought of that awful man, that vortex of contradictions. He only thawed out by parking *that* story on a mental shelf and starting something new.

In what language? Arabic. And if so, make it a short story. Plum wasn't up to being clever for over five thousand words in his adopted language.

Using what script? Plum was illiterate in Arabic. He threw down his pen and stood. Talk about adversity! Phonetic Roman, then. If all the whilom inhabitants of

Planet Earth decorated the landscape somewhere on Riverworld, there must be *dozens*, even *hundreds,* who would enjoy a good Arabic screed penned by guess and by gosh.

He returned to his table and started to scribble.

Plum took days to get up to speed. Even under better circumstances a five-thousand-word story needs a week to write. Hakim the Patient failed to understand. On his sixth visit, he tapped Wodehouse's finished pages. "I make nothing of your foolish ciphers. If this bears sense at all, read me this to prove it."

"I—I'm fairly horrible," Plum responded. "I've been told on good authority I should never read out loud."

"Try."

With a grimace Plum plucked up page one and began to orate. He faltered and droned, skipping lines, backtracking and scratching his head.

"Hah!" Hakim barked after two minutes of torment. "Give it to me! I know what needs to be done."

He left with Plum's half-finished work. Wodehouse sank in defeat. He had failed—and why not? How did he ever think otherwise? Would Hitler laugh at witticisms in pidgin German, penned in Hebrew? Gents like Lenin weren't famous for their senses of humor, were they? Hakim was no different. Hakim, who could keep him from reaching any audience at all!

In Plum's frame of mind the sight of his worktable was hateful. He got up and plunged into the garden, walking fast loops around the periphery, averting his face from the central tree. What had Hakim done with his wretched manuscript? Used it for toilet paper? Thrown it into the river?

Every fifth time he changed directions. Clockwise—counterclockwise—clockwise again. From the women's side of the wall, he heard laughter. The word "guffaw" sprang to mind, hard as it was to imagine girlish lungs guffawing. Life was sweet over there. The sun shone.

Perhaps if he spread-eagled himself across the tree, some guard would obligingly chuck a spear in his direction. "Hakim's a fake!" he'd shout to encourage the blighter. "He never wrote your scriptures! It's all lies!"

That would do it. Plum left the path he was burning in the grass, the better to make a target of himself.

As he reached the tree Hakim appeared at the labyrinth entry, his face creased with smiles. "Excellent! Wonderful!"

He handed over Plum's pages and left again, a man with a penchant for sudden departures. So it is with your general run of critic, Wodehouse thought to himself. You want them to omit no details of your excellent wonderfulness; this line, this joke, this felicity of expression, and instead they zoom off.

The world had just turned a hundred eighty degrees, so to speak. Plum did too. He went back into the hut. . . .

Girlish laughter. Girlish laughter *at his story?* Then they knew about him over there. *Someone* knew. What would she look like?

Perhaps a bit hearty. The sort of woman who brayed. Ah, no. Assuredly there was a bray-er, but why not *another* woman too? Who knew the density of population over there? Dozens of ears may have heard. Lips were lisping: "Wodehouse. Could it be the same? *That* Wodehouse?"

Plum was a lonely man, kept company by the creatures of his imagination. Take that dashed wall away, and he'd still be lonely. It was better this way. He could pretend there were people who thought about him. People he could excite.

No, no pretense. He *could* excite them. He *could* reach them. He sat at his table, fired with new ambition. A story? A *book!* In English, at least the first draft. No more weird mishmashes!

Once Plum immersed himself in his grand enterprise, time whizzed by, with occasional interruptions to tie on the old nosebag. He almost resented these breaks, made worse by the officiousness of the tiffin man, who never failed to collect his tobacco, his marijuana, his liquor, and/or his dreamgum. No altered mental states allowed in Druze-dom!

Hakim visited daily, and then absented himself on a tour of his domains. Plum scribbled on. Now and again he'd walk for exercise, having the sort of strappingly large body that insisted on its own health.

Chapter one took shape. It would remain chapter one. The chapters one of other authors became chapters twelve or chapters seventeen before their books were through, or got distributed in parcels through the work, or ditched entirely. Such was not the way of P.G. Wodehouse.

He launched chapter two. Hakim came back from his royal progress. He collected Plum's first closely written pages and felt the sting of the Wodehouse wrath. "Hey! What do you think you're doing?"

"You said this much was done. Maria wants to see it."

Plum insisted on promises. Hakim scowled, and left.

A guard returned the pages some hours later. Plus a pipe. Plus a pouch of tobacco. He turned and left. Plum danced a caper around his hut, puffed a bowlful, and got back to work.

He labored until the gilded evening dimmed and took his light away, and then took another walk, nodding cheerfully at Jim the Apache, the Smyrnese haberdasher, and a new arrival, a French Algerian with a smoldering resentment of everything Arabic. The Iraqi prince bowed grandly as Plum swung by, not a nice bow, but an accusation. Plum could not account for it. Jealousy? Word of the gift pipe had gotten around.

No butler shimmered into view at nine-thirty with whiskey-and-soda. Plum went to bed.

He was awakened by a *"Shhh!"* Someone was in the hut with him. "Please!" she whispered. "Don't make a sound."

Plum fumbled, then remembered he didn't need glasses anymore. He spoke to a scented silhouette. "How did you get here? Who are you?"

"I knew it was you. I had to see." She spoke English in the accents of the warm south, somewhere between Alps and Ganges. "I loved your story. The pipe was my idea."

"Oh." As he gained fuller consciousness, Plum was seized by terror. "This—you have to get back. This is madness! We'll be killed for it!"

The shadow shook her head. Plum's bed creaked as she sat at his side. "It does not occur to Hakim that resurrectees are random. He suspects purpose. You are either something dangerous or useful. Me? I'm one of the usefuls. If his alchemists can extract the essence of dreamgum and make his people children again, I will help mold them in ways—of freedom? So he says: freedom and goodness. He says he must put on the grand show of Druze-ism, but in his heart he is against it.

Survival! First he must stay alive here, where his position is unique."

Hers was a tidy synopsis of what Plum already had been told, but it touched too lightly on the one fact that put an edge on the knife. "He's a bally impostor. He never wrote their scriptures. He's just muddling along."

"You are always putting impostors in your Blandings Castle," the woman answered. "I think he wants this. He wants to be written up in allegory; warmly, a well-intentioned man. Your book will appeal to the new people we make. The orthodox will hate it. You will be a rod for their lightnings. Druze-land will be your prison, but your work will sneak out into the greater world."

"Until, not too guiltily, Hakim has me killed."

The visitor shook her head. "I don't see how he can pull it off. Creating a race of 'summer children' in the midst of this spiritual winter. He'll be killed too. And the new ones. But we'll be resurrected, knowing how to re-create ourselves with concentrated essence of dreamgum. The ratio of summer to winter will edge our way."

Plum made out the features of a comely face—though taxed by care, and less so than it might have been. She bent and kissed him. "You are purest summer—unless you have hidden depths."

Plum stammered. "No, no depth at all. I stay away from depth."

She smiled. "Yes, you are heroically shallow. Can you write your book? The book of the good impostor Hakim?"

Plum lurched clumsily, the better to pat his seductress's ankle. "He sent you. Your feet are dry. There's no way to get here dry-shod. There's a pool in the way. Except Hakim does it all the time. He's got a secret route."

The woman looked side to side. "I've never been on this half before. I wanted to come. It was made possible. I bring out the summer side of Hakim. Besides, I'm safe with you. I told Hakim you are not an ardent man. Anyone educated in an English boy's school and fond of wrestling and boxing—I told him you were assuredly a closet homosexual, or maybe a pedophile."

"Oh, I say—!"

She put a finger to his protesting lips. "That will make it easier. I must be your editor, you see."

"Are you—Maria?"

"Maria Montessori. World's foremost expert on the education of children!" She went on in bitter amusement. "If you were useless in Riverworld without paper, imagine me with no young minds to guide."

Wodehouse felt the warmth of her body. The hand he'd used to check her feet slid upward to take stock of her dimensions. This bed wasn't very big after all, even with him pressed against the wall in a semi-aroused state of anxiety. "Ahh," he said. "Ahh."

She went tilt. For a while there was confusion: knees and elbows being what they were. "Why Lenin?" Plum blurted after a first passionate clinch. "Why all this natter about Lenin and Hitler?"

"They stole my ideas about the plasticity of young minds. The New Communist Man. The Hitler youth. Get children early enough, and you make them anything!"

A kiss, and more lecture. "Of course their directions were wrong, but the concept! The tabula rasa! Did communism prove it, or not? If we make adults children again, and convert them into— You invented the words. *Summer people.* That's what we want."

"And you're sure about Hakim? You trust him?"

Maria laughed. "I can out-trick him any day. I'm here, aren't I? And he knows it. Let him kill me. I'd pop back with all my knowledge somewhere else, and start my own regime. So I'm not worried. Come now. Let's not talk about this. Goodness, you're a long-distance head-to-toe! And such baby-soft hair!"

Next day Plum zoomed through chapter two, and took a walk. The Iraqi prince stepped into his path. "Ah, the aristocrat's lapdog."

"Sorry?"

"I'm told you write about dukes and earls. The upper crust. Ordinary people not good enough for you."

"My dukes and earls are very ordinary," Wodehouse answered. "Really, I'm one with the masses. The masses who buy the *Saturday Evening Post*, anyhow."

"The despised masses. Hakim despises them. Don't you suppose he's told me? He only does bad things because they demand it. I've heard politicians whimper that sort of thing all my several lives. Have any of them had the courage to expect the best of their subjects? Or do they pander to the worst?"

"Some of each, I suppose," Plum muttered.

"Yes. And you know which kind of man Hakim is, and you write for him anyhow."

Plum colored. "I write what I write. Anybody who puts meaning into it is an idiot. You'd know if you'd ever read my stuff."

"And you spoke on Nazi radio in World War Two. Unfair of people to put meaning into that, right?"

Plum's blush deepened. "It was a mistake. I was isolated and naive. I didn't want people to worry about me. I didn't know my chipper bleat would give pain to Londoners who'd gotten blitzed."

"Stop pushing him around," Jim the Apache said from behind.

The princeling sneered. "I hear the voice of Hakim's Indian scout. The one who runs free, and tracks skulkers by their broken twigs. Your Arabic has improved."

"Don't let him bug you," Jim told Plum, ignoring the irksome Iraqi.

"Thanks. I'll try not."

"—Because when we have fights here, sometimes the guards execute everybody involved. I've seen it."

Plum made a face, but bad news or no, Jim's helpfulness deserved a reward. "Do you smoke? Would you share a bowl of shag with me?"

Jim smiled assent. Once in his hut and away from princely ears, Plum asked: "Er, about that broken twig business . . ."

"Maria's visit last night? I know nothing about it. There's a stone that pivots open, but I don't know about that either. Third on the left, this side of the pool."

Plum puffed and passed over his pipe. "I owe you. Concerning that woman—well, I've been pondering the archetypes. Tyrant, vamp, and fool. Publisher, editor, and writer. It's no different than in New York or London. The Doubleday gang didn't fling spears so enthusiastically, but you have to make allowances for local customs."

Plum sighed. "Maybe I shouldn't be here. Our Iraqi seems keen to take another "cheap trip." I could speed us both on our way."

Jim smiled, his brown face wreathed in smoke. "Hakim's spearmen have been practicing. They've gotten good. If it's true about people who get killed the same time, you and him could end up resurrecting side by side."

"I don't want that!" Plum laughed. He took another draw on the pipe, then traded it back. After five minutes of nicotine-tinged meditation, the Apache nodded thanks and left. Plum turned his hand to writing, and began chapter three.

Chapter four took shape. "Snookers" Van Doorp left his bedroom with the dead cat under his smoking jacket and bumped into the housemaid. Just then, a work-gang invaded Plum's hut, dismantled his bed, and began stringing a larger one "because you're so tall."

It was longer, and *wider*. Maria visited again that night, and left two hours later with chapters one to three. "You'll see," she whispered. "Ironwood is strong. We carve it into type for our printing press. This will look wonderful."

Plum instructed her in the publishing business. "First you frolic in the margins. Then I rewrite. Then your side sets type and runs off a proof. I look, and fuss, and fix all the mistakes that have crept in. Only after all that do you chug out the copies."

"I was an author in my day," Maria assured him. "Don't worry. I know what I'm doing."

She left. Plum heard the familiar sneers of the Iraqi prince just outside the door: "Oh, gua-a-a-ards! Look what we have here—*ugh!*"

Silence. Plum poked his head out of the hut and saw a body clutching itself in the grass. He scratched his head. Hadn't Maria Montessori been a pacifist in former times? There she was, twinkling off in utter haste. . . .

"*Ugh!*" Another figure was doing the damage; a

second riposte from the bushes and back again. The Iraqi bubbled a bit, and Plum withdrew to let the night shroud its secrets. In Hakim's gardens, this was ever the wisest course.

Plum was troubled to discover that murders no longer impeded his writing. His sleep, yes, but despite insomnia he insinuated Reverend Pancroft into chapter six, no matter that he had to fly the blighter home from France. The Toby Winkleman urchin insulted the cook, who quit the day of the Important Dinner. . . .

Maria Montessori edited with a light hand. On her third visit, she whispered about *Sijill* magazine, issue one, a Druze tract with news, views, a sermonette about the glories of Hakim—and Wodehouse's serialized book. "We'll send it down-River and up, to the Malagasies, the Rastafarians, the Phrygians, and the Shang. English, Esperanto, and French. Hakim needs food for his hordes. He'll put it to his neighbors—subscribe and pay in rations, or we attack."

"The tyrant publisher!" Plum sighed. "Didn't you write essays for peace? Didn't you sponsor a pacifist conference before World War Two?"

"Yes. And if I can make this work, we'll *have* peace," Maria Montessori answered.

A few days afterward, a guard delivered another pouch of tobacco and a proof of Plum's soon-to-be published pages. Perhaps because Fatima the copy editor knew little English, she did nothing to "correct" Wodehouse's immortal prose. All the errors had to do with commas, capitals, and italics. Plum fixed them, and swung his attention to chapter eight. Good old "Snookers" hid on the balcony, with no escape but to slide down the water pipe. . . .

Things went from bad to worse for Snookers, utter humiliation approaching in chapter twelve. New historical consultants popped in and became Wodehouse's neighbors. The *Sijill* rolled off its wooden press. Hakim's dhows and godowns paddled east and west, hawking a sugarcoated religion the Occult Master claimed not to believe.

Silence. Where were the raves to the editor? The press interviews? The literary luncheons? According to rumor, a hill-size node of metal had been dug up on the far side of the planet. Antipodeans used it to make steamships and radios. This business of ferrying the magazine beyond Hakim's borders facilitated gossip of all sorts: Druze immigrants confirmed talk about a metal steamer "approaching this way!"

None of this got into issue two. Maria's "institute" won six column-inches of glory, laud, and honor, touching only lightly on the facts: extract of dreamgum had made mental children of a few experimental subjects, who gibbered and ran mad in the ideal classroom she'd set up.

The good news was that this most potent of drugs had a permanent effect on their "winter" personalities. The bad news? It made them animals. "I have to find their souls," Maria told Plum on her next nocturnal visit. "I still have hope. Once they regain speech, we may discover what we did wrong. How we traumatized them. They might tell us."

"What does Hakim say?" Plum asked.

Maria sighed. "I have to repair my damage, or—it could be bad. I've lost influence. He's a politician. This business of summer people and winter people—he adopted the idea as his own for a while, but . . ."

"He took a flier, eh? And now he means to cut his losses."

She shook her head. "Not quite yet." Her eyes filled with tears. "Wouldn't I deserve it if he *did* punish me? But the makers of this world provided us with no experimental animals. What else could we do?"

"Shh. I hear voices. People are shouting out there."

"God!" Maria felt around the side of the bed for her clothes.

"Quick. Get under. I'll go see what's on."

A metal steamship is fast. At an unflagging twenty miles an hour, the *Potemkin* outpaced anything she had ever encountered. She was almost faster than rumor. No one in Hakim's domain had considered the possibility of such speed until the lights of her portholes gleamed on the River. Summoned from some women's-garden bed, Hakim called out the militia. An armed and vigilant citizenry crowded the shores. The *Potemkin* slid by, and dwindled, her name blazoned in characters few Druze could read. The valley narrowed to the left, and the mighty monster puffed on to the next regime in sequence.

Clouds bulked up for the predawn rain, and still the buzzing populace didn't go back to bed. In the men's garden, historical consultants and Druze guards chattered in excited clumps. Plum went in and told Maria the bad news. How could she sneak out of here?

For the purpose of these furtive rendezvous, someone had supplied her with the robes of a Druze elder. "Do I look male?" she asked nervously, wrapped to the nines. "I shall walk stiffly to the exit, as if I had a poker up my ass."

Plum winced. As a man she seemed woefully unconvincing. "Wait a minute. I'll create a diversion." He ran outside. "Jim! Jim! Let's fight."

"What?" Weary of the night's drama, the Apache had returned to his blanketed repose under the tree. He hoisted himself on one elbow.

Plum dropped to his knees and shouldered into him. "You bloody redskin. I'll take your scalp!"

"Hey!"

"Whoop it up. That's good!" Jim tumbled Wodehouse to the right. He stood. Plum stood too, bellowed, and charged again.

Jim kicked. Plum grabbed his foot and danced around. A gaggle of Druze guards converged on them. "Stop that! What are you doing?"

Plum dropped Jim's pedal appendage and squatted like a frog. *"Whan that Aprille with his shoures sote,"* he roared with a mad glint in his eye, and hopped in frog fashion. *"The droghte of Marche hath perced to the rote—"*

"You want to get killed?" Jim shouted. "Are you crazy?"

By now, Maria had made her exit. Plum rose and dusted himself. "Excuse me. I got excited. I'll be better now."

The guards muttered. "Go back in your hut!" Meekly, Plum accommodated them.

The next day Hakim was too busy to pass judgment on Plum's madness. A Druze spear-wallah came for the proofs for issue three, collecting them far ahead of the deadline. The next *Sijill* had to be hurried out, with Hakim's sermonette on the *Potemkin*'s night passage and what it meant. The neighboring kingdoms might get uppity, after all. They'd be less afraid of the Druze, after seeing how their technology was outclassed. They had to be preached back into a cooperative frame of mind.

Again the hawkers went out in their dhows, and came back with news: The *Potemkin* had interrupted its long voyage to the end of the river. The Rastafarians were entertaining the ship's sailors along their downstream shores.

The good news was that the magazine was a hot item among both Russians and Jamaicans, so much that the dhows returned laden with food. The slowest breezed into home port just ahead of the lights: Hours before the *Potemkin* had slipped anchor and reversed course.

From the steamship's bridge, an officer shouted in Esperanto, then English. "Bring us P.G. Wodehouse!" Such was Plum's isolation that his first inkling of this was when the garden guard was redoubled. The place bristled with spearmen.

"I could go to them," Plum announced to the Druze generality, who glinted at him in resentment, ice forming on their upper slopes. "I'd hate for there to be any fighting. Not for my sake. Jim, what's going on?"

Jim hustled to Plum's side, back from some palace excursion. "Hakim's digging in. He's being stubborn."

Clearly the Apache had more to say. "Yes?" Plum prompted him.

"You're a hostage. Hakim'll kill you if they attack. That's what he's told them."

"Cor!"

There was a fuss by the garden entry. "Let me through!" Maria announced in her queenliest tones. "I come from Hakim."

Plum converged on her. "What—?"

"Those Jamaicans!" she spluttered. "They put the

Russians up to it. You're just a cause célèbre. Something to make the war popular. You've got fans in the Russian crew who think *you're* what this is all about, and so they'll do anything. I know the truth, and Hakim does too. This ultimatum is all to humble the Druze, but what can he do? Spears against guns!"

"I'm supposed to feel sorry for the blighter?" Plum asked incredulously. "He's threatened—"

"I know. He's lost his soul to power. Nothing's too low for him anymore. I'm just the same. Nothing's too low for me, either." Maria Montessori undid a knot, and flung off her robes. Naked, she stepped to close the final distance. "Kiss me. We'll die together."

"Of all the bally—!"

It was the last straw for the outraged Druze guards. On the far side of the chiclet stones, a great gun boomed. On this side, arms dragged Plum and Maria to the tree trunk. "Kill the mockers! This is all their doing!"

"We'll try again together!" Maria shouted. "Another funny book!"

The gun boomed again. Masonry walls toppled in on Hakim's throne room. In the Occult Master's garden, spears flew simultaneously.

"—And so, here we are," Plum told President Firebrass of the Republic of Parolando. "I'd never heard about this 'simultaneous resurrection' business before. Have you?"

Firebrass shook his great head.

"Hakim's wishful thinking. But there's always a first time," Plum conceded.

Maria poured herself another cup of wine and curled into her seat by the fireplace. "These stores—mysterious strangers. Agents. The gods behind the curtains, who

move among us like spies. Parolando is full of rumors."
She looked at Plum. "What do you think about your
friend Jim?"

"Jim?"

"Who else could have arranged this unique 'cheap
trip' for us? Hakim himself?"

"Hakim! What can I do with that man?" President
Firebrass asked. "He sounds like a complete scoundrel."

Plum's eyes widened. "Yes! Maybe it was Jim after
all! I remember telling him: Tyrant, vamp, and fool.
Publisher, editor, and writer. Why else send the three of
us to be reborn in Riverworld's greatest literary mecca?"

Maria set down her glass. "You can do better than
Hakim for a publisher."

"I think so too." Plum beamed. "I can make my plots
work just fine without any villains at all. Why shouldn't
real life be the same?"

"I'll drink to that!" Maria, Plum, and President Firebrass
raised glasses in a final toast.

Two Thieves

Harry Turtledove

Alexios Komnenos folded his arms across his chest.
"You have heard my demands," he said in Arabic, the
only language he had in common with New Constantinople's
neighbors just down the River. "Obey them or face the
consequences."

"You are an infidel. We shall never yield to you."
Idris Alooma was the Sultan of Bornu's representative in
the town of New Constantinople. Tall and lean and
black, he towered over Alexios. To show his contempt,
he spat at the Basileus's feet.

Alexios's soldiers growled and brandished their flint-
tipped spears. He held up a hand. "Let the pagan go in
peace for now. Soon enough he will wake up naked and
bald somewhere along the River far from here." He used
the Greek his people spoke among themselves, then
translated for Idris Alooma's benefit.

The big black man laughed scornfully. "You may have
been plucked from hell to live beside us on the River
here, Christian dog, but you are the one whom Allah will
uproot when our armies meet." He turned on his heel and

marched back toward the stretch of the riverbank that owed allegiance to Bornu's Sultan, Musa ar-Rahman.

Alexios watched him go, wondering all the while if he should have let his men enjoy their sport. He tossed his head in a Greek no; he'd done the right thing. If Idris Alooma failed to return to Bornu town, Musa would take his revenge by torturing Michael Palaiologos to death and rebirth. Alexios Komnenos had nothing against killing, but killing to no purpose was stupid and wasteful.

He turned to his brother Isaac, who stood as usual at his right hand. The two men were near twins, especially since being restored to life along the River at the same youthful age. Both were a little below average size, but strongly muscled. Both had a narrow, foxy face beneath a broad forehead; both were swarthy and dark, Isaac a little less so than Alexios. But the best way to tell them apart was to note that Isaac's features were a trifle more open and friendly than Alexios's. Alexios had ruled during his remembered life; Isaac merely aided.

"It will be war," Alexios said now.

"So it would seem," Isaac agreed. "It will not be an easy war, either."

"No." Alexios's scowl was black as the beard he could no longer raise. He still sometimes felt like a eunuch without it. "Why were we resurrected alongside these filthy Muslims?" Were he less pious, he would have wondered about God's mercy. The folk upstream from New Constantinople were peaceful red-skinned pagans who wanted only to be left alone. Given Bornu on his other flank, he'd been happy to oblige them.

Isaac said, "They are infidels, but they are brave. If we meet them head-on, we will lose a great many of our best men, men we cannot afford to be without. That means that if anyone along this stretch of the River succeeds in uniting several little realms behind him, we will be vulnerable.''

''This I know.'' Alexios scowled again. *He* aimed to lead this stretch of the River. Along with a majority of Rhomaioi, he currently ruled a minority of peasants from the Egypt of Ptolemy III. As soon as they'd accepted Christianity, they made subjects as good as his own folk—maybe better, for their loyalties were less conditional. Some of them had spoken Greek even before their resurrection; they all did now.

''The war will not wait much longer,'' Isaac warned. ''If we do not begin it on our terms, Musa ar-Rahman will start it on his, for he loves us no better than we him.''

''This I also know.'' Alexios's nostrils flared as he took a long, deep breath. He let it out in a sigh. He didn't want to say what he had to say next: ''We shall begin it, brother of mine. But before we do, I aim to go to Shytown.''

Isaac's bushy eyebrows flew toward his hairline. ''You would deal with those—those aftermen?'' *Opisthanthropoi* was a word in no Greek lexicon; the folk of New Constantinople had coined it to describe people on the River who came from a time many centuries later than their own.

''God and the saints know I have no love for them,'' Alexios said. Aftermen were generally weak in faith, which made them unreliable, and strong in arcane gadgetry, which made them dangerous. Alexios sighed once more. ''But they are on Bornu's other flank. If they work with us, the pagans will fall like ripe wheat at harvesttime.''

''Let us make sure that we reap the full benefit thereof, though, not the men of Shytown,'' Isaac warned.

At last Alexios found something to amuse him. "Brother of mine, I was Basileus of the Romans for thirty-seven years. In all that time, did anyone ever out-trick me?"

Isaac did not answer. Alexios knew he had no answer. He'd stood off rebels from among his own people, Turks and Patzinaks and Normans; he'd even funneled through his Empire the western barbarians who called themselves Crusaders, and taken for the Rhomaioi most of the territory they'd won from the Seljuks in Anatolia. Maybe someone along the endless River was more cunning than he, but he had his doubts.

As if picking that boastful thought from his mind, Isaac said, "Do be cautious nonetheless. Shytown's Basileus is not a fool."

"Another truth. He does not style himself Emperor, though. While he is no Frank, he uses one of their titles—he calls himself *Mayor*."

"I wonder why?" Isaac mused.

"Who knows why the aftermen do as they do?" Alexios answered. "Their customs are even stranger than the Franks', and you know what it means for me to say that." No Franks lay anywhere close along the River, for which Alexios thanked God. Unwashed, ignorant, stinking, brutal savages—who happened to be inhumanly good at slaughtering anyone who got in their way. The Emperor rubbed his naked chin. "Where was I? Oh, yes, the customs of Shytown's aftermen. Do you know they didn't pick their Mayor by his courage or birth or anything sensible? No, they had all the people who wanted the job make speeches, and then chose by a show of hands from men and women both. 'Democracy,' they call it. It's idiocy, if you ask me."

"*Demokratia*." Isaac spat in the dirt. In the Greek the

two Komnenoi spoke, the word meant "mob rule." As Alexios said, it seemed a daft way to run a state, but Shytown flourished. Isaac added, "Do you really have to go there yourself?"

"Whom do you propose I send?" Alexios retorted. "The only other two men I might trust for the job are you and Michael Palaiologos. If I pull Michael out of Bornu town, Musa will surely divine what I aim to do. And you, brother of mine, make a better soldier than an ambassador. Meaning no disrespect, but in a dicker the Mayor would eat you up and pick his teeth with your bones."

Since that was true, Isaac could only give his brother a reproachful stare. He said, "How do you even propose to get to Shytown? You let Idris Alooma go, so the Muslim blacks will know trouble lies ahead for them. And Musa ar-Rahman is no fool either. He will be looking for you to try to stab him in the back like that. Were I he, I'd have rafts in the water day and night. Do you want to be fished out and tortured, then given time to heal and tortured again for years on end?"

"Do I want that? Of course not. But I have to get to Shytown, and I don't think I could pass myself off as a proper subject of Musa's to sneak across his domain." Alexios laughed. So did Isaac, but he sounded more dutiful than amused. Black men of Musa ar-Rahman's tribe made up about two thirds of the people of Bornu. Most of the rest were short, golden-skinned, flat-featured, and narrow-eyed. Alexios's chance of successfully impersonating a member of either group was effectively none.

"All right. It will have to be the River, then, but I don't like it," Isaac said.

Alexios laughed. "Here you are, Kaisar to my Basileus; if I fail, you become Emperor. And yet you caution me. What kind of brother are you?" He knew the answer to that: a loyal one. A loyal brother, especially among the treacherous Rhomaioi, was more precious than rubies. Alexios knew that, too. He clapped Isaac on the back with real affection. "Besides, I have an idea—"

The storm blew over not long before dawn. The River rode high and choppy in its banks. Debris drifted downstream—tree trunks, bamboo stalks, part of what had been a hut or a raft.

Isaac Komnenos chuckled. "If the Muslims were out watching for you last night, brother of mine, some of them will have drowned—so many the fewer to face when the time comes."

"True enough," Alexios answered. "I—" The morning roar of the grailstones interrupted him. Lambent blue fire shot into the air, to three times the height of a man. When it faded, the people of New Constantinople crowded forward to see what their grails contained today. Alexios took his with as much curiosity as anyone else.

He opened the hinged lid, smiled as savory steam tickled his nose. Black bread, honey, porridge with big bits of tuna and squid, a soft jar of wine, and a packet of the smokesticks his folk mostly traded to those who enjoyed sucking on them. And— "A firestarter!" he said happily. His grail had produced only a handful of them since his resurrection.

"A good omen," Isaac agreed.

"More than that," Alexios said. "A good weapon, too. I'll carry it along with my knife tonight. If a Bornu spots me, I'll burn out his tongue before he can shout the warning." That was bravado, and he knew it. Still, the new tool gave him one more string to his bow; without its appearance, he might not have thought to take one.

He spent the rest of the day going over his plans till he was sick of it and Isaac sicker. Most of what they talked about had to do with things that were unlikely to happen. Alexios had seen enough unlikely things in his life back on Earth to be sure some, at least, would come true: generally the ones that hadn't been planned for. He was a man who left as little as possible to chance.

The sun set in splendor over the mountains to the west. As dusk darkened toward true night, Alexios walked down to the River. A crew bossed by his brother waited for him there. When they started to prostrate themselves, he waved to show the gesture was unnecessary. "We have work to do here tonight, my friends."

He stripped off the reddish-purple kilt whose color was reserved for him alone in New Constantinople (any pieces of that hue that appeared on the grailstone were either saved for his use or traded away outside his little empire). To replace it, he covered himself with several dark-blue lengths of cloth, until only his head, hands, and feet remained bare.

Grunting and cursing, the work crew manhandled a yew into the River. They kept one last grassfiber line attached to it so it would not drift away downstream. Isaac Komnenos slapped Alexios on the back. "God go with you and bring you home again safe."

"You just say that because you don't want the work of ruling," Alexios said.

Isaac laughed. "Too right I don't, brother of mine. Do you have your reed?"

"Here." Alexios held up the yard-long piece of plant.

It wasn't actually a reed, as it would have been back on earth; it was a thin length of bamboo, with all the pith hollowed out. But it would serve.

Alexios slipped into the water. It was cool but not cold. The Basileus took hold of a root that trailed from the yew. At Isaac's shouted direction, one of the men cut the last rope with a sharp piece of flint. The yew began to drift down the River.

The land slid slowly past. Settlements in New Constantinople centered on the grailstones. Once the one from which he'd left dropped away behind him, darkness prevailed for most of the next mile. Alexios glanced over to the far side of the River. Lights there were even fewer; a broad stretch of that bank was inhabited by hunters and gatherers even more primitive than the nomadic Patzinaks. They weren't even fierce enough to make decent allies against Bornu; had they been so, Alexios would have tried to recruit them.

Something nibbled his leg. He jerked and thrashed in the water. A croaker let out the mournful call that gave the fish its name, then splashed away. The things were cowards and scavengers and not worth eating if anything better was available. Alexios was glad to be rid of this one.

It could have been worse. It could have been a dragonfish. Dragonfish did not usually attack boats or people in the River. When they did, the people attacked usually reappeared on a new stretch of River.

Another grailstone, another town of Rhomaioi. This one was called Thessaloniki, after the second city in Alexios's empire. The people had lit a bonfire; Alexios saw men and women dancing around it. Faintly, the music of turtlefish lyres and upraised voices reached his ears. He smiled. He would sooner have been dancing around that fire himself than where he was.

In the middle of the next stretch of quiet dark, another croaker swam snuffling up to Alexios, hoping, no doubt, that he was a piece of offal. He hit the fish with his fist. It nipped him on the leg before it fled. He hoped he wasn't bleeding. Blood in the water would draw a dragonfish to him if anything would.

The last town of Rhomaioi before the frontier with Bornu was Nikaia. More fires blazed at the frontier; a detachment of Rhomaioi kept watch against the infidels. Less than a hundred yards farther on, the black men had their own frontier garrison, of similar size to the one Alexios had posted.

The Bornu capered round their watchfires to the beat of bamboo-stalk drums with redfish leather skins. They brandished flint-tipped spears and shouted threats across the border to the Rhomaioi, most of whom, perhaps fortunately, could not understand them.

Alexios looked ahead. Before long, he spied torches on the River. The Bornu, he had learned since resurrection, came from a desert part of Africa; they did not take naturally to the water. But they were not stupid, either— they knew that if New Constantinople wanted to cut a deal with Shytown, the River was the logical avenue for emissaries.

The Basileus slid all the way under the water. He tried to get as far under the trunk of the yew as he could. Only the tip of his hollowed-out bamboo stuck up above the surface. The other end was in his mouth. He took deep, slow, steady breaths. A military manual from hundreds of years before his own time which he'd once read told how the Sklavenoi used this very trick to avoid detection by the Rhomaioi. Now, he thought, a Basileus of the Rhomaioi was turning it against barbarians.

He kept his eyes open, though the night-dark water all around him might as well have been ink. Then, through the crazily shifting mirror of the surface, he saw a flickering torchflame. He knew the black men were peering down into the River. If they saw his pale skin despite the gloomy kilts he'd draped round himself, if by some disaster they recognized his breathing tube for what it was . . . if either of those things happened, Isaac would become Basileus. Alexios just hoped the Bornu would eventually kill him, instead of torturing him almost to death, letting him heal, and starting over again.

The torchlight receded as the uprooted yew tree drifted on. Alexios sighed relief through hollow bamboo. He stayed submerged for some time, lest the noise of his emerging betray him to his foes.

But before long, he had to put up his head. He needed to watch the land by the River flow past, so he'd know when he'd gone by Bornu and entered the territory of Shytown. He also needed to keep an eye out for more rafts in the River. He would not have contented himself with a single line of pickets had he been Musa ar-Rahman, and he dared not assume the Sultan was less cautious than he.

Sure enough, he had to go under and breathe through his tube twice more. But the men of Bornu apparently found nothing suspicious about a tree floating downstream after a storm. Though once their torches seemed right overhead, they never probed the water with their spears.

After the third set of rafts, the Muslims had no further River defenses. Alexios drifted along past one of their settlements after another. He grew bored, and also chilly from having been in the water so long, but willingly endured both for the sake of the reward he might gain from this journey.

Bornu, by the look of things, fortified its border with Shytown more intensively than the one with New Constantinople. A palisade of bamboo and timber ran from the River toward the unclimbable mountains that sealed off the back of each domain.

Not long after he passed the palisade, Alexios kicked himself away from the yew and stroked toward the shore. He held on to his bamboo breathing tube: who could say when it might come in handy again?

He splashed up onto the riverbank. Shytown's sentries were alert; he'd hardly come out of the water before someone hailed him: "Who are you and what the devil are you doing here?"

He followed that, though he understood only a little of Shytown's language. The people of the Mayor's domain called it English, but it hardly resembled the English he'd learned from the Angles and Saxons of the Varangian Guard, men who'd abandoned England after William the Norman overthrew their kind. Having dealt with Robert Guiscard and his son Bohemund, Alexios did not love Normans, either.

He answered in the aftermen's dialect of English, as best he could: "I am Alexios Komnenos, Basileus of New Konstantinopolis. I will to see your Mayor."

"Say what?" It was a sudden, sharp exclamation, meaningless to Alexios. The sentry came up and looked him over. "Goddamn! Maybe you are him." He raised his voice: "Hey, Fred, Louie, come here! One of you take my slot, okay? This guy says he's Alexios from upstream, and he wants to see Mayor Daley. I'm gonna bring him to Hizzonor.''

Fred or Louie came up. Whoever he was, he had a torch. "Yeah, that's Alexios, all right—I seen him once. Okay, Pete, you found him; I guess you get to take him. Beats stayin' here, that's for damn sure.''

Alexios caught only part of that, but he gathered Pete would conduct him to the mayor. He fell into step with the Shytown sentry. All the way to Mayor Daley's residence, Pete bombarded him with questions. Why did he want to see the Mayor? Did it have to do with Bornu? If it didn't, what was it about? From one of his own subjects, Alexios would have found such prodding intolerable. But the folk of Shytown had a reputation for being both free of speech with their betters and insatiably inquisitive. Alexios found it politic to make his English poorer than it really was.

The Mayor dwelled in a fair-sized palace. Alexios thought the profusion of windows on the outside extravagant; houses in New Constantinople kept to the courtyard pattern of the lost imperial city. But enough guards ringed the place that theft was unlikely to be a problem.

Pete spoke to a guard by the door, too fast for Alexios to follow. Then he turned back and said, "Do you mind waiting till sunup? They don't want to wake Hizzonor yet.''

Alexios considered, decided to have a tantrum. He cursed in Greek before trying English again at the top of his lungs: "I am the Basileus, God dump you to hell! You keep me to wait like man with fish to sell?'' If the Mayor hadn't been awake, he ought to be now, *theou thelontos*.

After listening to some more ranting, the guard went

inside. Mayor Daley came out a few minutes later, accompanied by a thin man with red hair who wore a bone cross on a leather thong round his neck. Daley rumbled in his brand of English. The thin man spoke Latin, which Alexios also understood: "I am Father Boyle, Hizzonor's interpreter. He asks why whatever business this is couldn't wait until the morning."

"Because I am as much a ruler as he is, and I am here now," Alexios answered. "Tell him that." Because he is an upstart and I am Basileus of the Rhomaioi—he thought, though he kept that to himself.

Daley spoke again: "All right; let's get on with it."

Alexios waved aside the priest's translation; he'd understood that himself. He studied Hizzonor. Like everyone else along the River, Mayor Richard J. Daley was physically perfect and in the prime of youth. That failed to make him handsome; he looked like a bruiser. But his eyes— Maybe it was a trick of the torchlight, but Alexios didn't think so. Those cold gray eyes held more than a youth's experience. Alexios would have bet Hizzonor had lived a long life and done a lot of underhanded things in it. Isaac claimed his own eyes had that look, so no wonder he recognized it.

Aloud, he said, "We aim to fight Bornu soon; we want you to come in on our side. Between us, we can crush the black infidels, take control of their grails, and add to the wealth of both Shytown and New Constantinople. Is that interesting enough to get you out of bed early, Mayor?"

Daley didn't speak Latin; he had to wait for Father Boyle to translate. Even after the priest was done, the Mayor did not change expression. Yes, he's good, Alexios thought with reluctant admiration. Daley answered,

"Maybe. Depends on when you do it and what's in it for us. I don't have men to throw away on the Suicide Express."

Via Suicida made strange Latin, but Alexios understood: Daley didn't want men loyal to him killed and resurrected far, far up or down the River. Alexios didn't want that for his own retainers, either. He said, "That's why I propose alliance. Between us, we trap and outnumber the men of Bornu. Our casualties should be small."

"Yes, that might work," Daley said. "I also wouldn't mind seeing those shiftless blacks next door working for a living instead of sponging off their grails and lying around like they were in welfare heaven. So, yeah, I'm interested. Tell me more."

Even after Hizzonor's priest translated that, Alexios didn't get all of it; "welfare heaven" left him especially puzzled. Mayor Daley also seemed to despise the people of Bornu merely for being black. That confused Alexios. They couldn't help being black. But they had chosen false Islam of their own free will, and would (he continued to believe, despite resurrection along the River) one day suffer the pangs of hell for their error.

Reasons, however, didn't matter. He said, "Are we allies, then? Shall we fix the day for setting the fate of the black infidels?" If Hizzonor didn't like the Bornu because of their color, Alexios would remind him of it.

"It isn't quite so simple," Mayor Daley said. "The one thing the blacks are good for is keeping you and me from bumping up against each other. When we're neighbors, we're going to have to watch each other all the time. Musa's a nuisance to me now, what with his bucks coming in and stealing a white woman every so often, but he's only a nuisance, if you know what I mean. Having you next door might be downright dangerous.''

Alexios eyed Hizzonor with surprised respect. If he understood the idea of buffer states, he was indeed no one's fool. After some thought, Alexios said, "Let us agree in advance, then, on which of us will control each grailstone in Bornu. Quarrels settled ahead of time do not turn vexing later.''

But Mayor Daley shook his head. "That isn't good enough. I heard you were smart, and I see it's so. So sooner or later, Shytown and New Constantinople will likely fight. We're both going to want to take over as much as we can—we're like that. Am I right or wrong?''

"I think you're right," Alexios admitted. He'd seen the same, but had intended to keep quiet about it. Hizzonor's style was different, almost brutally direct. The Basileus asked, "What do you propose to do about the problem?''

"Here's what," Daley said. "A big war would wreck your country and mine both, and leave whichever of us won in bad shape against anybody strong who might come up or down the River at him. So let's keep it clean: We'll go together against the Bornu, sure. But at the same time, I'll name you Vice Mayor of Shytown and you'll name me—what do you call your number-two guy?''

"Kaisar," Alexios answered.

"Okay. That's what you'll name me, then. You see what I'm driving at?''

"I see," Alexios said slowly. If he took Mayor Daley's terms, whichever of them assassinated the other would rule New Constantinople and Shytown both. Life henceforward would be nervous for the two headmen, but their retainers would live. Alexios went on, "But, you see, I already have a Kaisar. He—"

"I got a Vice Mayor, too," Daley interrupted. "It's no big deal. This is important. It needs doing, if Shytown and New Constantinople are going to end up next door to each other. Am I right, or not?"

Alexios had been about to say that his Kaisar was his own brother, the only man he'd ever known upon whom he could rely absolutely. The last thing he wanted was to replace Isaac with someone mainly interested in killing him off. But Daley had made it clear that Shytown wouldn't help against Bornu unless he had his way. And if New Constantinople took on Bornu alone, then even if he won he'd be vulnerable to an attack from downstream.

Better the risk to his person than the one to his empire, he decided. "Let it be as you say," he told the Mayor. "Once Bornu is taken, you will name me Vice Mayor and I will appoint you Kaisar." And we shall see what happens after that, too, he added to himself.

Daley stuck out his hand. Alexios took it. The Mayor's clasp was brief, firm, and as mechanical as the gears and levers that raised the imperial throne in Constantinople high in the air to overawe barbarous envoys. Daley, worse luck, did not act like a barbarian—he did not show on his face what he was thinking. Alexios reminded himself that the aftermen had had hundreds of years past his own time in which to learn deceit. He hoped his own lifetime of practicing such arts would suffice.

Once the Mayor had what he wanted, he turned businesslike in a hurry. "Let's plan this thing out," he said. "If we're going to do it, we ought to do it right. I think we can, but we need to work things out beforehand. . . ."

The sun came up while Daley and Alexios were still

plotting. Only the roar from the grailstones made the Basileus notice he no longer needed torches to see. One of Daley's henchmen fetched him breakfast: fried eggs and bacon, toasted bread with fruit jam sweeter than honey, and the hot bitter brew called coffee. He didn't care for that, but drank for politeness' sake. After he finished it, he felt more awake and alert than the long night should have permitted.

Mayor Daley's title was anything but martial, but he had a sound grasp of strategy. If everything went as he and Alexios designed (which seldom happened in war), Bornu would be ground between them like grain between upper and lower millstones. And Daley's scheme for returning Alexios to New Constantinople was simplicity itself: "We'll send you as a sailor in one of our boats, and we'll tell the black boys they'll get instant war with us if they try searching anything of ours that floats. Think that'll work?"

"It should, by the Virgin," Alexios said. To his surprise, he found himself liking Hizzonor. Could the afterman have been trusted for a single instant out of Alexios's sight, he would have made a good Kaisar. As it was, he would make a bad enemy if he didn't get his way. Alexios smiled. Of course he intended to keep his promise to Daley. . . .

The army of Rhomaioi swept over the border a little before dawn. A few sentries shot arrows at the soldiers. More fled screeching into the interior of Bornu.

"Had it been my choice instead of Musa's, I would have had the Shytown boat searched and taken me off it were I found," Alexios said to Isaac. "But Mayor Daley was right there: the men of Bornu dared not antagonize

him and me at the same time, and so I came home
safely.''

"I'm glad of it, too," Isaac Komnenos answered.
"From all you've said since you got back, the *opisthan-
thropos* would be too much for a plain old honest soldier
like me." He laughed to show he didn't mean to be taken
altogether seriously.

Alexios laughed too. "One thing at a time, brother of
mine. The first thing we have to do is settle Musa
ar-Rahman. Only after Bornu ceases to be a problem will
Shytown become one . . . unless, of course, Hizzonor means
to sit this fight out, let us and the Muslims weaken
ourselves, and then pick up the remains." That he had
entertained that possibility earlier was a measure of
Daley's skill at lulling him. Something new to worry
about . . .

With every pace the Rhomaioi marched, they could see
farther. The sun rose as they drew near the grailstone
closest to the border. Bornu warriors boiled out of the
town that had grown up around the grailstone. Like
Alexios's men, they carried spears and bows, stone axes
and sword-clubs with wooden bodies and flint or obsidian
blades. Also like the Rhomaioi, they wore several layers
of kiltcloth as armor.

There the resemblance ended. Alexios's soldiers marched
in an orderly hollow diamond; the men of the outer ranks
carried shields of wood and fish-leather to protect themselves and their comrades from missile weapons. The
Bornu scorned both order and shields. Screaming "*Allahu
akbar!*"—"God is great"—they hurled themselves at
their Christian foes.

Isaac Komnenos waited till the black men were very
close before he shouted, "Loose!" Hundreds of arrows

flew as one. The archers reached over their shoulders for more shafts, shot again and again. Their bows, made from dragonfish mouthparts, were better than any they'd had in their previous lives.

Even so, not many Bornu fell. Draped as they were in kiltcloth, they were armored against most archery. But some were hit in the face, others wounded in arms or calves and thus out of the fight. The Rhomaioi suffered almost no casualties.

The black men's woes grew worse when the fighting came to close quarters. They were as brave as their foes, maybe braver—the Rhomaioi seldom showed more courage than an occasion demanded. But the Bornu fought as individuals; they had no notion of battle as anything but a series of single combats.

They paid dearly for their education. To Alexios and Isaac, the success of the army as a whole came first, with individual glory a long way behind. Alexios fought at the fore, true, but more to inspire his own men than out of love for combat. He cared more for the power that came through war than for war itself.

The Bornu flung themselves at him, one after another. He could read their thought: if he fell, the army's aggressive spirit would perish with him. He knew they were wrong; Isaac was no diplomat, but made a perfectly capable soldier. Alexios took the series of attacks to mean Bornu resistance would fall apart if he killed Musa ar-Rahman.

The Basileus carried a stout stone-headed club. It was a pragmatist's weapon, one that would break bones even through kiltcloth. A tall, screaming black man thrust a spear at his face. He ducked, stepped close, swung that club. A man's ribs were a bigger, less elusive target than his head. The black man moaned. Pink foam spurted from his nose and mouth as he crumpled. The advancing Rhomaioi trampled him into the dirt.

Quite suddenly, the Bornu quit fighting and turned to flight. Alexios was tempted to open his tight formation and pursue, but decided against it: let the defeated Muslims spread panic ahead of New Constantinople's army. Nor could he be sure the Bornu weren't trying to lead him into an ambuscade.

As the Rhomaioi approached, shrieking women fled from the village around the grailstone. That convinced Alexios he really had won a victory worth having. When a few of his warriors seemed about to break ranks and run after the women, he called, "We'll have as many of these wenches as we like once the Bornu are beaten. Till then, we risk ourselves if we chase them without discipline."

His lines held steady. Unlike the black men, the Rhomaioi knew what discipline was worth; they could put off immediate pleasure for the sake of a greater gain later. They made him proud.

Ahead in the far distance, smoke rose against the sky. "Is that what we hope for?" Isaac asked.

"It should be," Alexios answered. "Mayor Daley promised the men of Shytown would burn the palisade the Bornu built to keep them out. The aftermen seem clever with incendiaries, and to be acquainted with more of them than our liquid fire." Yet another thing to worry about, he thought. But not until later. Worry about Musa ar-Rahman came first.

Alexios detached a company of troops to fill grails on the grailstone of the captured town. Some of those grails belong to his own soldiers; others were seized from captured blacks. The Basileus pushed on with the main body of his force. The supply company had carts to carry the loaded grails (minus liquor, smoking hemp, and dreamgum) up to the rest of the army. The Bornu in the wake of the imperial forces would go hungry, but that was their hard luck.

"Do you think they'll try to attack us again, this side of their capital?" Isaac asked.

"I wouldn't, if I'd got myself into a mess like this," Alexios said. "But who can read Musa's mind with certainty? He might split his forces against us and Shytown, or he might try to beat one foe first and then turn back and quickly smite the other. But if it were me, I'd await attack where the works of the town favor defense. It's not as if we can starve him out in a hurry, worse luck."

Isaac chuckled. "Grails do make this whole business of sieges more complicated than it used to be."

Here and there, Bornu archers sniped from ambush at the advancing Rhomaioi. They did little damage. Alexios's scouts captured and hamstrung a couple of them and confiscated their grails. If the skirmishers were trying to slow off the Basileus's army, they failed.

Musa did as Alexios had guessed. After the first repulse, no sizable Bornu force appeared to challenge the men from New Constantinople. The second Bornu grailtown along the riverbank was all but deserted when the Rhomaioi reached it. The townsfolk had fled downstream with their grails. The same was true of the third town, where Alexios stopped to fill grails for the noon meal.

The fourth grailtown downstream from the border with New Constantinople was the capital of Bornu. Its grailstone was no bigger than any of the rest, so its normal population was like those of the other little cities, but Musa ar-Rahman had lavished far more care on it than on them. Its tall wall was built of stout timber and bamboo, and draped with kiltcloth to ward against torches. The second story of the Sultan's palace overtopped even the wall. That would be Musa's citadel if he lost the rest of the town, Alexios thought.

The wall was packed tight with black men who bellowed defiance at the Rhomaioi. Isaac Komnenos scowled up at them. "This place would be no joy to besiege even if they weren't able to feed themselves with their grails."

"I won't argue, brother of mine. However—" Alexios nodded to the musicians who accompanied the army. Shrill squeals from the flute, deep notes from the drum ordered the warriors to shift position. Alexios missed military trumpets, but not enough copper had been found in New Constantinople to make even one.

The front ranks of the army opened out, allowing the engineering detachment that had traveled in the middle of the hollow diamond to advance. They pushed their carts (quite different from those of the foragers) up toward the wall. Shieldmen moved forward with them, protecting them from the storm of missiles the Bornu loosed.

A man at the rear of each cart worked a kiltcloth bellows. Kiltcloth also lined the interior of the long bamboo tubes other engineers aimed toward the top of the wall. When the men at the bellows cried a warning, the shieldmen, as they'd practiced, skipped nimbly out of the way.

A golden liquid burst from the ends of the bamboo tubes. The aimers ignited it with carefully hoarded firestarters. Half a dozen streams of flowing fire rose to drip from the wall and the Bornu atop it.

Alexios watched in cold satisfaction as shrieking infidels dashed every which way in their agony, spreading the flames as they ran. The liquid fire dripped between lengths of kiltcloth. In moments, the wall itself began to burn.

Some of the black men had the courage and wit to stick to their posts. They poured buckets of water onto the burgeoning flames. The Basileus smiled at their cries of dismay, for the fire refused to go out. It was not the precise recipe the Rhomaioi had used in Constantinople; no one on this strange new world had yet found petroleum oozing up from between the rocks. But dragonfish oil made a good enough substitute. Mixed with naphtha, sulfur, and a few other ingredients so secret the engineer who knew them refused to name them even for Alexios, the oil made a hellbrew that burned until it consumed itself or until it was smothered with sand.

The Bornu, though, were ignorant of that trick and had no time to learn it. More and more of them scrambled or jumped off the wall as the flames spread. The Rhomaioi cheered the thick black smoke mounting to the sky.

Alexios gave new orders to the musicians. Their sharp notes pierced the din. The men of New Constantinople obediently formed themselves into a wedge-shaped formation. Here were soldiers you could do something with, Alexios thought—they were brave and obedient at the same time.

A section of the wall fell over with a rending crash. Sparks flew upward. The flutes screamed. Crying Alexios's name and "Christ with us," the Rhomaioi surged into the town.

Fighting raged fierce for a few minutes. Then the Bornu began to break and to stream toward the citadel. Alexios caught Isaac's eye. They both grinned. If the town wall, draped with kiltcloth, had burned, what a merry bonfire Musa ar-Rahman's palace would make. The Bornu capital was as good as theirs.

Some of the black men saw that, too. A detachment of perhaps fifty smashed headlong into Alexios's army, struggling desperately to force the men from New Constantinople outside the walls once more. At the head of the detachment was a hook-nosed man with full kiltcloth armor and gleaming copper rings in both ears and one nostril. Such a display of wealth could belong only to Musa.

The Sultan spied Alexios at the same instant Alexios recognized him. "To the death between us!" he shouted in Arabic. "Let the winner rule both folk!"

Alexios advanced on him. But when Musa ar-Rahman charged into what he thought was single combat, Isaac Komnenos and three other Rhomaioi also assailed him. Alexios crushed the Sultan's skull with his club, but was never sure afterward if that was the mortal blow.

The Bornu wailed in horror at the treachery. Alexios remained unfazed. Like the Frankish barbarians whose crusade he'd had to deflect, they were foolish enough to think war was about honor. War was about winning, nothing more.

Their ruler's death took the heart out of the black men. Soon screaming women impeded the army of New Constantinople more than the soldiery of Bornu. Men raised their hands and gave up their grails in token of surrender. "Keep as many alive as you can!" Alexios shouted. "If they die, we lose the food and other good things controlling them would give us."

Musa had been an exception to that rule. He was too cunning, too dangerous to keep around as a grail slave— better that he be reborn somewhere far from New

Constantinople and make trouble there. Mutilating him every few months was another alternative, but Alexios didn't care for it. He had his own notions of honor, and cruelty without cause was not part of them.

Before long, only the Sultan's palace still held out against the Rhomaioi. Alexios sent an Arabic-speaking herald forward with a message: "Yield your weapons and your grails and you will not be badly treated. Otherwise, we will use liquid fire against you. You may be born again afterward, but your deaths will be slow and hideous. Decide quickly, or we will use it anyhow."

He waited. Just as he was about to order the engineers forward, the palace doorway opened. Dejected black men began filing out. They threw their bows and spears and clubs in a pile to the right of the doorway. The pile became mountainously high. The weapons were as good as anything the Rhomaioi used. Alexios decided to store them against future need.

The foraging detail took charge of the black men's grails. The Muslims gave them up even more reluctantly than their arms. Without grails, they were at their conquerors' mercy. If they did not obey henceforward, they would not eat. Oh, a few might slip off and survive on River fish and fruits and tubers from the plants that grew from the riverbank back into the foothills. But a stretch of land that would support a thousand people with grails might only let a double handful live on it without them.

After the last of the weapons and grails were surrendered, Alexios's record-keepers began taking the names of the Bornu men, women, and adolescents alike. Bamboo pulp replaced the parchment and papyrus the scribes had used at their desks in Constantinople. The Franks, Alexios remembered, had been amazed at the minutiae his offi-

cials recorded. But how were you supposed to run a state
if you didn't keep track of the people it contained?

The sun began to set over the mountains to the west.
As the town's—now *his* town's—grailstone roared and
flamed, he let himself feel how tired he was. Then he had
to force himself back to abrupt alertness, for one of the
scouts who had gone downstream from the former Bornu
capital came pelting back, shouting, "An army's heading
our way!"

One of the black men must have learned some Greek
since being reborn along the River, for he made a dash
for the piled weapons. Rhomaioi sprang after him, speared
him down. He lay writhing in agony. "Finish him,"
Alexios said. One of his warriors smashed in the Bornu's
skull. Let some other king far away deal with a trouble-
maker, the Basileus thought.

Another scout panted into town. "It's the men of
Shytown," he said. The Rhomaioi cheered as if to make
their cries echo from the distant mountains. Alexios
instantly ordered the news translated into Arabic. The
Bornu sank even deeper into despair.

With a well-armed bodyguard around him, Alexios
went out to greet his allies. The Shytowners whooped
with glee when they recognized him in the failing light.
For the moment, all was concord in the two victorious
armies. But Mayor Daley also had protectors when he
stepped out to meet Alexios between his men and those
of the Basileus.

Daley spoke. Father Boyle turned his half-intelligible
words into Latin for Alexios: "It really did go just as we
planned. How often does that happen in war?"

"Not very," Alexios said, wondering how much the
afterman really knew of war. But that didn't matter, not

now. As Mayor Daley had said, they'd won. Alexios pushed through his bodyguards, held out his hand to the Mayor. Daley broke through the ranks of his own soldiers to clasp it. For one brief, proud moment, the alliance between them teetered on the edge of true friendship.

Then Daley said, "When do you think you can come to Shytown to be sworn in as Vice Mayor?"

A curious phrase, Alexios thought. But that was by the by. He focused again on what he would have to do, the gains and the probable costs. He said, "I think we would be wise first to consolidate and garrison what we have won today. Your men are already largely in place, since you are taking five of Bornu's Riverside grailstones to our four. But we still have to push away from the River to seize our extra inland stone to compensate. We may have a bit more fighting to do, though Musa concentrated his men along the River. I will join you—hmmm—in one week's time. Then you will visit New Constantinople to be anointed as our Kaisar."

Alexios held his voice steady only with effort. A foreigner as Kaisar of the Rhomaioi— It had happened once before, when Justinian II rewarded Tervel the Bulgar for backing in a civil war. Alexios still reckoned it disgraceful. But he'd needed Daley as Justinian had needed Tervel. He would pay the price . . . in his own fashion.

Father Boyle translated his words for the Mayor. Daley said something in the English of the *opisthanthropoi*. The priest dipped his head, then turned back to Alexios: "Hizzonor gives me leave to say a few words of my own to you. In our time and country, the land Constantinople ruled was more often called the Byzantine Empire than the Roman Empire. *Byzantine* became a word in our

English, too, meaning subtle, complex, and cunning diplomacy. Having worked with you now, Your Majesty, I can see how the word gained that definition.''

''You flatter me.'' Alexios's voice sounded uncommonly like a purr. The thing about flattery, though, was to enjoy it without letting it sway you. ''You may tell Hizzonor that he has no mean ability along these lines himself.''

Daley rumbled laughter. ''One horse thief knows another,'' he said. That made Alexios laugh too, and again friendship nearly flowered. But he saw that Daley's smile never quite reached the Mayor's unsettling eyes. The were two of a kind, all right, each trying to manipulate the other.

The Basileus nodded to Hizzonor once more, then backed into the company of his own bodyguard. Trouble would come very soon, he thought, if the men of Shytown didn't draw back from this grailtown. The agreed-upon boundary was halfway between it and the next one downstream.

Fatigue smote Alexios again, this time irresistibly. Tomorrow would be time enough to worry about borders.

Michael Palaiologos and other dignitaries from New Constantinople watched as Alexios Komnenos became Vice Mayor of Shytown: with Bornu gone, Palaiologos would serve as the Basileus's envoy to Mayor Daley. Only Isaac Komnenos stayed home for the ceremony, so treachery from Daley could not wipe out all the leaders of the Rhomaioi at once.

Alexios found himself envying his brother. The aftermen might be devious politicians and clever artisans, but they ran boring ceremonies. Hizzonor made a speech that went on and on. Alexios tried for a while to follow the English dialect the *opisthanthropoi* used, but gave up when he concluded Daley wasn't really saying anything.

The Basileus expected Father Boyle to administer the vice-mayoral oath to him. That gave him pause: some of his subjects considered followers of the Roman pope like Boyle schismatics. But in fact, a man dressed all in black kiltcloth swore him in; through Boyle, Daley introduced him as Judge Corcoran.

"Judge?" Alexios asked. "A secular title?"

"We separate church and state," Father Boyle answered. Alexios shrugged; that struck him as falling somewhere between incomprehensible and just plain crazy. But how the Shytowners ran their affairs wasn't his business.

"Raise your right hand," Judge Corcoran said. Alexios obeyed. The judge gave him the oath: "Do you solemnly swear to carry out the duties of Vice Mayor of Shytown honestly and to the best of your ability, so help you God?"

The duties of Vice Mayor were, in essence, none. The oath did not refer to any point that had set theologians from Constantinople at odds with those from Rome. In its way, it was admirably simple. Alexios said, "I swear."

Everyone cheered. Like the oath, Mayor Daley's way of celebrating was simple but effective. "Now let's get drunk," Hizzonor boomed. Servants carried in trays with flasks of wine and whiskey.

Since being reborn along the River, Alexios had developed a taste for whiskey. He liked the way it burned going down but warmed when it got to his middle. He sipped from a flask. "When you come to us," he told Daley, "I'll show you *our* way of doing things." Hizzonor nodded and reached for another whiskey himself.

* * *

When Mayor Daley descended from his boat to the riverbank, he advanced into New Constantinople through a double file of torchbearers. A chorus sang his praises. Pretty girls strewed flowers at his feet. He grinned enormously. "Fancy stuff," he said when he met Alexios in front of the imperial palace.

"Why not?" Alexios answered agreeably. "You've met my brother Isaac, I think—the current holder of the title Kaisar."

"No hard feelings, I hope," Daley said, perhaps sincerely—his own former Vice Mayor had been a nonentity, not his brother. But Isaac only smiled and shook his head. Hizzonor beamed. "Good, good."

"And here is the ecumenical patriarch of New Constantinople, Evstratios Garidas," Alexios said, pointing to a man in glittering gold kiltcloth. Most priests among the Rhomaioi took the loss of their beards here along the River very hard, but Garidas had always been smooth-chinned—in Constantinople, he'd been a eunuch. Between having his stones for the first time as an adult and the aphrodisiac effects of dreamgum, his chastity took a beating in the days after New Constantinople's folk were resurrected, but he remained a good and pious man.

Daley bowed politely. So did Father Boyle, which, given his probable attitude toward the church of Constantinople, might have required more discipline. The patriarch, his voice more than an octave deeper than Alexios remembered it from the imperial city, said, "Is the Mayor of Shytown prepared to take the oath as Kaisar of New Constantinople?" Alexios translated his Greek into Latin for Boyle, who turned it into the aftermens' English.

"I am," Hizzonor said, his voice solemn.

The oath Garidas had Mayor Daley swear was far more ornate and imposing than the one Judge Corcoran had given the Basileus. It invoked all three persons of the Trinity, the Virgin, and a squadron of saints (among them St. Andrew, patron of Constantinople), and called down upon the mayor anathema and damnation if he violated its terms by so much as an iota. "Will you, then, hold to these terms, in the name of the Father, the Son, and the Holy Spirit?" the patriarch finished.

Daley crossed himself. "By the Father, the Son, and the Holy Spirit, I will."

"Bend your head," Garidas said. When Hizzonor obeyed, the patriarch anointed him with fish oil made sweet-smelling with perfume from the grailstones.

Alexios set a circlet of woven grass dyed scarlet round Daley's head. "Hail to our Kaisar!" he cried. The people of New Constantinople cheered along with the delegation from Shytown. The chorus sent up a song of praise and thanksgiving.

"Now what?" the newly made Kaisar asked.

When do we celebrate, Alexios took him to mean. He said, "We have one thing left to do before the feast begins." Daley folded his arms across his beefy chest and composed himself to wait. The Basileus raised his voice: "By elevating Hizzonor to the rank of Kaisar, I have left my brother Isaac without a title to suit him. As he is both flesh of my flesh and always at my right hand, by your consent, people of New Constantinople, I propose for him the dignity of *Sebastokrator,* august ruler, said dignity to rank in honor *between* my rank of Basileus and that of the Kaisar."

"Let it be so!" the people shouted, as they'd been coached. *Sebastokrator,* a rank Alexios had invented back on Earth, was the title Isaac Komnenos had held most of his life there; in New Constantinople, the Basileus had resimplified the hierarchy. But the old title remained there in case it ever seemed useful, as it did today.

Alexios did not translate his proclamation of Isaac as Sebastokrator into Latin for Father Boyle; the longer Mayor Daley remained in blissful ignorance of what was going on around him, the happier the Basileus would have been. It transpired, however, that Father Boyle understood enough Greek to realize what was happening. That did not surprise Alexios; the Mayor was merely being prudent by having in his retinue someone who could follow the language of New Constantinople. Alexios had had a couple of English-speakers with him at Shytown.

He could gauge almost to the second when Hizzonor realized he'd been tricked. Daley must have had Celtic ancestors, for his skin was as fair as any Frankish Crusader's. All at once, he turned brick red. "What the hell!" he bellowed, a roar of outrage even Alexios had no trouble translating.

Evstratios Garidas had almost finished administering the oath to Isaac. He paused, looked a question to Alexios. "Continue, Your Holiness," the Basileus said calmly. Garidas continued. Only after he had finished anointing the newly named Sebastokrator, thus making Isaac's title indissoluble, did Alexios concern himself with his profanely displeased Kaisar.

Voice bland as butter, the Basileus turned to Mayor Daley. "Why are you unhappy? I named you Kaisar of New Constantinople as I promised. Had we gold, I'd have given you a crown rather than that fillet, but it is no less fine that the one Isaac wears."

Daley threw the red-dyed fillet on the ground and stamped on it. "You son of a bitch, you cheated me!"

"Before God, I did not," Alexios answered. "As a condition for our alliance, you required me to name you Kaisar. I agreed, and the alliance did all we hoped it would: Bornu is no more, and we have divided its lands fairly between Shytown and New Constantinople. Nowhere did you require me not to appoint a lord of rank intermediate between mine and yours. That I have done, for the security of my own realm. But cheat you? I deny it, and deny it with clear conscience."

The Mayor stared at him. Cool calculation alone should have been enough to calm Hizzonor's wrath; the Rhomaioi had him and his delegation at their mercy, if they chose to attack. But Daley's glance never went to the gathered men of New Constantinople; he watched Alexios alone. And then, to Alexios's amazement, Hizzonor threw back his head and shouted laughter to the sky. "You son of a bitch, you cheated me," he said again. The words were as they had been a minute before, but their tone altogether different.

The Mayor slapped the Basileus on the back, hard enough to stagger him. A couple of Alexios's guards growled and took a step toward Daley, but Alexios waved them back. "Now that you know I can, perhaps we'll have a better chance of living next to each other in peace," he told Hizzonor. "One thing I've noticed about you *opisthanthropoi* is that you think anyone from before your own time has to be foolish. Would you have proposed this arrangement of ours to one of your contemporaries? They would have seen through it to your true intentions, and so have I."

"Most of them wouldn't, by God," Daley said. He

did not mention that his true intentions were murderous,
any more than Alexios had. Sometimes that was part of
the game. Hizzonor laughed again, even louder than
before. "All right, I'm Kaisar and it doesn't matter worth
a damn. I know what I do the first thing I get back to
Shytown, though."

"What's that?" Alexios asked.

"Appoint myself an Associate Mayor—what else?"

It was the Basileus's turn to laugh. "Fair enough. *Now*
we feast."

Fool's Paradise

Ed Gorman

1

I heard the voice but I tried to ignore it. I didn't want to wake up. I was dreaming of the apartment on Eddy Street in the sunny autumn of 1921, a few weeks after my daughter Mary Jane was born, and of how tender and pretty my wife looked in those days before I betrayed her and ended our marriage.

Then it was more than just a voice, the summoning, it was quick, small hands shaking my shoulder and saying over and over, "Please, Mr. Hammett. Please wake up."

The first thing I smelled was the rain, the clean chill scent of it on the heavy green foliage along the River, and the dull tamping sound it made on the roof of the jerry-rigged wooden cabin where I lived.

I got one eye open and pulled myself up to one elbow for support and looked at the rabbity little man shaking me.

I hadn't liked him much back on earth—his work, I

mean; I obviously hadn't known him personally—and I didn't like him any better here on the Riverworld.

All the biographies have him as this tortured, romantic soul, but, like most people unfortunate enough to fit that description, he was a whiner, a schemer, and a tireless narcissist.

"I'm sorry I woke you up, Mr. Hammett."

"Yeah. I'll bet you are."

"I need your help, Mr. Hammett. Need it badly."

He always called me "Mr. Hammett." I suppose it was because of the hair. It went silver on me when I was young and no matter how much the ladies insisted it made me look "distinguished," it also made me look older than my years. Even now, even though like most folks on Riverworld I was only twenty-five, my hair was once again turning white.

I sat up on the blanket. I rubbed my eyes and allowed myself an expansive yawn. And then I punched him. Oh, it wasn't much of a punch, no teeth broken, no nose flattened, but it stunned him and pushed him back a foot or two, and that was good enough for me.

He touched his mouth tenderly, the tip of his tongue tasting the blood on his lower lip. "Why did you do that, Mr. Hammett?"

I've never been especially pleasant in the morning. My father was like that and so was my grandfather. I'm willing to blame it on my genes and not my soul. I'm especially unpleasant when somebody like my uninvited house guest wakes me up just at dawn.

I got to my feet, forgetting to duck in time. I raised the entire thatched roof with my white head.

He started to smirk, but I made a fist and his smirk dutifully vanished. I let the roof settle back down. I went

over and sat Indian-legged in the corner and poured
myself a drink of water. The rain still smelled clean and
good. I wished I could say as much for my guest.

Now that I was awake, I took my first good look at
him. He had an unpleasant reputation on Riverworld,
always seducing young girls and then deserting them, the
sort of woman-hating games Casanova the satyr always
played. At least Casanova had been forthright: he'd
wanted goaty sex. Poe wrapped it all up in a fog of
romance and dark feverish poetry.

"You stoned?"

"I resent that, Mr. Hammett."

"Knock off the theatrics and answer my question."

"No, I'm not stoned."

"You trying to tell me you're not a dreamgum addict
anymore?"

"I use it occasionally."

"Occasionally. Uh-huh."

"I know you don't think much of me."

I sighed. I hate sanctimony, mine or anybody else's,
and I realized suddenly that I was being awfully sanctimonious about this guy.

"Look," I said, "given the sort of life I led back on
earth, I don't have any right to make moral judgments
about anybody. And I sure as hell don't want to put on
the Roman collar and tell somebody he's a self-indulgent,
profligate twit who uses everybody he comes in contact
with."

He smiled. "I think there was a message for me
somewhere in there."

"Yes, I suppose there was."

"I know what I'm like, Mr. Hammett."

"You do, eh?"

"Believe or not, I'm not that way consciously. It just sort of—comes out that way. I mean, I don't really mean to use people . . . I just sort of . . . do."

I sighed again. "What can I do for you this fine, sunny morning, Mr. Poe?"

"I wish you'd call me Edgar. Everybody else does."

"I'll make a deal with you."

"What's that?"

"You call me Dashiell and I'll call you Edgar."

He smiled again. All the books have him as handsome, but he wasn't, not really; his mouth and his chin were too weak for handsome. But there was some force in the dark eyes that held real power, some kind of madness that was fascinating to observe. I'm sure it's a power he shared with snake charmers and wealthy ministers and politicians who wrap themselves in patriotism.

"All right, Dashiell," he said.

"You came here to tell me something."

"Yes."

"Then tell me."

"I'm afraid somebody is trying to kill Arda."

"That's an unlikely tale for the Riverworld. There not being any death here."

"No, not death as such, but if you kill a man, he's reborn elsewhere. And if you were to kill the woman a man loves and she's reborn elsewhere and he's never able to find her again because the Riverworld is so vast— well, that's just the same thing as her dying, isn't it?"

"I guess you're right about that." I looked down at his long, slender hands. Some people would call them artistic hands, I suppose. Anyway, his hands were trembling, and badly. "Why would anybody want to harm her?"

"I don't know." But the way he said it, fast and dismissive, I knew he was lying.

"I don't really do this sort of thing anymore, you know."

"You were a Pink."

"Pinkerton is the proper name. Pink is what the press called us, and I never much cared for that." I took some more water and then took a deep breath. "Maybe you don't know this, Edgar, but I ended up being a writer too. Not as good as you, maybe, but good enough that I was able to quit being a Pinkerton and support myself up to the end. Or thereabouts, anyway."

"What're you saying?"

"I'm saying that I'm out of practice."

"Last night, she was out walking and somebody shot an arrow at her. Missed her by no more than this." He indicated a small amount of space between thumb and forefinger. "And a week ago, somebody tried to drown her while she was bathing in the River. And a few days before that, somebody tried to push her off a mountain trail."

"Did she get a look at the person?"

"No. I wasn't there for any of it. But if I had been—" His messianic dark eyes looked away. "She has a hard time concentrating sometimes. And that can get dangerous when somebody is stalking you."

There's only one way you consistently lose your concentration on Riverworld.

"You mean you introduced her to dreamgum."

"No!" He was almost shouting. "She did it all on her own. I didn't even know she was doing it until it was too late."

Dreamgum comes to everybody in the grail. Most of

us decline it, not wanting to spend our lives in a phantas-magoria. Waking up on Riverworld is fantastic enough for most folks.

But I was getting sanctimonious again, a trait of mine Lillian hadn't much liked. But then, there had been many traits of Lillian's I hadn't much liked either, especially when, near the end of my life on earth, I deduced the real nature of our relationship.

"Who would want to hurt her?" I asked.

"I don't know."

"Or why?"

"I don't know that either."

"It couldn't be her imagination?"

"The arrow's in our cabin. I assumed you wanted to talk with her. I figured you could see the arrow then."

"I just can't help you, Edgar."

"Won't, you mean."

"If you like."

The tears were there, and they were so sudden that I didn't see how they could be fake, even given his theatrical nature.

"Oh, shit," I said. "It's bad enough when a woman uses tears on me. But a man—"

"Do you have any idea how much I love her, Dashiell? Any idea at all?"

Now, in addition to the tears, his whole body had started shaking. I looked at him and hated him. He was so goddamned weak. But then I realized how weak I was, just in a different way was all, and so I gave up my pulpit and said, "It's been a long time since I was a Pinkerton, Edgar. A long, long time."

"She really needs help, Dashiell. Otherwise, some-body will take her from me forever."

A nut-case poet and a dreamgum nymphette. Aren't they just the kind of clients all private ops dream of?

2

After swimming for twenty minutes or so, I climbed back to the bank and returned to my hut and got ready for the day.

By now, I was starting to like the idea of having a case. Riverworld is many things, but exciting is not one of them, at least not in my own particular little patch of it. Two cultures and historical eras are represented here, the first being a group of suburban businessmen and their families from the Baltimore area circa 1907, the second being a group of San Franciscans from the late 1950s. I was among the latter group when I died and was reborn on Riverworld, whatever and wherever Riverworld really is.

When I got back to the shore, I found the good Baltimore burghers engaged in carrying material for huts into the surrounding forest. Even here, even in this purgatory in which we found ourselves, the good industrious burghers wanted a suburb to themselves. They believed, and quite rightly, that half the people you found canoeing down the River were riffraff. How could I disagree when one of our last visitors had been Wyatt Earp, who very seriously proposed that we take the six prettiest women in camp and set up a whorehouse, which he of course would be happy to oversee for a goodly share of the action?

The rain didn't bother the good burghers. They had

been seized with an idea and nothing was going to stop them. They performed their task with the ceaseless and uncomplaining attitude of worker ants.

The San Franciscans were neither so robust nor so industrious. They sat beneath little canopies of leaves and fed on dreamgum and watched the River flow and waved to various folks floating by. One fellow told me that he'd once seen an entire UFO filled with little green Martians waving at him. Such are the rewards of dreamgum.

I waved to the burghers and I waved to the River watchers. I walked up the muddy, sloping hill to the small hut that sat on a bluff and overlooked a deep ravine. This was where Poe lived.

There was no door, just a long rag that offered minimal privacy. From behind it, apparently hearing me approach, a young woman said, "Come in, Mr. Hammett."

The interior stank of mud. The floor was covered with large, heavy, spade-shaped leaves that the burghers had been bringing back from the forest and charitably sharing with others, proving that not all capitalists are bad folks, even to Communists like me.

She was a fetching one, she was. She crouched near the back of the hut wearing some kind of white dress made grubby from life along the River. But even so, her sweet-sad face and her small but rich body marked her as a true beauty. "I told him you'd come."

"Edgar?"

"Yes. He doesn't have much faith in humanity, I'm afraid. But then, I wouldn't either. Not with the kind of life he's led. His stepfather used to beat him mercilessly for one thing. Edgar still has nightmares about it."

She was succeeding in making me feel sorry for Poe.

But he was easier to deal with when he came off as a self-indulgent artiste.

"What era are you from?" I asked.

"The 1930s. My father is a great admirer of yours. He's a judge and a very avid mystery reader." She reached out and touched a large pile of flowers that were dying inside the hut. Even their scent was gone here in the rain and the chill and the shadowed interior.

Then her face changed. Here she'd been this fetching young girl—the impolite name, in my time, being "jailbait" —and then she abruptly became this drawn, anxious young woman. "Look."

From somewhere among the leaves that gave the mud hut its floor, she produced a long arrow with a metal tip. Metals being as precious as they are on this world, I was impressed despite myself.

She handed it over. I rolled it around in my fingers and examined it, not worried about getting prints on it. Riverworld has a lousy crime lab.

The workmanship was very good, point, shaft, and nock perfectly designed. Having been an informal student of medieval history, I recognized the arrowhead as made of iron pile, the same metal an arrowsmith of the 1300s would have used.

"Edgar told you what happened?"

"Yes."

"Somebody's trying to kill me, Mr. Hammett."

"You could always call me Dashiell."

Her shy response was to tilt her head down in such a way that she looked younger and even more vulnerable.

She said, "I'm afraid. I don't want somebody to send me to some other time."

"I don't blame you."

She raised her eyes. "I think it's O'Brien."

"Who?"

"Richard O'Brien. One of the Baltimore businessmen. He's married, but that doesn't seem to bother him."

"Has he ever threatened you?"

"Not exactly. But he waits till Edgar goes down to the River and then he sneaks up here. He's a real pest."

"Pests aren't usually violent."

"Oh, he's very violent. Very violent. He grabbed Edgar one night and tried to drown him. This was before you were here, I think."

"Anybody else I should talk to?"

She thought a moment. She was about to speak when a small birdlike cry filled the air.

We sat in the rain-smelling silence and looked at each other, Edgar's sweet-sad little girlfriend and I. The bird cry had been plaintive, so much so that I touched my arm and felt tiny cold pebbles of goose bumps there.

"What kind of bird sound was that?" There were no birds on Riverworld.

She smiled. "That was Robert."

"Who's Robert?"

But I needn't have asked, because suddenly the long rag that served as a door was thrown back and there stood a boy of perhaps ten, brown as an American Indian, streaked with mud so fierce it looked like war paint. He had sandy blond hair and furtive blue eyes. His hips were wrapped in a towel held up by a magnetic clip. He managed to look both frightening and pathetic in the way of street urchins from time immemorial. Even given the soaking he'd taken in the rain, he smelled of sweat and feces.

From his belt dangled a knife holster, the stone blade it

held considerable and deadly. Filling his right hand, in almost comic contrast to the blade, was a handful of blue and yellow and pink flowers of the sort that grew on the periphery of the forest.

"These are for you," Robert said.

She smiled at him and put forth a frail hand. In her bony fingers, in the drab hut, the flowers were an explosion of bright summer colors.

"I'll see you later," the boy said. He stared at me as he spoke. He didn't try to hide his displeasure with my being there.

"But Robert—why don't I introduce you to Mr. Hammett?"

"No, thanks," he said.

And was gone, out the flapping rag of a door, down the brown mud slope into the cold silver rain.

"Poor Robert," she said after we heard the last of his flapping feet disappear in the thrum of rain.

"I'd say he's got more than a small crush on you."

"I feel so sorry for him. I was always falling in love with older men when I was his age. To adults it's always a joke, but when you're young—it's very painful."

"Who is he?"

She shrugged. "He lives with the woman they call the Witch of the Woods."

"I've heard of her."

"She's no witch. Just a very dirty woman with a bunch of mumbo-jumbo she spouts to scare the children away."

I lifted the arrow. "Maybe I'll see her when I go into the woods. Maybe she can tell me something about this." I smiled. "Being a witch and all, I mean."

I stood up, careful of my head. Riverworld huts were not designed for people of the twentieth century.

"I guess I'll start with O'Brien."

"Be careful of him. He's a very tricky man."

I thought of my years in prison, there at the last when simply apologizing for being a Communist would have been sufficient to free me. I'd known a lot of tricky men in that time, both in prison and on the congressional committee that saw to it I was incarcerated. I thought of old Dick Nixon, actually not the wily man he seemed to be, but rather a sad frantic soul who'd been loved too much by his mother and not enough by his father. What was it Wilde said about parents—sometimes we even forgive them?

"I think I can handle him," I said.

"This is very nice of you."

I raised the cloth hanging down in the doorway. "Don't take any unnecessary chances."

She smiled. "You don't have to worry now. Edgar gave me this."

From beneath one of the fronds, a huge stone knife appeared in her slender hand. "And he also told me where to put it. Right between a man's legs."

She said it with such style and vigor that I almost grabbed my own sac out of pure protective response. The subject of castration does not set lightly on a man's ears.

"I just hope I get a chance to test myself," she said. "See if I'm really this helpless little girl or if I'm a really strong young woman."

I laughed. "Somehow I think you'll pass the test just fine."

She laughed too. "So do I, actually. I just pity the man who tries anything."

I nodded good-bye and went outside the tent. I started down the slope in the grass. The grass smelled strong and leafy. The sky was a shifting kaleidoscope of dark clouds and turbulence. As a child, I'd always been afraid of storms, the sudden chill and scent of rain overwhelming me. I suppose this dated back to the time my sister Reba had been lost for half an hour, my parents searching the neighborhood for her frantically as a storm gathered in the east. Storms would always mean that my sweet sister Reba was lost, even though I was now an adult and Reba had long ago been found safe at a neighbor's house.

3

The campsite was as shabby as everything else on the Riverworld. We brought all our skills with us, true, but we lacked the materials we needed. The "suburbs" was a good example, being little more than a large circle of huts in a forest clearing. At the eastern edge of it a man stood holding a crude spear while behind him a group of four children appeared to be playing marbles as they squatted around a small circle of bald, muddy earth.

The man with the spear stepped forward and said, "You're Mr. Hammett."

"That I am."

"Not to be unpleasant, Mr. Hammett, but we prefer to stay to ourselves. That's why we have a sentry posted twenty-four hours a day."

If he was supposed to be fierce, he wasn't doing his job very well. He was big, yes, but he was deferential, and that's never good in a would-be bully.

"I'd like to see Mr. O'Brien."

He grinned. He looked like an oversize kid. "Well, you saved us both some trouble there."

"I don't understand."

"O'Brien isn't here—" He angled the spear in the direction of the mud huts. At that moment, a boy ran between two of the huts, chased by a laughing young girl. "He's down-river a ways." He nodded toward the River. "And I can't stop you from going there. All I have to do is guard the compound."

"Exactly what do you find so offensive about us, anyway, living apart, I mean?"

"Oh, it's nothing personal, Mr. Hammett. It's just that we're good fundamentalist Baltimore Christians and you're from San Francisco. Worlds apart, I'm afraid. But we don't hate you. Every day the parson leads us in a prayer for your souls."

"Well, that's damned civilized of you."

He winced at "damned" and then started considering the possibility that I was mocking him.

I left him that way and went down-river.

Before I emerged from the forest and found the narrow, winding path running parallel to the water, I heard a *thwock*ing sound. I had no idea what it was.

I followed the path, by now long used to the rain dripping like plump crystals from the green overhanging leaves, and where the path arced wide around an imposing furry bush, I found O'Brien.

He was big and Irish and mean-looking in a somewhat studied and theatrical way.

He held a large bow from which he launched arrows into a rain-blackened tree trunk. The arrow penetrating the wood was the *thwock*ing sound I'd heard. A sad-looking little woman who looked much older than she probably was fetched his arrows and brought them back to him. It looked as if it took all her strength to jerk them free of the tree. There was something arrogant about working a worn-out woman this way.

The woman saw me first. She was ferrying his last arrow back when she glanced up and nodded in my direction.

He turned, facing me fully this time. "Who the hell are you?"

"He's Mr. Hammett," the woman said. "He's a famous writer about thirty years ahead of us."

"Shut up, you stupid bitch," he said, handing her his bow and then stepping over toward me. "You know how sick I am of you always butting in?"

The woman looked as if she'd been lashed.

I stopped about five feet from him. "You're O'Brien?"

"What if I am?"

"I need to talk to you."

"About what?"

"About something personal." I nodded to the woman. "Maybe your wife could use a little rest."

"Since when is my wife your business?"

The woman, weary and dirty and nervous, came up to him as if he were a great stone god and she the eternal supplicant. "I'll go back to the campsite and rest."

"Yes, as if you don't get enough rest already."

I had the sense that he was about to slap her. I wasn't tough and never had been tough, but I disliked him enough to take satisfaction in punching him, even if he later knocked me out.

He settled on shoving her. She started to pitch to the ground, but I grabbed her arm and kept her upright. She peered at me from eyes eternal with grief and fear. You saw women like this throughout the West of my day, their lives over well before they reached sixteen, little more than slaves to violent husbands and sad frantic children, living on hot black coffee and words unspoken and prayers unanswered.

I wanted to hold her, nothing sexual, just hold her for the sake of kindness, something she'd been so long denied.

And I then took a swing at him. I hadn't planned it, I was barely aware of it in fact, but just as my fist started toward his face, she nudged me, so that the arc of my fist went past him.

"I don't want to see you get hurt, Mr. Hammett," she said, and went quickly around the big furry bush in the slanting silver rain, and was gone.

"You supposed to be a tough guy?" O'Brien laughed.

"You could always treat her a little better."

"You see what she looks like? She let's herself become an old woman. It was the same back in Baltimore. Hell, she didn't look so bad when she was reborn on the River, but she started going to hell all over again." He grinned. "I want some nice fresh nooky while my loins are still up to it."

"Meaning Arda?"

His eyes narrowed. His flat nose, which oddly enough lent him a brutal handsomeness, managed to look even fiercer. "What about Arda?"

"Somebody's trying to hurt her." I reached down on the ground and picked up one of the arrows he'd been shooting. It was identical to the one Arda had shown me in her hut. I raised my eyes to his. "Somebody shot an arrow at her recently."

"She needs a man."

"She's got a man."

"You mean Poe?" He made a face. "He's a nancy if I ever saw one."

"She doesn't seem to think so."

"What the hell's your interest in all this, anyway?"

"She's under the impression that somebody is trying to take her from Poe." I held up the arrow. "This is the kind of arrow her assailant used."

"Are you saying I shot the arrow?"

"It's a possibility."

He grabbed at me then, but he was too paunchy to move quickly and so I was able to move right as he moved left.

"Arda wants you to leave her alone."

"That's my business."

"You've got a wife of your own. Why don't you try spending a little time with her?"

But I was getting sanctimonious again. I thought of my own wife, the one I'd left back there on Eddy Street along with my daughter, when I went off all liquored up to accept the accolades of Lillian and all her slick friends. I was in no position to give even a crud like O'Brien any moral preachments.

He snatched the arrow from my hand and said, "If I was you, I'd be getting out of here."

"Just remember what I said. Arda wants you to leave her alone."

"I'd say that's up to me."

He then turned around and picked up his bow and shot an arrow straight into the hard, shiny heart of the tree. It wasn't difficult to imagine him shooting an arrow into me.

4

The next twenty minutes, I followed a path that took me to the center of the forest. Out of boredom more than anything, I'd started following various paths to see where they'd take me. Back in the real world, I'd studied a lot of maps, especially when I'd worked for Pinkerton on various railroads, and being a pathfinder held a real fascination for me. Anyway, as I said, Riverworld wasn't exactly overrun with spellbinding things to do.

I was taking a wide leg in the path, one that ran beneath a heavy canopy of trees, when I spotted the woman. She was lying on the ground, faceup.

Even from here, I could see that she looked grubby and strange. I could also see a trickle of blood on the side of her face that was being washed away by the rain dripping from the leaves above.

I ran to her and knelt next to her and started to turn her over for a better look at her crabbed, filthy face when—

When one of the highwayman's more venerable tricks was pulled on me.

Leave a helpless woman of whatever age in the middle of a path and what gallant man can resist coming to her aid?

Well, I came to her aid, all right, and that was when somebody stepped out from behind one of the trees and hit me squarely over the head.

All I had time for was a small lightning bolt of pain, and then all was darkness.

5

I came to in a large hut. A fire burned in a dugout in the center of the mud floor. The warmth of the flames felt good. The only bad thing was the stench of the place. Whoever lived here was not what I'd call cleanly.

Two women sat on the other side of the flapping fire, watching me. The flames gave their flesh the brown tint of American Indians, and their shining black eyes only enhanced the impression. They sat buried deep in towels. One had a pipe stuck in the corner of her mouth. This was the grubby one. Her sister—I assumed this because their facial similarities were remarkable—had no pipe and was bald. The hues of the fire danced red and yellow on her shiny dome.

"You're Mr. Hammett."

"I guess so."

"We're glad to meet you, Mr. Hammett."

"Yeah, I could tell that by the way you slugged me."

"We just had to be sure." The bald one had done all the talking thus far.

"Sure of what?"

"That you looked up to the task." This time the gray-haired one spoke. "I'm Elena, by the way, and this is my sister Stephanie."

I struggled to a sitting position. Elena handed me a cup of something steaming. I peered inside. I didn't see anything crawling around in there, so I started sipping it. It was tea and it was good, very good.

"I know you probably think we're Indians, but we're not," Stephanie said. "We're French, actually. Our parents came to Baltimore from a small town just outside Paris. Anyway, we got to the Riverworld along with Mr. Poe and all the others. Unfortunately, we had nothing in common with them back there and we have nothing in common with them now."

I looked at Elena. "You're the Witch of the Woods?"

Her sister giggled.

"Don't encourage her. That's what she wants you to do. She's starting to believe all the myths people have started about her," Stephanie said.

"Then she's not a witch?"

Stephanie giggled again. "Hardly." She smiled. "Though I'll bet Mr. Poe wishes she was."

"Why's that?" I asked.

"Because the other night in the woods Elena caught him with another girl. If she were really a witch, Mr. Poe could ask her to put a spell on Arda so she wouldn't be angry with his infidelity."

I thought of Arda, of her sad little face and eyes, and of dramatic Poe seemingly so faithful to her. Even with Arda, he couldn't leave other girls alone.

I sipped more tea and said, "You were going to tell me why you slugged me."

"Easily enough explained, Mr. Hammett," Stephanie said. "We want you to steal something for us tonight, and we just wanted to make sure that you were stronger than you looked."

"We heard that you were a Pinkerton, but frankly, you don't look all that hearty to us."

"Well, maybe I can put on a few pounds for you."

Both women giggled this time.

"What is it you want me to steal?"

"We're not sure," Stephanie said. "And that's the problem."

Elena offered more tea. I accepted.

Elena said, "There's a little boy named Robert who lives in the woods here."

"Yes, I met him."

"Well, Robert's actually a very nice little boy, but he has a secret."

"A secret?"

"Yes, and it's one he won't share with us," Stephanie said.

"Then how do you know he has a secret?"

"Because the other night we saw Mr. O'Brien beating him."

"Beating Robert?"

"Yes," Stephanie said. "I like to run through the woods at night, playing the witch, I mean. Gives people something to talk about and it's kind of fun. Anyway, I was going through the woods and I saw Robert tied to a tree and Mr. O'Brien slapping him again and again. I tried to stop him, but Mr. O'Brien just pushed me away. He doesn't seem to be frightened by witches."

"It's because you're *not* a witch," Elena reminded her.

"Anyway, he kept telling Robert over and over to tell him the secret. But Robert wouldn't. He's very brave for a little boy." She sighed. "Then he took something from Robert. A piece of paper. He ripped it out of the boy's pocket and then took off running. I'd been hiding in the bushes, watching it all, and so when he left, I ran up and freed Robert."

"Robert didn't tell you what O'Brien had stolen?"

"No, and in fact, when I brought it up, he started crying and ran off."

"So what you want me to steal is—"

"—is the piece of paper that Mr. O'Brien took from poor little Robert the other night."

"Great," I said. "Now I have two clients."

"You're being sarcastic, aren't you, Mr. Hammett?" Elena said. "About it being 'great' that you have two clients?"

"Of course he's being sarcastic, Elena. Pinkertons are always sarcastic."

"Don't you want to help poor little Robert, Mr. Hammett? Don't you?" Elena said.

And exactly what was I going to say to that?

6

It took me the rest of the day to find Robert and then I found him only coincidentally, following the trail to the huge stone mushroom where he stood staring at the River.

I moved over to him as carefully as I could. I didn't want to spook him. But when he sensed me, he turned around, saw me, frowned, and then took off running.

He followed a path along the River. The rain made running risky. Several times in escaping, he slipped. Several times in pursuing, I slipped.

I knew that he'd elude me completely if I didn't resort to something unpleasant. I stopped, stooped, and picked up a stone. I threw it with pleasing accuracy and caught him just below the back of the knee. The shock and pain were enough to bring him down, and just as he reached the mud, I pounced.

When I jerked him to his feet and slammed him against a tree trunk, he was completely covered with mud. He looked as if he were doing a turn in blackface.

He was out of breath and so was I, and so we stood there, his mud washing away in the slanting silver rain, exhaling ragged and sour breath at each other.

"O'Brien took a piece of paper from you the other night," I said. "I want to know what the paper said."

"None of your business."

"Kid, I could break your arm."

"Go ahead. I don't give a shit."

"Somebody's trying to kill Arda. Don't you give a shit about that?"

"I love Arda."

He said it in a way most boys wouldn't. Most boys would be too inhibited and shy to say it out that way. But there was so much need and so much pain in his quick urchin words that I sensed he needed to say them out loud, and often.

"She likes you too. She told me."

His eyes scanned the muddy path we'd just come down. "That's the problem."

"What is?"

"I love her, but she only likes me."

I got cute in the way adults usually get cute with youngsters who talk about romantic love. "You don't think she's a little old for you?"

"She may be a little old for me, but then, she's too young for Poe."

"I guess you've got a point there."

He looked sad then, and I wished I hadn't gotten cute and I wished I knew the right thing to say.

"You like it here on Riverworld?"

He shrugged. "It's not any worse than where I lived in Baltimore. At least it doesn't have rats." He raised his eyes to me and spoke in a voice far too weary for his age. "I never loved anybody before."

"It can be pretty painful."

"I get sick to my stomach, it's so painful. She shouldn't love him, she should love me."

I had to keep reminding myself that he was only ten years old.

I said, "Have you ever hated her?"

He looked baffled. "Hated her? No. I said I love her. And I do."

"Well, sometimes when you love somebody very intensely you can also hate them intensely because they have so much power over you."

"That doesn't make any sense."

"It may not make sense, but it's true."

He smiled. "When I hear things like that, I wonder if I ever want to be an adult."

I laughed. "I think that's a myth."

"What is?"

"That there's any such thing as adults. We're just bigger versions of kids. Anyway, being a so-called adult is the shits. It really is."

"You really think somebody wants to kill her?"

"Well, if they don't, they're sure doing a good job of pretending they do."

"I better not find out who it is. I'll kill him myself if I do." He touched the formidable knife shod in his leather holster.

I paused a moment and said, "Tell me about the paper O'Brien took from you."

"That's between me and O'Brien."

"I thought maybe we were becoming friends."

"That doesn't have anything to do with it. That paper's a secret." His face hardened, as did his gaze. "I'll get it back from him one way or another."

"He could hurt you."

"I'm not afraid of him."

"You're not going to tell me about the paper?"

"No."

"You don't want me to help you?"

He shrugged. "O'Brien isn't any more afraid of you than he is of me."

"But still, the two of us—"

He smiled again. "Believe it or not, Mr. Hammett, there were a lot of people afraid of me back in Baltimore."

"I believe it."

"I may not be big or especially tough, but I'm determined." He touched his knife again. "And when somebody pisses me off—" He shrugged again. " Well, I can be pretty relentless."

"I'll bet you can, kid, I'll bet you can."

And that's where I left him, there on the trail.

I nodded good-bye and set off back the way I'd come. He gave me a minute or two and then started following me through the underbrush. I tried to shake him up a few times by breaking into a run. He got panicky and made too much noise in the undergrowth. If I hadn't noticed him before, I sure would have now. But he was only ten, and for that age he was a regular Leatherstocking. When I was ten, I was living in my nice snug, middle-class home and hunting ducks with my father in the salt marsh along Chesapeake Bay.

I didn't have to support and sustain myself the way poor little Robert did.

7

I lay for two hours in my hut listening to the rain. It brought back memories of San Francisco when I was still living with my wife and daughter, who as a baby always asked, "Wet, Daddy? Is wet, Daddy?" when she saw crystal raindrops bead on the windows of our small apartment.

I slept, too, at least for a time, but it was the troubled sleep of an unhappy man, and when I came awake I did so with a yelp, the rock cracking my knee where it landed.

In the gloom and sweat of the hut, I jerked upward and grabbed the rock. Somebody had wrapped a note around it and then wrapped twine around rock and paper alike.

The note read: THE CLEARING BY THE GRAILSTONE AT DUSK.

There was one inherent problem with the instructions. Given the rain and the gloom, how could I tell when dusk actually settled in?

I waited two hours in the top of a leafy tree by the clearing. A minty aroma of leaf filled my nostrils. The bark was as slimy as a dragon's back.

Dark came. The rain continued. There is a melancholy that only cold rain can inspire in me, and it was with me there in that tree. I wanted to talk to my wife and daughter.

She wore cape and cowl, and at first I did not recognize her as she ran across the clearing from one edge of the forest to the other.

Just as I realized that I was seeing Arda, a small shape in the shadows stepped forth and fired off an arrow.

I heard the dead *chunk*ing sound of arrowhead sinking into flesh.

Then she screamed, a strangled sound muffled by the fact that she was already pitching to the wet earth.

By now I knew who her assailant was, too. I wanted to go after Robert and slap him around to sate my rage, but I knew I'd better first attend to Arda.

She was light in my arms as I carried her upslope to the hut where she and Poe lived.

Poe must have heard us coming. Before we reached the hut, he was in the doorway. Then, dramatic as always, he ran toward us with his arms outstretched.

He ran alongside me as I bore her to the hut.

He didn't offer to share my burden, nor did he do much but coo little plaintive nonsense words in her direction.

Inside, we propped her up by the fire.

"Can you take the arrow out?" Poe asked, face yellow from flames. He was frantic.

"I thought maybe you'd want to do it. She's your woman."

"It would make me . . . sick. Feeling it slide out that way. I wouldn't be any good at it." There was pleading in both his voice and eyes.

I sighed. Excising the arrow wasn't something I relished either.

I went over to her and knelt down. She was unconscious. I felt her forehead. She was feverish already from the poison. Her pulse was faint.

I worked as quickly as I could.

When I was halfway through, I heard a noise in the doorway and looked up.

Robert, without his bow, stood there watching me. "How's she doing, Mr. Hammett?"

He trembled with tears.

"Why the hell would you care, kid? After what you did to her?"

He started to say something else, but I said, "Shut the hell up. I'm trying to concentrate."

In the firelight, his eyes glistened with tears. Then the doorway was empty. He was gone.

It took about twenty minutes, and twice she came awake and started crying pretty hard and looked up at Poe with a love so obvious it embarrassed me to see.

Why the hell did she want some gigolo like Poe?

He stayed on the other side of the hut. He hadn't been kidding about not wanting to see. He wouldn't even glance down at the wound.

I got the arrow out and the wound cleaned and the shoulder covered up.

I was just about to get to my feet when I saw her eyes flutter open. She pulled me gently to her and pressed her soft warm lips to my ear and told me then the whole story.

The rain hit the water like bullets. There was no moon.

I found him down on the bank, just sitting there, not caring about being wet or cold or alone.

I sat down next to him in the darkness.

The rain was cold and ceaseless.

I said, "She told me."

"I figured she would."

"She could have been killed."

"I know." He sighed. "The other times were easy. We didn't have to do anything. She just told him that somebody tried to drown her and push her off a cliff and shot an arrow at her. She didn't actually have to get hurt or anything."

"But this time she asked you to really wound her."

"Right," he said.

She'd explained it all to me, back there in the hut she shared with Poe. She knew he was constantly unfaithful. She tried everything to stop him. Nothing worked.

She and her friend Robert concocted all the tales of somebody trying to kill her. She thought that that would work for sure. Poe would be so worried about her, he'd give up running around. For a few weeks Poe was true to her, but then he went right back to slipping out at night and meeting other girls in the forest.

That's when Arda came up with the idea of getting herself wounded. Robert would steal O'Brien's bow and arrow—just as he'd stolen an arrow before to show to Poe—but this time he'd actually wound her.

Faced with Arda's injury, surely not even Poe could be unfaithful any longer.

But then Robert got angry with her one night because he knew she didn't love him the way she loved Poe. He wrote Poe a letter telling him about the plan Arda and he had concocted. O'Brien saw him writing this and snatched the paper away. He planned to use it as blackmail with Arda. She would sleep with him or he would turn Robert's letter over to Poe. Robert felt terrible. He knew he should never have written the letter, knew he would never have actually given it to Poe.

But now O'Brien's having the letter is moot.

By now, back in their hut, Arda would have told Poe everything.

"He'll sneak off again on her, won't he, Mr. Hammett?"

"Poe, you mean?"

"Uh-huh."

"I'm afraid he will, Robert."

"I don't like him much."

"Neither do I."

"I just wish I didn't love her so much."

"Someday you won't love her at all."

"You mean I'll be able to look at her and my stomach won't get all knotted up?"

"You'll be able to look at her and wonder why the hell you wasted all that time loving her in the first place."

"Has that ever happened to you?"

"Many times."

"She's awfully pretty."

"Awfully pretty," I said.

"And she's nice to be in love with, because she doesn't care when you hang around all the time."

"Well, there's something to be said for that, I guess."

He sighed. "Maybe I'm not ready to stop loving her yet, Mr. Hammett."

"It doesn't sound like you are, Robert."

"Maybe someday she'll see Poe for what he really is."

"Maybe she will, Robert."

"And then maybe she'll want to marry me."

"That's always a possibility, Robert."

He kept quiet for a long time, then looked up at me and said, "You don't understand this any better than I do, do you, Mr. Hammett?"

I sure as hell had to laugh at that one. I tousled his hair and said, "I sure as hell don't, Robert. I sure as hell don't."

The Merry Men
of Riverworld

John Gregory Betancourt

The man in green paused dramatically at the top of the rocky cliff, one hand shading his eyes against the sun. His shoulder-length hair, the color of wheat, ruffled faintly in the breeze. He carried a yew longbow and had a quiver of bamboo-fletched arrows slung across his shoulder. With the sun on his face and a thick, dark forest at his back, he cut quite a striking figure.

Below, the River wound like an endless silver ribbon as far as he could see. On its far bank, half a mile up, stood a town—a ramshackle accumulation of forty or fifty log houses. Smoke rose from clay-brick chimneys, and men and women dressed in brightly colored robes moved among the buildings.

He heard a woman's low voice singing a tune he didn't recognize in a language he didn't know. His men would have warned him if there was any danger, but he still didn't like surprises. He'd speak to Will or Tuck about it later.

Slowly, he dropped his right hand from his eyes. In a single movement he whirled, drew his bow, and nocked an arrow.

237

It was a half-naked woman with skin the color of chocolate, and she was carrying a bundle of bamboo. She dropped the bamboo in a clattering heap, her mouth gaping in surprise and fear. Her hair was long and black, Robin saw, and she wore a grass skirt. Her naked breasts were small and deeply tanned.

"Ya linya!" she breathed. *"Me ton fevin!"*

Putting down his bow, Robin leaped onto a low boulder and looked her up and down. His voice was low, powerful, when he asked, "Do you speak the king's English?"

The woman started to back away.

Robin gave a whistle. The woods around them suddenly erupted with motion—two dozen men from the trees, from the bushes, seemingly from the very air itself. All wore green and carried longbows.

"I am Robin Hood," he said. "Welcome to Sherwood, m'lady!"

Screeching in terror, the woman turned and fled into the trees. Robin threw back his head and laughed.

"Sir Robin!" said the tall man he called Little John. "On the River—"

Robin turned to follow his friend's gaze.

Coming around a bend in the river was one of the strangest-looking riverboats he'd ever seen. They had encountered three others on the River, but this one—

It was huge, easily two hundred feet from pointed prow to broad, flat stern, with a large wheel on either side and a third wheel churning water at the rear. Its three tall decks had intricate woodwork, and twin smokestacks rose from a central pilot's cabin. Sunlight glinted off glass windows and what looked like brass railings. Several dozen men moved about various tasks on the upper two decks, while sword-bearing guards maintained a vigilant watch on the lowest.

"Incredible," Robin said. He stared, a thoughtful look on his face.

"What do you think?" a portly Friar Tuck asked.

"I've never seen anything like it," Will Scarlet said.

"Who could have built it?" asked Little John.

"A better question is, where did they get the metal," said Mutch. He'd been a civil engineer in the last life and tended toward practical questions. "Did you see those windows? That was glass! Real *glass*!"

"I think," Robin said, sitting down, "we're going to wait for the riverboat's return. Will, Ben—scout the hill. There should be a grailstone on the other side. If the natives are peaceful, we'll spend the night here."

"Yes, Robin," Will Scarlet said. He and Ben Taylor slipped into the forest like shadows.

While Robin stared out across the River, deep in thought, the rest of his men began setting up camp: clearing the area, gathering wood, building a circle of stones to hold their fire. After a minute Robin opened his pack, took out a small square of cigarette paper, a tiny clay jar with a stopper, and a carved fishbone pen. He opened the jar, dipped his pen into a thin grayish ink, and began to write. His script was tiny, meticulous.

When he finished, he wrapped the paper around an arrow's shaft, tied it in place with human-hair string, and returned the arrow to his quiver. Now it was just a matter of time.

The natives turned out to be surprisingly friendly, considering the language barrier. They were a shy people, quiet and simple in their ways, all living in grass huts around a grailstone. They allowed Robin and his men to fit their grails into the unused slots in the grailstone, then clustered at the far side of the village to keep a wary vigil.

Robin counted twenty-five men and thirty women. He noticed each man kept a long, bone-tipped spear close at hand, though none made a hostile move.

"Polynesian," Friar Tuck suggested, "or from another of the Pacific Islands." He had been a sociologist before being recruited into the merry men: one of the reasons he'd joined was to see more of the people resurrected along the River's banks. "Probably never saw a white man in their natural lives. . . ."

Nodding, Robin collected his grail from the grailstone after the charge had come. "What do you think the chances are they'll attack?"

Tuck hesitated. "They were a friendly people. But I wouldn't want to press our luck."

"Come on, then," Robin told the rest of his men. "Back to the River. We shouldn't push our welcome by eating in front of them."

He led the way back to the cliff. Will Scarlet was standing guard, keeping an eye out for the riverboat.

"No sign of it," he reported.

Robin nodded slowly. "I'm sure they're on a scouting mission this time," he said. "They'll be back."

"In such a craft?" Little John said, his bushy black eyebrows coming together in a frown. "They could go to the ends of the River. Why shouldn't they return here?"

"Any of a dozen reasons." Robin hunkered down and opened his grail. There were thin crispy wafers, little packets of what looked like peanut butter, strips of some dried, cured meat, and a little flask of brandy . . . as well as the usual tobacco, marijuana, and dreamgum.

Robin took a chew of the meat and continued. "First, that riverboat's one of the most valuable pieces of equipment on the River—but it burns wood. They'll have to put ashore whenever they run low. I'm betting they only stop at prearranged safe bases, and if they're scouting new territory they won't stop at all. They'll head home when they start to run low on fuel. Maybe two days, maybe three. Second, they didn't have enough people on board for an extended journey. If it were my riverboat and I were going far, I'd pack it with armed men. Every petty tyrant on the River will try to steal it, given half a chance."

"Shades of Robert Fulton . . ." Little John murmured to himself.

"Unless you're wrong," Will Scarlet told Robin.

Robin flashed a dazzling grin. "Of course," he said. "If it hasn't returned in a week, we'll push on."

In the old days, before the Resurrection, Robin had been a classically trained actor named Edmond Hope Bryor. He'd played minor parts on stage for twenty-two years, since the age of six, before his big move to Hollywood and the silver screen. After three tragic love stories, eight forgettable westerns (critics admired the horses more than his acting talent), and one gangster movie where a young Spencer Tracy shot him in the end, he made the great leap to the *enfant terrible* of acting: television.

Cast as Robin Hood for the fledgling Dupont Network's twice-a-week *Robin Hood and His Merry Men* would have made Edmond Bryor a hero to tens of thousands of children. He'd known that when he signed onto the project. He'd also known he was going nowhere fast in movies, just as he'd gone nowhere fast on stage.

Only Diablo, the ill-tempered white stallion the producer insisted he ride, threw him on the first day of shooting *Robin Hood and His Merry Men*. Edmond had no real memories after that, just a vision of the soundstage floor rushing up to meet him. A broken neck, he assumed; instant death or close to it.

In three years of wandering the River's banks, he hadn't met anyone he'd known in the old life to verify his suspicions. It was just as well, he often thought; he'd given up his old life and assumed a new one: that of Robin Hood. It was the role he was born to play, a dream from the childhood he'd never truly outgrown.

As the only son of two thespians, he'd been molded to their ideals, with elocution lessons, dance lessons, and music lessons instead of play time. He knew it had warped him in subtle ways. Awakening on the River, he'd decided to start over again, to live the sort of life he'd always wanted for himself, full of adventure and romance. And so his wanderings began.

He assumed the name Robin Hood and began journeying up the River, righting any wrongs he found, on the pretense of searching for King Richard the Lionhearted. Playacting, yes, but it was curiously satisfying. Along the way he'd found others willing to share that quest, and he'd filled his band of merry men from their numbers. It seemed his dream was contagious. He'd even talked a politics-weary Abraham Lincoln into abandoning a new political career and assuming the role of Little John. They'd been fast friends ever since.

* * *

Two nights later, a light hand touched Robin's shoulder. He was awake instantly, gazing up into Mutch's stoic face.

"You were right," Mutch said. "It's come back."

Robin leaped to his feet and ran to the cliff, as close to the edge as he dared stand. The riverboat was easy to spot; its windows shone with a clear yellow light, like beacons in the darkness. What kind of lamps, he wondered, did they have on board? What kind of people could civilize a world so quickly?

"Build up the fire," he said.

The others obeyed, throwing wood onto the embers, fanning them until a huge bonfire blazed.

By the time the riverboat drew even with the cliffs, Robin had his bow strung and his special arrow nocked. He'd had two weeks of intense archery training for his television show; the producers had planned to bill him as the greatest archer of the twentieth century. To his surprise, he'd found he had a talent for it, and he'd honed that talent to perfection in three more years of practice along the River.

He aimed, then let his arrow fly. For an instant his eyes lost it in the darkness, then it hit the pilothouse's door with a *thunk* audible all the way across the water.

The door opened. A short, broad man was silhouetted for an instant. He saw the arrow and its note, grabbed them, and slammed the door closed. The riverboat's paddlewheels continued their steady chugging.

"They didn't stop," Tuck said.

"They will."

"What if they don't understand English?" he persisted.

Mutch said, "The riverboat is an American invention. They will speak English."

Little John asked, "What did you tell them, Sir Robin?"

"I'm sure you'd approve—the truth."

He inclined his large head. "Ah, but which one?"

Robin smiled. "Mine."

The riverboat slowed, but did not stop. It almost seemed as if some debate raged within. Five minutes passed, then ten, then fifteen. Finally it began to turn, the huge rear paddlewheel coming to a halt. It began to drift slowly down-River with the current, away from them.

"What does *that* mean?" Friar Tuck demanded.

"It means they don't want to meet us in the dark," Little John said. "They will float with the current until dawn, then paddle back up to see us."

"My thought exactly," Robin said. He sat, crossing his legs. "We wait."

The riverboat reappeared an hour after dawn, chugging faintly, smoke from its stack leaving twin gray smears in the air. Robin stood and began to wave his bow. His men did the same.

The riverboat slowed, its paddles turning just enough to keep abreast of Robin and his men. Sailors dressed in black and white swarmed across the deck. They broke out a small boat, lowered it, and two men began to row briskly toward the cliffs. Two more men aboard, armed with short curved swords, kept a vigilant watch on Robin and his men.

Robin began to make his way down to the rocky shore. The others followed. He arrived just as the boat reached the shallows and waded out to help pull them to shore.

"Bonjour," one of the men with swords said. *"Je m'appelle Claude de Ves. Je suis—"*

Robin shook his head, interrupting. "I don't speak French. Do you speak English?"

"A little," he said in a heavy accent. "I am Claude de Ves of the—how you say?—ah, the riverboat *Belle Dame*."

"Who is your captain?" Robin asked.

"Monsieur Jules Verne."

"The author?"

"Oui."

The name meant nothing to Little John and most of the others, Robin saw. Quickly he explained about the famous French technologist and writer, who had foreseen the invention of everything from the submarine to atomic power.

"This is a man," Little John vowed, "that I would truly like to meet."

"Yes, he is a great man," Claude said. "Your letter—*alors*, I do not know the word—but the captain, he wishes to meet with you."

"Excellent!" Robin said. "It should not take more than four or five trips to get us all over—"

"You are the leader?" Claude asked.

"Yes."

"Monsieur Verne wishes only you to visit."

Robin looked at Little John. "What do you think?"

"If this Verne is as great a man as you say, you will have nothing to fear."

"My thought exactly." Robin looked at Claude de Ves. "Very well, your condition is acceptable." He clambered into the rowboat and sat. His men pushed them out into deeper water, and Verne's men maneuvered them around and began to row toward the riverboat with powerful strokes.

Once Robin glanced back and saw Little John standing

there, staring back at him with an unreadable expression. Robin waved, and shouted, "I'll be back soon."

The riverboat itself was a technological marvel, but up close Robin began to notice subtle details that marked it as the product of a more primitive technology than he had at first suspected. The glass in the windows was cloudy and full of bubbles. The brass had been beaten to shape the rails; mallet marks were clearly visible. As he climbed onto the lower deck, he noted the square-headed nails in the ladder. The riverboat had been built by hand, he was sure, and represented the product of a fantastic amount of sheer physical labor.

"Monsieur Verne is in his cabin," Claude said. He led Robin to a hatch, then rapped sharply on its frame.

A feeble voice answered.

Claude undogged the hatch and stood back so Robin could enter first. Robin ducked through.

It took his eyes a moment to adjust to the gloom inside. When he could see, he discovered a pale man with short, wiry black hair propped up in bed. There was a sweet smell in the air, almost like meat left in the sun too long. Infection, Robin thought.

"Monsieur Verne?" he asked.

Jules Verne nodded. Despite his sickness, his blue eyes held a fire Robin could not deny. Verne held the note Robin had attached to the arrow.

"You claim to be Sir Robin of Locksley?" he asked in nearly unaccented English.

"I am he," Robin said. "I am delighted to meet you, sir."

"Draw up that chair and we will talk," Verne said.

Robin did so. "You have a nineteenth-century British accent, I would say. How do you explain that?"

Robin shrugged. "Would you understand Saxon?"

"Touché."

"And it's a twentieth-century accent, by the way." Almost before he knew it, Robin found himself telling how he'd adopted the role of Robin Hood, of his adventures and misadventures along the River as he and his men sought to right the wrongs of this new world. Verne nodded now and then, an avid listener.

"Life is indeed mostly a series of curious events," he said. "I needed someone such as you a week ago. Indeed, I nearly died because of it."

"What do you mean?" Robin asked.

Verne sighed and sank back on his bed, closing his eyes. Suddenly he looked tired, frail. When he spoke again it was with the voice of an old man.

"When I awakened on the River and found myself young," he said, "it seemed almost as though God had created this world for me alone. . . ."

Now (Verne said) I could do those things of which I had only dreamed throughout my life. All my research, all my books and writings, they had led me inexorably toward this moment.

I vowed to create a perfect society. This new civilization would be modeled on mankind's old one, but with all its various flaws and imperfections cured. Mankind had been given a fresh chance here, I felt, and it would be up to us to make the best of it.

I was fortunate enough to be resurrected among a group consisting primarily of Frenchmen from the late nineteenth century. Also among us were Russians from some twenty or thirty years in our future, Chinese from yet another age (I could not pinpoint their place in history; alas, my schooling in matters Oriental was somewhat lacking), and a few others from what seemed random periods in our world's history.

The Chinese immediately banded together and left, seeking whatever it is Chinamen seek; to my regret, we never circumvented the language barrier. The Russians, on the other hand, stayed with us. One among them, a fiery youth with an unpronounceable name who had us call him Lenin, began preaching socialism to the masses, but his voice fell on deaf ears. Most people were content to live natural lives, eating food from the metal Providers; sunning themselves on the riverbanks, eating the dreamsticks, and fornicating in a hedonistic frenzy.

Lenin was murdered his second week there. But what he'd said interested me. The idea of all men being equal is, of course, ridiculous; but the organizational system he outlined seemed workable, even practical in our current circumstances.

I combined his thoughts with my own. As I talked to my fellows, I found among them a number of engineers who were sympathetic to my new ideas. Their names would be meaningless to you, for they were in no way famous, but they were sturdy men, well schooled in their fields and not afraid of hard work.

First we moved away from the general population, to a more remote Provider in the hills. Here we began a systematic analysis of the land and its raw potential. There were deposits of iron, tin, and copper within easy reach. Trees could provide wood for fires and tools. And, I must admit, we made use of whatever human corpses came our way—bones were our first tools.

Over the next few months, we set about creating a community based on scientific planning. As we discussed matters, we reached a general consensus that our resurrection was a test of some kind, and that to prove our species worthy we must strive to create a more perfect society from the materials available.

Needless to say, it was difficult. But as more people joined us, we found strength in numbers. Houses were erected; a stockade was built to protect us from our neighbors and whatever marauding animals this world might harbor. Soon we were smelting bronze, then iron. Sand, with some refinement, proved suitable for the crude glass you see in the *Belle Dame*'s windows. In three months we had a prosperous town, with every man and woman working ten hours a day toward the common good. My dream was coming true, shaping itself before my very eyes.

Of course, our society was a technocracy. Our Technocrat Council of Engineers ruled, with me at its head. When it occurred to us that we should try to bring all the best elements of this new world together in one place, we sent out emissaries. Our scientific ambassadors ranged for a thousand miles up and down the River, persuading whatever engineers and scientists they found to join our cause.

Again, the plan worked. People from all ages flocked to our incipient city. The vast laboratories we set up were something to see! We had mills, running water, and even a number of working clocks and watches within a year. Every success fueled our drive forward. A railway was begun to link the Providers. Hot-air balloons scouted the air. Cartographers began to chart our new world. And, finally, we began to build this riverboat.

No, don't interrupt—let me finish my tale. I am near the end now.

Perhaps we were too giddy with our successes. We allowed anyone to join us who wanted to—*anyone*. That was the mistake. We woke up one morning to find our little society drowning in an unskilled "proletariat," to borrow Lenin's word.

Among those who had joined us was a man called Capone. He came with a group of followers. He was small, quiet, a smooth talker. He offered to set up a bureaucracy to deal with our population as a whole. Indeed, we had already seen the need for administration and police . . . but none on the Council truly wanted to oversee such mundane matters. We were all scientists, visionaries, men looking toward the future. Each of us had pet projects to oversee. Letting Capone handle such matters seemed the ideal solution, as it would allow us to concentrate on our work.

Capone gave us all bodyguards. At the time it seemed like a good idea, since there were grumblings from the masses, but I understood his plan now. He wanted to isolate us from the population so he could control us. I'd heard of many twentieth-century inventions by this point— men walking on the moon, satellites, computers, television— and I wanted all these scientific miracles and more. Perhaps that's what blinded me. I wanted to leap centuries in months, to claw my way to the highest point of mankind's technological achievement in the span of a few years.

Perhaps it truly was punishment for my hubris. Perhaps it was blind stupidity. I awakened one morning to find myself a prisoner. My bodyguards had become prison guards. I—and the other technocrats—were no longer in control. In the space of a single night, our government fell in a bloodless coup. Al Capone had taken over.

He was a clever man, I admit. When we met with him in the Technocrat Council's chambers—we on the floor, he on a low throne—he made it clear who was in charge. When Leonardo da Vinci dared speak against him, Capone bludgeoned him to death with a wooden club. The blood, the blood! It was horrible . . . the most horrible moment of my life.

I longed to see Capone dead, but there was nothing any of us could do but agree to whatever he demanded. Perhaps we should have spoken against him, should have joined Leonardo in death. That would have been the proper thing to do. Even though I knew I would be resurrected somewhere else along the River, I could not stand up against him. I'm ashamed to say I *was* afraid of death, and of the pain he would administer before it.

Capone kept us on tight leashes after that. We never appeared alone in public, never spoke to anyone except on scientific projects, and then always under the close scrutiny of our guards. Capone wanted my pet project, the riverboat, completed as quickly as possible; I assume that's why I had what little freedom I did. Most of the other technocrats were locked in their rooms, forced to work on blueprints for machines that others would fully execute in their absence.

The greater body of engineers and working scientists, I found out later, had deduced most of what had happened. Capone was a greedy pig. He renamed our little city New Chicago and began taxing everyone on their tobacco, marijuana, and dreamgum. Anyone who didn't have a useful skill suddenly found himself drafted into a labor gang and sent into the hills to mine metal or cut lumber to fuel New Chicago's technological machinery.

The next year was, indeed, a grim one. But the riverboat was nearing completion, and though Capone had decided to turn it into a floating brothel and casino, its presence offered hope to many of our scientists.

On the night before the *Belle Dame*'s test voyage, they staged a revolt. Using crossbows they had made in their spare time, they shot the guards on the building where I and the other technocrats were quartered and set us free.

It took seconds for them to explain their mad plan. We would seize the riverboat and set off to start a new technocratic state. This time we would not repeat the mistakes that had brought Capone to power. This time we really *would* create a perfect world.

To make things short, Capone somehow found out about the rescue attempt. He sent the bulk of his men to stop us—to *kill* us, rather, since the riverboat was finished. If none of the scientists could be trusted, our usefulness to him was ended.

It came down to hand-to-hand fighting. I had written about it, had studied fisticuffs, but still found myself little prepared for true mortal combat. One of Capone's lieutenants slashed my belly open with a sword. I fell, unconscious.

I awakened here, aboard the *Belle Dame*. A handful of men had rallied around my fallen body, fought their way free to the riverboat, and launched. We were searching the river for another suitable site for our technocracy when you encountered us.

* * *

THE MERRY MEN OF RIVERWORLD

Robin sat in thought when Jules Verne finished his tale. Every word of it rang true; he had no doubts about its veracity.

"What you are looking for," Robin said at last, "is a place like the last one, with abundant metals and wood, with easy access to the River, and a Provider—what we call a grail."

"That is correct." Verne leaned forward again, wincing a bit from pain. "Do you know of such a place?"

"We've traveled thousands of miles along the River, always heading upstream," Robin said. "I've kept an eye out for metal along the way, and I know of places where lead and copper have been found. But iron ore? No, there's none."

Verne sank back, face ashen. "Then perhaps we truly *are* lost," he said. "Providence led us to that spot, and in our pride we failed to see the dangers we courted."

"Providence may be brought us together for a reason. Don't you wonder at the convenience of it all?"

"What do you mean?"

Robin stood and began to pace. "You have been driven from your town by a thug and his men. After that you meet me, a man with a band of loyal followers who are looking to fix the wrongs of the world. Can you think of a more appropriate partnership?"

"Are you thinking what I am, sir?"

"If you're thinking we might be able to wrest control of New Chicago from Capone—then yes."

"I must think on it," Verne said. "Violence has never been the answer to the world's problems."

"But sometimes it is the only solution," Robin said.

Verne closed his eyes. "Find Claude," he said. "I will have him bring your men aboard. We will talk again later."

* * *

That afternoon Will Scarlet, who had spent a year training as a medic before dropping out of the program, went to see Jules Verne. Robin hoped he'd be able to help the technocrat. Will was the closest thing to a doctor on board.

While they waiting for the prognosis, Robin met with Little John in the salon. It was a beautifully decorated room; the tables all had floral designs inlaid with ivory taken from the bones of the giant fish that lived at the bottom of the River. Robin had seen such fish only twice . . . once when a twenty-foot-long corpse had washed ashore; another time when a fisherman had been devoured whole while Robin and his men were passing through his town. Robin wondered how Verne had gotten so many of their bones that he could afford to waste them on decorations. Perhaps the riverfish were more numerous around New Chicago.

Robin and Little John drew up chairs and sat facing each other. The two always conferred on major decisions; the former president was a wise man, brilliant in many ways, and his advice carried a great deal of weight with Robin.

"I'm not sure I like the sound of this Capone fellow," Little John said.

"We'll handle him easily enough."

"Edmond—listen to what you're saying."

"I heard myself."

"You're an actor, not a hero. I admit it's been fun to play this game with you, to romp through the hills as Robin Hood and his men would have done. It's been grand, a chance to live out my childhood daydreams. But perhaps the time has come to end this charade. We aren't bandits from the greenwood, we're civilized men. And Capone will not be easy to scare off.''

"I don't want to scare him. I want him locked up—or, lacking that, dead and resurrected a million miles away.''

"I doubt we are capable of doing it.''

"Have you forgotten all we've accomplished?''

Lincoln's bushy brows knit together. ''We've scared a few peasants into giving up grail-slavery. We've broken up a few drunken brawls. We've explored a thousand miles of this damned endless River. That's *all*. We aren't an avenging army, and we're not the fist of God. This man Capone is a dangerous criminal. He has surrounded himself with a private army, if what Verne told you is true. Twenty against two hundred is suicide.''

"So you're saying we should leave him there, building the biggest criminal empire in the history of mankind?''

"I'm not saying that, either. I'm saying we can't recapture a city by treating it like a romp. It will take planning, strategy, and a lot of patience.''

"What about luck?''

"You're impossible!''

"Little John—''

"Call me Abraham!''

"Little Abraham, then. I've always felt I should have a calling. My life was more or less forced on me—first by my parents, then by my acting troupe, then by a string of agents. I've always known I was meant for something greater. Since our resurrection, that feeling has come over me stronger than ever. My assuming the role of Robin Hood, our finding Verne and this riverboat, *everything*—it's all been leading up to this moment. It's destiny. The dice are rolling, and I can hear them.''

Lincoln stood. "It's time to put away your childish

dreams," he said. "If we are going to take New Chicago from Capone, we will need a man to lead us, not a character from storybooks."

"Are you sure?"

"That I am." Abraham Lincoln turned and stalked from the room.

Robin Hood, né Edmond Bryor, sat alone for a long time, deep in thought.

Will Scarlet's prognosis was promising: he had cleaned and dressed Jules Verne's wound, then sewed it up properly, and now felt certain his patient would recover completely in time. "His problem was loss of blood and a bad infection," he reported. "Luckily no vital organs were damaged."

It was welcome news to Robin. "Is there anything else you can do?" he asked.

"Let him sleep. It's the best thing for him right now."

"Good," Robin said, nodding. "Stay with him. Let me know if you need anything."

Two days later Jules Verne sent word that he wished to see Robin again. Verne looked vastly improved, Robin thought when he entered the cabin. The color had returned to his cheeks, and his voice was stronger and more authoritative.

"I have decided to agree to your plan," Verne said with no preamble. "We will return and try to win back New Chicago. I will leave the details to you—I am a man of science, not violence, as recent events have shown. Whatever you need, I will arrange it. Now, what are your plans?"

"I have none as yet," Robin said. "Little John and I

must study the town, count our resources, and estimate the enemy's strength before committing to anything.''

"Very wise." Verne nodded slowly. "I have instructed Claude de Ves to give you any help you need. Our diverse talents stand at your disposal, sir.''

"Thank you," Robin said. "Your trust in me is not misplaced. You won't be disappointed.''

Robin held no false illusions about himself or the task at hand: he knew it would be difficult, that the fighting would probably be bloody and violent, that some of his men—perhaps even he himself—would die as a result. But he also knew Capone needed to be removed from power, and that he was the one man capable of carrying it off successfully.

The next day, Claude de Ves gave Robin and his men a tour of the riverboat. They saw the steam engines driving the paddlewheels and the huge bins where they kept wood for fuel; they saw the pilothouse and the luxurious salons; they saw the cabins and the empty cargo holds.

The riverboat had tremendous potential, Robin decided, but they wouldn't be able to use it in their attack. It was too large and too obvious—Capone would have too much time to prepare for a fight if he saw it coming. Besides, Verne and his men would be easily overwhelmed by Capone's superior forces. No, Robin decided, given the odds against them, they would have to rely on their wits to gain the upper hand.

The riverboat paddled up-River for three weeks, crossing hundreds of miles, passing thousands of different cultures. Aztecs, Minoans, modern Japanese, seventeenth-century Indians . . . the sheer volume of people was staggering.

During that time Robin drilled his men and Verne's mercilessly in the art of the longbow. They made straw targets in the shape of men and shot them again and again behind the pilothouse. The pilothouse's back wall became filled with chips and holes from being hit by countless arrowheads.

In the evenings Robin and his men worked on making more bows and arrows, aided by Verne's crew. Eventually every man and woman on board had two longbows and two dozen arrows. Robin felt certain—and Little John tended to agree—that they would need everyone aboard to retake New Chicago.

When they were a week's walk from New Chicago, the *Belle Dame* slowed and once again put in to shore. This time Robin was the only one to leave. The riverboat would return in three weeks' time to pick him up; in the meantime it would wait far down-River, where Little John and Will Scarlet and the others would continue to drill Verne's men in archery.

Robin's mission was simple: he would scout the land, see New Chicago, get an estimate of Capone's strength, and return.

The trip to New Chicago proved disappointingly uneventful. The native populations along the River were sparse—most, Robin learned, had migrated to New Chicago during its early days. Since Al Capone's rise to power, the remaining people had migrated down-River . . . rumors of slave camps, spread by a few escapees, did the trick.

As he walked, every possible plan for taking Chicago ran through Robin's head. Storming the walls . . . poisoning

Capone's food . . . leading a slave revolt . . . all seemed equally mad, and equally improbable.

One day out from the New Chicago, he blundered into a patrol of Capone's thugs: six men, all armed with swords and shields. They ringed Robin at once, weapons drawn.

"Throw down your weapons," their leader said with a cruel sneer, "and we may let you live."

Robin stood with his back to a tree, his bow drawn, an arrow nocked and ready to fire.

"Not a chance," Robin said. "Another step and you're a dead man." His arrow targeted the man's chest. "An arrow will go through that shield you're holding like a hot knife through butter."

The man shifted a bit uneasily. "Here now," he began. "You can't—"

"I heard there's a city ahead where men with certain skills can find a good life," Robin went on. "Is that true, or not?"

"What skills do you have?"

"I make weapons."

"What sort?"

"Everything from bows to guns."

"Guns, you say?"

"That's right."

Grinning, the man stepped back and sheathed his sword. "Why didn't you say so, friend? We've had problems with the natives around here, so we can't be too careful. You'll be welcome in New Chicago, all right— the boss always has a place for another man with useful skills."

Robin lowered his bow. "I should think so," he said.

* * *

That New Chicago was a pearl buried in a pigsty was Robin's first impression. The original town, surrounded by a stockade, was exactly as Verne had described it. The streets were wide, the houses laid out along tree-lined avenues radiating from a large central plaza. The huge council building—now Capone's palace—stood at the exact center of town.

Around the stockade, though, lay a huge slum. Gaunt-faced men and women stared as Robin and Capone's men strode past. Thousands of hovels, flimsy constructions of logs, clay from the River, and bamboo, had been built between New Chicago and the River with no concern for order or sanitation. The reek of human waste was nauseating.

Robin covered his mouth and nose with a bit of cloth. Is there no degradation to which man will not fall? he wondered.

"Don't worry," the man to his right whispered, as though in answer to his unspoken thought. "You can't smell Pisstown from the city most days."

"Good," Robin said.

At the stockade's gate, guards took Robin's longbow and quiver of arrows. Robin didn't protest; he knew it was a small price to pay for the information he would gain.

To his surprise, he was taken almost at once to a small whitewashed building fronting the central plaza. Two guards escorted him to an office. An engraved brass plaque beside the door said A. EICHMANN.

"Come in," a young man with sandy hair said in a heavy German accent. "Please, sit."

Robin lowered himself into a straight-backed wooden

chair. It creaked faintly under his weight. He allowed his gaze to travel leisurely around the room—it was bare except for the desk—then back to Eichmann's thin, unsmiling face.

Eichmann had a paper in front of him. He dipped a pen into a clay inkwell, then asked, "Name?"

"Robin Huntington," Robin said, and spelled it. Eichmann's pen made scritch-scratch sounds.

"Date of death?"

"The year of our Lord eighteen hundred and forty-six."

Eichmann noted it down, then paused to study him. "Skills?"

"I was a master gunsmith."

"Excellent, excellent." Eichmann wrote that down, too, then deposited the form in a small tray on the corner of his desk. Opening a drawer, he removed a card. The paper looked thick and coarse, but words had been printed on it with a printing press of some sort. Eichmann wrote Robin's name on the card, along with a series of numbers.

"This is your identification card," he explained. "Carry it with you at all times. You will need it to enter and leave buildings, use the Provider for your meals, and requisition tools and equipment for your work." He smiled. "You're lucky you're a gunsmith—the boss is big on weapons. He wants pistols as quickly as possible, and if you work hard to keep him happy, you'll find the benefits and privileges are enormous. As it is, you'll be among the elite of the scientific teams."

"That sounds good to me," Robin said.

Eichmann gestured to the guards. "Find him a room in the dormitories," he said.

* * *

The next morning, in the gunshop, Robin met the three other gunsmiths working for Capone. The head of the gun project, a Dutchman named Emile van Deskol who had died in 1865, gave Robin a tour of their shop. A dozen apprentices, varying in age from about seventeen to twenty or twenty-one, were hand-carving rifle stocks and pistol grips, and chipping flint for flintlocks. A few pistol barrels had been cast in iron, and their bores were being smoothed and polished.

"As you can see," Emile said, "our progress is slow. The iron is poor, our casting methods worse, and the work is tedious and time-consuming. It will be months if not years before we have a single working pistol."

Robin frowned. He was no expert, but progress on the weapons seemed far more rapid than that. He made no mention of his suspicions, though.

"This will be your area," Emile said, indicating an empty table and bench at the back of the shop. "Each of us works on weapons of our own design. Any tools you need will be requisitioned, as well as assistants. Life is cheap; the more people we put to gainful employment, the better, if you understand me."

"I believe I do." Robin began to smile. Emile had a pretty good racket of his own going on . . . as long as he looked busy and useful, he would be immune to Capone's bullying. In the meantime he'd pull as many people up from the slum of Pisstown as he could.

Robin knew, then, that he'd found an ally. He just had to convince Emile of that fact.

After the ten-hour workday, as the others hurried out to place their grails in the grailstone, the Dutchman took Robin's arm and held him back. Robin paused, curious.

Emile said, "You're no gunsmith."

"I don't know what you mean," Robin said.

"I've been watching you, and you don't have the faintest idea of what you're doing. If you are here to spy on us—" Emile began.

"Actually, I am." Robin lowered his voice. "I was sent here by Jules Verne."

Emile took a step back as if struck. "Verne—he is still alive?"

"Yes. He wants to capture Capone and free New Chicago."

"I would welcome the day!" There were tears on Emile's face. "Verne was a good friend of mine. Where is he? I want to know all that has happened to him!"

Quickly Robin gave him a summary of Verne's life since he'd escaped on the riverboat. The Dutchman kept nodding happily.

"I have something to show you," Emile said when Robin finished. He led the way into the back room. Several of the floorboards were loose; he pulled them up, revealing a crawlway. Inside were dozens of pistols and muskets.

"These are our rejects," he said proudly. "They all work perfectly, so of course we cannot give them to Capone. When he comes to see our progress, we fire the defective guns for him. When they explode, we tell him it is a problem with the forging process. When it is refined further, we say, the guns will work." He chuckled. "He is a fool. One of Capone's men even lost an eye to a bit of flying metal."

"How many guns do you have?" Robin asked.

"Thirteen flintlock pistols, eight rifles."

"I need to leave here in five days to rejoin Verne and

his men. We'll return ten days after that. Will you be ready to help us?''

"Yes," Emile breathed. "All we need is a signal."

"A flaming arrow at dawn," Robin said. "Watch for it. Two minutes after it crosses the sky, join us in the attack."

Emile and the other two gunsmiths covered for Robin over the next few days. As a gunsmith—even a new one—Robin found he had rights and privileges denied most other residents of New Chicago. He found he could move freely through the city, poking into its darker corners, mapping the streets in his mind. He even visited the roofs of several buildings, "for stargazing is my hobby," as he put it.

There were countless places from which his men might strike. One of the smaller gates on the northern side of New Chicago seemed to offer the best possibilities for invasion: it was barred from the inside each night, with a single guard posted to watch over it.

Robin also learned that Al Capone left his palace early each morning to look over pet projects, accompanied by Eichmann and a few other trusted lieutenants. Such a routine begged closer examination, so Robin visited the city library one morning (several dozen authors were re-creating famous works from memory, and interested readers could inspect new drafts of *Moby Dick*, *War and Peace*, *Ubik*, and *Little House on the Prairie*). Since the library faced out on the central plaza, he had a clear view as Capone—a small, round-faced man with powerful arms and shoulders—crossed the square. The gangster smoked constantly, his words interspersed with short, sharp hand motions. It took maybe three minutes for

Capone and his men to cross from the palace to Eichmann's office building.

Robin stared up at the rooftops surrounding the square and thought about ambushes. Yes, he thought, the more he studied the matter, the higher he believed their chance of success.

On his fifth night in New Chicago, Emile drew him aside again. "I have it arranged for you to leave tomorrow," he said. "We need more flint. You will be going to a high-quality outcropping you spotted some weeks ago in your wanderings, and two of our apprentices will accompany you to carry it back."

"What about guards?"

"Seven men will accompany you for the first day. When you reach the edge of Capone's territory, six of them will turn back. Capone has an entire city to watch over, and cannot spare guards for such minor missions as this." Emile winked. "Besides, in my confidential reports to Eichmann, I have told him how happy you are here, and how hard you are working. They like loyalty in men such as us, eh?" He gave a hearty laugh.

Dawn the next morning found Robin and two seventeen-year-old apprentice gunsmiths standing at the main gates. As Emile had promised, everything was arranged: the guards were waiting, and they even returned Robin's bow.

"You'll be standing double duty," said the guard who was to accompany them the whole time, a grizzled, tough-looking mercenary named O'Brien. "Keep the kiddies in line, keep yourself in line, and we won't have no trouble."

"Sounds good to me," Robin said.

* * *

Their fourth night out, Robin put an arrow in O'Brien's back as the man lay sleeping. Fast, quick, and painless by this world's standards: Robin felt not a moment's remorse. It wasn't like death here was permanent, he thought. O'Brien would awaken the following day, naked and confused, next to a grail hundreds or even thousands of miles away.

The two apprentices stared at Robin, clearly terrified. They tensed to run.

"Relax," Robin told them. "I'm not going to kill you. I'm on a secret mission and had to get rid of our guard. You can either stick with me for the next few weeks . . . and you'll be richly rewarded when we're through . . . or you can return to New Chicago. If you go back, though, be warned that Emile will have naught to do with you. He knows about what's going on, and even arranged this whole trip. You'll be stuck in Pisstown or sent to a labor camp for the rest of your lives."

"We will go with you," they both said at once.

Robin nodded; he'd expected that answer. "Search O'Brien's body and split whatever valuables he has. The sword and shield are mine. Then hide the body where it won't be found."

Both boys hurried to obey. Robin sat back and watched. He didn't know if they'd stick with him, hightail it back for New Chicago at their first chance, or just flee to another settlement somewhere down-River. It didn't really matter, he thought; he'd be back aboard the *Belle Dame* the next day. Even if the boys tried to warn Capone, he'd beat them to New Chicago on the riverboat.

* * *

The *Belle Dame* was anchored in the middle of the River exactly as they had agreed it would be. Little John and the others were practicing on deck. Arrows were nocked, fired, nocked, and fired again at the straw targets. Verne's men had improved vastly in the ten days he'd been away, Robin noticed.

The apprentices merely gaped. Robin clapped them on their backs. "What do you think now?" he asked.

"But this is Monsieur Verne's boat!" Jacques, the younger of the two, finally said.

"And there is Monsieur Verne!" cried Pierre. He gazed at Robbin in awe. "You are a spy for Monsieur Verne!"

"That's right." Robin cupped hands to his mouth and hallooed to the *Belle Dame*. Everyone on the deck dropped what they were doing and crowded to the rails, waving excitedly.

A boat was rapidly dispatched, and in twenty minutes Robin and the boys had been transported safely aboard.

Jules Verne was the first to shake Robin's hand. "Congratulations!" he boomed. He looked completely well, his cheeks ruddy, his long brown hair whipping wildly in the breeze. "I knew you would return safely!"

"And I have good news," Robin said. "It will be easier than we thought to capture the city."

"Do not keep us in suspense! What have you discovered?"

Robin climbed two of the steps toward the second deck and turned. His men and the *Belle Dame*'s crew all stared at him avidly. Taking a deep breath, he began to tell, in simple language, exactly what had transpired, and exactly how he planned to take the city back. Claude de Ves gave a running translation for the members of Verne's crew who didn't speak English well enough to follow.

There were startled gasps when he told of the flintlocks and the ally he had found in Emile van Deskol. "And so," Robin said, "I think we stand more than a chance of taking New Chicago from Capone. I *know* we can do it. It will be hard, it will be brutal, and some of us will undoubtedly die. But in this world where death is but an inconvenience, we have nothing to fear. Come, let's drink to our success!"

To the cheers of the men, he led the way into the salon, where enough liquor had been stored for everyone aboard to share a toast. When it was done, Jules Verne led everyone in three cheers for Robin.

And Robin himself, riding high on the crest of their emotion, felt as though he were flying, as though he would never come down.

"I will need a few things," Robin said.

It was the next afternoon; he and Jules Verne were in the riverboat's salon. The *Belle Dame* was headed up-River for New Chicago at full speed.

"If it's within my power, you know I will get them for you," Verne said.

"First," Robin said, "I need something like a portable periscope, to watch Capone and his men from cover."

"We have mirrors on board," Verne said. "It is simple enough to mount two of them in a box, arranged so you can look over walls or around corners."

"Second, I need a thin sheet of metal, perhaps an inch wide and eight inches long—but it must be strong at the same time."

"We have extra brass railings aboard. One can be cut to that size."

"And I need something flammable—an oil-soaked rag would be ideal—and matches to ignite it quickly."

"Will flint and steel suffice?"

"If that's all you have, it must."

"It is; we have found no sulfur deposits yet. What else?"

"Nothing but luck."

"That, my friend," Jules Verne said, "must rest with Providence."

When they neared New Chicago, the crew doused all lights and ran the riverboat in darkness. Robin moved forward, studying the shoreline. Here and there fires from human settlements glimmered faintly through the trees. Overhead, alien constellations shone palely down, providing a wan sort of light that made the River's waves shimmer ever so faintly silver.

Several crewmen sat silently in the prow, dangling their feet overboard, calling instructions back to the pilothouse. The pilot avoided sandbanks as best he could. Twice Robin heard the *Belle Dame*'s keel scrape sand.

At last they rounded a bend in the River and New Chicago, some three or four miles distant as yet, came into view. Its thousands of lights and campfires gave the sky a glow visible for leagues in every direction.

"I think we should land here," Robin said. "We're about an hour's walk away. We can be there well before dawn."

"Good," said Verne. He hefted his longbow. "This time I am ready for Capone."

"No," Robin said. "I want you to stay aboard. You're too valuable to risk in the fighting."

"I did not journey all this way—" Verne began.

Mutch said, "Think of your wounds, sir. They're not fully healed. If you rip out the stitches..."

Claude de Ves whispered something in French in Verne's ear. Jules Verne frowned, but finally nodded and turned to Robin.

"You all seem united against me in this matter," he said. "So be it. Take all the men you require; I will remain aboard the *Belle Dame* until success is assured."

"What if you're attacked?" Robin asked. "Surely you need *some* crew to protect the riverboat."

"The *Belle Dame* carries a few surprises for anyone foolish enough to attack her," Verne said with a wink. "As for my crew, I need five strong men, no more."

"Very well," Robin said, "though I would gladly leave twice that number."

Verne rose with sudden determination. "Let us see to the boats," he said. "The sooner New Chicago is freed, the happier I will be."

On deck, Verne gave the orders and the riverboat put in as close to shore as it could. The crew broke out four boats this time. Robin and his men went ashore first, then Verne's men followed. The *Belle Dame* pulled back and began to drift down-River with the current, away from New Chicago. Verne would hide around the River's bend until dawn.

Robin found himself in command of no fewer than fifty-two archers. A skeleton crew of eight—including Jacques, Pierre, and Verne—had remained aboard the *Belle Dame*.

As the men gathered together for the march to New Chicago, Robin quietly asked Claude de Ves what he'd said to Verne in the salon.

"Eh?" De Ves chuckled. "Merely that he is too valuable to chance in such an attack as this. We will need his mind to restore the city and the technocracy to its former glory. How can he do that if he is dead—from old wounds, or from new ones?''

''Very logical.''

''Indeed, it is logic to which Monsieur Verne listens best.''

Robin divided the party into three groups, one led by Claude de Ves, one by Little John, and one by himself. ''We stand less chance of being spotted if we move quickly and in small groups,'' he told them. ''Little John, follow me in five minutes. Claude, follow five minutes after Little John.''

They nodded their understanding. De Ves translated for the Frenchmen.

''Remember,'' Robin told his group, ''we will be the first ones to run into any trouble. Should guards challenge us, shoot first and ask questions later. We have plenty of arrows; don't be afraid to waste them.''

He looked his men over one last time, making eye contact with each and every one. They all hefted their bows, shifting impatiently, like hounds eager for the hunt. At last Robin nodded, convinced they were ready. With a sharp whistle, he turned and padded softly into the darkness. They followed right on his heels.

The journey took one of the longest hours of Robin's life.

Every noise in the night, every creaking branch, every rustle of leaves grated on his nerves. He would pause, motioning his men to silence, and listen. Usually it was the wind, or a passing animal. Twice patrols of Capone's men passed within yards of where they crouched; Capone's men talked loudly to one another, their swords and shields making occasional metallic clangs. They were arrogant in their strength, convinced they were invulnerable here, Robin thought. He let them pass unharmed to maintain the night's façade of normality.

They circled the stinking mire of Pisstown, keeping upwind as much as possible. The northern side of the stockade faced out on a sea of tree stumps sprinkled with little copses of saplings; the forest had been cleared for hundreds of yards around New Chicago for its wood. Like phantoms they drifted from hiding place to hiding place until they were twenty yards from the stockade walls.

While the others waited under cover, Robin and Will Scarlet jogged over to the side gate Robin had scouted during his time in the city. Robin pressed his ear to the wood and heard deep snoring from the other side. The lone guard had fallen asleep at his post.

He mimed it to Will, who had taken out the long, thin strip of brass Verne's men had prepared. Nodding, Will inserted the strip between the door and frame, working it carefully upward. It caught on the bar. Will shifted left, then right, then up again, and the bar lifted out of place.

Using his fingertips, Robin pushed the door back. Will reached inside, caught the bar, and lowered it silently. They both slipped inside.

Next to the gate they found a guard sprawled in a high-backed wooden chair, his mouth open. He was snoring softly. Robin nocked an arrow and leaned forward until its tip pricked the man's throat. He came awake with a frightened mew.

"One more sound and you're dead," Robin said. "Will, tie him up."

Will Scarlet did as instructed. In minutes the guard was firmly bound and gagged with strips cut from his own clothing. He could do nothing but stare at them with wide eyes.

Turning, Robin pushed the gate completely open and motioned toward the saplings. In groups of three and four, the rest of his band crossed into the stockade.

As they entered, Robin reminded everyone where to go and what to do. "Watch for a flaming arrow," he said. "That will be our sign that the attack has begun."

His men dispersed, melting into the dark streets and alleyways like a fine mist.

Dawn brought a cool gray sky, with a brisk wind that held the promise of rain. Robin, Little John, and five others sprawled on the roof of a building that overlooked the central plaza. Their bows were strung; arrows lay close at hand.

"He'll come from the central doorway," Robin was saying. He passed the little periscope Verne had made to each man in turn; they looked over the roof's peak with it, down into the plaza. "He'll have at least four others with him, possibly more. The best time to strike is when they're in the center of the plaza. I'll give the signal. Agreed?"

"I'm not sure assassination is the answer," Little John said.

Robin turned to look at his friend. "Abe, he's a criminal and a murderer."

Lincoln bit his lip.

"If I thought we could safely take him prisoner," Robin went on, "I'd try it. You know I don't want Capone free to raise another criminal empire somewhere else along the River. But I also have to balance our possible losses against his. This is the best way."

Little John shook his head sadly. "Perhaps you are right. Even so, I find the idea of assassinating him distasteful."

"It's not murder," Mutch pointed out. "He won't die."

"But he'll feel it nevertheless."

"True," Robin said. He retrieved the periscope from Mutch and took up watch. A second later, the palace's main doors opened.

Robin let his voice drop to a whisper. "Get ready. They're coming out!" He selected his arrow and prepared to stand and fire. Around him, his men did the same.

"On the count of three," he said. "Everyone aim for Capone. He's the short, round-faced man in the center. One . . . two . . . three!"

And on three, all seven rose and fired.

Either the whistle of arrows in flight or the sudden movement on the rooftop gave Capone the warning he needed. The gangster jerked one of his men around, and that man rather than Capone took two arrows in the chest and one in the leg. It was Eichmann, Robin saw. The German staggered, a startled look on his face, then collapsed.

"Guards!" Capone was shouting. He grabbed another man as a shield. "Bring out da guards! Archers on da roofs! Guards!"

Robin fired a second time, just missing Capone's head by a hand's breadth. The gangster continued his retreat, still bellowing for help.

Meantime, Robin's men had killed the rest of Capone's lieutenants. Their bodies lay in the plaza, surrounded by growing pools of blood, arrows protruding at odd angles from their bodies.

Robin calmly nocked a third arrow, took careful aim, and let it fly. This time he hit the lieutenant Capone was using as a shield, killing him instantly. The gangster continued to drag the corpse in front of him, though, and made it up the palace steps and through the doors unscathed.

"Get down!" Robin said. His men crouched out of sight once more. "Damn, damn, damn," he said, pounding his leg with his fist. "I should have had him!"

"It wasn't meant to be," Little John said.

Robin grimaced. "We'll take him later, if we can," he said. "It's time to start the second phase of our attack. Mutch?"

Mutch produced flint and steel. Robin pulled an arrow with an oil-soaked rag bound tightly around its shaft. Mutch struck sparks until the rag caught fire, then Robin rose and fired. It arched across the sky, bright as a flare, a clear signal for everyone else involved in the plan.

"Let's hope the others succeed in their tasks better than we did," he said grimly. "I'll lead the guards away. Little John, you stay here and keep watch, in case Capone comes back out. The rest of you, scatter and keep an eye out for danger. If you can, rally the people to our cause."

With a cry of, "God save the king!" Robin rose and ran across the top of the roof. With an Indian war-whoop, he leaped to the next building's roof. Shouts came from below as the guards spotted him and gave chase.

Robin grinned and sprinted toward the next building, ten feet away and six feet lower. He'd lead them a merry chase, all right. He reached the edge, leaped, and hung over thirty feet of emptiness. Then, with a grunt, he hit the other building's roof and scrambled for purchase. His feet slipped on the wood shingles and he fell forward, grasping for a handhold. He slid six feet before he found one.

Pulling himself up, he glanced over the edge. Twenty or thirty guards were watching for him, swords drawn. A cry went up, and Robin began to run again.

He led them from rooftop to rooftop. Over the next ten minutes, he found the number of guards had grown alarmingly—there were at least a hundred men following him below, waiting for him to slip or get himself trapped.

At last he reached the end of his chase, as he found himself on the roof of a meeting hall. He stood on the top of the roof, looking around in seeming confusion, as if he didn't know where to go from there. Then he climbed down to an open window in the second story and climbed inside.

The guards rushed the building *en masse*. As they entered, Robin dashed across the balcony that overlooked the ground floor, drawing their attention.

Then in the center of the balcony, Robin held up his hands and shouted for their silence. A bit to his surprise, the guards paused and stared at him.

"I have come," he shouted, "to free this city from tyranny! Look around you—you are surrounded by my men! Lay down your weapons or you will all be killed!"

For the first time, Capone's men began to look around the meeting hall. Robin's archers had been waiting motionlessly up against the walls. Now forty-five of them stepped forward, arrows nocked.

A sudden, confused babble of voices rose from the guards. Bewildered questions—puzzled demands—angry threats.

Robin shouted them down. "Drop your weapons and put your hands on your heads!" he instructed. "This is your last warning!"

One by one swords began to thud against the floorboards. Two of Robin's men moved forward and began collecting them, while the others kept the guards covered.

Chuckling, Robin descended to take charge.

Outside, he could already hear scattered gunshots, as the smiths and their apprentices took care of what other guards remained. It would only be a matter of mopping up after this.

The city had completely fallen to Robin and his men. By noon the last of the fighting had ended, as the few holdouts among Capone's men were disarmed and locked into the meeting hall with the others. All told, three hundred and forty-four of Capone's guards and lieutenants had been rounded up. Another sixteen lay dead, and eighteen more were wounded and not expected to live through the night . . . mostly due to New Chicagoans settling old grudges with their former captors. The whole city had joined in the revolt at the end. Robin hadn't lost a single man.

Of Capone, though, there was no sign. Robin assumed he'd somehow made his way from the city and fled. With such complete victory in hand, though, it seemed a minor detail. They'd send out patrols to try to find him later. Considering all he'd done to the land and people, Robin thought Capone would have few friends willing to aid his escape.

That afternoon, as the *Belle Dame* sailed close under its skeleton crew, Robin's men raised a red flag over the council building as a signal that all was well. A long whistle blared from the *Belle Dame* in reply.

Musicians were already playing in the streets, and men and women were dancing in the plaza with joyous abandon. The gates to the city had been thrown wide; most of the population of New Chicago and Pisstown had come in to join the celebration.

Emile van Deskol and the other gunsmiths and their apprentices had organized themselves into a police force, and the threat of their guns kept order. Truly, a new age had come to New Chicago.

"Look!" Mutch said, grabbing Robin's arm and pointing toward the River.

It took Robin a minute to see what he meant. Two outriggers had cast off from shore and were sailing toward the *Belle Dame*. In the lead boat . . . was Al Capone!

Robin counted quickly. The outriggers held a total of twelve men . . . all armed killers. The *Belle Dame* had a crew of eight at the moment, and two were little more than boys. They wouldn't stand a chance against Capone and his men.

"They must have been waiting near the water," Mutch said. "We weren't guarding anything but the city. They saw their chance to escape and took it . . . and the *Belle Dame* just happened along at the wrong time."

Robin felt an electric shock run through his body. "We've got to stop them!" he cried. "If they gain control of the riverboat—"

"Get two boats ready," Little John said. "I'll fetch some of our boys with guns. It's not too late. We can still stop Capone."

Robin and Mutch raced for the water.

* * *

Ten minutes had passed by the time twenty armed men made it to the outriggers from New Chicago. Robin had to stand helplessly and watch as Verne and his men scurried across the *Belle Dame*, shutting hatches, fastening wooden shutters over the windows, doing anything and everything they could to protect themselves before Capone and his men could board. At last Verne ushered everyone into the pilothouse, slammed the hatch, and (Robin assumed) bolted it closed from the inside. Perhaps Verne would be able to hold out long enough for Robin to save him.

As Capone's outriggers pulled even with the *Belle Dame* and the gangster and his men began to climb aboard, a curious thing began to happen. Robin had to blink and rub his eyes to make sure he wasn't seeing things.

The riverboat was sinking.

Or perhaps *submerging* was the appropriate word, since it didn't seem to be happening in any way like a disaster: there were no explosions as cold water hit the steam boilers, and the craft was descending evenly, prow and stern simultaneously. The newsreels Robin had seen of ships sinking had always shown them turning tail-up and then vanishing into the depths.

"It's a submarine, too," Mutch breathed.

"But the smokestacks . . ." Robin said.

"Perhaps they stick out of the water at all times," Mutch said.

"I don't understand," Little John said. "Is it sinking or not?"

"It's not!" Robin let out a relieved laugh. "He's brilliant! *That's* how he knew his ship could never be taken by force—he can submerge it whenever he's attacked!''

"Keep us clear of the riverboat," Mutch said. "When she goes down, the sudden undertow might be enough to capsize us."

They circled the *Belle Dame* from a hundred yards away, watching as she continued to sink. Capone and his men had abandoned their outriggers when they boarded; now they could only climb higher and higher as first one deck, then another fell awash.

At last they stood on the pilothouse's roof, pounding futilely on the wood with their swords, screaming obscenities at Verne and his infernal riverboat. Then the water covered even the pilothouse, and they found themselves floundering in the river.

"Riverfish . . ." Little John murmured. "The riverboat has stirred them up."

"Where?" Mutch asked.

He pointed, and Robin saw them too: four or five dark shapes moving swiftly through the water. In seconds they reached Capone and his men and pulled them under. The water turned bright red.

Robin swallowed and found a lump in his throat. He found he'd been unconsciously rooting for Capone to make it to shore. Devoured by riverfish . . . that wasn't a fate he would have wished on anyone, even Al Capone.

Over the next few weeks, things gradually returned to normal in New Chicago. The people went back to their jobs, trials were held for Capone's men (all were sentenced to five years at hard labor in the mining camps), and Jules Verne himself restored the scientific council, to continue the press toward new research and the reinvention of all mankind had lost.

Robin and his men were declared Heroes of the City and awarded every honor Jules Verne could think of. Verne himself pinned the Nemo Medal on Robin's chest in a holiday to celebrate ten days of liberty for the city.

At the end of the evening, as Robin and his men returned to their temporary quarters, Robin found his thoughts wandering toward the River and what lay ahead once more. He knew it was time to leave, to continue his journey.

"I've been thinking," he said at last, "that it's time we were moving on. What say you, men?"

They all cheered mightily. The merry men had increased to thirty-eight during their stay in New Chicago: it seemed many were sick of the city and longed for freedom and the open road to adventure.

At dawn the next morning Robin and his men gathered at the gate to the city. Jules Verne and most of the people of New Chicago had come to see them off. There were more than a few sad farewells.

"Robin," Little John said solemnly, "I don't know how to say this, so I'll put it plainly."

Robin turned. "Is something wrong?" he asked.

"I've decided to remain here," Little John said.

Robin stared. "What?" he cried.

Abraham Lincoln took off his cap. "I'm sorry, Robin," he said in his low, powerful voice. "I've been looking for my place in this world, and I think I've found it here. Jules Verne and his scientists need people like me. Their problems came from their system of government. They never planned for the common man. If their quest for scientific enlightenment had paid more attention to people instead of machines, Capone never could have taken over from them.''

"But what could you do?'' Robin asked.

"I've already spoken to Mr. Verne. He has agreed to let me draft a constitution to govern this city and its people. Democracy must be kept alive, and New Chicago will be its headquarters. Do you understand now why I must stay?''

"I think I do,'' Robin said solemnly. He put his hand on Lincoln's shoulder. "I wish you all the best, my friend." The two embraced briefly. "Good-bye, Abraham.''

"Good-bye, Robin.''

Robin swallowed, took a step back, and looked over the rest of his merry men. One of the newest additions, a tall, thin youth with straight black hair and a ready smile, stood at the back. "Little John,'' Robin told him. "Henceforth you will be our new Little John.''

"*Pardon, Monsieur Robin?*'' Little John said, looking confused. One of the other merry men translated for him, and a slow smile spread across his face as he understood. "*Merci!*'' he cried. "*Merci bien, Robin!*''

Robin sighed mentally, but didn't let it show. He'd work on it. After all, how bad could a Frenchman playing Little John be? It couldn't be worse than the first Little John, who'd tried to introduce the merry men to something he called "the Ministry of Funny Walks.''

And so, his band stronger than ever, Robin Hood headed from New Chicago, continuing his quest for justice and King Richard the Lionhearted.

Unfinished Business

Robert Weinberg

1

"Company's coming," shouted Jim Bowie, spotting a shimmering in the air a few feet from where he stood. Along with nearly five hundred other citizens of New Athens, he was waiting by the town grailstone for lunch to appear. Translations, though fairly commonplace, always caused a ripple among the villagers when they took place. No one ever adjusted to people materializing out of thin air.

The crowd, equally divided between men and women all looking approximately twenty-five years old, hastily backed away from the huge stone mushroom. Barely five seconds after Bowie's warning, a man's nude and hairless body materialized next to the massive grailstone. Attached to his wrist was the ever-present lunch bucket, while close at hand appeared a half-dozen towels. As his form hardened into reality, the grailstone roared like thunder, blue fire streaking a score of feet up into the air.

"Luncheon is served," announced Bill Mason cheerfully. Carefully circling around the unconscious newcomer, he scrambled onto the grailstone and retrieved his bucket. Opening it, he peered carefully inside. "Hey, Bowie, I got a bottle of bourbon. I'll trade it to you for some of that chocolate you've been hoarding."

The stranger momentarily forgotten, the villagers hurried to their grails. Bowie followed suit. There would be plenty of time to talk to the new arrival later. On Riverworld, there was always time. Lunch came first.

Groaning, the translated man rubbed his head and sat up. Bowie, checking the contents of his lunch bucket, kept one eye on the stranger. A few months earlier, a new arrival went berserk seconds after his arrival. He slaughtered three citizens of New Athens before finally being dispatched. Ever since, Bowie made sure he had his knife handy after a resurrection.

Meanwhile, his friend Socrates, always the Good Samaritan, knelt by the stranger. The philosopher's small, ugly face creased with concern. "Would you like something to eat?" Bowie heard the Greek inquire in Esperanto, the lingua franca of the River. "Resurrection gives one an appetite. Or so I have been told."

The newcomer, a tall, lanky man with pleasant features and blue-gray eyes, groggily shook his head. "No, thanks," he replied in the same language. "The last thing I remember is a bunch of cannibals hacking at me with knives. Best I could tell, they wanted me to stay for dinner." The man laughed out loud. "Actually, I guess they wanted me *for* dinner. Kinda put me off eating for a while."

"Cannibals!" gasped a nearby woman, her features turning a delicate shade of green. "But the food from the grailstones . . ."

"Each to his own nature," said Socrates with a shrug. "Some people are harder to please than others."

Opening his grail, the philosopher pulled out a bacon, lettuce, and tomato sandwich. Taking a deep bite, he waved the food at the other man. "Are you firm in your resolve? Or perhaps a cup of coffee would suit you better?"

"Maybe in a few minutes," replied the stranger, his gaze sweeping the crowd. It came to rest on Bowie, unmistakable with his fair skin and wavy red hair. "I thought I heard your name," the man muttered in amazement.

Bowie frowned. That voice sounded familiar.

"Don't you recognize me, Jim?" the man cried out, his voice thick with emotion. "You old son of a bitch."

Bowie gasped in amazement. Everyone on Riverworld had been reborn at age twenty-five and without any facial hair. The man whose voice he heard had been fifty the last time they had been together. He stared at the new arrival, trying to fit his image to the one he remembered. It was the stranger's eyes, blue-gray like his own—"killer's eyes," the Mexicans had called them—that decided him. His mouth curved in a huge grin. "I'll be a ring-tailed alligator!" he exclaimed. "Davy Crockett."

Tears in both their eyes, they embraced. "Long time since the Alamo," said Bowie.

"Not long enough," replied Crockett grimly. "But we can talk about that later. How you been?"

Before Bowie could answer, Crockett turned to Socrates. "I'll take that coffee now, friend. And maybe a bite or two from that sandwich. Running into old buddies always makes me hungry."

"Back on Earth," said Bowie a few minutes later,

watching his old friend wolf down anything offered him by the generous villagers, "everything made you hungry. Can't say you've changed very much."

"Been eating a lot better since Resurrection Day," said Crockett between bites. "Life's a mite easier when you don't gotta hunt for your grub."

He waved a hand about, taking in the whole area. "Who lives in these parts?" he asked, eyeing several of the better-looking women. Around their waists, they wore their towels like loincloths, leaving their breasts bare. Crockett grinned. "Foreigners, I take it. Not that I mind their style of clothing."

Bowie chuckled. "To them, we're the outsiders. Most of the folks are ancient Greeks like my buddy, Socrates. Some from Athens, the others from Sparta. The rest are a scattering of Texans from our era, some fifteenth-century Frenchies, and a few dozen others drawn from all periods and places. That Bill Mason over there comes from the twentieth century. He told me that we became famous after we died. Got our names in all the history books and stuff like that."

"They wrote a song about me," said Crockett smugly. "Learned some of the lyrics from a pretty young lady back down the River a-pace. You want to hear the words?"

Without waiting for an answer, he started singing. Bowie grimaced. Resurrection had not improved Crockett's voice. He still sounded like a bullfrog in pain.

"Enough torture," he said after the frontiersman finished the first verse. "Time to head back to our cabin. Me an' Socrates and Mason share a place. There's plenty of room. You want to stay with us?"

"Others won't mind?" asked Crockett. "Don't want to impose none."

"It's fine with me," said Mason, wandering over and hearing the question. He shook Crockett's hand. A short, stocky man with light-blond hair, he was dwarfed by both of the six-foot Westerners. "I taught history back on Earth. Getting to talk with people like you is a dream come true."

"I also have no objection," added Socrates. He smiled. A sturdily built man with small face and round eyes, he was grotesquely ugly. "Our home is yours."

"Mighty kind of you fellas," said Crockett. He smiled and nodded at an attractive woman walking past. "No women problems or stuff like that?"

"I've been seeing a few ladies," said Bowie, his blue eyes twinkling, "but nothing serious. I don't like being tied down. Same applies to Bill. Socrates is on the run from his wife."

"All men should marry," declared the philosopher solemnly. "If you get a good wife, you become happy and content. If you get a bad one, you become a philosopher." Ruefully, he shrugged his shoulders and smiled. "I am a *notorious* philosopher."

Crockett chuckled. "I'm convinced. Your place easy to find?"

"It's up the slope about a hundred yards from town," answered Bowie. "Why? Where you going?"

"That little lady over there has been givin' me the eye while you gents have been jawing away," said Crockett, scooping up his grail and towels. "Thought I'd spend a little time getting to know her better. I'll be around by evenin'."

Then, for an instant, all of the good humor departed

from his face and his voice grew ice cold. "That's when we'll talk about the Alamo, Jim. And our buddy, Santy Anna."

2

Five men gathered around a roaring campfire late that night. Crockett had shown up at Bowie's cabin at sundown, grinning broadly but refusing to say anything about his day's activities. "I'm too much of a gentleman to do any bragging," he replied to their questions.

None of the others saw any reason to mention to the frontiersman that his lady fair was Clio of Athens, notorious in the community for her voracious sexual appetites. He would learn soon enough, as had both Bowie and Mason. And many others.

The fifth member of their group was a soft-spoken man who answered to the name of Isaac. A tall, well-built man with distinguished features and dark-brown hair, he had the saddest eyes Bowie had ever seen. Solitary by nature, he lived by himself at the edge of the forest. Though not a dreamgum addict, he was haunted by terrible nightmares that he refused to discuss with anyone. Oftentimes, in the midnight hours, his screams would drift down into the village, causing all those who heard them to shiver in fear. Many of the Greeks considered him cursed by the gods.

A few nights each week, Isaac would drift over to Bowie's cabin to sit silently at their fire. Though he was fluent in Latin, Greek and Esperanto, the man rarely spoke unless addressed directly, and even then his answers were short and to the point. Socrates theorized that Isaac hungered for the warmth of human companionship but not the responsibilities of friendship. Bowie, who had encountered similar men on the frontier, always made their visitor welcome.

"Do you remember dying?" asked Crockett, casually stirring the raging fire with a bamboo stick. "Not here and now, but the first time. On Earth?"

Though he addressed them all, he obviously aimed the question at Bowie. And the Texan was the one who answered.

"I was pretty well gone by the time the Mexicans came huntin' me. What with pneumonia and my broken ribs and all, my cards were laid out on the table. Not that it mattered much to those troopers. They had blood in their eyes, if you know what I mean." Bowie paused, as if sorting out details in his mind. "Propped myself up against the back wall when I heard them coming. Better than dyin' in bed, I figured. When they finally stumbled on me, I shot the lead man in the chest, then gutted a second with my knife. That's when my legs gave out and I crashed to the floor. I must've died right then, 'cause the next thing I remember is waking up naked on the grass down by the River, like everyone else, four years ago."

"They dragged your body into the courtyard and tossed it into the air on their bayonets," said Crockett. Shuddering, he stared directly into the fire. "The soldiers mutilated your corpse pretty bad. Did the same with several of the others. It was pretty gruesome stuff. I saw the whole thing."

"You saw it?" said Bowie, amazed. "Then you didn't die when the Mexe's overran the fort."

"Nope. Me and three others surrendered once we saw things were hopeless. It seemed the best thing to do."

"But all the history books say you perished at the Alamo," interrupted Bill Mason.

"Goes to show you can't believe everything you read," said Crockett with a faint smile. Then his features turned grim. "For all practical purposes, I died there. Santy Anna wasn't in a forgiving mood that day. His men murdered us quick enough."

"What?" exclaimed Bill. "Why?"

"Before they attacked, the General told his soldiers, 'No prisoners.' He meant what he said. So when we were brought before him, Santy Anna didn't even look up. He just repeated his command. Damned Mex troopers bayoneted us right there. With my dyin' breath, I swore I'd get even with that coldhearted bastard. And ever since Resurrection Day, I've been a-huntin' for him."

"What do you plan to do if you find him?" asked Mason. "The logistics of this place takes a lot of the sting out of revenge. Kill a man, and he's reborn elsewhere. Cut off his hand and it grows back."

"I've got me some ideas about that," said Crockett, his teeth flashing in a nasty grin. "Locating the General is the problem. Hell of a lot of people living on this River."

"All of mankind up to around the year two thousand," said Bill Mason. "At least, that's what some people claim. Thirty or forty billion, give or take a few."

"Bigger numbers than I can handle," said Crockett. "Still, I'm a patient man. If it takes a thousand years of searching, I'll find him. That's a promise."

"Why bother?" asked Bowie, a bitter edge to his

voice. "Bill's right. Revenge don't mean much anymore. It ain't worth the trouble."

Crockett sighed deeply and shook his head. "That don't sound like the Jim Bowie I knew. Folks said he killt six, seven men in duels back in Louisiana before heading west. Same man believed in rightin' wrongs and makin' the guilty pay for their misdeeds. He never worried whether they was headin' to heaven or hell. Or if it was too much trouble."

Bowie shrugged. "Life is different now. The edge is gone. First time around, life meant something, 'cause you knew death lurked in the background. It kept you on your toes, if you catch my drift. I'm not complaining, but this sure ain't what I expected from the great Hereafter. Damned place is boring."

"Is the problem with this world?" asked Socrates unexpectedly, "or perhaps with ourselves?"

"Huh?" said Bowie, scowling. "What do you mean by that?"

"Are you a man who makes things happen?" replied the philosopher, "or one who is satisfied to sit back and let events and circumstances manipulate him?"

Bowie hesitated, pondering his reply. "I always thought of myself as master of my own destiny," he finally stated. "No one ever told Jim Bowie what he could or couldn't do."

"Yet you find yourself bored on this world of endless opportunity," said Socrates with a mere glimmer of sarcasm in his voice. "How very strange."

"Endless opportunity?" repeated Isaac, catching them all by surprise. It was the first time anyone could remember the mystery man speaking other than in answer to a direct question. "I don't understand."

"For what reason has all mankind been re-created on this great River?" asked Socrates, his eyes glowing with excitement. "To strive toward perfection as we are told by the disciples of the Church of the Second Chance? A noble goal, but one I suspect out of the reach of most of us.

"Or are we here to finish that which we left undone when we died? Can any of us truly say that we perished with all of our dreams, our goals, our ambitions satisfied? Who among us has not some business left unfinished? Perhaps Crockett's quest for vengeance is not the most noble of enterprises, but it gives his life purpose."

"Carpe diem," said Bill Mason. "Seize the day."

"Exactly," said Socrates. "An excellent thought. We must be true to our own nature. The shortest way to live with honor is to be in reality what we appear to be."

"That's the way I figure it," said Crockett. "Come on, Jim. You can sit around here growing fat or help me find Santy Anna and give him what he deserves."

Bowie sat for a moment, mulling over Socrates' words. The Greek philosopher had an uncanny knack of ferreting out the truth with a few simple questions. For months, Bowie had been feeling restless. Life in New Athens offered no challenge for a frontiersman. Crockett's appearance only served to underscore the emptiness of his own existence.

Searching for Santa Anna meant nothing to him. Unlike Crockett, he had no personal score to settle with the Mexican. His past had died at the Alamo. He was free of old grudges, old hates. Yet, thinking that, he suddenly realized he wanted to leave anyway.

In an instant of epiphany, Bowie realized that the reason for his departure didn't matter. It was the trip itself that counted, not the final destination. The meaning of life was in the living, not the ending. Perhaps that was why all mankind had been reborn on the banks of a seemingly endless river.

"Well," he said, a smile slowly forming on his lips, "I guess I could use a change of scenery."

With a whoop of excitement, Crockett grabbed Bowie by the shoulders. "Now that's more like it! The two of us, together again, lookin' for trouble."

"Hey," said Bill Mason. "Count me in. I'm no adventurer, but there's a few people on the River I'd like to find. Jack Ruby and Lee Harvey Oswald, for starters."

"Why not," said Crockett. "No reason we can't hunt for those fellas too. Whoever the hell they are."

"I, too, would like to join your party," said Isaac unexpectedly. For the first time since Bowie met the man, there was a glimmer of hope in his haunted eyes. "My nightmares are driving me mad. Only one man can put those dreams to rest. He, too, must live somewhere along the River."

Bowie glanced over at Socrates. "What about you, my friend? Want to come along? Or are you satisfied to remain here?"

"In my old age," said the philosopher, a sarcastic edge to his voice, "the good citizens of Athens voted to put me to death for corrupting the youth of that city. Too many of those same people were resurrected in this community.

"Lately they again grumble about my endless questions. They think I mock the gods. Unfortunately, they are right. One taste of hemlock is enough. Better that I travel with you than risk a second sentence. If I die, let it be because of my own stupidity, not another's.

"Besides," he added. "I have asked many people, 'What is justice?' In all my years, I have yet to receive a satisfactory reply. Perhaps somewhere on the River is an answer to my question."

"Then it's settled," said Crockett. "Tomorrow we'll build us a canoe and head out."

"Wait a minute," said Bowie, raising his hands for silence. "I agreed to help you find the General, but I ain't planning to commit suicide. How many times you die already, searchin' on your own?"

"Seven," answered Crockett. "Or maybe eight. I lost count a while back."

"I figured as much," said Bowie, his mind racing. Crockett hadn't changed much since his days on the frontier. He had grand ideas but little patience for details. "Only way we'll accomplish anything is by staying alive. Maybe death ain't permanent anymore, but it'll scatter our party to the four winds. So we gotta make plans, big plans. Traveling by canoe ain't the answer. We'll need a boat, a good one, and a crew to sail her."

"A boat?" said Crockett. "And crew? Why?"

"I've learned quite a bit from some of the other folk translated here during the past few years. Not all the people on the River are as friendly as the citizens of New Athens. Take those cannibal friends of yours, for example. The five of us don't stand much of a chance on our own. There's strength in numbers. That's why a crew is important."

"The Spartans," interrupted Bill Mason excitedly. "Ever since they defeated those Viking raiders last year, they've been looking for new worlds to conquer."

"My thoughts exactly," said Bowie. "I watched them in action. They're tough, disciplined fighters who know how to fight as a unit. Precisely the type of men we want."

"And anxious for adventure," said Socrates. "Let me talk to Lysander of Sparta tomorrow. He was the admiral of their fleet and knows the finest sailors. Though I suspect that insufferable bore will insist we take him along as well."

"What about a ship?" asked Crockett. "Or you got that all planned too."

"Maybe," said Bowie, smiling. "Just maybe I do."

3

The next morning, Bowie, Crockett, and Mason walked down-River a mile to the next grailstone. "That's where Thorberg Scafhogg lives," said Bowie, as they strolled along the beach. "We sometimes get together for a few drinks."

Seeing the disapproving look that crossed Crockett's face, Bowie raised his hands in protest. "I know what you're thinking, and it ain't like that. No more drunken binges for me. I learned my lesson at the Alamo. Damned near broke all my ribs when I fell off the ramparts. Ended doin' more damage to myself than the Mexicans."

Bowie's face grew solemn. "Besides, in those days I didn't care much if I lived or died. Not after the cholera took my wife and baby girl. Liquor helped me forget. All that's changed since the resurrection. Life's different knowing that Maria is alive somewhere out there. I've mended my ways." The Texan smiled. "Maybe I should think about joining the Church of the Second Chance."

"Yeah," said Crockett, arching his eyebrows. "What do you think of those preacher folks? Hold much to their theory of us being re-created so we can all strive toward sainthood?" Davy laughed. "Hard to imagine old Andy Jackson, the devil himself, with a halo."

"Having a second chance at life strikes me as a fine idea," said Bowie. "Not to mention a third, fourth, and who knows how many more tries. But, people is people. No matter how many times they're reborn, they ain't gonna change much. At least, that's the way I see it."

"Who's this Thorberg you mentioned?" asked Crockett, changing the subject. "And what's he to us?"

"Around twelve months ago," replied Bill Mason, "a fleet of six Viking ships came sailing down the River. Commanded by Olaf Tryggvason, a Norwegian king from the tenth century, they were looking to establish an empire in this territory. The raiders had conquered two other valleys, and they figured we'd be no more trouble. None of them counted on the Spartans."

"Must have been about a thousand Norsemen looking for plunder on those boats," said Bowie, continuing the tale. "They never encountered any organized opposition before. Stormed ashore, not expecting any resistance. Three thousand Greeks, combat-hardened veterans of years of intercity warfare, met them on the beaches. The sands ran red with blood."

"The Vikings fought heroically," said Mason, "but without much discipline. They battled as individuals. The Spartans, raised and trained in groups, worked in unison. Individually, they didn't match up against their opponents. But collectively they overwhelmed them.

"By the time King Olaf fell, most of his followers were dead. The remaining few, mostly artisans and craftsmen who kept the ships in good condition, surrendered. Lysander of Sparta offered them a choice. Join our community, freely sharing their knowledge of science and engineering, or perish by the sword. In a world where death means nothing, mercy no longer exists. The Norwegians, to a man, chose to live. Thorberg Scafhogg was one of that bunch.''

"Their boats?'' asked Crockett.

"Burned during the battle,'' replied Mason. "Fortunately, afterward, we were able to save most of the rivets and bolts.''

On Riverworld, where minerals were almost nonexistent, iron was more valued than gold. Without it, modern technology could not exist. Wars were fought for metal.

"Where'd they get the ore?'' asked Crockett. "Can't dig for it. Grass is too darned tough.''

"You know those firestarters that sometimes appear in the grails? Rumor has it that an American named Edison tried all sorts of experiments to discover their secrets. Got killed a couple of times, but he kept on trying. Never did find out how they worked. But what he did learn was equally important.

"Edison discovered that if you place a burned-out firestarter in a grail, most of the housing gets cooked off, leaving a small amount of iron and copper. Not much, but considering that everyone in the valley started out with one firestarter and usually got another every six months or so, that accounted for a good amount of material in a few years.

"The Vikings used the metal to make rivets and bolts, along with a few axes. Those went to the best fighters and a few shipwrights. Scafhogg, their most famous craftsman, got one. He uses it still.

"Norsemen dislike saws, preferring axes for cutting wood. Wait till you see Thorberg use his blade. The man's a genius with it."

"Ain't his only talent," said Bowie. The Texan pulled a long knife out of a dragonfish scabbard. The burnished steel blade blazed in the morning sunshine.

"He made it for me usin' a picture I drew," Bowie continued. "Same way Rezin designed the original. Not perfectly balanced, but it's sure better than a hornfish sword. Only Bowie knife on the whole river, I suspect."

"I'll say," replied Crockett. "You think maybe this Thorberg could make me a rifle?"

"Probably," said Bowie. "We even cooked up some gunpowder for explosives a while back. But what you planning to use for ammunition? Wooden bullets?"

"Damn," said Crockett. "Ain't proper for a man to be without a gun. I miss my Betsy."

"There's Scafhogg now," interrupted Mason, pointing to a figure in the distance. "That's a title given him by King Olaf in the tenth century," he added as an after-thought. "It means, 'Smoothing Stroke,' referring to his shipbuilding skills."

A hundred feet away, a squat, heavyset man stood beside a long wood workbench, busily chopping into a slab of oak with a glittering steel ax. Powerful muscles rippled in his arms and shoulders as he worked. A long blond braid tossed to and fro across his back with each motion.

"Ho, Thorberg," cried Bowie as they drew closer.

The Norseman paused and looked up. The harsh, angular lines of his face softened when he spotted the Texan. "Ho, Bowie," he called in return. "Welcome to you and your friends."

They spent the next ten minutes on introductions and idle

gossip. Thorberg spoke Esperanto with a thick accent, and oftentimes it was difficult to make out what he said. However, the master builder possessed a keen mind and quick wit. He expressed pleasure in meeting Crockett, and even submitted to listening to a verse of the sharpshooter's theme song. Bowie agonized through the rendition. He wondered idly if this miracle picture device called television ever featured a show on *his* life. Mentally, he promised to put that question to Bill Mason once they were alone.

The serenade over, Thorberg showed them his latest project, a massive oak chair he was constructing for one of the villagers. As he spoke, he slashed at the wood backboard with his ax, trimming it away with the precision of a fine surgeon.

"And what brings you to my humble home?" he asked, brushing a tiny sliver of wood from his hair. "Not merely the desire to show Crockett examples of my work, I suspect."

"We want you to build a boat," said Bowie, seeing no reason to equivocate. "A longboat, like the ones you constructed for King Olaf and his men. We're planning a trip downstream."

The Norseman didn't seem the least bit surprised. "Follow me," he said.

Turning, he headed away from the River and into the forest. He seemed to know exactly where he was going. Five minutes of brisk walking brought them to the base of a huge oak tree, towering well over a hundred feet into the air.

"Here is the keel for your ship," he declared proudly. "I knew from the day we met that someday you would ask this task from me. It was in your eyes. Sooner or later, all true men must challenge the great River."

"Mighty big tree," said Davy Crockett. "Gonna be an awfully long boat."

"On Earth, for King Olaf, I built one twice the size," said Thorberg. "A mighty dragon ship he named *Long Serpent*."

The Viking waved his hands at the surrounding forest. "The gods sensed your plans long ago. They provided us with many fine oaks for the planks and arches of the vessel."

Bowie nodded. Not that he believed in the Norse deities, but he found it highly unusual that both bamboo and oak thrived in the valleys. It was as if the unseen masters of this world challenged men to build boats and explore the River. The Texan wondered if he would ever know the truth. Or if he really wanted to.

"And what do you require in return?" he asked Thorberg, pushing the speculation from his mind. No use contemplating questions without answers.

"To sail with you," answered Thorberg immediately, not surprising any of them. "You need a master helmsman to steer your ship. I am that man.

"After all," he added, "none of you has any experience guiding a longboat on this River. I already piloted such a vessel for King Olaf's fleet."

"You're hired," said Bowie with a laugh. "How long will it take to construct this marvel?"

"With the help of the other shipwrights," said Thorberg after a short pause, "three months. Add to that another two weeks to train the crew. In a little more than a hundred days, we can set sail."

Bowie turned to Crockett. "Your revenge hold till then?"

"You betcha," replied the frontiersman. "I don't mind setting a spell, knowing the reward is waiting at the end."

"Then it's decided," declared Bowie. "Thorberg, you

assemble your friends and start working. Any assistance you need, let me know. In the meanwhile, we'll recruit a crew and gather our supplies."

Enthusiasm for the project welled up within the Texan, filling him with excitement. For the first time since Resurrection Day, he felt truly alive. It was good to be working for a cause again. Any cause.

"You picked out a name for this ship already?" asked Crockett, grinning.

"I think so," said Bowie. "Unless you gents object, I plan on callin' the boat *Unfinished Business*. Because that's what it's all about—unfinished business."

4

Exactly one hundred and ten days later, they set sail. Along with Bowie and his friends, the crew consisted of sixty Greek sailors under the command of Lysander of Sparta. Most of the men had served for the Greek Admiral on Earth and were hardened veterans of the long war between Sparta and Athens.

It was agreed upon by all concerned that Bowie would serve as leader of the expedition. A true man of the people, the Texan was one of the few men in New Athens without enemies. He, in turn, appointed Lysander as his second-in-command. The Greek soldier was a tough, capable sailor who hungered for action and adventure. A sixty-year-old man resurrected in a twenty-five-year-old body, his optimistic expectations provided an interesting contrast to Socrates' cynical views of the human condition.

The two men often engaged in long, heated debates contrasting Athenian democracy and Spartan militarism.

Thorberg's ship proved to be a marvel of Viking engineering. A hundred feet long and twenty feet at the beam, the longboat had ports for twenty-five oars per side. There was a solitary mast fitted between two heavy oak blocks, the leeson and the mast partner. Sail raised, the speedy, maneuverable ship made ten knots with a following wind.

Like all such ships, it was built from the outside in. The T-shaped keel, cut from the giant oak Thorberg had shown Bowie, was bowed in the middle so that in a battle the ship could be spun around on its axis. Attached to it was a thin shell of oak planks, each one cut from a single tree, bark to core. The boards were affixed to the stempost and sternpost by roundhead nails and bolts, then joined to one another in an overlap fashion with twisted and tarred ironwood vines. The resulting hull was incredibly light but remained watertight no matter how rough the going.

The boat weighed less than thirty tons when fully loaded with crew and supplies, and it drew less than three feet of water. To Bowie and his friends, the ship appeared to almost fly over the river. Thorberg even constructed wooden rollers, kept in the rear cargo area, on which the longboat could be dragged onto the beach when necessary.

At the stern was a rudder, some ten feet long, cut from a solid piece of oak. On the nearby poop deck stood a powerful ballista. The mast was only thirty feet high, but the sail, made from dragonfish membrane, stretched forty feet across.

The Spartans adjusted easily to the new ship. With its single sail and bank of oars, it resembled the triremes that they had sailed for Sparta. After several trial runs with the new crew, Thorberg pronounced them worthy of his vessel. A hundred and nine days after starting work, the Viking shipwright informed Bowie that all was ready.

Anxious to get going, the Texan immediately ordered their supplies loaded onto the boat. Not believing in long good-byes, he decided to set sail the following morning.

The whole population of New Athens turned out to see them off. The faces of the crowd reflected a mix of emotions, ranging from anger to joy, envy to disdain. Bowie no longer cared. Never a patient man, he was happy to be on his way.

Finally, the last of the supplies were loaded, the crew were at their oars, Thorberg at his rudder. All that remained was to lift anchor and set sail. Bowie lifted a hand in farewell.

"Speech," called a voice from the shore. "Speech, speech," echoed many others.

Momentarily taken aback, Bowie hesitated, not sure what to say. Socrates, standing next to him on the poop deck, suffered no such modesty. He stepped forward immediately.

"My friends, good countrymen," his voice rang out, silencing the cries of the crowd, "today the bravest sons of New Athens set sail on a great adventure. We go in search of the gods, those magical beings whom many of you foolishly insist resurrected us on the banks of this mighty river. Personally, I cannot imagine we will find them, for as you well know, I strongly doubt that they exist."

Most of the crowd nodded politely, not listening in the least to what the philosopher said. A few even applauded politely. However, Bowie noticed a number of unhappy faces. "Make ready to cast off," he muttered to Thorberg as the boos started.

"Once before, I stood before such a noble assembly," Socrates continued. "On that particular afternoon, you graciously condemned me to death for corrupting the youth of Athens." The boos were growing louder, but the philosopher ignored them. "A model citizen, I obeyed your command. In my heart, though, I knew that if hemlock was given to all those in Athens guilty of a similar crime, the city would stand empty of life!"

By now, the crowd had turned ugly. En masse, the citizens surged forward, seeking to pull the boat back to shore and rip Socrates to pieces. Pieces of debris tossed by the angry Greeks pelted the ship. "Up anchor," commanded Bowie hurriedly, as a stone whizzed by his head. *"Fast."*

The longship darted into the current like an arrow taking flight. In seconds, it sped out into the center of the River. "If I encounter the gods," shouted Socrates in derision, "I will surely warn them of your hospitality."

"Nice and diplomatic," said Bowie with a heavy sigh, as the banks of New Athens slipped far behind. "From now on, do me one favor. Clear any speeches with me first."

"I could not bear to leave them without a few words of wisdom," said Socrates, sounding not the least bit contrite. "At least our departure will be remembered for years to come."

"You can say that again, frogface," declared Davy Crockett, joining them. He had been at the front of the boat during the speech. In a drink match with the frontiersman a month before, Socrates had let slip his nickname on Earth. Ever since, Crockett insisted on using it all the time.

"Reminds me of the time when the good people of Tennessee voted me out of office," Davy continued.

"For my concession speech, I told the ungrateful scum to go to hell. Then I gathered up some friends and rode off for Texas."

"Another diplomat," said Bowie, smiling. "No wonder you got killed so often since Resurrection Day. Telling the truth ain't the way to win many friends."

"I won't argue with that," said Crockett. "But that's one of the joys of living on this river. You can be as honest as you like and not worry about the consequences." He paused for an instant, then continued. "Though you make a good point about wakin' up naked and hairless more often than not. Maybe a course of moderation is best."

"Nothing to excess," added Socrates.

"Amen to that," said Bowie, and then addressed his attention to the River. The great voyage had begun.

5

The first few weeks passed swiftly. They made good time, stopping at several villages each day. Bronze Age civilizations dominated this section of the River, and the travelers found courteous welcomes from the numerous Chinese settlements encountered on their journey.

Whenever possible, Bowie and his men made use of the woodland grailstones for their meals. It cut down on their dependence on supplies and provided a meeting ground with the inhabitants of the region. For safety, they slept on the boat beneath dragonfish leather tents.

Socrates spent his time ashore debating philosophy with anyone willing to argue. That rarely proved to be a problem. He usually attracted a crowd. One of the mainstays of the human condition anywhere on the River seemed to be a willingness to speculate on the meaning of life and the whys and wherefores of the great Resurrection.

Always he asked, "What is justice?" Nowhere did he find an answer that satisfied him.

Davy Crockett roamed through each new town looking for his nemesis, Santa Anna. Isaac accompanied the frontiersman, his sad eyes searching the throngs of people they met for a man only he could identify. Neither of them reported any success.

Bowie enforced only one rule: No passengers without good reason. He knew otherwise the boat would quickly fill with prostitutes and camp followers. The Texan made it quite clear to all involved that he had no objections to sex, but that it belonged on shore, not on their ship. Anyone who found the rules too restrictive could leave. No one did.

Actually, the Spartans thrived on tight discipline. Raised in a communistic state that placed duty above all else, the crew prided themselves in their mental as well as physical toughness. Lysander lost no opportunity in reminding his men of their heritage. "Remember," he lectured them whenever someone complained about short rations or the nightly downpour. "We are not rabble. We are Spartans."

As often as he was able, Bowie conferred with the town elders on what lay ahead on their journey. Oftentimes, the leaders of the community knew conditions five or ten villages farther on. While their voyage so far had been peaceful, Bowie knew that sooner or later they would encounter trouble. He wanted to be prepared for danger before it occurred.

Unfortunately, not everyone knew what loomed past

the beach's end. On the twentieth day of their voyage, they left a friendly Chinese village with no knowledge of what lay beyond the next bend in the River. Content in their own lives, the townspeople had never attempted to explore any farther than the natural boundaries of their village. Other expeditions that had passed through their valley from locations up-River never returned.

Nervously, Bowie watched as the huge mountain walls narrowed as they came to the end of the Chinese enclave. Thorberg, aware of the uncertainty of their situation, kept the longboat at the center of the river. He hoped their position would give them a few extra seconds to prepare for any attack from either shore. The Norseman kept both hands tight on the rudder. The narrower the River became, the faster the current. Even without sails or oars, they were moving at better than fifteen knots.

"Keep alert," Lysander warned his men, walking up and down the boat. "Remember. We are Spartans."

They sped into the next valley, their boat riding high on the whitecapped waves. "Watch for rapids," said Thorberg, wrestling with the steering paddle. "Shout if you see any rocks."

Mountains crowded in on them from both sides. The cliffs towered up so high that they seemed to meet many thousands of feet above their heads. Only a thin line of sunlight trickled down into the ravine, casting a twilight glow across the land.

The entire valley was little more than thin strips of beach, with the inevitable grailstones spaced a mile apart. There were no signs of people, or of human habitation.

"Empty," declared Bowie, beads of sweat trickling down his back. The *Unfinished Business* skipped along the water, heading for the next break in the mountains.

"Nobody's here," said Crockett. "But what's ahead?"

They found out in less than an hour. Though powerful currents and strong waves buffeted their ship, the long-boat had been built to withstand major storms at sea. They made it through the narrow gorge at the end of the uninhabited valley with nothing more than a light soaking to mark their passage. And discovered themselves in a huge, placid lake, some ten miles long and four miles wide.

"Out oars," commanded Lysander immediately. His Spartans, ever ready, were rowing in seconds.

"Not much of a current here," said Thorberg, relaxing his grip on the rudder. "The worst is past."

"Maybe, maybe not," said Bill Mason, his gaze fixed on the nearer shore. A massive wooden palisade ran along much of the beach, cutting if off completely from the water. Patrolling the walls were leather-clad men, armed with spears and swords. The soldiers watched their passing silently, making no move in response. From somewhere behind the fortifications, a horn sounded. A hundred feet farther down-River, a second responded. And then another a hundred feet beyond that.

"Signaling our approach," said Bowie. "Lysander, pick up the tempo."

"I'm headin' for the crow's nest," said Crockett, and scrambled up handholds in the short mast to the lookout perch at its top. The frontiersman had the keenest vision on board.

"Walls across the lake as well," he called down a few seconds later. "Pretty much the same construction as here. Looks like the same people rule both sides of the River."

The waterway curved to the right a half-mile ahead. "Keep to the middle of the stream," Bowie said to Thorberg, the sound of many horns echoing on the beach.

"Ships up ahead," cried Crockett. "Two of them, 'bout the same size as ours. Heading out from shore pretty fast."

"They look friendly?" asked Bowie, already knowing the answer.

"Not likely. They're loaded with armed men. Lots of them. Plenty of folks on the beach cheering them on. Looks like they know what they're doin'. We ain't the first ones passed this way, Jim."

"Pirates," said Bowie, disgusted.

"Or worse," said Socrates, pulling on a dragonleather buckler and helmet. He slashed the air a few times with a hornfish sword, accustoming himself to the weight of the blade. "They could be grail-slavers."

Bowie cursed. Born in the American South during the late eighteenth century, he considered slavery perfectly acceptable when applied to others. Faced with the same prospect for himself, he exploded with rage.

"Load the ballista," he bellowed. "Ready the grenades. If these bastards want a fight, we'll teach them a thing or two about warfare!"

"Spartans, prepare for battle," ordered Lysander, pulling on his armor and unsheathing his sword. Half the crew stopped rowing and donned their gear while the others kept up the pace. As soon as the first group finished, they took over the oars as their fellows made ready. The entire process took only a few minutes, and without any noticeable reduction in the boat's speed.

The *Unfinished Business* rounded the River bend into war. Huge stones, thrown by catapults on the beach, splashed in the water nearby. Giant arrows roared overhead. Propelled by three banks of oarsmen, the two enemy vessels bore down on them from both sides. On shore, thousands screamed in excitement.

"Roman triremes," said Isaac, anger clouding his usually despondent features. Clad in dragonfish leather and armed with two short swords, he no longer looked the man of peace. "Their ships are much heavier than ours. And legionnaires are no sailors. If we can steer free, they won't catch us. Beware, though," he said ominously, "if they get close enough to send on boarding parties. On land or sea, the soldiers of Rome fight like cornered tigers."

"Sounds like you admire them," said Bowie, his gaze fixed on the approaching warships.

"I spent most of my life with the legions," answered Isaac, pride ringing in his words. Then his voice grew harsh. "But then, one day, I recognized the error of my ways."

The big man turned away before Bowie could follow with another question. After that, it was time for action.

"Surrender!" bellowed the captain of one of the triremes, now less than a hundred yards away. "Surrender and you won't be harmed."

"The hell we won't," said Bowie with a snort. He looked over at Bill Mason, waiting for orders by the ballista. The history teacher, to everyone's surprise, was an excellent shot with the giant crossbow. He attributed his skill to a cryptic organization named the SCA. Bowie assumed the group was related in some way to TV, the AMA, and IRS, all mentioned in passing by the often unintelligible man from the future.

"You ready, Bill?" he asked, a terrible calmness descending upon him. Bowie recognized the feeling. It was the same icy madness that possessed him back on Earth during his many duels. Rezin, his brother, called it a killing rage. "Let's burn those bastards out of the water. Fire!"

Mason fired. With a shriek, a fiery crossbow bolt hurtled across the water at the nearest boat. The historian had added several unique touches to the giant arrow. Hollow chambers made it scream, while a mixture of grease, mulch, and gunpowder set it ablaze with an explosive fire. Mason called his special arrows "Molotov cocktails," and he promised deadly results.

The first arrow missed. It flew over the nearer trireme's sail and landed harmlessly in the water. Still, it alerted the ship's captain of the potential deadly danger to his ship. On the deck of the *Unfinished Business*, they could see the Roman sailors scrambling to the mast. But not in time.

With a roar, the second ballista bolt slammed into the pirate's sail. Instantly, a dozen tongues of fire licked at the wood frame and dragonfish membrane. Black smoke billowed as the ship's deck ignited.

Screaming in fear, the Roman sailors dove off the burning boat and into the River. Valiantly, a few men remained and tried to fight the fire, but with little success. The trireme drifted helplessly out of control, no longer a threat.

" 'Ware the second ship!" yelled Crockett, clambering down from the mast. "It's moving up fast."

Masked by the black smoke from the first trireme, the other ship hurtled forward over the water like a shark sensing blood. It was less than a hundred feet from the *Unfinished Business* and closing fast, its bow headed directly at theirs. They were on a collision course that would destroy both boats.

"Pull in your oars!" Lysander shouted to the Spartans. "Before they are snapped to kindling!"

Grunting with effort, Thorberg wrenched at the rudder with all of his strength. Shuddering, the longboat swerved to the right. At the same time, the captain of the trireme angled his boat to the left.

With a crunch of colliding wood, the bows of the two ships met, sending the crews of both tumbling to the deck. But the force of the blow had been muted by the sudden shifts in direction. Neither boat was badly damaged. Instead, they floated only yards away from each other, as the sailors on board scrambled for their weapons.

The Romans recovered first. With a roar of triumph, they slammed a portable bridge onto the deck of the *Unfinished Business*. A metal spike embedded in the far end of the gangplank held the ships together. In seconds, troops poured over the plank and onto the longboat.

The first two soldiers died as their feet touched the deck. Socrates, his face devoid of emotion, thrust his sword into one man's eye, killing him instantly. Without pausing, the Greek whirled about and caught the second boarder with a backhand blow to the head. The man staggered off balance, letting down his guard. Socrates' blade caught him in the throat, ripping it to shreds. For all of his reputation as a philosopher, the Athenian had served in three campaigns and was known throughout Greece as a ruthless, deadly fighter.

Other attackers fared little better. By now, Lysander had rallied his warriors with the cry of "Spartans, forward!" The Greeks responded with a flurry of action that cleared the deck of invaders. But there were hundreds more Romans, ready to take their place. They crowded onto the portable gangplank linking the two ships. Unless that bridge was destroyed, the *Unfinished Business* was doomed.

Two swords flashing, Isaac leapt onto the narrow platform. Eyes wild, features contorted with anger, he made no effort to protect himself from his enemy's attacks. Instead he fought with an insane rage to match that of a Norse Berserker. Slashing left and right, he killed a man with each blow. The narrow width of the gangplank made it impossible for more than one to confront him at one time. And no one man could stop him.

Soldiers tried, and soldiers died. Others, seeing their death in his eyes, scrambled back to the safety of their own ship. Single-handed, Isaac cleared the boarding ramp and held it. Blood spurting from a dozen wounds, he glared at the crew of the trireme, as if daring them to do their worst. Then, before any could respond, he leaped back onto the deck of the *Unfinished Business*.

"Pull us free," yelled Bowie unnecessarily. Already, a dozen Spartans struggled with the grappling hook that held the boarding ramp in place. Oak panels shrieked in protest as the metal claws tore free. Cheering wildly, the Greeks shoved the platform off the longboat and into the River.

"Spartans, to your oars," commanded Lysander. It was time for a quick getaway.

Casually, Davy Crockett lifted a small bag made of leaves and dried clay from a storage box on the poop deck. A short vine fuse dangled from its side. Balancing the object in one hand, he lit the fuse with the firestarter he held in the other. Shrugging his shoulders, he tossed it over the gap separating the two boats. It exploded a second later. Surprised Romans screamed in pain as hundreds of small fragments of quartz and flint filled the air.

"Darned things work pretty good," commented Crockett, lighting a second grenade. Unconcerned, he watched the fuse sputter. "Short fuses, though."

With a flick of the wrist, he lobbed it at the trireme. Bowie sighed in relief as the bomb exploded among their enemies. Crockett was a bit too casual about death and destruction.

"Let's get out of here," said Bowie as the Spartans started rowing, "before Crockett blows us to hell and gone."

6

Two weeks and a thousand miles later, they learned more than they wanted to know about revenge. Anxious for several days of shore leave, they anchored the *Unfinished Business* at a peaceful Egyptian village. While the crew relaxed in town, Bowie questioned the town elders on the route ahead. Nearby, Socrates coached Davy Crockett on the finer points of swordplay.

Bowie had just concluded his meeting when Bill Mason appeared in the doorway of the council chambers. The historian's face was white as a sheet, and there was a haunted look in his eyes that Bowie found disturbing.

"You free for a little while?" Mason asked, his voice trembling.

"Sure," answered Bowie. "What's up?"

"There's two women I want you to meet," replied Mason mysteriously. He beckoned to Socrates and Crockett. "Can you two come with me? It's important."

Mason refused to say anything more. The four of them walked swiftly through the small town and entered the ever-present forest that stretched from the end of the beach to the mountains approximately a mile from the water. It took them about twenty minutes to reach their destination.

"The villagers told me about these women and their captive," said Mason as they closed in on a rough cabin sheltered among the huge trees. "Not willing to believe what I heard, I came here this morning. And soon wished I hadn't."

"Care to explain what you mean by that, Bill?" asked Davy Crockett, his gaze jumping from place to place. The veteran Indian fighter always stayed alert in the woods.

"Just listen to the women's story," said Mason. "You'll understand my meaning quick enough."

The shelter appeared deserted. A crude shack constructed out of untrimmed logs, its most prominent feature was a large wooden cage a few feet from the door. There was no sign of anyone about.

Something moved inside the cage. "Never heard of no animals on the River," said Crockett, his eyes narrowing. He peered between the bars. "Damn it," he said, shock and horror mixing equally in his voice, "there's a man inside. Blinded, with his fingers and toes hacked off!"

"That's so the bugger can't escape." The speaker was a well-built woman, with curly long brunette hair that fell past her shoulders. She stood in the doorway of the cabin, holding a loaded crossbow in her hands. She appeared quite capable of using it.

"I don't mean you gents no harm," she continued, speaking Esperanto with a thick Cockney accent, "but too many men come round planning to set our friend here go free. Can't allow that either. So I stay ready for trouble."

"If we want to free that poor soul," said Bowie, anger welling up within him, "one crossbow will not stop us."

"That's why my friend in the woods got you covered with another, guv'nor," said the woman, with a smile. "Say hello to the nice gentlemen, Cathy," she called to her unseen ally behind them.

"No tricks, kind sirs," replied a second woman out of

their line of sight. "I could take all four of you in less time than you could reach dear Mary."

"None of your heroics, please," said the woman named Mary. "I recognize our visitor from this morning. These, I take it, must be the friends of yours you wanted us to meet? Well, then, gentlemen, have a seat. Listen to my story, and afterward tell me if you want to set this bastard free."

"Please, do as she asks," said Bill Mason. "It's important that you hear their tale."

"All right," said Davy Crockett, settling down on the grass. "But I don't holds with keepin' a man caged like a wild animal. No matter what he's done."

"Depends on your point of view," said Mary. "Me, I was never much for violence either. Me and Cathy there, we made our living on our backs." She chuckled. "Plenty of times we did it standin' up, as well."

"As long as the gents paid us," added Cathy, "that's all that mattered."

"Wasn't a good life, but weren't as bad as some in those days," said Mary. "At least we never went 'ungry."

"England, 1888," added Mason softly.

"Anyhows, Cathy's life was cut short on September thirtieth. One of her gentlemen friends cut her throat. Same as happened to me in my flat on November sixth."

"Leather Apron they called him in the papers after the first murder," said Cathy, her voice shrill. "I 'eard all about it from one of the girls who could read. Never gave the story much attention. Not my concern, I thought."

"He cooked and ate one of Cathy's kidneys," said Mary, her tone matter-of-fact mentioning the atrocity. "Bugger wrote letters to the news agency all about it. Called himself Jack the Ripper."

Bowie shivered in spite of himself. What madman ate parts of his victims and chose a title like "the Ripper"?

"The crimes became famous in England," said Mason, ever the historian. "Jack the Ripper killed five women, Mary being the last of them, terribly mutilating the bodies, in the space of a few months. Then he vanished, leaving no clues to his identity. Many people speculated on who he was, but no one ever learned the truth."

"I never saws him," said Mary. "Bugger cut my throat from behind. Don't remember a thing. Like the rest of you, I died then woke up naked on the beach, here.

"First day was strange. Wasn't many of us Brits around. Mostly these Egyptian gents and ladies. Weird, with everybody naked and all that. I wandered about a bit, trying to find somebody who understood English. That's when I stumbled upon Cathy. Even without hair, we recognized each other right away. Rememberin' how she died made me realize that Red Jack probably did me in as well. Seemed awfully strange, the two of us brought back to life in the same spot. Imagine our surprise when, with a little searching, we discovered that all five of the Ripper's victims had been resurrected in this location."

"I don't like the sounds of this nohow," said Crockett.

"Nothing happened the first month," continued Mary, "other than us trying to adjust to this new world. Egyptians turned out to be right nice to us. We got along fine. And then the killings started."

"The Ripper?" asked Bowie.

"One and the same," said Mary. "The five of us recognized his handiwork right off. Not only the victims got resurrected here, but their murderer as well. The bastard killed his prey from behind, slashing open their throats with his knife. Afterward, he mutilated the bodies. Cut them to shreds, tearing their insides apart. And, of course, his victims were always women.''

"It took us six weeks to catch 'im,'' said Cathy. "Six long weeks of watching and waiting for the bugger to make a mistake. He finally did, and we bagged 'im. Caught the bastard red-handed.'' The woman laughed at her grisly pun. "Bloody mess it was, too.''

"Who was he?'' asked Mason.

"Some middle-class prig whose father died from the clap,'' said Mary. "He blamed the old man's death on whores in general and figured he'd eliminate the problem with a knife.''

"I thought the mentally ill were cured before their resurrection,'' said Bowie.

"He weren't insane,'' replied Mary, "at least not by his own standards. The Ripper felt he was doing society a favor. Thought the same when he returned to life. Damned maniac considered women to be servants of the devil. He felt it his sacred obligation to punish immoral behavior.''

"Lots of that goin' round,'' said Davy Crockett. "Must have kept him busy.''

"He killed twelve women in those six weeks,'' said Mary, her voice grim. "Soon as we had him, the bastard tried to commit suicide. He might be mad, but he weren't crazy. Ripper knew that death wasn't final on the River. Instead, he'd be born somewhere else, without anyone knowing a thing about him. What more could a murderer ask? This resurrection business meant he could kill all he liked, without ever being punished.''

"Death offered him a perfect method of escape,'' added Cathy. "That's why we couldn't let him die. Pharaoh gave the Ripper to us to do what we wanted. According to him, we that suffered from the Ripper's crimes on Earth deserved to set his punishment in the afterlife. It was Mary who came up with the plan.''

"You decided to keep him alive," said Bowie, comprehension growing within him. "So he couldn't harm anyone else.''

"Right you are, guv," said Mary. "Weren't even plannin' to hurt him. We might be lowborn, but we ain't savages. Then the Ripper tried killin' Annie Chapman during an escape attempt. That's when we cut off his fingers and toes and put out his eyes. And put him in that cage there. Haven't had any problems since then.

"The five of us take turns guarding him. Mostly makin' sure he don't succeed in killing himself. It ain't much fun, but somebody's got to do it.''

The woman lowered her crossbow. "You've heard my story. Still want to set the Ripper free?''

Slowly, Bowie shook his head. "No. But there must be a better way to handle—''

"I'm waiting to hear one," interrupted Mary. "Whatever gods resurrected us all, they didn't provide any easy answers. Your friend told me the name of your boat. Well, that's the way I see our problem. If we let the Ripper die, he's reborn to kill again. And keeping him alive ain't much better. Either way, he's unfinished business.''

Silently, Davy Crockett stared at the mutilated man huddled at the far side of the cage. The Ripper chewed his dreamgum, lost in the mad world of his own mind. The frontiersman shook his head and turned away from the bars. "What do you do when his fingers and toes grow back?'' he asked.

"We cut them off again," said Mary. "And again and again and again.''

On the way back to the boat, Socrates, who had not

said a word during their entire confrontation, voiced the
thought that was in all of their minds. "That," he
declared sadly, "whatever it may be, is not justice."

7

After the encounter with the Ripper and his captors,
Davy Crockett quit talking about Santa Anna and revenge.
Evidently, the frontiersman started having second thoughts
about his mission. A number of times during the next week,
Bowie spotted his friend engaged in deep conversation with
Socrates. Crockett never smiled during those talks.

The whole purpose of their adventure came into question a thousand miles farther down the River. The *Unfinished Business* was docked in a Chinese village for the
usual reasons. The Spartans, under Lysander, had marched
off down the beach to compete in athletic contests.
Crockett and Mason, Socrates and Thorberg remained on
board, playing bridge with a deck of handmade cards.
The historian had taught the others the game a few weeks
back, and ever since they played whenever possible.
Isaac, silent as ever, watched.

As usual, Bowie spent most of his time meeting with
the village elders. Each stop on the River fueled his
desire to discover what lay farther on. For all of the
dangers and uncertainties of the trip, he was no longer
bored. And, on Riverworld, that meant a great deal.

Returning back to the ship late that afternoon, Bowie
found himself in the company of a short, slender male
Caucasian. "M'sieur Bowie, I am led to believe?" the

stranger asked. Though he spoke Esperanto, there was no question he was a Frenchman.

"That's me," the Texan answered. "Do I know you?"

"Not in the least," the Frenchman replied. "I am Maurice LeBlanc, formerly a mathematician from Tours, France, circa 1900."

"Interesting enough," said Bowie, continuing toward the boat. "But what's it to me?"

"This morning I saw your vessel arrive. Later, from a friend on the high council, I learned your story. You and your friends are engaged on a noble enterprise, to be sure! It would be a great honor if you would allow me to join on this voyage."

"Sorry," said Bowie. "No hitchhikers." He had learned the phrase from Mason and used it frequently. Half the people they met wanted to sail on the *Unfinished Business*. "We don't have the room."

"Of course, of course," said LeBlanc. "But I have, as you say, unfinished business along the River. And, to that end, I am willing to pay for my passage."

Bowie smiled, impressed in spite of himself with the Frenchman's pluck. "Only thing worth much on the River is metal," he declared, looking LeBlanc up and down with a critical eye. "Which you don't got."

"A-ha," said LeBlanc with a sly smile of triumph. "Your materialism betrays you, *mon ami*. On this strange new world of ours, one thing is worth more than iron and steel. *Information*."

"Keep talkin'," said Bowie. They were in sight of the ship now, but he was in no hurry to get there. "What do you know that I want to hear?"

"According to my friend on the council, you require news of a certain Mexican politician named Santa Anna.

I am acquainted with the whereabouts of the General. In trade for transportation, I will gladly tell you all I know about him. Including his present location.''

Bowie laughed. ''Who you lookin' for on the River, Frenchie?''

''Another mathematician,'' replied LeBlanc, ''by the name of Pierre de Fermat. I would like to discuss with him a certain theorem, his last theorem, which perplexed Earthly mathematicians, myself included, for centuries. I must know the truth.''

''Odd sort of reason to head off down the River,'' said Bowie, shaking his head. ''But I was never one much for numbers. Come with me and let's see what the others think.''

No one objected to LeBlanc's terms. On a planet with thirty-five billion people, searching for one man was akin to looking for a single grain of sand on the beach. The Frenchman was right. Knowledge was worth more than anything else on the Riverworld, even iron. They unanimously voted him a member of the expedition in return for his cooperation.

''Six times I have died since Resurrection Day,'' LeBlanc declared, making himself comfortable on the poop deck. ''By nature, I am the quiet, retiring type. I dislike fighting and violence of any kind. However, I am also a Frenchman, and from time to time, I find myself forced to make a stand against the barbarism of my fellow man. Above all, I believe in liberty, fraternity, equality.''

''Why do I have a difficult time imaginin' you a mild-mannered sort of guy?'' asked Crockett, grinning. ''You sure about that, LeBlanc?''

''Perhaps my years with the Foreign Legion betray me more than I care to admit,'' said the Frenchman, a twinkle in his eyes. "I assure you, I only lose my temper in good cause."

"You're my type of fella, LeBlanc," said Crockett. "Betcha keep that temper in control a coupla hours every week."

"About that," admitted the Frenchman. "Which has led to my violent demise several times on this uncivilized world. What concerns us today is my most recent death, only a few weeks ago."

LeBlanc's cheerful features turned serious. "If, as many have surmised, the civilizations on the River follow a somewhat historical order, I translated here from a valley several million miles away. It was the home of a nation of seventeenth-century Indians from South America. During my sojourn there, these normally peaceful natives were fighting for their lives against a horde of invaders from the north who had already overrun a dozen nearby valleys. At the time of my death, in a minor skirmish with the enemy, a large party of reinforcements had just arrived from the south. In my humble opinion, a major war was brewing.

"One of probably hundreds taking place along the River," said Bowie. "Resurrection sure didn't change mankind's basic nature. We sure the hell were an ornery bunch."

"Not that I ain't interested in your adventures, LeBlanc," said Crockett, "but how does Santa Anna fit in the picture?"

"I am coming to that," said the Frenchman. "The invading armada, and that term was singularly appropriate, consisted of a fleet of ships carrying sixteenth-century Spaniards under the leadership of Philip II of Spain. Their terms to the Indians were quite explicit: convert to Catholicism or die. Aiding the King in his mission was the infamous leader of the Inquisition, Torquemada."

Socrates sighed. "How many tears the gods must shed over the crimes committed in their names."

"My native friends were helpless against the invaders. Only the timely arrival of the southern forces saved them from annihilation. Can you guess who led that rescue force?"

Crockett groaned. "Santy Anna. He always claimed to be a man of the people. Even the Indians."

"Three men commanded the relief troops. You guessed correctly about Santa Anna. The other two were Simón Bolívar, whose name I recognized, and a man unknown to me, Che Guevara. All of them seemed dedicated to saving the Indians from Philip and Torquemada."

"Great news," said Crockett bitterly. "How can I kill that son of a bitch if he's a hero? Besides, killing him wouldn't serve much purpose if he's just born again somewhere else."

The frontiersman rose to his feet. "Maybe this trip wasn't such a great idea after all. Maybe whatever business we left unfinished on Earth deserved to be forgotten."

"You suggesting we abandon the voyage?" asked Bowie.

"I don't know," replied Crockett. "Suddenly, though, I'm not so sure we should continue. Besides, if LeBlanc's right, Santa Anna's five million miles away. That's a mighty long trip."

"We must continue," said Isaac softly. His gaze swept the group and came to rest on Bowie. "You understand why."

"I think so," admitted the Texan, sorrow filling his voice. "You were there, weren't you?"

Isaac nodded. "*I was there.*"

A minute passed before he continued. "A captain of the Roman legions, I served in Judea under Pontius

Pilate. The squadron I commanded handled the execution of Rome's enemies. On that fateful day in Jerusalem, we were commanded to execute three men—two thieves and a rabble-rouser. A good soldier, I followed my orders. The three were crucified.''

Isaac drew in a deep breath, his voice crackling with emotion as he continued. "I personally drove the nails into his hands, the man called Yeshua. As I had done with many others over the years. Only this time, instead of cursing or shrieking in pain, he whispered words of absolution to me. 'I forgive you, my son,' he said. 'You only do God's will.' " Tears trickled down Isaac's face. "And, then afterward, when we raised the cross, the look in his eyes . . . the look in his eyes . . ."

The Roman stopped for a moment, unable to continue. No one made a sound. There was nothing that anyone could say to lessen the pain.

"I must find him," said Isaac. "He lives again somewhere on this world. Only he can grant me peace. That is why I cannot stop searching. Why I will not stop searching."

"Well," said Bill Mason, groping for the right words, "I still never found Jack Ruby. And, I'd like to ask King Richard III a few questions about the Tower of London."

"Do not forget Fermat," added LeBlanc. "Mathematics demands I continue the hunt."

"Maybe revenge ain't the answer," said Crockett. "But who knows? Maybe by the time we caught up with Santy Anna, the General might be up to his old tricks again. Forget everything I said before. What's a few million miles to Davy Crockett, king of the Wild Frontier?"

Bowie grinned. "For a minute there, I almost worried that you boys might make the wrong decision. Glad to see you woke up in time. Life without challenges ain't worth

living. And, since dyin' is out of the question, I figure we
might as well live the best we can. Now, enough of this
jawing. Let's round up those Spartans and get going.''

Socrates, as always, had to have the last word. ''Can it
be,'' he asked solemnly, the barest trace of a smile
betraying his true feelings, ''that we humans misunder-
stand the whole reason for our resurrection? Perhaps
whatever Powers exist created this entire Riverworld not
for our redemption but for theirs. Our meanderings and
wanderings may be reflections on the true purpose of a
much greater drama. At times, I suspect that the Lords of
the River are manipulating us for their own devices. I
wonder if we are not merely actors seeking to complete
the gods' . . . unfinished business?''